Praise for
FREDERICK BUSCH
and
THE STORIES OF
FREDERICK BUSCH

"Frederick Busch's short stories are wonderful things, composed by a fine and far-seeing intelligence that never averts its eyes. His is a first-rate inquirer into the sorrows of ordinary people living ordinary lives and all of it in stripped-down prose—not minimalist but nuclear. Any reader coming to these stories for the first time is in for a revelation: the work of one of the great storytellers of our time."   —Ward Just

"These stories illuminate a generous belief that everyone's experience— from that of an influential politician to the hardworking mechanic living paycheck to paycheck—is epic. . . . Busch reminds us that no matter where or how we live, our lives are both unforgiving and magical, and that just as despair is ordinary, so too is hope."
                    —Emily Rapp, *Boston Sunday Globe Books*

"[Busch's] stories hum with sorrow, quake with wit, exude a rare magnitude of compassion even as they force his readers to face unsettling truths. . . . Busch's stories read like sneak attacks, loping along with their easy diction and commonplace settings, then landing a late-in-the-game emotional wallop that makes the reader reframe everything that's come before. You thought you were on a lazy stroll, but you turn out to have been walking through a minefield. . . . You can count on Busch's prose to be startlingly revelatory, and the brilliance of his sentences endures even out of context. . . . [T]his collection will make more people see Frederick Busch for the master he was, one whose talent for subtle impact was downright maximal."
                    —Katie Arnold-Ratliff, *New York Times Book Review*

"Fred Busch faced every emotion with an open heart and tirelessly energetic language. Never unkind to his characters, he forgave inadequacy if it was genuine, an honest struggle. And of all the writers I can think of, Fred was the most impatient with inauthentic feeling. That richness of spirit, that passion and wit, made his stories indispensable. This book is a great a gift to keep his voice with us and to bring it to those who've never had the pleasure of hearing it." —Rosellen Brown

"[His stories] depict a range of small human dramas evoked with emotional intelligence and perfect pitch."

—Amanda Heller, *Boston Globe*

THE STORIES OF
FREDERICK BUSCH

THE STORIES OF
FREDERICK
BUSCH

EDITED AND WITH AN INTRODUCTION BY

ELIZABETH STROUT

W. W. NORTON & COMPANY
New York   London

Printed in the United States of America
First published as a Norton paperback 2015

For information about permission to reproduce selections from this book,
write to Permissions, W. W. Norton & Company, Inc.,
500 Fifth Avenue, New York, NY 10110

For information about special discounts for bulk purchases, please contact W. W. Norton
Special Sales at specialsales@wwnorton.com or 800-233-4830

Manufacturing by RR Donnelley, Harrisonburg
Book design by Helene Berinsky
Production manager: Julia Druskin

Library of Congress Cataloging-in-Publication Data
Busch, Frederick, 1941–2006.
[Short stories. Selections]
The Stories of Frederick Busch / edited and with an introduction by Elizabeth Strout. —
First edition.
pages cm
ISBN 978-0-393-23954-6 (hardcover : alk. paper) I. Strout,
Elizabeth, editor of compilation. II. Title.
PS3552.U814A6 2014
813'.54—dc23

2013041070

ISBN 978-0-393-35076-0 pbk.

W. W. Norton & Company, Inc.
500 Fifth Avenue, New York, N.Y. 10110
www.wwnorton.com

W. W. Norton & Company Ltd.
Castle House, 75/76 Wells Street, London W1T 3QT

1 2 3 4 5 6 7 8 9 0

CONTENTS

THE STORIES OF
FREDERICK BUSCH

INTRODUCTION

"Be brave," Frederick Busch admonished aspiring writers in an interview he gave in 2003. "Keep your knees unbent." Courage on the page mattered to this writer, and those reading through this collection of stories will find Busch's writing to be relentlessly brave. "Love and serve your characters," he said in the same interview. That will be found here, too, how he loved his characters and served them well. The undercurrent of tenderness toward these characters, combined with the daring presentation of them in their stripped down struggles, is what makes a Busch story its own inimitable experience to read. At the time of his death at the age of sixty-four, Frederick Busch had written twenty-seven books; seven of them were story collections. While he was a prize-winning novelist, the stories here have been chosen as a collection that represents the span of his life spent as a short story writer. This career began, he was to famously say, in the fourth grade when his stony-faced teacher suddenly smiled at him after he wrote a poem that pleased her. He claimed to have written steadily since then. But it would be a mistake to assume that Busch spent a lifetime as a writer in order for the world to smile upon him. These are not stories about a flowering dog wood tree, as his fourth grade poem had been. These stories are intended for the brave reader. These are stories for grown-ups.

Born in Brooklyn, New York, Busch spent the majority of his adult years living in central New York State. Much of his work portrays the landscape of this rural and rugged and often bleak, often beautiful, terrain. There are other stories here—though they are fewer in number—that reflect his childhood spent in the Midwood and Flatbush sections of Brooklyn, where his father was a lawyer and his mother a teacher. Certain themes naturally arise when one reads the work of a writer, and readers of Busch will see the recurrence of the man who is openly truculent, often self-lacerating, always aware of his failings. Busch, who cited Hemingway as one of his influences, also cites Hemingway's phrase *"It's that some of them stay little boys so long . . . . . the great American boy-men,"* as an epigraph in the beginning of one of his collections, and it is no surprise. Busch's men are often boy-men: men trying to be adults, trying to be good, and always, or often, it seems, falling short. They are men struggling to get the upper hand against their recalcitrant boy-part, that part that still views the world with bafflement in spite of their experience. It is their awareness of this aspect of themselves—and Busch's awareness—that gives a particular type of sufficiency and fullness to his stories.

It also makes the women who love these men despair. The women found here are a varied lot, but they are fundamentally good. No one can accuse Busch of not liking his women. You can feel his sympathy for them as their husbands, ex-husbands, boyfriends, make them weep, make them yell, or cause them to walk out. While there may be the inattentive mother, the straying wife—more apt to be found in the Brooklyn stories—by and large the women in these stories love their men. If a boy-man survives his poor actions, it is often because of a woman's love. More often than not it is a woman keeping the children cared for, and if the husband or boyfriend at times seems like another needful child, Busch portrays this need with clear eyes.

THE FIRST LINE of the first story in this collection is a fairly direct route to the Busch world view. "What to know about pain is how little we

deserve it, how simple it is to give, how hard to lose." There is no sum-
ming up of Busch's work, but these lines serve to open the causeway the
reader will find himself riding across. These stories abound with pain
undeserved—parents who have lost children through death or mental
illness, children who have suffered the neglect, not always benign, of
adults pursuing their own needs rapaciously—and these stories are
filled, too, with the understanding that pain is hard to lose. But what
Busch does especially well is to tell stories of how simple pain is to give.
Because he writes with a large heart, the only judgment present comes
from the characters themselves, certainly not from the writer. In his
display of how easy it is to hurt another, we find that undercurrent of
tenderness; Busch is not condemning. He—in his authorial role—
seems as bewildered by all this as anyone. No one, the subtext of this
voice might be saying, starts out life with the desire to cause anyone
pain. And yet we hurt people all the time. The mere act of living, Busch
seems to imply, means that this will be true.

Perhaps it is one reason that dogs appear so frequently in these pages.
The black labs, and yellow labs, and big shaggy Newfoundlands inhab-
iting these rural settings are not hurting anyone. They are pure in their
innocence, pure in their loyalty. They are not complicated, they are just
good, although, Busch's world being what it is, people are not always
good to them. In the story "Dog Songs" there are twenty-six dogs living
in a yellow trailer; they come to a bad end at the hand of the town deputy
who fears they may have been perverted by their owners, one of whom is
hoping for a sex change. The opposite is true, of course, the love these dogs
have for mankind is never ending. Through the eyes of the protagonist,
a judge lying in a hospital bed after driving—perhaps suicidal, he cannot remember—into a tree with a woman other than his wife, dwells on
the image of these dogs which had earlier been destroyed. "He thought,
when he thought of the dogs, that their lips and tails and even their postures signaled their devotion. . . . . . And as the deputies flung them . . . .
and their bodies flew, they looked ardent." Even in death, the innocence
of these dogs is excruciating. They are the angels in the Busch universe.

The heroes are those people just trying to do their best, and you will find a lot of them here. One of his better known stories, "Ralph the Duck," starts with a dog vomiting early in the morning. A wife is sleeping on the couch. The husband, a security guard at the local college, is determined to make her coffee when she wakes, determined to behave in a way that will cause her to forgive whatever he has done to hurt her the day before. But first the dog has to be let out, and let back in. The dog is interested in a dead deer carcass in the woods, and the protagonist man, a first person narrator, knows the dog will return to the carcass. "He loved what made him sick." The dog is not the only one, and undoubtedly this is the point. The college girl loves her professor who has discarded her; she's taken pills, making herself very sick. The protagonist must save her, and presumably he does. But he is sick with fury in doing so, and we learn why by the time the story concludes. The wife, patient in her own grief, is willing to endure her husband's behavior; she is the adult here, the unconditional giver of love, though one assumes at times she is just as sick of it all as anyone else, and takes a night's respite on the couch. Still, they endure. They endure, this couple, as do many couples in the book, and sometimes we are given to believe that is enough. Other times a relationship does not endure, and Busch is not afraid to let us know that the pain we so easily inflict, that is not so easily removed, will lead us to our ultimate destination: that of being alone.

Busch was writing many of these stories during a time when it was fashionable for short stories to be what was referred to as minimalist. He was, after all, a contemporary of Raymond Carver, Tobias Wolff, Ann Beattie, Richard Bausch, and others, who were also writing in the vein of a short story form that was pared down, plain-spoken, often first-person, and told of single-event moments in what we call ordinary life. It is natural that Busch would write stories reflecting his time in history, and he did, all the while looking back over his shoulder, as any writer does, at those he believed helped shape his own particular use of the American language. In his case, these influences were, in particular,

Melville and Hemingway. But he would just as naturally have been influenced by those writing next to him. And of course being a minimalist in the story form meant just that: the form was kept to a minimum. In the case of Busch, the stories mostly dwell on the domestic.

Even in the story "Reruns" where a wife has left her psychiatrist husband, and gone to Beruit, where she is kidnapped and taken hostage, the story remains tightly oriented in the town of Sherwood New York, not particularly interested in the international aspects of the world. The husband himself realizes, "We are so far from every place." Later he reports, "I couldn't have named one hostage." His life is taking place in the town with three traffic lights; his life is taking place inside his office where he admits, "Being crazy's a family project," and inside his house where a member of the state department sits in the kitchen, and in the next room the daughters watch their mother on television.

So-called ordinary life, though, is large, and the array of situations and conflicts presented in these stories is impressive. Again and again we are reminded that we have no idea what goes on behind closed doors, or what goes on in the mind of another. Busch once said that what he most enjoyed as a writer was "knowing that I made someone see something in a different way." It's hard to imagine any reader of these stories driving past a farmhouse in upstate New York—or anywhere—without seeing it another way, which is to say honoring the possibilities that lie inside, those aspects of life that are unsayable, otherwise unknowable.

In "Name the Name" a man who is a traveling teacher, required by the state to attend to local school age children who for whatever reasons cannot make it to the classroom, takes us through an ordinary (extraordinary) day. First he goes to the home of a young pregnant girl, whose mother makes him reheated coffee, "a woman too embarrassed to look at my face. She wore polyester pants with a black and white check, a man's gray sweatshirt over a heavy flannel shirt, and big slippers lined with synthetic fur; on top of each slipper was the face of a dog with a pink tongue. She wore no socks and the chapped red roughness of her ankles was an intimacy between us." From there the teacher goes to the hospital to teach a bedridden girl poetry that she writes on her chalk-board is "bologna." And he finishes his day by going to the county jail where the sixteen year old young man he is there to teach is his own son. While there was a flirtation with a nurse at the hospital, as there are often flirtations or hints of sexual liaisons outside the family, it seems the family unit is the engine running most of these stories, with the boy-man head of the household often weary.

It can be argued—and Busch seems both aware of this and in charge of it—that the claustrophobic self-loathing of these men comes close at times to narcissism; a fascination with the self that can't transcend its setting. This is when the Brooklyn based stories provide a change of tone as well as their change in location. You will find Brooklyn trees seen through Brooklyn windows, men wearing pol-ished wing tips, cigarettes smoked while holding glasses of brandy, and the sound of Electrolux vacuum cleaners. The men seem more cheerful, in spite of their heart conditions, or the wives they betray, or the lovers whose needs they cannot fulfill. Probably this comes from the fact that these stories tend to be narrated by a younger character, looking up at these people as a young person often does, believing that grown-ups are actually adults. The boy-man aspect is in abey-ance. They tell the tale of a time gone by.

And eventually the other stories will do the same. The era that Busch writes of is, of course, passing. He noted this himself in an essay he wrote in 1984, "Fiction That's Glossier," bemoaning what he found in the fiction section of what was then the current magazines. He found gossip instead of beauty. He found technology instead of narrative. He found stories that merely stated problems, working "like a small machine of limited function." He worried that the "new anti-Freudian psychopiddle that began in the 60's and flourished during the 70's, when it was stylish to be selfish, healthy, pretty and pretty much alone in your concerns" was now all the readers wanted. What Busch wanted was to communicate. This is why he praised Hemingway for "responsible writing, a writing that is about the essential transaction between writer and reader. It is about being human in a time of despair."

Busch has been referred to as a "writer's writer," and it is hard to know exactly what this means. Ostensibly it means that he is read mainly by writers—and for good reason; one can learn a lot about dialogue, character, setting, about how little it takes on the page to render something correctly. But probably it also means that his sales were not high enough for him to be considered a writer who reached a large number of mainstream readers. This is too bad, because any reader, whether they are a writer, or a lover of humanity, a consumer of literature for the sake of it alone, has a great deal to find in here. Through the abilities of Busch, and his unfaltering benevolence, we learn that not only was he brave, he tells us something we should know: Most of us are brave. It is worth celebrating.

HARDWATER
COUNTRY

◆

WIDOW WATER

WHAT TO KNOW about pain is how little we do to deserve it, how simple it is to give, how hard to lose. I'm a plumber. I dig for what's wrong. I should know. And what I think of now as I remember pain is the fat young man and his child, their staggering house, the basement filled with death and dark water, the small perfect boy on the stone cellar steps who wept, the widow's coffee gone cold.

They called on Friday to complain that the pump in their basement wouldn't work. Theirs is shallow-well country, a couple of miles from the college, a place near the fast wide river that once ran the mill that all the houses of the town depended on. The railroad came, the town grew, the large white clapboard houses spread. By the time their seedlings were in the middle growth, the mill had failed, the houses had run to blisters of rotted wood on the siding and to gaps in the black and green roofs. The old ones were nearly all dead and the railroad came twice a day, from Utica to Binghamton, to Utica from Binghamton, carrying sometimes some freight, sometimes a car of men who maintained the nearly useless track. And the new people came, took their children for walks on the river to the stone foundations of the mill. They looked at the water and went home. People now don't know the water as they should. I'm a plumber, I should know.

I told him I couldn't come on a Friday afternoon in April, when the rains were opening seams and seals and cellars all through the country. Bella was making coffee for us while I took the call, and I snapped my fingers for her to turn around. She did, all broad—not fat, though—and full of colors—red in her face, yellow in her hair going gray, the gold in her tooth, her eyes blue as pottery—and I pointed at the phone. She mouthed a mimic "Today, today, today," and I nodded, and she nodded back and poured the almost boiling water out into the instant coffee, which dissolved.

He said, "So you see, sir, we can use your help."

I said, "Yessir, sounds like a problem."

"No water, and we've got a boy who isn't toilet-trained. It gets kind of messy."

"I imagine."

"So do you think you could . . ."

"Yessir?"

"Come kind of soon?"

"Oh, I'll come kind of soon. It just won't be today."

"You're sure you couldn't . . ."

"Yessir?"

"Come today?"

"Yessir."

"Yes sir, what?"

"Yessir, I'm sure I can't come."

Bella rapped on the table with her big knuckles to tell me to come and sit. I nodded, pointed at the telephone, waited for him to try once more. He was from the college—he would try once more.

He said, "But no water—for how long? The weekend? All week?"

I heard a woman whisper in the background with the harshness of a wife making peace, and then he said, "Uh—I mean, do you know when you can come?"

I said, "When're you up?"

"Excuse me?"

"When do you wake up?"

"We'll be up. Just tell me when."

I said, "I'll be there tomorrow morning, early, if that's all right."

"I mean, how early?"

"You get up, Mr. Samuels, and you have yourself a comfortable breakfast, and I'll be there for a cup of your coffee."

He hung on the line, waiting for more. I gave him nothing more, and he said, "Thanks. I mean, we'll see you tomorrow, then. Thank you."

"Thank *you* for calling, Mr. Samuels, and I'll see you soon."

He said, "Not soon enough," and chuckled and didn't mean the laugh.

I chuckled back and meant it, because coffee was waiting, and Bella, and a quiet hour before I went back out to clear a lonely lady's pipe in a fifty-foot well. I said, "Good-bye, Mr. Samuels."

He said, "Yes," which meant he was listening to his whispering wife, not me, and then he said, "Yes, good-bye, thank you very much, see you soon."

I blew on my coffee and Bella turned the radio off—she'd been listening to it low to hear if she'd won the fur coat someone in Oneida was giving away—and we sat and ate bran muffins with her blueberry jam and talked about nothing much; we said most of it by sitting and eating too much together after so many years of coffee and preserves.

After a while she said, "A professor with a problem."

"His pump won't turn off. Somebody sold him a good big Gould brand-new when he moved in last summer, and now it won't turn off and he's mad as hell."

"Well, I can understand that. They hear that motor banging away and think it's going to explode and burn their house down. They're city people, I suppose."

"Aren't they ever. I know the house. McGregory's old place near the Keeper farm. It needs work."

"Which they wouldn't know how to do."

"Or be able to afford," I said. "He's a young one and a new professor. He wouldn't earn much more than the boys on Buildings and Grounds. I'll bill him—he won't have the money in the house or at the bank, probably—and we'll wait a couple of months."

Bella said, "We can wait."

"We will."

"What did you tell him to do?"

"I told him to unplug the pump."

"He wasn't satisfied."

"I guess I wouldn't be."

"Abe," she said, "what's it like to be young as that?"

I said, "Unhappy."

She said, "But happy, too."

"A little of that."

She bent her gray and gold head over the brown mug of dark brown coffee and picked at the richness of a moist muffin. She said, still looking down, "It's hard."

I said, "It gets easier."

She looked up and nodded, grinned her golden tooth at me, said, "Doesn't it?"

THEN I SPENT the afternoon driving to New Hartford to the ice-cream plant for twenty-five pounds of sliced dry ice. I had them cut the ice into ten-inch-long slivers about three-quarters of an inch around, wrapped the ice in heavy brown paper, and drove it back to Brookfield and the widow's jammed drill point. It's all hard-water country here, and the crimped-pipe points they drive down for wells get sealed with calcium scales if you wait enough years, and the pressure falls, the people call, they worry about having to drill new wells and how much it will cost and when they can flush the toilets again. They worry how long they'll have to wait.

I went in the cellar door without telling her I was there, disconnected the elbow joint, went back out for the ice, and when I had carried the second bundle in, she was standing by her silent well in the damp of her basement, surrounded by furniture draped in plastic sheets, fire-wood stacked, cardboard boxes of web-crusted Mason jars, the growing heaps of whatever in her life she couldn't use.

She was small and white and dressed in sweaters and a thin green housecoat. She said, "Whatever do you mean to do?" Her hands were folded across her little chest, and she rubbed her gnarled throat. "Is my well dead?"

"No, ma'am. I'd like you to go upstairs while I do my small miracle here. Because I'd like you not to worry. Won't you go upstairs?"

She said, "I live alone—"

I said, "You don't have to worry."

"I don't know what to do about—this kind of thing. It gets more and more of a problem—this—all this." She waved her hand at what she lived in and then hung her hands at her sides.

I said, "You go on up and watch the television. I'm going to fix it up. I'll do a little fixing here and come back tonight and hook her up again, and you be ready to make me my after-dinner coffee when I come back. You'll have water enough to do it with."

"Just go back upstairs?" she said.

"You go on up while I make it good. And I don't want you worrying."

"All right, then," she said, "I'll go back up. I get awfully upset now. When these—things. These—I don't know what to do anymore." She looked at me like something that was new. Then she said, "I knew your father, I think. Was he big like you?"

"You know it," I said. "Bigger. Didn't he court you one time?"

"I think everybody must have courted me one time."

"You were frisky," I said.

"Not like now," she said. Her lips were white on her white face, the flesh looked like flower petals. Pinch them and they crumble, wet dust.

"Don't you feel so good now?"

"I mean kids now."

"Oh?"

"They have a different notion of frisky now."

"Yes they do," I said. "I guess they do."

"But I don't feel so good," she said. "This. Things like this. I wish they wouldn't happen. Now. I'm very old."

I said, "It keeps on coming, doesn't it?"

"I can hear it come. When the well stopped, I thought it was a sign. When you get like me, you can hear it come."

I said, "Now listen: You go up. You wrap a blanket around you and talk on the telephone or watch the TV. Because I guarantee. You knew my father. You knew my father's word. Take mine. I guarantee."

"Well, if you're guaranteeing."

I said, "That's my girl." She was past politeness so she didn't smile or come back out of herself to say goodbye. She walked to the stairs and when she started to shuffle and haul the long way up, I turned away to the well pipe, calling, "You make sure and have my coffee ready tonight. You wait and make my after-dinner coffee, hear? There'll be water for it." I waited until she went up, and it was something of a wait. She was too tired for stairs. I thought to tell Bella that it looked like the widow hadn't long.

But when she was gone, I worked. I put my ear to the pipe and heard the sounds of hollowness, the emptiness under the earth that's not quite silence—like the whisper you hear in the long-distance wires of the telephone before the relays connect. Then I opened the brown paper packages and started forcing the lengths of dry ice down into the pipe. I carried and shoved, drove the ice first with my fingers and then with a piece of copper tube, and I filled the well pipe until nothing more would go. My fingers were red, and the smoke from dry ice misted up until I stood in an underground fog. When nothing more would fit, I capped the pipe, kicked the rest of the ice down into the sump—it steamed as if she lived above a fire, as if always her house were smoldering—and I went out, drove home.

I went by the hill roads, and near Excell's farm I turned the motor off, drifted down the dirt road in neutral, watching. The deer had come down from the high hills and they were moving carefully through the fields of last year's corn stumps, grazing like cattle at dusk, too many to count. When the truck stopped I heard the rustle as they pulled the tough silk. Then I started the motor—they jumped, stiffened, watched me for a while, went back to eating: A man could come and kill them, they had so little fear—and I drove home to Bella and a tight house, long dinner, silence for most of the meal, then talk about the children while I washed the dishes and she put them away.

AND THEN I drove back to the house that was dark except for one lighted window. The light was yellow and not strong. I turned the engine off and coasted in. I went downstairs on the tips of my toes because, I told myself, there was a sense of silence there, and I hoped she was having some rest. I uncapped the well pipe and gases blew back, a stink of the deepest cold, and then there was a sound of climbing, of filling up, and water banged to her house again. I put the funnel and hose on the mouth of the pipe and filled my jeep can, then capped the check valve, close the pipe that delivered the water upstairs, poured water from the jeep can through the funnel to prime the pump, switched it on, watched the pressure needle climb to thirty-eight pounds, opened the faucet to the upstairs pipes, and heard it gush.

I hurried to get the jeep can and hose and funnel and tools to the truck, and I had closed the cellar door and driven off before she made the porch to call me. I wanted to get back to Bella and tell her what a man she was married to—who could know so well the truths of ice and make a dead well live.

SATURDAY MORNING the pickup trucks were going to the dump, and the men would leave off trash and hard fill, stand at tailgates, spitting, talking, complaining, shooting at rats or nothing, firing off, picking for scrap, and I drove to see the professor and his catastrophe.

His house was tilted. It needed jacks. The asbestos siding was probably all that kept the snow out. His drain-pipes were broken, and I could see the damp spots where water wasn't carried off but spilled to the roof of his small porch to eat its way in and gradually soften the house for bad winter leaks. The lawn at the side of his drive was rutted and soft, needed gravel. The barn he used for garage would have to be coated with creosote or it would rot and fall. A child's bright toys lay in his yard like litter. The cornfield behind his house went off to soft meadow and low hills, and everything was clean and growing behind where they lived; for the view they had, they might as well have owned the countryside. What they didn't own was their house.

He met me at the back steps, all puffy and breasted in his T-shirt, face in the midst of a curly black beard, dirty glasses over his eyes like a mask. He shook my hand as if I were his surgeon. He asked me to have coffee, and I told him I wouldn't now. A little boy came out, and he was beautiful: blond hair and sweetly shaped head, bright brown eyes, as red from weather as his father was pale, a sturdy body with a rounded stomach you would want to cup your hand on as if it were a breast, and teeth as white as bone. He stood behind his father and circled an arm around his father's heavy thigh, put his forehead in his father's buttocks, and then peeped out at me. He said, "Is this the fixing man? Will he fix our pump?"

Samuels put his hand behind him and squeezed the boy's head. He said, "This is the plumber, Mac." He raised his eyebrows at me and smiled, and I liked the way he loved the boy and knew how the boy embarrassed him too.

I kneeled down and said, "Hey, Mac."

The boy hid his face in his father's behind.

I said, "Mac, do you play in that sandbox over there?"

His face came out and he said, very politely, "Would you like to play with me?"

I said, "I have to look at your pump, Mac."

He nodded. He was serious now. He said, "Daddy broke it last night, and we can't fix it again."

I carried my tool pack to the cellar door—the galvanized sheeting on top of it was coming loose, several nails had gone, the weather was getting behind it and would eat the wood away—and I opened it up and started down the stone steps to the inside cellar door. They came behind me, then Samuels went ahead of me, turning on lights, scuffing through the mud and puddles on his concrete floor. The pump was on the wall to the left as I came in. The converted coal furnace in front of me leaked oil where the oilfeed came in. Stone foundation cracking that was two hundred years old, vent windows shut when they should have been opened to stop the dry rot, beams with the adze scars in them powdering almost as we watched: that was his cellar—and packing cartons and scraps of wood, broken chairs, a table with no legs. There was a stink of something very bad.

I looked at the pump, breathed out, then I looked at Mac. He breathed out too. He sounded like me. I grinned at him and he grinned back.

"We're the workers," he said. "Okay? You and me will be the workers. But Daddy can't fix anymore. Mommy said so."

Samuels said, "We'll leave him alone now, Mac."

I said, "How old is he?"

Mac said, "Six years old."

Samuels said, "Three. Almost three and a half."

"And lots of boy," I said.

Mac said, "I'm a worker."

Samuels said, "All right, Mac."

Mac said, "Can't stay here? Daddy? I'm a *work*er."

Samuels said, "Would we be in the way? I'd like to learn a little about the thing if I can."

Mac shook his head and smiled at me. He said, "What are we going to do with our Daddy?"

Samuels said, "Okay, buddy."

Mac raised his brows and shrugged his little arms.

Samuels said, "Out, Mac. Into the yard. Play in the sandbox for a while." He said, "Okay? I'll call you when we need some help."

"Sure!" Mac said.

He walked up the steps, arms slanted out to balance himself, little thighs pushing up on the steps. From outside, where we couldn't see him anymore, the boy called, "Bye and I love you," and ran away.

Samuels held his arms folded across his chest, covering his fleshy breasts. He uncrossed his arms to push his glasses up on his face when they slipped from the bridge of his flat nose. He said, "The water here—I tried to use the instruction book last night, after I talked to you. I guess I shouldn't have done that, huh?"

"Depends on what you did, Mr. Samuels." I unrolled the tool pack, got ready to work.

"I figured it wouldn't turn off on account of an air block in the pipes. The instructions mentioned that."

"Oh."

"So I unplugged the pump as you told me to, and then I drained all the water out—that's how the floor got so wet. Then it all ran into that hole over there."

"The sump."

"Oh, *that's* what a sump is. Then that motor like an outboard engine with the pipe—"

"The sump pump. The water collects in the hole and pushes the float up and the motor cuts in and pumps the water out the side of the house—over there, behind your hot-water heater."

"Oh."

"Except your sump pump isn't plugged in."

"Oh. I wondered. And I was fooling with the motor and this black ball fell off into the water."

"The float. So it wouldn't turn itself *off* if you did keep it plugged in. Don't you worry, Mr. Samuels, we'll pump her out later. Did you do anything else to the well pump?"

He pushed his glasses up and recrossed his arms. "I didn't know what else to do. I couldn't make it start again. We didn't have any water all night. There wasn't any pressure on the gauge."

"No. You have to prime it."

"Prime it?"

"I'll show you, Mr. Samuels. First, you better let me look. Right?"

"Sorry. Sorry. Do you mind if I stay here, though?" He smiled. He blushed under his whiskers. "I really have to learn something about how—this whole thing." He waved his arms around him and then covered up.

I said, "You can stay, sure. Stay."

I started to work a wrench on the heavy casing bolts, and when I'd got the motor apart from the casing, water began to run to the floor from the discharge pipe over the galvanized tank.

He said, "Should I . . ."

"Excuse me?"

"There's water coming down. Should I do anything about it?"

I said, "No, thank you. No. You just watch, thank you."

After a while the trickle slowed, and I pulled the halves apart. I took the rubber diaphragm off, put the flashlight on the motor, poked with a screwdriver, found nothing. I expected nothing. It had to be in the jet. I put the light on that and looked in and saw it, nodded, waited for him to ask.

He said, "You found it?"

"Yessir. The jet's blocked. That's what it sounded like when you called. Wouldn't let the pressure build up, so the gauge wouldn't know when to stop. It's set at forty pounds, and the block wouldn't let it up past—oh, twenty-eight or thirty, I'd say. Am I right?"

"Uh, I don't know. I don't know *any*thing about these things."

I said, "When this needle hits forty, it's what you should be getting. Forty pounds of pressure per square inch. If you'd read the gauge you'd have seen it to be about thirty, I calculate. That would've told you the whole thing."

"I thought the gauge was broken."

"They generally don't break. Generally, these things work. Usually it's something simpler than machines when you can't get water up."

He pushed his glasses and covered up, said, "God, what I don't know."

I said, "It's hard to live in a house, isn't it? But you'll learn."

"Jesus, I hope so. I don't know. I hope so. We never lived in a house before."

"What'd you live in? Apartment houses?"

"Yeah—where you call the janitor downstairs and he comes up while you're at work and you never see him. Like magic. It's just all better by the time you get home."

"Well, we'll get this better for you."

He frowned and nodded very seriously. "I'll bet you will," he said. It was a gift he gave me, a bribe.

I said, "So why don't you go on up and ask the missus for about three inches of aluminum foil. Would you do that? And a coat hanger, if you don't mind."

"Coat hanger?"

"Yessir. If you don't mind."

He walked across the floor to the wooden steps that went upstairs above the furnace; he tried to hide the sway and bounce of his body in the way that he walked, the boy coming down the outside concrete steps as the father went up the inside ones. "Do you need any help?" the boy said.

I said, "Mac, you old helper. Hello."

"Do you need any help?"

"I had a boy like you."

"A little bit big, like me?"

"Little bit big. Except now he's almost a daddy too."

He said, "Is he *your* daddy now?"

I said, "Not yet."

"Not yet?"

"Not for a while."

"Oh. Well, then what happened to him?"

"He just got big. He grew up."

"Does he go to the college?"

"He's bigger than that, even."

Mac smiled and showed his hand, fingers held together. "*That* big? *So* big?"

"Bigger," I said.

Mac said, "That's a big boy you have."

SAMUELS HANDED ME the foil and coat hanger. I rolled the foil around a cigar until it was a cylinder, and I stuck it in the well side of the nozzle. I opened the hanger and straightened her out.

Mac said, "What's he doing, Daddy?"

Samuels said, "I don't know. I don't know, Mac. Why don't you go outside? I don't know."

I said, "Mr. Samuels, I wonder if you would hold that foil firmly in there and cup your hand under it while I give her a shove."

He held. Mac watched him. I pushed at the other side of the jet, felt it, pushed again, and it rolled down the aluminum foil to his palm: a flat wet pebble half the size of the nail on his little finger. He said, "That's it? That's all it is? This is what ruined my life for two days?"

I said, "That's all it ever takes, Mr. Samuels. It came up with the water—you have to have gravel where there's water—and it lodged in the jet, kept the pressure from building up. If it happens again, I'll put a screen in at the check valve. May never happen again. If it does, we'll know what to do, won't we?"

Samuels said, "I wonder when I'll ever know what to do around here."

I said, "You'll learn."

I fastened the halves of the pump together, then went out for my jeep can, still half full from the widow's house. I came back in and I unscrewed the pipe plug at the top of the pump and poured the water in, put the plug back on, connected the pump to the switch.

Mac jumped, then stood still, holding to his father's leg.

The pump chirred, caught on the water from the widow's well, drew, and we all watched the pressure climb to forty, heard the motor cut out, heard the water climb in the copper pipes to the rest of the house as I opened the valve.

I was putting away tools when I heard Samuels say, "Now keep away from there!" I heard the *whack* of his hand on Mac's flesh, and heard the weeping start, in the back of the boy's throat, and then the wail. Samuels said, "That's *filthy* in there—Christ knows what you've dragged up. And I *told* you not to mess with things you don't know anything about. Dammit!"

Mac wailed louder. I watched his face clench and grow red, ugly. He put his left sleeve in his mouth and chewed on it, backed away to the stone steps, fumbled with his feet and stepped backwards up one step. "But *Dad*-dy," he said. "But *Dad*-dy." Then he stood on the steps and chewed his sleeve and cried.

Samuels said, "God, look at that."

I said, "There's that smell you've been smelling, Mr. Samuels. Mouse. He must've fallen into the sump and starved to death and rotted there. That's what you've been smelling."

"God. Mac—go up and wash your hands. Mac! Go upstairs and wash your hands. I mean *now*!"

The small brown lump of paws and tail and teeth, its stomach swollen, the rest looking almost dissolved, lay in its puddle on the floor beside the sump. The stink of its death was everywhere. The pump cut in and built the pressure up again. Mac stood on the cellar steps and cried. His father pushed his glasses up and looked at the corpse of the rotted mouse and hugged his arms around himself and looked at his son. I walked past Samuels, turned away from the weeping boy, and pushed up at the lever that the float, if he had left it there, would have released on the sump pump. Nothing happened, and I stayed where I was, waiting, until I remembered to plug the sump pump in. I pushed the lever again, its motor started, the filthy reeking water dropped, the wide black rubber pipe it passed through on the ceiling swung like something alive as all that dying passed along it and out.

I picked the mouse up by its tail after the pump had stopped and Samuels, waiting for my approval, watching my face, had pulled out the plug. I carried my tools under my arm and the jeep can in my hand. I nodded to Samuels and he was going to speak, then didn't, just nodded back. I walked past Mac on the steps, not crying anymore, but wet-faced and stunned. I bent down as I passed him. I whispered, "What shall we do with your Daddy?" and went on, not smiling.

I walked to the truck in their unkempt drive that went to the barn that would fall. I carried the corpse. I thought to get home to Bella and say how sorry I was for the sorrow I'd made and couldn't take back. I spun the dripping mouse by its tail and flung it beyond the barn into Keeper's field of corn stumps. It rose and sank from the air and was gone. I had primed the earth. It didn't need the prime.

THE LESSON OF THE
HÔTEL LOTTI

M Y MOTHER'S LOVER was always exhausted, and yet he generated
for me, and I think for her too, a sense of the most inexhaustible
gentleness, and the strong calm I grew up thinking a prerequisite for
love. He was a lawyer with offices at the foot of Manhattan, a neighborhood he knew intimately and talked about compellingly. The son of
Austrian immigrants, a Jew, he lectured gently on Trinity Church and
practiced maritime law, a field not famous for its renunciations of the
more vulgar bigotries. He was the same age as my mother, fifty-five,
when they started practicing deceptions and certainly cruelties upon his
wife. And when my mother died at sixty-two, a couple of years after he
did, she had suffered the most dreadful solitude, for he was necessary.

I was unplanned, unexpected, and apparently less than desirable.
Born when my mother was thirty-nine, I was doubtless part of what
happened not long thereafter. My father, who owned yards—a pleasure-
craft boat yard, two lumberyards, and part of an undistinguished Cali-
fornia vineyard—left my mother, and me, for a woman with inherited
land in a suburb of London called Edgware. I have been there, for
reasons I don't need to make clear; it looks like Flatbush Avenue in
Brooklyn, though less permanent—every other house seems to be in a
state of rebuilding or repair—and I never will need to go back. I grew

up as much my mother's younger sister as her child. And the older I became, the more accomplished I was said to be, so my mother grew more fatigued by the world, more easily dismayed.

I have composed some recollections, for the sake of sentiment—I don't want to lose *anything* now—and so I think that I recall him standing silently at the door of our apartment on East 50th Street, late one night, as they returned from the theater. He seemed reluctant to walk farther in. I think I remember his smile: lips tightly closed (he had bad teeth), the long frown-lines from the nose to the corners of his mouth (they later became the boundaries of jowls), the pale blue eyes content but ready not to be. I think I can call him ironic, in the sense that he inspired, and dealt with, several emotions at once; he never surrendered to sarcasm. He looks larger in this possible early recollection than he was but, then, I feel smaller, when I remember him, than I am. He was nearly six feet tall, but because of his short legs he looked less large when I knew him well. His head was bald, the fringe gone chestnut and white. His face was square, his neck solid but not thick. His nose was wide without being bulbous. He was a slender man with a broad chest and strong shoulders, and he dressed in dark expensive suits. His voice was deep; it could snap and yap and snarl, or it could rumble soothingly as he spoke of what he loved, and nearly always when he talked to me it was with a graveled gentleness I have heard no other man use.

For years, my mother spoke of "my attorney," or "my legal adviser," or, as I grew older, "our lawyer." Then it became "Leonard Marcus says" and then "Leonard." He came to my graduation from the Brearley School, and I introduced him as "my Uncle Leonard," although my mother had never called him that. The night of my graduation, the three of us had dinner at the Russian Tea Room and went to a revival of *Our American Friend*. I thereafter left for a party with classmates, and when I came home early because I had decided to age quickly by finding myself bored with my intimate companions of four years, I found my mother waiting in the living room for a talk.

For a talk: a separate category in our lives, signaled by a silver drinks tray on the coffee table, a round stone ashtray, and a packet of Player's cigarettes, which my mother had come more and more to smoke too many of—perhaps to remind her, in distress, of the England my father had fled to. The sailor on the packet had blue eyes, and on his hatband was the word HERO.

She wore a long challis housecoat and no slippers, and sat in a corner of the sofa with a plaid blanket held across her lap; I had bought the blanket for her in England during my pointless pilgrimage there the summer before. We greeted each other matter-of-factly, per our tacit agreement not to become hysterical until it was clearly a necessity, and for a few minutes we discussed how remarkably mature I had become, in contrast to my friends, in the course of a single evening. She made herself a drink—Calvados and soda with ice—and I made my own sophisticated bourbon and ginger ale. She lit a Player's Navy Cut, hissed smoke out at me, and then caught her breath as I took a package of Kools from my bag and lit up too.

"Well, well," she said.

I shrugged.

"About Leonard," she said.

"Where is he?"

"Leonard's at home with his wife."

I puffed as if the cigarette were a pipe. My face beat hot, and I'm sure I felt the same sense of landslide felt by children who in their teens are asked, "Did you ever think you might be adopted, darling?" But I managed to say, as if it weren't the second commencement of the day, "Gee, I didn't know he was married, Anya."

"Leonard is a married man," my mother said, nodding, and with a note of pride in her voice—a sound I would hear again when I came home from Vassar to discuss with her my first and unspectacular coupling, with a boy from Union College.

"Has he been married—uh—all the time?"

My mother nodded and drank some brandy, said across the rim of her glass, "We have always been having an *affaire*." Her French was manifest and overaccented; she was an educated woman, and never untheatrical. "He is not your uncle, darling."

"Well, that's all right, Anya."

"Susu," she said.

"Anya, would you mind very much calling me Suzanne?" I said.

So I was Suzanne, and he was not Uncle Leonard, nor simply our attorney, Leonard Marcus. And shortly, we were a domestic routine. Once the declaration had been made, it wasn't mentioned again—by me, because I was in awe of an *affaire* conducted by a woman with varicose veins who was my humdrum, pretty, and flustered mother; by her, because I tried very hard that summer to rarely be home.

I worked at the neighborhood Gristede's during the day, and at night I kept moving—the evening jazz concerts at the Museum of Modern Art, or Shakespeare in the Park, or films at the Thalia, or shopping for frights on Eighth Street in the Village, or posed and dramaturgical dates ending with kisses on the Staten Island ferry slip and several near-misses—and near-disasters—in the cars and homes of boys who belonged to poetry clubs at Lafayette or to rugby clubs at Yale.

I felt, in part, like an elder sister, or a mother even, who was giving Anya as much privacy as possible with her beau. And then, in late August, when I was beginning to shop for school and to face the fact that going to Poughkeepsie frightened me, I returned to the apartment on a Saturday afternoon after swimming at Rye with friends—I had, by then, forgiven them their youth—to find Leonard on the sofa in the living room, and Anya in a true state of fear.

His head was what I saw first, propped on a crocheted pillow that leaned against the arm rest. It was white, and I saw blue veins near the surface of the skin, and beads of perspiration that looked like oil; they didn't run or drip. He wore his polished black wingtips, and it was their position that frightened me. They didn't touch, nor did they lie as if he sprawled at rest; they were apart because his legs were slightly apart, the dark blue poplin suit soaked onto them by sweat, to show how thin his thighs and calves were. There was a terrible weakness in his posture, a sense of the exhaustion of resources. His hands lay on his stomach, barely, as if he hadn't strength enough to lift his arms. His breathing was shallow—I looked to be certain that he breathed. He opened his eyes, and their blueness made his pallor seem worse. He smiled and then his lips made the shape one makes to whistle. He was showing me that he knew how he looked, and that he felt as ill as he appeared, and that he, and disability, and us together—me poised over and before him in uselessness and perplexity—were something of a joke we each understood. But no noise came from his lips. I touched my own lips with my index finger, as if hushing him, as if dispelling the confession he would make, and I turned away quickly to find Anya in the bedroom, where I knew she would be, smoking Player's and crossing her legs.

I sat on the bed beside her. But she sat up taut, so I moved away. "It's the heat," she said.

"It looks like more than the heat, Anya."

"It's the heat *because* it's more than the heat. He has a bad heart. He's been seeing doctors."

"What are they planning to do?"

"Nothing. Medication. They say he's too old for the kind of surgery he needs."

And that, as much as Leonard's condition, was what made her start to weep. I think she had been waiting in that darkened bedroom filled with cigarette smoke and the hum of air-conditioning for someone to whom she could state that cruelty: that she, a slender woman in shorts and a halter, a woman with a young throat atop a body that was no disgrace despite the varicose veins, a woman who for years had conducted in perfect French an *affaire* with a man of gentle elegance—she, such a woman, now faced the continuation of a lesson she had received when my father left us years before. The lesson was about things running down—respect and trust and strength, and finally time.

I said, "Anya, can I ask you something?"

She sniffed and wiped her face with the back of a pale beautiful wrist. "When you ask if you can ask, Susu—Suzanne—it means you know you shouldn't ask it. Do you really need to?"

I said, "Do you and Leonard make love?"

She exploded into tears then, perhaps because her answer—not the impertinence or heartlessness of the question—was another segment of the lesson she must learn. "We used to," she said, as she tried to catch her breath.

"He can't anymore?"

"Suzanne!"

And her genuine dignity, a surprising muscularity of tone, her wonderful slight carriage, the beauty of her hair and neck, and certainly the specter of Poughkeepsie and my sense of the blackness beyond what I managed to know—all brought me into her arms, leaning over her, smelling her hair, wishing that I wept only for her.

HER LETTERS TO SCHOOL described his frailty and determination. My visits home confirmed them. They were together a great deal, and Leonard came to 50th Street with gifts—a book, a pen from Mark Cross, a scarf purchased at Liberty on one of his transatlantic trips. I grew accustomed, over that first year of school and then the others, to his slower walk, a loss of tension in his bearing, his need to pause and catch his breath, the permanent pallor of his face, his need for naps. His illness aged my mother, and I accepted that as well: I felt ten years older than I was, and it seemed appropriate to me that my mother should not look young. Leonard worked harder than before, and Anya tried to convince him to retire.

I was studying in my room at home one weekend, with the door ajar, when I heard her ask him, again, to slow his pace. He snapped at her, "I have to provide for a *wife*—remember? She's getting on, like us."

That was in my sophomore or junior year, and on the New York Central to Poughkeepsie that Sunday evening I stared out the window at the Hudson, which in the last sunlight looked like ice although it was nearly May, and I thought as hard as I could about Leonard's wife. I knew that he had been married to her for some thirty years. I knew that their child was grown and away. I knew that they maintained a home in Westchester County but that Leonard, complaining of fatigue, had furnished an apartment in the east forties where he stayed during the week. I knew that he often found a reason for staying in the city over weekends as well—that is, he found an alibi to broadcast in Westchester; I knew the reason. I wondered how much his wife knew, and I fell asleep refusing to believe that she didn't know it all.

I spent a week preparing for final exams, and made use of one of Leonard's lectures. This one had been on the Dead Sea scrolls. He had lent me three books and had told me what he knew. As I studied, I heard the low sweet voice, smelled the breath of decay, saw the round-shouldered posture he more and more assumed, and the sad ironic smile—a kind of shyness, I concluded—on the handsome white face. And I studied history, and Platonic posturings—"'But, sirs, it may be that the difficulty is not to flee from death, but from guilt. Guilt is swifter than death'"—and thought, again, that Dryden really needn't have bothered. I was studying Leonard Marcus, my mother's lover, and wondering why he, who had in spirit left his wife, was of a different category of being from my father, who had left his wife in fact. It pleases me to remember that, although I couldn't answer the question, I knew that Leonard Marcus *was* different. And thinking of my small rattled mother, or of Leonard's low devoted tones caressing the history of the Jefferson Administration, say, or of the angry assertion of his wife's need for money in old age, I am now—callow an impulse as it is—proud.

Leonard was not allowed to drink, and I had sworn myself to ignore his married life. We renounced those imperatives together in New York after he had returned from a business trip to Paris, and after I had begun my first semester at Columbia Law. Leonard called me at John Jay Hall and asked me to meet him at the Top of the Towers. I dressed nervously and too stylishly, and was quiet as we rode the elevator to the top of the Beekman Arms. We sat at a little table on the terrace and looked over the stone balustrade at the river, which, from that enormous distance, looked clean. The entire city looked clean and manageable, and knowing that it was an illusion helped me swear to myself that for this shrinking man who always, now, was out of breath, I would sustain whatever illusions he required of me. The winds up there were strong, despite the heat of late September, and I thought Leonard shivered. But when I suggested that we move indoors, he smiled that shy smile, shrugged his shoulders, and ordered drinks. He bought me a brandy Alexander, as if I were half child and we were combining the magic of a milkshake and the necessity that a dignified law student enjoy strong drink.

I felt like someone's daughter.

Leonard held my hand, then put it down as you would place Baccarat on a marble table—with deference to its quality, with care because it was fragile. And he began—precisely as if he were telling me of the rebel zealot Jesus, or of the building of Washington, or of the regulations governing off-shore fishing in Europe—to deliver another lecture. But this one was about his life.

"My wife is named Belle. Did you know that? She's a very tall woman, nearly as tall as you are. But she has bad feet, something to do with the instep, it's terribly painful, and she tends to shuffle. For some reason, that makes her look shorter. When I tell you this, you should try to see her as someone who is short. She has friends on Long Island, younger than she—younger than I—who are very much involved in the restoration of Colonial furniture. Do you care about Colonial furniture?" He actually paused, waited to know, and I am quite certain that he did wonder, even at the moment, about my interests. I shook my head and lit another Chesterfield—he had to cup his hands around mine to shelter the flame from the wind—and then Leonard continued.

"This happened last week, before I went to Paris. Did you know I'd been there? I'll have to tell you about it. A ship seems to have disappeared, although the client insists it was sold to the Egyptians, under Panamanian registry, for purposes involving proscribed shipments to

Northern Ireland. Our adversaries insist that the bill of lading was received and entered at Marseilles. The original owners are Americans—it's out of Eric Ambler, did you ever read him?" He laughed and threw his hands up, shook his head. "It's nonsense, and they're all crooks. But I want you to know about last week, before my trip. Belle was supposed to spend the weekend with her friends, and they asked if I could drive out with them. It was time to say yes, and I did, and we met at their apartment, at University Place, to go together to their house on the Island. You know how I've been—sometimes my energy is pretty poor." This time he didn't smile.

"Without going into details, let me say that I was pretty punk about it. Just as we were about to leave, I told Belle that I was too tired for the drive and that I'd go back to my apartment. She was furious, but she wasn't surprised." He looked at me so intensely that I looked away. "I want you to understand some of the complexities of our assumptions, Belle's and mine. At any rate, I did go back, and they went on to Long Island.

"My understanding is that Belle became worried about me"—he signaled for more drinks, brandy Alexander for me, white wine for him—"and woke up the poor host and made him drive her all the way back to New York at two in the morning, in a nasty rain. She has a key, of course, and let herself into my apartment."

"You weren't there," I said.

"No."

"Because you moved in with Anya after I went uptown to Columbia."

"That's not inaccurate."

"You keep the other place—"

"As a cover. In an Eric Ambler novel, it would be called that, yes." Leonard tried to smile, sipped his wine, frowned at it.

"And you sort of live part-time with Anya?"

He shrugged, raised his eyebrows, said, "It's a simple clarity for a complex situation—but, yes. Yes."

"Can I be your law clerk, Leonard?"

He grinned, with all his teeth this time, saying, "You mean you're my student? You flatter me that much?"

"Meaning I admire you very much."

He said, "You'll be *Law Review* and start someplace so prestigious—"

"Can I? Can I ask you again at the end of the year?"

He blushed, like a young man having drinks with a girl at one of the city's romantic saloons, and he said, "Yes. Please."

"Thank you, Leonard."

"But listen," he said. "She came into an empty apartment and looked around—it's tiny, a sofa bed, a kitchenette, a bathroom and closet. But she looked. And not only wasn't I there, there were barely signs that I'd *been* there. I don't know precisely what she began to know, but she began to know it. It was four in the morning by then. She sat there, by herself, not reading, not looking at television. She simply sat. Probably in the dark. And then, around six, she called the police and asked what to do. They told her she could file a missing persons report. What would that achieve? she asked. Nothing, they told her, except list me as missing and cause my name to be checked in emergency rooms and at the medical examiner's office. She thought there was no point in that, she said. She said she knew that if I were sick or dead she'd find out fairly soon. Then she went down to Grand Central and rode home. She reached me at the office later that morning. I assured her that I had been all right. I told her not to worry herself."

"And she accepted that?"

"She said she supposed foreign clients had arrived on a late plane and that I had to meet them."

"You let her believe that?"

"I didn't really answer. I told her I'd be home that weekend and told her to take care of herself, and we hung up."

"Leonard, she believed you?"

"We believe what we need to, I suppose."

"Is that true?"

He clasped his hands before him, in the air. The tips of his fingers were white and substanceless beneath the skin; they held the imprint of whatever they pressed upon. Shrugging his shoulders, he said, "It *sounds* true."

"Leonard, everything sounds true if you say it right."

"Dealing with other people's truth *can* be a self-indulgent process," he said. And then, as if to assure me that his remark was not meant merely to discipline me, he added, "We have been self-indulgent, I suppose, in a sense. Though we've been waiting for this. We're waiting now." And I didn't know which *we*—my mother and he, or someone else's mother and he—he meant.

I finished my drink, and he ordered another round, and then he finished his. We sat in silence through the arrival of the drinks, and through our consumption of them, and through the waiter's arrival with more. I smoked a lot and tried to think hard. Leonard waited patiently for me to have a reaction, or to discern what it was. I lit another cigarette—he cupped his hands for me again—and I blew smoke out, feeling that my tongue was raw, my throat sore, my head filled with childish exclamations and masterful formulations and the tune of a Robert Hall radio jingle. It was dark over the river now, but bright on the terrace, and ships were glimmering like fish as their super-structures caught the light the river absorbed. I said, "Life is confusing, Leonard," and he was decent enough to try to keep his lips from curving. But he couldn't, and then I couldn't, and we laughed—whooped, really—until he walked around to my chair, leaned from behind to kiss my cheek, and then gripped my arm to help me up and get me to a cab.

A year after his death—he died in his sleep, and in Westchester—I was spending the weekend helping my mother clean and cook for a party she'd decided it was necessary to give. As I vacuumed and put things away, grinding my teeth because I should have been uptown at my desk, I looked, thinking of my books, at the bedside bookcase. I saw *Judgment on Deltchev* by Eric Ambler. I thought of the Beekman Towers and Leonard's lesson; I had been trying to understand it since he'd offered it to me, and particularly since his death—since the funeral we felt we couldn't attend. I think our absence would have provoked his hesitant smile, but also grave pity for Anya and, I think, actual understanding of her relief at not having to watch him buried. Anya knew of his death when she read it in the *Times*.

With the vacuum cleaner bellowing, I opened the book, saw Balkan names and descriptions of fear and subterfuge, and then a shade of baby blue—a piece of note-paper. I laughed, because only in stories and in the most arcane probate cases will a letter from the dead fall from among the pages of a book. But I was sure that I had found such a letter, and I did not laugh anymore. In the roar of Anya's Electrolux, air pouring from an unstoppered vent, the old motor getting louder as it got hotter, I sat on my mother's bed and opened the folded single sheet. It was six-by-nine—perhaps half an inch longer each way—and where it had been folded, yellow-brown had supplanted the blue. A lion was engraved in the upper left-hand corner, and in the right it said *Hôtel Lotti, 7 et 9, Rue de Castiglione, Paris*. And below, nothing. No message I could read, no reminder, no clue. It was simply a bookmark, a convenience—it had nothing to say.

I smelled the motor grinding and meat cooking in the kitchen and the harsh intimate scent of Anya's Russia Leather. I was made physically sick by the blankness of the paper, its neat precise folds in which the brown discolorations pooled. I folded it and put it back in the book, and I thought of Leonard in a hotel room that smelled of paint. He lay on the long wide wooden bed in the Hôtel Lotti. Over a chair hung his trousers, wrinkled from the airplane, and on the bathroom doorknob hung his jacket, heavy with passport case and pens. He was in undershorts and undershirt, and his long black hose were held to his thin white calves by garters, black and tight. His feet nearly touched, and one arm lay on his chest while the other held *Judgment on Deltchev*. He was reading of failures and fealties, the corruptions of the sub-rosa world, and Anya was on 50th Street, and I was studying torts, and the man who had fathered me was living in Edgware, and I knew who my father was. I heard the shallow breathing and saw his thin white skull on the wide pillow, the dwindling body enclosed by the patterned wall-paper of the Hôtel Lotti.

I was holding the paperback book when Anya came in to find me sitting on her bed. The noise of the vacuum cleaner broke around me like beach thunder. Her throat was slack now, and the flesh of her upper arms soft. In her black dressing gown she seemed pretentious and pathetic, too made up, as if she had costumed herself for solitude and, at the same time, me.

She turned her head to the side as she looked at me; it was a dog's motion of puzzlement, a gesture new for her, another sign of age in us both. She asked me, I think, what the matter was. But her voice did not carry through the sound of the machine.

That was when I whispered, into all that mechanical rage, to all her worn-out loneliness, that I'd been studying too hard and needed to rest. I thought of Leonard Marcus' wife and tried to picture her as short.

That was when Anya mimed across the machine to me the question I read on her lips.

She said: What? What?

FAMILY CIRCLE

IAN'S GRANDFATHER summoned him with sneezes. Bright silver light from the leaded windows behind his grandfather made the dust a steady snow, falling from nowhere onto the old man's shoulders and the polished wood desk. Large in the morning light, he sat under an avalanche of shiny fineness, always being buried where he sat—slow storms of dust fell over him into his shadow on the smooth golden oak, disappearing—always untouched. From the doorway the old man was magical, and Ian watched as his grandfather crossed his arms and held himself by the shoulders and squeezed at the brown tweed cloth he wore and hunched his shoulders and pushed his chin down onto his chest and shuddered and closed his eyes and shook out the sneeze with an open-mouthed roar. He wiped the coarse sleeve across his mouth and nose—the left arm now hugged his heart—and like a cat licking fur, he rubbed the same sleeve on the desk, slowly back and forth, cleaning. When he saw Ian in the doorway, a little higher than the sculpted metal knob, the old man said, "What? *What?*" and Ian blew away.

IAN'S MOTHER WAS changing Stuart's diaper—here they called it nappy, but his mother said it smelled the same in England as it did in America—and Ian stood in his room and looked around the corner of the high cupboard that, with a dark green curtain, divided where he slept from the smaller room where his mother and Stuart had a double bed and a crib. He watched as she rolled Stuart over and swabbed him with a wash rag, then turned him over again to poke him in the stomach.

Ian held himself and watched. Then he stopped smiling and backed away in his high black Wellingtons and his tight American jeans and went down the wooden steps into the main room, where they had their little kitchen and their dining table and couch and the fire that smoked. There were wooden beams on the low white ceiling, and dark chunks of wood floated in the white plaster walls. Ian stood in the room and they laughed upstairs. He took an apple down from the little refrigerator top and the sharp knife from the table. He sliced the apple, then took bread from the cupboard and made two sandwiches—chunks of thick-skinned apple between slices of bread. He put them on the wide white plates and carried them up the steps. At the doorway to his room he called, "It's okay, Mom, I got breakfast for us. The baby can wait for his. I got us our breakfast first because we're bigger."

BRENDA WAS in the field with the six horses, spreading hay from two bales in a wheelbarrow that she had slid, squeaking, from the old stables next door to the stone coalhouse and the little stone cottage where Ian and his mother and Stuart were staying. Next to their cottage was the big house, with its chimneys at either end. The grandfather stood in front of his house, looking down the walk and over the yew hedge and the stone fence to where Brenda, small and skinny in her dark green duffel coat and jeans and Wellingtons, fed the horses in the rain. He saw what the boy saw—a pony trying to enter the white and black mare.

Ian, in his yellow slicker and hat, sitting under the overturned canvas-and-tubing sun chaise, called, "He's putting a baby into her, Grampa. We'll have puppies soon, won't we?" The mare kicked away at the pony.

High in his dark tweed sportcoat, rocking on his shoes with their built-up commando soles, the grandfather looked at the boy, and ran his big hand over his pink scalp and the black and white strands that crossed over it. "Puppies," he said. "Ian, when horses have babies, they're called *foals*. Foals, lad. Can you say that?"

Ian said, "Foals."

His grandfather watched Brenda stand in the circle of mud and manure while the horses and ponies ate at the six stations of hay she'd made. At some signal no one ever saw, one horse would think of changing his station and another would respond, moving from his so that the first one could move, and then they all would move, in a slow rainy dance, while Brenda stood there in the center.

"Brenda's good," the grandfather said.

Ian's mother came up from the cottage, carrying Stuart, both of them covered by the white canvas raincoat she held like a tent. She said, "Brenda's got a crooked nose."

His grandfather said, "Got it the good way—she was twice kicked, had it broken twice, never set, never in hospital for it. She's as tough as you. She's tougher."

"She's twenty-five years old, Daddy."

"Aye, all of that. She qualifies, all right."

His mother said, "For *what?*"

His grandfather hugged his chest and ducked his face and wrenched his mouth about and let the sneeze curl out of his mouth and nose. He wiped his face with his sleeve.

Stuart said, "Toooo!"

His mother said, "Punishment."

His grandfather said, "Dinner," and went inside.

BRENDA WAS wearing a black halter and her dungarees and boots, and a scarf held her long brown hair in place behind her, on the neck. She rode out with three pony-trekkers shifting and wobbling like potato sacks on their thin saddles. She led them across the two-lane road and up a small access road that went to the foot of the fells. She waved to Ian. She had dropped the butt of her filtered cigarette on the dust and stones inside the green metal gate Ian closed for her, then stood on, climbing the rungs, waving back.

When Ian jumped off the gate, the morning sun was high and hot. Sheep across the road moaned, and a truck coming down the 1:7 hill from the quarry at Broughton Moor filled the fields with the sound of its straining. The boy turned and saw that the small herd of two-year-old cattle in the outer field had followed him, were standing in a semicircle behind him, heads lowered, watching. As he moved, a white and gray heifer jumped backward and threw its face up.

"Hello," the boy said. "Hello." Ian held a handful of weed up to them and said, "Hello."

All their eyes watched.

IAN's MOTHER lay on the sun chaise in a bathing suit that was held together at the stomach by a metal ring. Her eyes were closed and her face was covered with tiny drops of oiled sweat. Her toes danced to the music from Brenda's big brown radio which sat atop a stone wall, all that was left of a shed outside the old stables. Brenda rubbed oil onto tack, and Ian's mother lay with almost a smile on her face, moving her feet. Stuart sat on the cobbles near Brenda, holding a red and white ball against his face, watching Brenda's hands move. Ian, in Wellingtons and shorts, made a tiny house of stones and twigs. Everyone was quiet, and the radio played, and then the green metal gate two pastures down squeaked above the music and Brenda, without looking, said, "Oh, it must be another gifted horseman. I suppose I shall have to book the lot of rubbish for a ride."

Ian stood up to watch, then ran down to the gravel where cars were parked below the big house. He shouted, "Mommy, it's the police. It's the police, Mommy!"

Brenda went down to him, lighting a cigarette, then standing with it sticking out of her mouth, her lips curled hard to hold it. "It's taxi, Ian." She called back to his mother, "Has our Ian not seen taxis before?"

The driver let the man out at the second gate, the wooden one close by the stream that Brenda had told him was a dike and that his grand-father called a beck. But Ian's mother had said he could call it a stream because that's what they had in America.

The heavy man walked up, carrying a brown leather bag with two straps, rolling a little sideways when he walked.

Brenda said, "Ian, is that what your dad looks like?"

THEY WALKED UP the access road, following the rich brown mounds of horse droppings, going along the stone fences, and then through the rocky fields where there were no fences and the road took them high enough to look down steep grazing grounds with teeth of gray rock coming through the grass, and then, on their left, the hills going higher, green and gray, and then the moors beginning, ferny and darker with moss, wet, and beyond them the blueness of mountains, grainy and clear in the bright late afternoon. His father held his hand and he stopped them near a tiny fall of water which came over rocks into a small pool that drained beneath the road and ran on the other side down to the sheep below. His father said, "Are you tired?"

Ian said, "I came up here plenty of times."

His father nodded. He pulled a thick-bladed weed up, peeled it back, wetted it, put the end in his mouth, and blew. Nothing came out. He said, "It used to make a whistle when I was a kid."

Ian said, "It's probably a different kind of plant in America."

"Everything's different here, huh?"

"And they call them different things. They don't say boots, they say Wellingtons. Grampa got me these in Ulverston. We go shopping there. Will you get boots, Daddy?"

"You think I should?"

"If you stay here, yes. Do you have enough money?"

"Yes, love, thank you."

"Because Grampa gave me some English money if you need it."

"Thank you, love."

"If you want to stay here and go for a hike or something."

"Hey, I missed you a lot, Ian."

"They have all these swamps here. Brenda calls them boggy."

"Ian, I was really missing you. And Stu, and Mommy."

Ian walked ahead of his father, past the waterfall. The boy said, "Come on, Daddy. Only next time you have to wear boots. Wellingtons. All right?"

THE GRANDFATHER SAT at the desk, writing with a black fountain pen on long white paper. The dust fell onto him and disappeared into his shadow, into the words that he wrote. Ian stood at the door, his hand on the knob, watching. The grandfather didn't look up. He said, "Come here."

Inside, where the books stood in all their shelves and the newspapers were curled on the table near the wide red-cushioned chair, Ian stood beside the desk and watched the dark hairs on his grandfather's hands as they moved in the shadows. He said, "Hi."

"Can you read what I'm writing?"

"I'm not old enough to read that kind. The letters are too scribbly."

"I'm writing a book. What do you think of that?"

"Is it a good book?"

His grandfather looked over the heavy tweed on his arm at Ian's face. He said, "Is that a good question?"

Ian looked up at him. He said, "That's all I could think of."

His grandfather stood up from his chair. Ian moved back. His grandfather waved his hand inside his sport-coat pocket and took out a puddle of coins. He held the palm up to his face, poked through it, pinched a big copper two-pence piece, and held it out for Ian to take. He said, "Damned good question. It's all I could think of too." He sat down, pushed himself closer to the desk, looked at the page, and then at the papers beside it. He said, "Say thank you and disappear."

"Thank you, Grampa. Should I say disappear?"

The grandfather hugged himself and ducked his head and shook, and the sneeze belched out. He panted, then rubbed his arm over the page, making some of the words run. He wiped his mouth and hugged his chest for the next one.

AT DINNER IN the big house, they could hear Stuart crying in his room in the cottage. The grandfather brought the pork roast in from the kitchen. He said, "Anna, do you want to see to Stuart?"

Ian's mother said, "No, dear. You ask me that nearly every night, and I tell you that he's all right. That's how he goes to sleep."

The grandfather said, "Do you remember that ruckus, Harry?"

Ian's father said, "It hasn't been that long."

Brenda smoked a cigarette and said, "Did you pick the wine?"

The grandfather said, "Absolutely. And with care."

"It's too dry."

Carving, his grandfather looked up, raised his gray eyebrows, smiled. He said, "You've got the taste of a Yorkshire pig-farmer."

Brenda said, "I'm the daughter of a Yorkshire pig-farmer."

Ian said, "Brenda says she saw a pig eat a chicken once."

"A pig will take a chunk from a fair-sized man," Brenda said.

The grandfather passed a plate to Ian's father. He said, "Let's see a man take a bit of a pig, then, Harry."

Ian's mother said, "You have such elegance, Daddy."

"Yes I do, don't I? Sort of careless elegance. It's what the landed gentry are supposed to show. But I wish I had a little more land and a little less gentry."

Ian's father said, "Should I cut your meat, Ian?"

Ian said, "Yes, please."

Ian's mother said, "I'll do it. Pass my your plate."

"Can Daddy do it?"

His father put his hands in his trouser pockets and sat lower in his chair.

Brenda said, "I wonder if anyone would like a cigarette?"

Ian passed his plate. His grandfather bowed low, sat up straighter, crossed his chest with arms, and sneezed onto the roast.

Ian's mother said, "I think you've *got* a little less gentry, Daddy. God. I won't want second helpings, thank you."

Brenda held the cigarette with her lips and said, "I think the old boy's allergic to horses."

IN THE STONE BARN, half of its roof burned away and never replaced, hay stacked in the covered part, Ian, in the cool darkness, while sun ran like water into the open side, swam in the bales, jumped from one layer to another, wriggled between them, hid. Yellow seed popped into the air as he played, and each time he buried himself he came back up with more long stalks on his short-sleeved shirt and his arms. He chanted to himself, "Don-ta-don," rolling and sidling, pulling hay away with his hands, then heaping it back over himself, "Don-ta-don." He said, "Don-ta-don," and was a diving thing, a creature of animal strength and warlike thrusts which hid and then revealed itself; fearless, it nevertheless sought the lower bales and the spaces between them nearest to the floor. And when the smell of strong cigarettes came up the dirt path behind the barn on the hillside, and when Brenda's voice came, singing hoarsely and low, the creature went to ground.

She pulled a bale out by its strings and laid it along her right shoulderblade and flank. Bursting up from cover, the hiding thing called, "Yah-*hah*!" Brenda straightened, took the cigarette from her mouth as she eased the bale back down, said quietly, "Ian, I have asked you not to muck about in the hay. Now you come down off of there and help me scatter this to the rubbishy creatures, will you?"

She stooped under the bale, got it up again and, the cigarette in her mouth, walked away behind the barn. Ian followed her, his arms against his sides, shedding his camouflage, leaving a trail.

IN THEIR COTTAGE, Ian's father arranged his sticks on the wide slate fireplace around the circular brazier. He had tiny twigs on the right, against the plaster wall, then larger twigs that were thin, then small branch pieces, then pieces of sapling that he and Ian had dragged down from the hillside forest behind the houses, then round rough pieces of rotten tree that were almost dry and might burn. He had a bucket of coal chunks, and wrinkled pages of *The Times*. Around some paper, he laid the littlest sticks. Stuart put a piece of sapling on while Ian's mother sat on the wide old couch and drank whiskey from a teacup. Ian sat next to his mother, his knees a little together, his eyes on his father, but his mouth a bit open, as if he thought of something else.

Ian's father said, "No, Stuart!"

Ian's mother said, "Come here, Stu."

Stuart pushed another piece of wood into the tepee shape and his father said, "*Stu*art!"

Ian's mother said, "Come here Stu."

Ian's father said, "Would you mind getting him, Anna? If you want me to make this damned thing."

She said, "I didn't ask for the fire, Harry. If it's too much of a mess with Stuart around, let's skip it. I don't care."

Ian said, "Can I match the fire, Mommy? Can I light the match?"

His mother said, "Ask your father. He handles the hearth and home."

His father stood up, looked at her, then at Ian, squatted down again in front of the slate shelf and said, "Come on, Ian, before the monster strikes again." Ian stood beside his father, held the yellow box of Swan Vestas, then opened it and took one, started to scratch it alight, then stood again, his hands at his sides, as his father took the box, closed it, handed him the single match and the box, and said, "Okay, my friend, light us up."

Ian struck toward himself. His father held his hand and showed him to strike away. Ian tried it three times, and on the fourth the match lit. He dropped the yellow box, stepped backward, then moved himself to the paper and twigs, bent down, singed his fingers, dropped the match into the metal grate, and closed his eyes. His father held the finger inside the circle of his fist, then kissed the finger, picked up the yellow box and handed it back. Ian took out a match, closed the box, struck,

struck, struck, lit the match, stooped to the fireplace, singed his finger, dropped the lighted match onto the paper, which caught, and then he stood again to be held by his father's fist while the paper roared, burnt the small sticks up, and everything went out.

His mother said, "It almost did it."

Ian said, "I lit all right, didn't I?"

His father said, "You did fine. I built it wrong."

His mother said, "I love you."

Ian turned. He said, "Who?"

IN HIS WHITE jockey shorts and undershirt, his long feet bare, Ian moved in the house while swallows called outside and the morning warmed. He opened the door from the stairs to the main room and watched his father, under heavy gray wool blankets on the couch, rolling slowly in his sleep as if his sleep were sea.

His father's mouth was open, and Ian moved closer to look inside. Then he went back to the door and upstairs silently, and he stood at Stuart's cot. The quilt was off, and Stuart's bottom stuck into the air above his gathered knees, mouth closed, face wholly still. Ian went on his toes to the double bed his mother slept in, her mouth open, her brows bunched into lines. He waited, and then he went on his toes again down the stairs and silently to the little refrigerator for apples and the table loaf and the long sharp knife. He heard his father say, "Ian?"

Ian said, "I'm making breakfast for everyone, Daddy. I'm making enough."

ON THE TREKKING path through the moors they crisscrossed with sheep tracks, going over one, then another, then descending later to the first, the horses walking around great gray lumps of wrinkled granite and cliffs of slate and later on, delicate hooves under rolling round bodies, slowly dancing over a fast beck that ran in a deep narrow valley for a mile. On the sheep track over the valley, and with the sheep above and below them, shaggy, turd-smeared, expressionless, terrified in place but hungry enough not to move, they rode: Brenda first, her small silver earrings pitching light, then the grandfather, then Ian's father behind him, then Ian, holding the edge of the saddle and leaning onto the pony's neck. Behind him were the long stretches of swamp and thick green grass, the little bolls of fell cotton where the water was murkiest on the surface, and the distances back to the cottage where his mother and Stuart were alone.

Ian's grandfather rode high and straight-backed, his toes pushing in his black pointed boots back against his horse's motion. Ian's father bobbed like a toy rider on a toy horse. Ian held on. Brenda rode ahead, then waited near a cluster of junipers, gray-brown and tense on the sky. When the other riders reached her, Brenda let her horse move out ahead again a little quickly, and Ian's grandfather's horse went too, more quickly than the others. Ian's father pulled on the reins and slowed, and Ian and his father went one behind the other, slowly, over the ridge of junipers, until they caught up to the others at the wide clear tarn where Brenda's white and gray horse was drinking, and where the grandfather looked toward them and then turned his back. As they came up, Brenda said to Ian, "There's tadpoles in there. You want to have a look before we go—if your father thinks it's all right. Walk in shallow and mind you don't slip."

Ian's father smiled, and Brenda helped Ian down, and he waded in, slipping on the wet stones and slimy vegetation. Brenda drove the horses back away from the water and tied them away from the yews, which she said they could die from eating. She gave Ian's father a cigarette and she lit it for him. Ian, in the water to his ankles, teetering, watched.

Brenda said, "Will you all be going home, then, Harry?"

She blew smoke out. Ian heard it over her teeth.

His father said, "Anna's the one who knows that."

Ian stood in the cold mountain lake and watched a black bird hanging in the wind, not moving much.

The grandfather said, "I think you've got some ground to cover yet, Harry."

Ian watched. He saw Brenda blow smoke out through her teeth and throw the cigarette into the water. He saw the grandfather watch it float.

IN THE PARKING LOT behind the Church Inn, near the small iron tables, Ian, in his shorts and Wellingtons, squatted at a mound of gravel in front of his grandfather's Morris Minor estate wagon. With the edges of his hands, Ian channeled and heaped the stones. His father drank from a pint of bitter and his mother drank whiskey. Ian put a stick in the center of the mound, then made a double line of little rocks which led toward the center. He ran a little green steel Land Rover back and forth on his road. His parents stood and talked, and closer to the whitewashed walls of the inn Brenda and the grandfather sat at a table.

Ian's mother said, "Dad's going to get in trouble. He really doesn't know."

Ian's father said, "Oh. I thought they were already—you know."

His mother said, "No, she has a room there, in a sort of a separate wing upstairs. It opens into the hallways of the cottage. She lives there and mostly cooks for herself. Sometimes she eats with him, but that's all."

"Are you sure?"

"Poor Daddy. He's sixty-five, going on twenty-five, and it won't work for him."

"She's quite a girl."

"You noticed."

Ian pushed a large rock with the Land Rover and it fell onto the fence he'd made for his road. He pushed the pebbles back with the edges of his hands, then started again to move the stone. A waitress came out with red terrycloth table mats to hang on the washline nearby, and Ian's parents smiled to her. Ian kept working. He heard his father say, "I noticed you. You and the kids. That's what I came over here for."

At the tables behind the public room the grandfather sneezed. He choked one, and then two fast shouts came after, like shots. Ian stood up to look past the clothesline and over low hedges. The grandfather was talking to Brenda, rubbing the sleeve of his brown tweed coat.

AFTER BRENDA HAD shoveled and swept, had stacked the push broom and shovel and rake, and had put the wheelbarrow away, Ian went into the stone stable and closed the double doors behind him. The walls were whitewashed halfway around, and the opposite doors, leading into the field with its small stream, were open, so that cool winds and the white clean stones of the walls made everything smell good. The gelding, the oldest and largest of the horses, dark brown and dull in the shadows of his wooden stall, ate and blew out; the noise of his feeding was a river sound. Ian smelled the ammonia and the hay of the horses, and he breathed deeply. He heard the horses in the field, and he heard his mother.

She said, "Ian?"

Ian said, "Hello."

"Hello."

Ian said, "Are we going home to America?"

"Where's that?"

BRENDA LIT IAN'S father's cigarette and threw the wooden match onto the cobbles in front of the cottage. Ian sat inside on the wooden windowseat and watched, and his mother, on the sofa between him and the room, facing in, sat with a heavy book that Ian's grandfather had given her. She read while Stuart played with coal from the scuttle. The rain was heavy, and Brenda wore her duffel coat with the hood up, but Ian's father wore only his sweater with the reindeer on it as they shoveled and swept inside the stables, then loaded the muck and wheeled it out to the lower stable where they sometimes kept foals.

Stuart spat out a small piece of coal, and Ian's mother lit a cigarette, holding it in her mouth with one hand, working the match back and forth with the other. Beyond her was Ian, who looked at her and then out at the rain beating into the cobbles, and his father helping Brenda with her work, and then the fence and five slow horses wheeling silently from pile of hay to pile, in their dance.

Ian watched everything. He saw his grandfather go down the walk from the house, come around past where the cars were parked, then walk on the cobbles in his leather shoes that clicked, the collar of his brown tweed jacket up against the rain, his gray hair soaking onto his head, showing only pink there by the time he'd knocked on their door and walked in.

The grandfather said, "That child is eating coal." He shut the door, turned his collar down, opened his buttons, rebuttoned them, shook his arms in place at his sides, walked into the middle of the small room to stop where he looked at Ian's mother and, behind her, at Ian, who turned around and pulled his knees up and held them in place with his hands. "Is it good for him? Large pieces like that?" Stuart held the coal up to the grandfather, who was looking at Ian's mother.

She said, "No, Daddy. Pick him up, then."

Ian's grandfather picked Stuart up, and Stuart tried to rub the coal into his grandfather's smooth face. But he stopped when his grandfather snarled and shook him in his arms. The grandfather said, "I've been thinking about you and your family, Anna. I've decided what *I* think is best. God knows you haven't been asking but I want to tell you something. I've wanted to give you some sort of advice for weeks. Before your Harry came to retrieve you."

The mother said, "It sounds like I'm a stick. Or a dead duck."

His grandfather said, "And he's a game dog? Ah. No. No. But for some time. Thinking about this." He put Stuart down, and Stuart rubbed his coal into his grandfather's green twill pants. The grandfather slowly kicked at him as he spoke. "I didn't know you smoked anymore, Anna."

Ian's mother said, "We're all taking it up these days."

His grandfather said, "Ah. *There* we're in tune. What we say now rhymes, in a manner of speaking. I mean to say that while I'd prefer *not* to say it, because I hate to sound as much of a fool as I often am, I nevertheless know what you mean. Which is why I've been thinking so much about—it."

Ian's mother patted the end of her cigarette into a small brass ashtray on the sofa. She said, "You're a sexy old pig, aren't you?"

The grandfather nodded. He rubbed his nose. He said, "It's best for all of us in the family that your family be whole. And home. In the States. Don't you agree?"

Ian's mother said, "I've thought that. Couldn't you tell, really? No, you couldn't tell. You were busy counting your hormones. Old pig. But I've thought about it. It's impossible to tell someone. Like this. In a situation like this. To have the courage or blandness to say: Let's take this awkward and embarrassing and slightly hopeless situation and— whatever you do say." His mother shook her head.

The grandfather put his hands in his sportcoat pockets, then took his right hand out to rub the tip of his nose back and forth. He slowly pushed the toe of his pebbly bright brown shoe into Stuart's stomach as Stuart rubbed a piece of coal along his trouser bottoms. He said, "Right. I suppose it's time to lay claim. Try to." He pushed the back of his hand into his nose, and Ian's mother stood up and leaned her fingers on the front of his dark brown shirt. The grandfather said, "Do I represent the family honor handsomely?" Ian's mother nodded. Her mouth was down and tight, as if she held a cigarette between her lips. Ian's grandfather asked, "Do you think the family is in senile decay?" He rubbed his nose. Then he went to the door and outside.

THE DAY'S RAIN had made the stables cold, and Brenda had left the lights off while she and Ian's father did the mucking out. Ian's mother said, "Why don't you wait in the house, love?" But Ian backed against a stall post and stood there, watching his father hold a cigarette in his mouth. Brenda lighted her own and threw the wooden match onto the cobbled floor. The grandfather moved to step on it, and Ian's mother moved back and so did Brenda. Ian's father stepped around toward him, stopped on the other side of the stall, and then they all waited.

The grandfather said, "Put out that silly cigarette."

Ian's father and Brenda said, "Me?"

Ian's mother laughed. Stuart moved against her and she shifted him to her other side. She said, "Brenda, I'm going to write to you. All right?"

Brenda, in the corner where the tools stood, stared at Ian's mother, then said, "Don't expect me to write back. I can hardly spell me name. And I can't testify that you'll have the address right by then."

The grandfather crossed his arms on his chest, shivered, ducked his head down, closed his eyes, and belched the sneezes out. Ian saw his mother close her eyes and shake her head. Then the grandfather sneezed onto his arm and pressed his arm against his nose. The gelding backed out, then moved again toward the front of his stall. Ian's grandfather sneezed again, and the gelding came out fast, a hoof stabbing, then banging onto the cobblestones, stabbing back. Ian stayed where he was, leaning against the post. Brenda said, "Get out," very softly as she walked so smoothly she seemed to be skating on ice instead of lifting floppy boots. She said, "Everybody move slowly. Get out."

Ian's mother said, "Ian."

His father came across the circle with his arm out.

The grandfather sneezed into both of his hands.

Ian stood against the post.

Brenda said, "Get out now. Everybody get out."

WHAT YOU MIGHT AS
WELL CALL LOVE

JUST LIKE A CURSE, rain fell for two weeks, hissing on shingles and in nearly naked trees, and the river, dammed by brush and rotted elms, began to rise. Sun sometimes shone, and sometimes the rain held off an hour, but the ground was always spongy, and mud was on everything. The river wound around the hamlet, in some places close to backyards, in others separated from yards by hillocks and cabbage fields. It was a dark autumn, and always cold; the cabbage stank in the early mornings and late at night. And the water table rose in response to the rain and pushed through deep foundation stones and up through cracked cement cellar floors, pooled around furnaces and freezers and water heaters, triggered sump pumps which gargled out the water which ran back into the ground and reappeared inside, rising slowly, in the darkness of the cellars looking black.

On the second day of flooding, Ethan came home from school with the mimeo'd message about the outbreak of head lice in the elementary grades. Marge had come up from sweeping pooled water in the cellar and her black boots glistened as she read the notice and cross-examined Ethan about school, while, forcing his head down, she raked through the fine brown hair, seeking nits.

"What's a nit?" Ethan said.

"You're clean," she said. "A nit is the egg of a louse."

"Louse?"

"A louse is one lice. Lice are a lot of louses."

"What's a *person* who's a louse, then?"

"A nitwit. Please go up and change your clothes."

"Can I look at the flood?"

"There *isn't* any flood. There's water in the cellar and go upstairs and change your clothes. Please. Everything's fine."

"How come you were down there, then, Mom?"

"I was sweeping water into the sump. It collects some places, and doesn't go into the sump. If that happens, it doesn't get pumped out. See? Please go up?"

"But doesn't it come back *in*?"

Marge sat on the floor and took one boot off. "That is not a nine-year-old question," she said. "Up."

Ethan said, "It's a nitwit question." He gave her his grown-up smile, irony and all, ruffled her thick light hair, and went up. Marge took off her other boot and leaned against the wall, stretching out her legs, to wait for Ben to come home.

HE CAME IN A red-and-black woolen shirt that was darkening with rainwater, and wire-rimmed glasses that were sheeted over, and thirty feet of black plastic pipe taped in a big crooked circle. As Marge held the door, Ben backed and sidled and swore—"Sell. We sell, and we move someplace where we can live on top of a hill and *nothing* runs in"—and then he was inside their small kitchen, talking in a low rant and forcing the pipe around the table to the cellar door.

Marge said, "You got it."

"The pipe? You noticed, huh?"

"According to Ethan, who is correct, the water is welling *up*."

"What?"

"That water's coming *up* from the ground."

"You noticed that too, huh?" Ben was down on the cellar steps now, pulling the pipe after him and grunting.

In a far, partly lighted corner, water ran in black smears down the wall stones and onto the cement floor. In the center of the floor, a hole three feet deep, about eighteen inches in diameter, received the run-off from the walls and floor. Tied to various beam jacks and ancient wooden posts, some with bark still on them, held in a web of white sash cord, was the sump pump with its copper float; when water in the sump reached a certain level, the float came up and the pump started. Water ran from it through black plastic pipe such as Ben wrestled with, and up through a broken storm window above their heads, and out onto the ground beside the house. The motor went on and off twice as they watched, and Ben cleared his throat and sniffed as if the need for pumping, the sound of the little motor, the invasion of water, were making his sinuses pour.

He lugged the pipe around the furnace to the other side of the cellar. There water pooled deeper than anywhere else, in a declivity that didn't permit it to run to the sump. They looked at it, and as Ben began to swear Marge went upstairs and put her boots on.

Ben stood above the center of the pool which shimmered, bubbled slightly, in the light of a bulb on the ceiling. In the pool was a silted corroding pipe. He leaned the circle of black plastic pipe against the furnace, squatted in the water, almost sitting in it, and jammed a plastic joint into the pipe in the floor. "It fits!" he called. "I guessed, and I was right, and it *fits*! I'm telling you, Marge, I'm going to pipe the goddamn water right the hell out of this old well or whatever the hell it is, *directly* into the faithful sump and its obedient pump, chug chug master, and we are *home*! There will be *no* pooling of water in my house without written permission. The furnace will continue to roar, *all* the necessary machines will function, including us, and the home fires will burn. Marge?"

She stood a few feet away from him, and when he noticed her he smiled, and then they both were silent as he pushed the elbow joint deeper into the rusted socket. There was the sound of dripping, and of the pump cutting on and off, and then the louder yammer of the water pump forcing water upstairs from their well because the pressure to the faucets was low, and then, at the same time, the whir of the furnace fan. Then the machines completed their cycles and stopped, and there was only the sound of their breathing, of trickles and drips.

Ben cut the tape from the black plastic pipe and Marge took one end to stretch it away from him. She wove it among lolly columns and beam supports to where it would empty into the sump. "Mere victory," Ben said. "Nothing great. Maybe a small cathedral's worth of vision and ability and strength. Thank you."

Marge, looking at the open end of the pipe, which still was dry, which carried nothing from the rusted drain into the sump, said, "It does flow up."

"Water doesn't flow up."

"It *wells* up. It seeps. It's like a spring, Ben, when the water table's high. It comes up around the pipe you put there. It just comes up."

"Jesus, Marge."

She walked back to where he stood at the elbow joint and, stooping, pointed. In the silt around the pipe into which he had shoved the white plastic joint, water was bubbling up, stirring mossy brown sediment. The pool of dark water widened. Ben took the big janitor's broom that leaned against the furnace and he began to sweep, long hard angry strokes, so that the pool ran over the lip of its margins and flowed along the inclines of the cellar, into the sump. He said, breathing hard, "It doesn't work."

"Nice try, though."

"I really thought it would work. I thought seventeen dollars' worth."

"It was a good idea," Marge said.

"I should have listened."

"Ethan figured it out."

"Yeah? He's nine and I'm only thirty-five."

"Ben has the advantage of years," she said.

He threw the broom into the pool, which was widening again, and said, "I don't really think it'll get into the furnace."

"No," she said, "it probably won't."

"We'll check on it."

They were walking up the narrow steps.

"There's an epidemic of head lice in school," Marge said.

"Ethan's okay?"

"So far. But it's really contagious."

"Son of a bitch!" Ben said.

Marge said, "I'd rather have locusts than lice."

"You're right," Ben said at the top of the stairs. "There's a better tone to locusts than lice."

"And it seems more suitable to floods, anyway," Marge said.

Ethan was waiting in the kitchen. "I thought you said there wasn't any flood, Mom."

She sat on the floor, thin, with long arms, looking like a child as she took her black boots off. She said, "There isn't."

"Didn't you and Dad just talk about one?"

"It's a flood for grown-ups," Ben said. "It isn't a flood for kids."

"Nitwit," Ethan said.

And Ben roared, *"What?"*

Marge said, "It's a joke, Ben. It's a joke Ethan and I were having. Ethan, why don't you go upstairs and change your clothes?"

"I just did. Remember?"

"Why don't you go upstairs and read *John Sevier, Pioneer Boy?*"

"I finished it last night. Mom, would you and Dad like some privacy? I can go upstairs and work on my carrier."

Marge told Ben, "It's an atomic supercarrier which is capable of holding a hundred and ten assorted fighters and long-range patrol planes, plus surface-to-air missiles. One inch to forty feet. Good-bye, Ethan. I love you."

THEY WERE SITTING in the kitchen with whiskey and ice, and Ben was telling Marge about an issue of the pharmaceuticals firm's company magazine he was putting together, for which he was not only editor but photographer and writer. He said, "Substitute teaching may just be the worst work in the world, and *I* wouldn't do it. I don't blame you for hating it. I'm saying, for *me*, right now, even though I did worse work in New York, this one is an ugly boring stupid horrible job. I mean, I think I'm running out of sick leave from calling in with phony flus every other day."

"And you don't get paid enough," she said.

"Nope."

"And neither do I, when I do get work."

"Nope."

"And we're out seventeen bucks for plastic pipe."

"Thank you," he said, "for recollecting that. For diving deep into your memory to retrieve that data."

"Datum."

Ben said, "Do I need another drink or do you?"

"Why don't we both do that, and skip the fight we don't even feel like having, and discuss what to have for dinner."

"Let's go out for pizza," Ben said. "Ethan loves it."

"Because it'll cost more money."

"Which we haven't got."

"Almost. We almost haven't got it, you're right."

Wind threw rainwater, as if it were solid, at the backdoor window, and Ben said, "Fucking rain."

Marge stood, poured more whiskey over fresh ice for them, pulled at the hem of her sweater, and remained standing as she said, "I would like us to consider having another child."

Ben said nothing, drank a large swallow, stared at her. He offered a smile, the sort you use in case a bearer of bad news might be joking, then he withdrew it. The pump went on and off, then on again, then off. "It always sounds like it's grinding something," Ben said.

Marge said, "I realize this isn't the best time to broach the subject. But it's not a complete surprise."

"No. I was just hoping I could evade it for a while. Maybe until the rain stops?"

"Well, the rain keeps making me think about babies. It's the *threat*. Do you know what I mean? What if something, I keep thinking, what if something happens."

"You mean to Ethan?"

Marge's eyes filled and instantly were red at the rims. She nodded.

"We won't *let* anything happen to him," Ben said, as if he were accused of neglect.

"We can't stop the lice," she said. "We can't stop the rain."

"We're *old*, Marge. Aren't we pretty old to be having kids?"

"We're poor, and it's a nuisance, taking care of a baby again. But a thirty-five-year-old woman can deliver a child safely, a normal child, without risking her health."

"Not without risk."

"Without risking that *much*."

"Is that true?"

She drank some whiskey. She said, "I can find out."

IN A KHAKI SLICKER and rubber boots, wearing a tweed hat, Ben walked the river. Behind him, the cabbage field went slightly uphill and then descended to their yard and the backyards of seven other small box-shaped hundred-and-fifty-year-old farmhouses that had rank-smelling cellars and sodden lintels and rotting beams. In the late summer, when the cabbages were young and small, aquamarine, not stinking, thousands of small white cabbage butterflies hovered in the field, invisible until one of them caught the sun and then drew attention to the others, and what had seemed to be hundreds of rows of blue-green vegetables set into rock-studded light brown soil suddenly would seem an ocean of little butterflies that surged around the houses and their small yards. Now the cabbages were bulbous and dark, part of the muddy field that, despite its slope, could not keep the water table from rising through stone toward a furnace's fuel jet.

Ben broke through a natural fence of brush, some red poisonous berries still glistening but most fruit gone, and the vegetation a tangle of blackthorn and exploded milkweed and powdering log, pulped fungus. He sank in down to his calves and had to work himself loose. His boots freed with slow-motion sucking sounds, and there was a released smell of gases from the rotted roots and weed. He went downhill the last few yards, a steep muddy incline leading to the river's edge—higher than it ever had been—where sinuous dying elms stood on both sides of the river, which roared like machines. Debris floated past, chunks of log, plastic milk bottles, a bran-colored kitten, turning. The surface was like a skin, for although it sped, there was an undercurrent, other water, deeper, moving more quickly. The surface was Prussian blue and silver, bright, dangerous-looking, like a reptile's skin. The water below was muddy and poisoned by cesspools rising with the flood.

It was deeper than ever, and faster, high enough to cover a tall man, swift enough to drown him as it had the kitten. Ben threw a heavy rounded chalky rock into the water. It made no ripple or splash, but disappeared. Slowly, as if he balanced at great heights, Ben walked along the river toward the red iron bridge at the south end of town. He passed behind the homes of two widows, and the only man he knew who was always glad—Henry Quail, seventy, fat, smelling of chewing tobacco and sweat and Irish whiskey. Because of his cleft palate, Henry was hard to understand, and few people asked him to speak. Henry patrolled the roads in his long green pickup truck, answered fire alarms in his red reflecting vest and yellow hardhat, helped repair tractors, collected his Social Security, made large and undeclared sums for cutting the horns off cattle, and was always bright-faced drunk.

In the large backyard of the second widow, water had collected six inches deep at least. A pyramid of logs, waiting to be split—probably by Henry Quail—had fallen, and some of the logs were submerged in the pool. Then the field between the river and the hamlet climbed again, steeply, and there was no cabbage; at first there were rows of corn stubble which, as the snows melted, the deer might come to crop at dusk, and then there was only tangled brush and high weed as the land rose to close Ben in at the river's turning.

The elms were bare above him, close together, soon to die and fall. Some willow flourished there, the empty branches hanging like awful hair, suddenly shuddering as the wind picked up. The temperature was dropping as darkness fell, and a mist hung above the water, higher than a man could reach, thick and smelling of cabbage and silt and old plants. The fog looked yellow in the dusk light. The roar of the river grew as Ben went on and arrived at the dam.

At first it looked as if the silver-blue skin of the water had grown tumorous. Then he saw, just under the surface, tangled trees, woven vines, and bushes locked into one another, small logs and larger ones, pieces of siding, detergent boxes, green garbage, bones. All were holding the river high, though a million gallons flowed past him as Ben watched. He closed his eyes and opened them, lost the peculiar focus he'd found, and saw simply a silvery blue skin that writhed.

He went on to the bridge, from which children in summer fished and where Ben had stood to watch Ethan and some friends wade on the sun-heated slippery rocks. Now they would, as soon as a foot went into the water, be seized and beaten, pulled away, spinning, to surface half a mile downstream, under the railroad trestle, features erased by rocks and trees, bloody tubes of meat digested and released.

Ben reached toward a stump and knocked on it three times. He said, "Please."

THEY ATE DINNER in the living room, in front of the Franklin stove. The third time Ethan smacked his lips while chewing hamburger Stroganoff, Marge made good on her threat and marched Ethan into the kitchen, where he sat in the yellow light of one lamp and finished his meal alone. Ben and Marge, in the living room, said nothing; they ate and looked at the bright flare of fire visible where the stove doors met. Ethan's chair scraped, something creaked, and then there was a silence. "Where's he going?" Ben whispered.

"Maybe his room."

"I didn't hear him on the steps."

"Well, there's noplace else to go. He has to go past us to get to the TV—"

"Yeah," Ben said, standing, "but he doesn't have to go past us to go *out*."

"Ethan takes care," Marge said. "He wouldn't want to get soaked— oh, come *on*, Ben, he is *not* going to the river."

Ben said, "If the sump pump starts in now, to punctuate all this dread and criminality, I'll disconnect it." The sump pump started in, they heard it grinding downstairs. Ben said, "I can't disconnect it or the cellar will flood and the furnace'll go out."

"What dread?" Marge said. "What criminality?"

"No, it's just, with the river rising, with the goddamn *cellar* rising, I don't like it that we aren't together. Happy."

"Ben," she said, "do you know how unhappy he would be if there weren't consequences? Discipline? Rules he has to follow?"

"Yeah, but he can't follow them."

"He will. It's called learning."

Ben put another log into the stove and sat down again, then stood up. The sump pump was on. "But what if he does go to the river?"

"He won't. Go look for him if you're worried. It isn't such a big house, you know. Go look."

Ben sipped coffee and rubbed the back of his neck. "Do you understand that when you talk to me like that, when you patronize me, even if it's *Ethan*, I can't go do what I think is right?"

"You asked me and I told you."

"Bitch," Ben said. He put his coffee on the table in front of the sofa and went around it, clumsily and blushing. He leaned over, one knee on the cushion, to kiss her on the cheek chastely. "I forgive you your transgressions," he said.

Marge said, "Asshole." She held his head and struck her tongue out slowly, and slowly licked his lips from side to side. Ben sat down beside her, moved in closer, and kissed her mouth.

"That's right," he said when they'd stopped.

"That's right," she said.

"Yes. As usual," he said.

"Yes."

As if to hold her trophy up, while Ben breathed deeply on the sofa beside her, Marge called, "Ethan!"

When there was no answer, Ben shook his head. She called again. Ben shouted, as if in rage, *Ethan!*"

The high small voice came back from far away: "Yes?"

"Where is he?" Ben said.

"Yes?"

Ben said, "Is that from outside? He *is* outside."

But Marge was already up, walking toward the kitchen and the cellar door, and she was on the steps before Ben had stood to follow her. Downstairs, in the light of the one bulb at the far end of the cellar, in the grinding chatter of the pump, Ethan swept water from the drain that Ben had uselessly capped. The water rolled with a loud hush across the gray floor and spilled over into the sump and was pumped out to seep back in again. There was a new smell downstairs, among the smells of wet wood and soaked stone and hot motor—the sharp tang of mildew. Ethan, in Marge's high black boots, continued to sweep. Marge in her fur-lined slippers, Ben in his still soaked boots, both with wet feet, stood watching him—the long pale intelligent face, the slender arms and legs, big hands. In Marge's boots, in the weak cellar light, in the pool of black water, Ethan looked very small.

"Hi," he said. Then he smiled, and his ill-brushed teeth shone beige.

Ben cleared his throat. "We thought you went out, honey."

Marge reached back to slap Ben's buttocks, to warn him into silence. "How's it going?" she said.

Ethan said, "I don't think I'm making any progress. But you guys were so upset about the water, I thought maybe I could, you know, do something."

"No," Ben said, "you're doing fine."

"Really fine," Marge said. "You're a helper, all right."

Ben rubbed the back of his neck and stepped away so that Marge couldn't reach him. "Ethan," he said, "you know where babies come from?"

Ethan said, "Mom told me. You could check with her if you want to."

The boy swept more water into the sump, and the pump went on again.

"Okay," Ben said, "I will."

Marge turned and walked to the foot of the steps. Ben stood, watching Ethan sweep. Then he turned too and followed his wife. When Marge was in the kitchen, and Ben was halfway there, Ethan called, "Hey, Dad? Dad?"

"Yes, sir."

"Tell me what she says, okay?"

THAT NIGHT THE skies shook and darkness was total: no moon, no stars, no road lights visible from the bedroom window, the bedroom itself extinguished, and their eyes squeezed shut. They did not touch; when they rolled on the mattress or tugged at blankets or pushed a pillow flat, they grunted as if hurt. They slept finally, then awakened to hear field mice running in the eaves and between the walls at the head of the bed. It was the dry scraping sound of panic. It rhymed with the grinding chirr of the pump in the lath and beams and floorboard between them and the flooded cellar. Marge turned her bedside lamp on, and the walls jumped in toward them. Ben whispered, "Don't read. Just lie there. If you say you're awake, you won't be able to sleep at all."

Wearing Ben's undershirt and squinting from the blackened eyes of an exhausted athlete, Marge reached up to turn off the light.

"You look nice," he whispered.

"You always like me to wear your clothes."

"So I can own you."

"So you can *protect* me."

"Probably that too."

Marge said, "If the mice desert it, and come in here, does that mean the world is sinking?"

Ben said into his pillow, "The world will be fine."

After a minute, after another minute, with the darkness humid around them and expanding into the darkness of the flooded world outside, Marge said, "Can you promise me that? Can you *promise*?"

"I promise," Ben said.

"You better mean that."

"I do. But no babies. No more babies."

She prayed at him: "Then you better mean it, Ben."

He wanted it to end with his praying back *I do*, but he lay still and saw the yellow school bus, Ethan on board, rolling off the rain-slicked road. Ben opened his eyes so as not to see the children bouncing in the bus, pips in a fat collapsing gourd. He saw the darkness. He closed his eyes and against his will he looked closer, supplying details, squeezing his eyes. He saw the battered heads of bleeding children, and black hair, yellow hair, brown hair, hair cut short and hair tied in thin bright ribbon, all of it pasty with blood and teeming with lice, the lice jumping in blood and tracking it tinily on the wrinkled brown lunch bags that lay on cracked seats and in muddy aisles. He heard Ethan cry, not in the house with them now, but in his dream, in the future, in the world that possessed more of him than Ben thought it right to have to yield, and he pushed himself from the pillow. He almost said *I do*. But he turned—Marge said, "Ben?"—and in the darkness, with the pump going on and off, with mice hurtling furiously between the walls, he wrestled her, tore at the shared shirt, buried his mouth in her neck and labored with his lips and teeth, dropping upon her with no question and no answer, hearing nothing for the first time that night, making what you might as well call love.

TOO LATE
AMERICAN
BOYHOOD BLUES

◆

THE SETTLEMENT OF MARS

IT BEGAN FOR ME in a woman's bed, and my father was there though she wasn't. I was nine years old, and starting to age. "Separate vacations," then, meant only adventure to me. My bespectacled mother would travel west to attend a conference about birds; she would stare through heavy binoculars at what was distant and nameable. My father and I would drive through Massachusetts and New Hampshire into Maine, where he and Bill Brown, a friend from the army, would climb Mount Katahdin and I would stay behind at the Brown family's farm.

And it was adventure—in the days away from New York, and in the drive alone with my father in the light-green '49 Chevrolet, and in my mother's absence. For she seemed to be usually angry at someone, and my father struck me as usually pleased with the world, and surely with me. And though I knew enough to understand that his life was something of a secret he didn't tell me, I also knew enough at nine to accept his silence as a gift: peace, which my mother withheld by offering the truth, in codes I couldn't crack, of her discontent.

I remember the dreamy, slow progress of the car on heat-shimmered highways, and my elbow—this never was permitted when we all drove together on Long Island—permanently stuck from the high window.

We slept one night in a motel that smelled like iodine, we ate lobster rolls and hot dogs, I discussed the probable settlement of Mars, and my father nodded gravely toward my knowledge of the future.

He gave me close escapes—the long, gray Hudson which almost hit us, because my father looked only ahead when he drove, never to the side or rear, as we pulled out of a service station; the time we had a flat and the jack collapsed twice, the car crashing onto the wheel hub, my father swearing—"God*damn* it!"—for the first time in my hearing; and the time he let the car drift into a ditch at the side of the road, pitching us nose-down, rear left-side wheel in the air, shaken and stranded until a farmer on a high tractor towed us out and sent us smiling together on our way. My father bared his teeth to say, "It's a lucky thing Mother isn't here," while I regretted the decorum I had learned from him—I was not to speak without respect of the woman with binoculars who had journeyed from us.

I thought of those binoculars as we approached the vague shapes of weathered gray buildings, wished that I could stare ahead through them and see what my life, for the next little while, might offer. But the black Zeiss 12 × 50s were thousands of miles from us, and really further than that: they were in my memory of silent bruised field trips, when my father's interest would be in covering ground, and my mother's would be expressed in the spraddle-legged stiffness with which she stared at birds up a slope I knew my father wanted to be climbing.

Bill Brown was short and mild in silver-rimmed glasses. He wore a striped engineer's cap with a long bill, and he smiled at everything my father said. Molly Brown was taller than Bill, and was enormously fat, with wobbling arm flesh and shaking jowls and perpetual streaked flushes on her soft round cheeks. Their daughter, Paula, was fourteen and tall and lean and beautiful. She had breasts. Sweat, such an intimate fact to me, stained the underarms of her sleeveless shirt. She wore dungarees that clung to her buttocks. She rolled the cuffs to just below her knees, and I saw the dusk sun light up golden hairs on her shins. She had been assigned to babysit me for the visit. I could not imagine being babysat by so much of everything I had heard rumored, and was beginning to notice in playgrounds, secrets of the other world.

We ate mashed potatoes and a roast that seemed to heat the kitchen, which, like the other rooms in the house, smelled of unwashed bodies and damp earth. I slept that first night on a cot in Paula's room, and I was too tired even to be embarrassed, much less thrilled, by the proximity; I slept in purest fatigue, as if I had journeyed on foot for weeks to another country, in which the air was thin. Next day, we walked the Brown's land—I could not take my eyes from Paula's spiny back and strong thighs as we climbed fences, as she helped me, her child-assignment, up and over and down—and we ate too much hot food, and drank Kool-Aid (forbidden, because too sugary, at home), and we sat around a lot. I rejoiced in such purposelessness, and I suspected that my father enjoyed it too, for our weekend days at home were slanted toward mission; starting each Saturday morning, we tumbled down the long tilted surfaces of the day into weeding and pruning and sweeping and traveling in the silent car to far-off fields to see if something my mother knew to be special was fluttering over marshes in New Jersey or forests in upstate New York.

My father, who made radio advertisements, spoke a little about his work, and Bill Brown said in his pleased soft voice that he had heard my father's ads. But when Bill said, "Where do you get those crazy ideas, Frank?" my father turned the conversation to potato farming, and the moth collection which Bill and Molly kept together, and the maintenance of trucks. I knew that my father understood nothing about engines. He was being generous again, and he was hiding again while someone else talked of nothing that mattered to the private man who had taught me how to throw a baseball, and how to pack a knapsack, and how—I know this now—to shelter inside other people's words. And there was Paula, too, smoking cigarettes without reprimand, swinging beside me on the high-backed wooden bench that was fastened by chains to the ceiling of their porch. I breathed her smoke as now I'd breathe in perfume on smooth, heated skin.

In reply to a question, my father said, "Angie's in Colorado.

"All the way out there," Molly said.

Bill said, "Well."

"Yes, she had a fine opportunity," my father said. "They gave her a scholarship to this conference about bird migration, I guess it is, and she just couldn't say no."

"I'd like to go there sometime," Paula said, sighing smoke out.

"Wouldn't you, though?" Molly growled in her rich voice. "Meet some Colorado boys and such, I suspect?"

"Give them a chance to meet a State of Maine *girl*, don't forget," Paula said. "Uncle Frank, didn't you want to go to Colorado?"

My father's deep voice rumbled softly. "Not when I can meet a State of Maine girl right here, hon. And don't forget, your father and I already spent some time in Colorado."

"Amen that it's over," Bill said.

"I saw your father learn his manners from a mule out there, didn't I, Bill?"

"Son of a bitch stepped so hard on my foot, he broke every damned bone inside it. Just squatted there, Frank, you remember? Son of a bitch didn't have the sense to get off once he'd crushed it. It took Frank jumping up and down and kicking him just to make him wake and look down and notice he already done his worst and he could move along. Leisurely, as I remember. He must have been thinking or something. I *still* get the bowlegged limps in wet weather. I wouldn't cook a mule and eat one if I was starved to death."

"Well, didn't she—" Paula said.

"Angie," I said. I felt my father look at me across the dark porch.

"Didn't Angie want to come up here and meet us?" Paula asked.

Molly said, "Couldn't you think of any personal questions you would like for Frank to answer for you?"

"Well, I guess I'm *sorry*, then."

"That's right," Molly said.

"It was one hell of a basic training," Bill said. He said it in a rush.

"They had us with this new mountain division they were starting up. Taught us every goddamned thing you could want to know about carrying howitzers up onto mountains by muleback. How to get killed while skiing. All of it. Then, they take about three hundred of us or so and send us by boat over to some hot jungle. Ship all our gear with us too, of course. So we land there in the Philippine Islands with snowshoes, skis, camouflage parkas, light machine guns in white canvas *covers*, for gosh-sakes, and they ask us if we'd win the war for them."

"It took us a while," my father said.

"Didn't it now?"

Bill went inside and returned with a bottle and glasses. He sat down next to my father, and I heard the gurgle, then a smacking of lips and, from my father, a low groan of pleasure, of uncontrol, which I hadn't heard before. New information was promised by that sound, and I folded my arms across my chest for warmth and settled in to learn, from the invisibility darkness offered, and from the rhythm of the rattle of bottle and glass.

I was jealous that Paula wanted boys in Colorado when I was there, and I was resigned—it was like fighting gravity, I knew—to not bulking sizably enough. Their voices seemed to sink into the cold black air and the smell of Paula's cigarettes, and I heard few whole words—nothing, surely, about my vanished mother, or about my father and me—and what I knew next was the stubbly friction of my father's cheek as he kissed me goodbye and whispered that he'd see me soon. I though that we were home and that he was putting me to bed. Then, when I heard the coarse noise of Bill's truck, I opened my eyes and saw that I was on the canvas cot in Paula's room in a bright morning in Maine. I was certain that he was leaving me there to grow up as a farmer, and I almost said aloud the first words that occurred to me: "What about school? Do I go to school *here*?" School meant breakfast, meant wearing clothes taken from the oak highboy in the room in Stony Brook, Long Island, meant coming downstairs to see my father making coffee while my mother rattled at *The Times*. The enormity of such stranding drove me in several directions as I came from the cot, "What about school?" still held, like scalding soup, behind my teeth and on my wounded tongue.

Paula, at the doorway, shaking a blouse down over her brassiere—I could not move my eyes from the awful power of her underwear—called through the cloth, "Don't you be frightened. You fell asleep and you slept deep. Frank and Daddy're climbing, is all. Remember?" Though the cotton finally fell to hide her chest and stomach, I stared there, at strong hidden matters. We ate eggs fried in butter on a wood-fired stove while Molly drank coffee and talked about a dull moth which lived on Katahdin and which Bill might bring home. I stared at Paula's lips as they closed around corners of toast and yellow runny yolks.

We shoveled manure into the wheelbarrow Paula let me push, and we fed their dozen cows. One of them she'd named Bobo, and I held straw to Bobo's wet mouth and pretended to enjoy how her nose dripped. I listened to the running-water noises of their stomachs, and I looked at the long stringy muscles in Paula's tanned bare arms. Her face, long like her mother's, but with high cheekbones and wide light eyes, was always in repose, as if she dreamed as she worked while naming for me the nature of her chores and the functions of equipment. I watched the sweat that glistened under her arms and on her broad forehead, and she sounded then like my father, when he took me to his office on a school holiday: I was told about the surfaces of everything I saw, but not of his relation to them, and therefore their relation to me. In Jefferson, Maine, as on East Fifty-second Street in Manhattan, as in Stony Brook, New York, the world was puzzling and seductive, and I couldn't put my hands on it, and hold.

We went across a blurred meadow that vibrated with black flies and tiny white butterflies that rose and fell like tides. On the crest of a little hill, under gray trees with wide branches and no leaves or fruit, Paula lay flat, groaning as if she were old, and stared up through bug-clouds and barren limbs and harsh sun. "Here," she said, patting the sparse fine grass beside her. "Look."

I lay down next to her as tentatively as I might lie now beside a woman whom I'd know I finally couldn't hold. Her arm was almost touching mine, and I thought I could feel its heat. Then the arm rose to point, and I smelled her sweat. "Look," she said again. "He looks like he's resting awhile, but he's hanging onto the air. That's work. He's drifting for food. He'll see a mole from there and strike it too."

Squint as hard as I might, there was nothing for me but bright spots the sun made inside my eyes. I tried to change the focus, as if I looked through my mother's binoculars, but I saw only a branch above us, and it was blurry too. I blinked again; nothing looked right.

"I guess I saw enough birds in my life," I told her.

"That's right, isn't it? Your mother's a bird-watcher. In Colorado, too. I guess there's trouble *there*."

"They're taking separate vacations this year."

"They sure are. That's what I mean about trouble. Man and wife *live* together. That's why they get married. They watch birds together, if that's what they do, and they climb up mountains together, and they sleep together in the same bed. Do Frank and Angie sleep in the same bed?"

I was rigid lest our arms touch, and the question made me stiffer. "I don't see *your* mother climbing any mountains," I said.

"Well, she's too fat, honey. Otherwise she would. And if this wasn't a trip for your father and mine to take alone, a kind of special treat for them, you can bet me and Momma would be there, living out of a little canvas tent and cooking for when Daddy came back down, bug-bit and chewed up by rocks. And you won't find but one bed for the two of them. I still hear them sometimes at night. You know. Do you?"

"Oh, sure. I hear my mom and dad too." That was true: I heard them talking in the living room, or washing dishes after a party, or playing music on the Victrola. "Sure," I said, suspecting that I was soon to learn things terrible and delicious, and worried not only because I was ashamed of what I didn't hear, but because, if I *did* hear them, I wouldn't know what they meant. The tree limb was blurred, still, and I moved to rub my eyes.

Then that girl of smells—her cigarette smoke lay over the odor of the arm she'd raised—and of fleshy swellings and mysterious belly and the awesome mechanics of brassieres, the girl who knew about me and my frights, about my parents and their now-profound deficiencies, said gently, "Come on back to my room. I'll show you something."

When she stood, she took my hand; hers was rough and dry and strong. She pulled me back over field and fences, and I thrilled to the feel of flesh as much as I hated the maternity with which she towed me. But I thought, too, that something alarming was about to be disclosed. I couldn't wait to be told, though I was scared.

Molly was putting clothes through a mangle near the rain barrel, and she waved as we passed. We went through cool shadows into the room Paula had decorated with Dick Powell's picture, and Gable's, and on the far wall a blurred someone with a moustache wore tights and feathered hat and held a sword.

"My library," she said, opening the closet. "Here." And on shelves, stacked, and in shaggy feathering heaps on the closet floor, were little yellowing books and bright comics and magazines that told the truth about the life of Claudette Colbert and Cary Grant. I doubt that she knew what I needed, for she was mostly a teenage kid on a little farm in Maine. She wasn't magical, except to me in her skin, although she was smarter than I about the life I nearly knew I led. But something made her take me from the swarm of sun and insects, the high-hanging invisible bird of prey—that place where, she possibly knew, I sensed how much of my life was a secret to me—and she installed me on the dirty floor of a dirty house, in deepening afternoon, half-inside a closet where, squinting, I fell away from the world and into pictures, words.

I read small glossy-jacketed books, little type on crumbling wartime paper, with some line drawings, about Flash Gordon and Ming the Merciless and the plight of the always-kidnapped Dale. I read about death rays and rockets that went to Mars from Venus as quickly as they had to for the sake of mild creatures with six arms who were victimized by Ming's high greed. Dale and the other women had very pointed breasts and often said, "Oh, Flash, do you really think so?"

And there was Captain Marvel, whose curling forelock was so much like Superman's, but whom I preferred because I thought we looked alike and because he never had to bother to change his clothes to get mighty: he said *Shazam!* and a lightning bolt made him muscular and capable of rescuing women with long legs. I read of Superboy, whose folks in Smallville were so proud of him. Littler worlds, manageable by me, and on my behalf by people who could change, whether in phone booths or storerooms or explosions of light, into what they needed to be: Aqua-Man, Spider Man, the Green Lantern, wide-nostriled Wonder Woman in her glass airplane, and always Flash and Dale, "Oh, Flash, do you really think so?"

For a while, Paula sat behind me, cross-legged on her bed, reading fan magazines and murmuring of Gary Cooper's wardrobe and the number of people Victor Mature could lift into the air. When she went out, she spoke and I answered, but I don't remember what we said. I leaned forward in the darkness, squinting and forgetting to worry that I had to screw my face around my eyes in order to see, and I stayed where I was, which was away.

They had a radio, and we listened to it for a while after dinner, and then Molly showed me, in a room off the kitchen, board after board on which dead moths were stiffly pegged. I squinted at them and said "Wow," and while Paula and Molly sat in sweaters on the porch and talked, I squatted in the closet's mouth, under weak yellow light, and started Edgar Rice Burroughs's *The Chessmen of Mars*. When Paula entered to change into nightclothes, I was lured from the cruel pursuit of Dejah Thoris by Gahan of Gathol, for the whisper of cloth over skin was a new music. But I went back with relief to "The dazzling sunlight of Barsoom clothed Manator in an aureole of splendor as the girl and her captors rode into the city through the Gate of Enemies."

When Paula warned me that the lights were going off, I stumbled toward my cot, and when they were out I undressed and went to sleep, telling myself stories. And next day, after breakfast and a halfhearted attempt to follow her through chores, I walked over the blurred field to the rank shade of Paula's room, and I sat in the closet doorway, reading of Martian prisons, and heroes who hacked and slew, unaware that I had neither sniffed nor stared at her, and worried only that I might not finish the book and start another before my father and Bill returned. They didn't, and we ate roast beef hash and pulpy carrots, and Molly worked in the shed on the motor of their kitchen blender while Paula listened to "Henry Aldrich" and I attended to rescues performed by the Warlord of Mars.

It was the next afternoon when my father and Bill returned in the truck. They were dirty and tired and beaming, and they smelled like woodsmoke. My father hugged me and kissed me so hard that he hurt me with his unshaved cheeks. He swatted my bottom and rubbed my shoulders with his big hands. Bill presented Molly with a dirty little moth and she clapped her hands and trilled. Paula smoked cigarettes and sat on the porch between Bill and my father, listening, as if she actually cared, to Bill's description of how well my father had done to follow him up Abel's Slide, where the chunks of stone were like steps too high to walk, too short and smooth to climb, and up which you had to spring, my father broke in to say, "Like a goat in a competition. I thought my stomach would burst, following this—this *kid*. That's you, Bill, part mountain goat and part boy. I don't know how you stayed young for so long. You were the oldest man in the outfit, and what you did was you stayed where you were and I got ancient."

"Nah. Frank, you're in pretty good shape. For someone who makes his living by sitting on his backside. I'll tell you that. You did swell."

"Well, you did better. How's that?"

Bill swallowed beer and nodded. "I'd say that's right."

And they both laughed hard, in a way the rest of us could only smile at and watch.

"Damn," my father said, smiling so wide. *"Damn!"*

My head felt hot and the skin of my face was too tight for whatever beat beneath it. They were shimmering shapes in the afternoon light, and I rubbed my eyes to make them work in some other way. But what I saw was as through a membrane. Perhaps it was Paula's cool hand on my face that did it, and the surge of smells, the distant mystery of her older skin and knowledge which I suddenly remembered to be mastered by. Perhaps it was the distance my father had traveled over and from which, as I learned from the privacies of his laughter, he still had not returned. Perhaps it was Molly, sitting on the porch steps next to Bill, her hand on his thigh. Or perhaps it was the bird I couldn't see which hung over Jefferson, Maine, drifting to dive. I pushed my face against Paula's hard hand and I rubbed at my eyes and I started to weep long coughing noises which frightened me as much as they must have startled the others.

My father's hobbed climbing boots banged on the porch as he hurried to hold me, but I didn't see him because I knew that if I opened my eyes I would know how far the blindness had progressed. I didn't want to know anything more. He carried me inside while I wailed like a hysterical child—which is what I was, and what I'm sure I felt relieved to be. I listened to their voices when they'd stilled my weeping and asked me questions about pain. I swallowed aspirin with Kool-Aid and heard my father discover the comics and the books I'd read while on my separate vacation. And the relief in his voice, and the smile I heard riding on his breath, served to clench my jaw and lock my hands above my eyes. Because he knew, and they knew, and I still didn't, though I now suspected, because I always trusted him, that I wouldn't die and probably wouldn't go blind.

"Just think of your mother's glasses, love," he whispered while the others walked from the room. He sat on the bed and stroked my face around my fists, which still stayed on my eyes. "Mother has weak eyes, and these things can be passed along—the kids can get them from their parents."

"You mean I caught it from her?"

The bed I was in, Paula's bed—I smelled her on the pillow and the sheets—shook as he nodded and continued to stroke my face. "*Like* that. Just about, yes. I bet when we go home, and we go to the eye doctor, he'll put a chart up for you to read. Did you have these tests in school? He'll ask you to read the letters, and he'll say you didn't see them too clearly, and he'll tell us to get you some glasses. And that's *all*. I promise. It isn't meningitis, it isn't polio—"

"Polio?" I said. "*Polio?*"

"No," he said. "No. No, it isn't a *sickness*. I'm sorry I said that. I was worried for a minute, but now I'm not, I promise. You hear? I'm promising you. Your eyes are weak. Your head'll feel better from the aspirin—it's just eyestrain, love. It's nothing more."

"Yeah," I said. "Some dumb vacation. I should have gone with Mommy."

I lay in a woman's bed, and in the warmth of her secrets, and in the rich smell of what was coming to me. And my father sat there as his large hands gentled my face. His hands never left me. I dropped my fists, though I kept my eyes closed tight. I felt his strong fingers, roughened by rocks, as they ran along my eyebrows, touched my cheeks, my hairline, my forehead, then eyebrows again, over and over, until, with great gentleness, they dropped upon the locked lids, and he said, "No, no, this is where you should be." So I hid beneath my father's hands, and I rested awhile.

RISE AND FALL

HIS FATHER ROSE early and climbed the attic stairs to bathe in the farthest tub of their house. He came home from work for dinner at seven o'clock. In between for Jay Reese it was school, and his mother in the late afternoon; at every hour, though, he was the kind of boy who liked living alone. But especially after the war—during which he had lived by himself with his mother—while he was being six and seven and eight, his father was the figure disappearing in the early part of the morning, and then coming home from the practice of the law while the day went dark.

He remembered his father in two weekend costumes from those days in the Midwood section of Flatbush, in Brooklyn in New York, when the old trees made the air green in summer and were a network of traps, during the autumn and early winter, for the pink Spaulding rubber ball the boys would bat, with a sawed-off broomstick, as far down the narrow street as they could. In hot weather, his father would, on Saturdays, wear one of two seersucker suits. There was a brown-and-white stripe, there was a gray-and-white stripe, and each jacket buttoned tight at the waist, and the trousers of each would cling to his father's thin calves. He always thought it was his father's garters and long hose that made the trousers cling. With the brown suit his father would wear a Panama hat; with the gray, a fedora made of gray straw. And, often, there his father would be, emerging from the hot brown cars of the BMT subway at the elevated Avenue H station, obviously not thinking of his older son because he was always surprised to see that he had pedaled over the Avenue H footbridge down the leafy streets past the wide brick or stucco houses where, on Saturdays, so many fathers mowed lawns or clipped hedges or threw baseballs to kids. His father worked on Saturdays until Jay was nearly out of college, and his father, on so many of those Saturdays, in the early afternoon, tall and strong and bald and handsome in a way that used to be called manly, came out of the BMT and was surprised to see his son. They went home in, for the father, a march, and a slow ticking of bicycle gears for the son, who made his legs act patient as he wobbled his front wheel so that he might go slowly and not fall down. They were nearly side-by-side.

The other costume he recalled—the son was the sort of grownup who would dwell on melancholy matters and tatters torn back from the past—was his heavy winter coat. It was a camouflage coat, and his father had worn it in the Second World War. Jay spent a good deal of time in looking the coat over carefully for blood. It was an unbloodied coat, however, and on Sunday mornings in winter, after his father had looked at *The Times*, and while his mother tried to sneak into her own life in another room for a few private moments, his father, if there was snow on the ground, would tell Jay and his little brother, Jonas, to get dressed for the cold. Jay would dress himself, and his father would slide Jonas into a snowsuit that left him immobile, a two-year-old doll bundled under wool and nylon and rubber except for his nose and sad eyes and solemn mouth. Jay would wear a dull plaid mackinaw over sweater and flannel shirt, and the corduroy knickers that slid into the tops of his boots. His father, also in a mackinaw and woolen pants and boots, would add the camouflage shell, khaki on one side and snow-white on the other. His father always wore the snow-side out, and only when Jay was grown would he wonder what purpose such camouflage, in Brooklyn, New York, in the 1940s and '50s, might serve.

His father pulled Jonas on their small wooden sled, while Jay, like a warrior, carried the longer sled at port-arms across Avenue I, and toward the footbridge at Avenue H, over which pedestrians might walk while, underneath, the freight trains of the Long Island Railroad rumbled, heading for the Atlantic Avenue terminal and then out of Brooklyn to the rest of the world. It was a great concrete slab, that arching bridge, with meshwire sides and both a railed ramp and a set of concrete steps. You could stand on it and look down as the train came by, throwing heat and sound. Next to the steps was a patch of waste ground, beside a small pale apartment house. And in the area between the apartments and the bridge, fathers stood and talked easily, without intimacy, or they read their Sunday papers, swaying as though they hung onto hand-straps aboard the BMT, and no trains ran below, and children—Jay, alone, and then sometimes with Jonas tucked before him, seated, or clinging prone to his back—rode shrieking down the long gradual hill to stop in the deeper snow some twenty feet or so from the double set of tracks.

And one day, in the winter, after Christmastime, Jay remembered, he and Jonas and their father went to the bridge to sled and were met by a group of puzzled fathers and children. They stood, looking at the newcomers and then back to the waste ground from which the sleds were launched, to see the new fence. There was something miraculous about it, because although children had walked and biked there, and though certain fathers, Jay's among them, had walked on the bridge twice a day all week, no one, apparently, had seen the fence erected. It was very high, and was attached, on the right, to the bridge itself, and, on the left, to a 10- or 12-foot metal pole beside the apartment house. It was a tall wire fence of the sort that keeps people out of, or trapped inside, the recess yards of public schools. Many of them stood at the fence and held the heavy, woven mesh. And then Jay's father pointed out to the others that the overhead electric wires, running beneath the bridge and above the tracks, were different—they had new hues of glass transformer, and large metal boxes of a different shape were affixed to creosoted poles, and the wire itself was a thicker and shinier black. They agreed, the fathers, while their children stamped and whined and looked about, that these were "high power lines," though no one knew the meaning of what they agreed on. To keep the children of the Avenue H neighborhood safe, their sledding ground was closed.

Of course, children learned to sneak under the fence soon enough, and to climb over the side of the bridge and hang by their hands and pull themselves, dangling in the air, to the side of the hill and then tumble until their balance was caught, and then be safely standing on what was forbidden. Some threw sleds over in winter and then climbed over the bridge—for a while, Jay was among them. Some climbed over in warmer weather to huddle under the bridge, as if it rained and they were camping, in order to have a hidden place for smoking their Old Gold cigarettes. And two boys, who came from across Ocean Avenue, climbed over and shinnied along the girders beneath the bridge and fell onto the lines and were burned to death by the electricity. A man who lived in the apartment house, a Silesian bookbinder named Jankowicz who bound Jay's mother's magazines into volumes, had reported to Jay's parents that when the police lifted the bodies up to the bridge and took them off in a long green truck, the limbs were stiff and the flesh was dark, "like they was cooked," his mother reported that Jankowicz had said. She reported it a lot. And Jay thought of roasted bellies and crusts of dark buttock and he stopped climbing over the bridge. But that was later, after the day when the fathers and sons stood interdicted by a fence in a neighborhood that was largely without such barriers. It was a witty but to him forgivable formulation, as Jay thought of it later on, waxing sentimental over his father's wardrobe and his early life in the quiet, gentle district where they'd lived: the world had, one weekend, announced to the children of children of immigrants, many of whom thought of themselves as living in the almost-prosperous not-quite-suburbs, that they could descend as swiftly as they wished, in silence or in frightened laughter; the danger, said the diamond-shapes of thick linked fence, the bright black wire, the energy that snaked within it, was in trying to rise.

JONAS, HIS BROTHER, had soared. Like their father, he went to law school and then was a clerk, of sorts, in a shabby firm of men whose wages came from defending the malfeasances and tax shelters of businessmen with overseas interests. Jonas was in fact above that kind of law, at least as often as he could be. He moved on, a junior partner in a firm whose practice was exclusively international law. And then, on lower Broadway in Manhattan, across the street from Trinity Church and hard by Brooks Brothers, Jonas rented quarters for himself and a secretary and two other men, and he became Reese, Kupkind & Slatauer, and at meetings of the New York Bar Association, he served on the foreign law committee. He took taxis to work, from Yorkville, and when they spoke by telephone every few months—each might have sworn, Jay suspected, that they'd spoken within the past week—Jonas reported savagely to Jay on how, from families still in the old neighborhood, he had learned of sweeping ethnic shifts, brown skins edging out white, and rumors of voodoo practiced within three-quarters of a mile of the synagogue that Eleanor Roosevelt herself had opened with a garbled Hebrew phrase in 1953.

Jay had gone to Moravian and then to the medical college of the University of Pennsylvania. To their father, going to any out-of-town college was a step up from his own attendance at Brooklyn College. Moravian was a major school to him, therefore, and the move to Penn had been pure triumph. Jonas's acceptance, with a scholarship, by Reed, had actually made their father weep. When they were together, and drinking too much, Jonas went wet at the eyes, remembering their father's tears. Jonas had come home for law school, attending Columbia while living at International House, uptown, and then moving to an apartment at 112th and Riverside. Jay had gone from Penn to a residency in Syracuse, at Upstate Hospital, and then he had moved downstate into Duchess County, near Poughkeepsie, where he practiced pediatrics and lived in a large white house that had been started in the eighteenth century and, according to Jay, had rarely been lived in since. He claimed to Jonas that most of his money went toward making up for years of rot and structural decline. He never talked about the tall, coal-colored woman he had married in Philadelphia, and had lived with for two years, and who had left him for a man in Durham, North Carolina.

Jonas married too. His wife was named Norma, their daughter Joanne, their son Joseph. The grandparents were healthy and transplanted and long-lived in Miami. The boys were men now, Jonas thirty-seven and Jay forty-two, and progress seemed assured. If they were not what might be called a successful family, and there is always someone who wants to say that, then they surely were not a failure. They lived in America and were making their way.

IN THE PART OF Duchess County from which Jay commuted to Vassar Hospital in Poughkeepsie, there were still large areas of forest, and there were dirt roads that tore a car apart in winter and that in summer were half-grown-over with weeds and hanging brush. Jay lived nearly in the woods, except for the half-acre of lawn around the house, and the long scrubby hillside climbing away to the west. He almost never mowed the lawn, so he lived within a swollen circle of meadow that, from time to time, he engaged someone with a tractor to come and cut. It was a Sunday in June, and he had driven home from morning rounds in his old crimson Alfa-Romeo with the top down. He was wearing khakis with white porch-paint on them, and was even getting some of the paint onto the four fluted pillars at the front of his house. He worked with his back to the hillside forest and the road that went through it, listening to Elgar on the big radio he'd put at the edge of his drippy brush's reach, beside the cooler in which four Beck's beer bottles glistened. Paint spattered onto the green V-necked hospital shirt he'd swiped, and it flew onto his chin and, he was sure, up into his five o'clock shadow. One more white hair, he thought, and he smiled charitably at the notion of getting old because—he caught himself and warned himself and kept on smiling anyway—he wasn't taking his whitening whiskers and aging body very seriously at all. I will pay for that, he thought. Janet Baker was singing the Elgar Sea Pictures, and, as her voice soared, he dropped his thought about age and he shouted, in a strong and utterly off-key praying, to accompany the song about horses running on a beach.

Nell drove up his hill in her very old Jeep, with the big front grille that looked like a sneer. He not only heard her above the music and his own noise, but he saw, in the corner of his vision, the plume of dusty roadbed that she trailed, like smoke, below her. He put the brush down and stood, paint-smeared fingers on his hips, to watch her arrive. He watched her all he could. She was wearing dirty jeans and boots with flat heels and a tank-top knitted shirt, and he thought again that she must have more muscles than he, and yet she looked so smooth at the shoulders. He could see the bones below the neck. Baker rose again; she sounded like a cello. Through her, Jay said, "You have the chest of a bird. I can see all of your bones."

Nell grew red, as she often did, but looked down at her body and then shook her head, as if she disapproved. She shrugged and started walking again, and soon she was there. As usual, they didn't know what to do. She pulled her hair back and refastened the clip that held it in a clump above her neck. Her hair was very close to black, and very fine, and it was always falling down. "You must be wooing me again, to talk like that."

He reached to turn the radio off and pulled the cooler to him, across the patch he'd just painted. He handed her a bottle of beer. She nodded and unscrewed the cap and started to drink. He said, "What else? I invited you to marry me, and you declined. I take that very personally."

"I would hope so," she said.

"It's a kind of combat," he said. "Do you remember this from when you were teen-aged? You'd have a crush on someone and they'd be going with somebody else, or they'd just be too obtuse to notice you, and you'd spend most of your time being cruel to them and teasing them and vilifying them because you wanted them to just react? In almost any way at all? Do you remember that? I do. I think I must have done it a lot. Forgive me."

She finished the beer too quickly and belched a little. "All right," she said. "How's the porch? Oh. Oh, that's not really good, is it?"

"Paint's paint."

"Jay, you're putting latex over enamel. And you haven't even scraped the enamel. You got paint all over everything. You're incompetent. No. It's worse than that. You don't care about this."

He handed her another beer and opened one for himself. The sweat ran down his forehead, and sap beetles whirred slowly in the sun to land on the sticky paint and die there. He heard the tapping of a woodpecker, and a lot of other birds he never bothered to identify: they called, he listened, and that was all he required.

"And," she said, frowning, looking too serious, "you got paint on your face, and you got it in your hair—Jay! You got paint all over your goddamned *hair*."

"Do you love me?"

"No."

"Really. Do you *like* me?"

"No."

"So marry me, then. We'd be the Great American Marriage. Can you tolerate me in small doses?"

"I don't think so. No."

"Perfect. We can get the blood tests tomorrow. Or I can do them here, heh heh."

"Pig. Painting pig. I will not be married to you."

Then Jay said, "No. I meant it."

She slowly nodded her head.

"Okay," he said. "Now tell me what you really think about my paint job."

And she did smile, then, so they sat down on the hill below the house, their faces in the sun, and they shared the last bottle of beer while Nell complained, as usual, about the bookstore she ran in Spruce Plains—that she wasn't bankrupt yet was the best she could report—and Jay described a child in the emergency room, body covered from waist to neck with a deep gouging rash that itched and hurt simultaneously, and that his family physician couldn't cure. He had remembered the article on gypsy moth larvae as the child's mother was describing how calamine didn't stop the discomfort. He'd swabbed the crusted lotion away and rubbed on a topical cortisone cream, explaining that the larvae of gypsy moths produce histamines, and they had set up an allergic reaction in the child, who had run shirtless through chest-high grass where the moths had laid their eggs.

"Pretty nice, huh?"

"You're a good detective," she said. "I like the way you look for clues. I like the way you enjoy it when you find them."

"Me too. It's the best thing I do. It's the only fun, really, except when little kids hug me and get better."

"You should have children," she said.

"And you have one I could use. You want to do a deal with me? Nell, are you listening?"

"Yes. I am."

"Okay. I have no idea what else I should say."

She stood and she jumped on him and bore him down. She lay on top of him and kissed him crookedly, half on the mouth and half beneath his nose. Then she pushed off him and left him slanted on his hillside, and she backed her Jeep and drove down the road. He lay there a while and looked up into the light, then he rolled over onto his hands and knees, got up, and walked back up to his porch, where he dipped his brush into the wrong kind of paint and continued to apply it to the unprepared surfaces. He turned the radio on, and the Fountains of Rome played. He smacked the radio hard, and it slid into wet paint. "Baby music," he said. He took a deep breath and then he apologized to Respighi. I don't need a baby, he told himself. I have one. He paints my porch. He paints my radio. What I have to find, really, he said to himself, putting the brush into a jar of turpentine that he needed, he realized, for enamel paint, but not for the latex he'd been using, and then pressing down the paint can's cover to save the wrong paint for the rest of the job, what I have to locate around here is somebody who could pass for an adult.

He tried his brother, Jonas, who was inside Jay's house, sitting in the livingroom and reading at old copies of *Science* and *Esquire*, sitting in an armless rocker that Jay had stripped but never refinished. Jonas sat as if he were in a waiting room in a country doctor's house. Jonas wore the trousers to the suit he'd arrived in—it was a blue-and-white Brooks crisp seersucker—and the same black polished penny loafers he had worn last night, and the same wrinkled blue oxford cloth shirt that he now wore rolled to just above the elbows. He was smoking a small cigar with a filter on it, and the air around him was the color of steel. He seemed to derive no pleasure from smoking, but he worked away at it, squinting against the smoke, blowing out as if it all were distasteful to him, but necessary. Maybe it was, Jay thought. Jonas had come in a long, wide Lincoln that matched the light blue of his suit. He had come before Jay was back from his evening with Nell, and he'd been sitting, although the door was unlocked, on the unscraped and as yet unpainted front porch. Buckets and brushes were waiting to be used there, and so was the radio, and Jonas had been sitting against one of the pillars, legs crossed before him, smoke around his face like bugs, listening to jazz on some disc jockey's dawn patrol. They had said hello while Peggy Lee sang her instructions that some poor sucker had better go out and get her some money like the other men do.

Inside, though Jay had wanted to sleep, or at least not talk, they had sat up late together. They had drunk beer and had sat in the old shabby kitchen, with its damp sticky surfaces, and ants behind the long rusted sink, and mildew on the wallpaper, gashes in the linoleum—Jay liked to say that he was taking his time in bringing the house up to snuff: he had lived there for seven years—and they'd discussed how Jonas had just run away from home.

Jay asked, "Did you leave them a note or something? So they'd know you weren't dead?"

Jonas shook his head.

Jay said, "No? You didn't?"

Jonas said, "No. I didn't. Okay?"

"Did you want to talk to me or what? Because I could go upstairs and we could sit around and not say anything tomorrow, if you're busy tonight."

Jonas waved his hand at Jay's temper, then he looked at him. This was something Jay thought lawyers did with juries—the red, wounded little-boy's eyes, peering into you. Jonas rarely pleaded trials, however, and Jay knew that. Jonas did good research and wrote fine contracts and argued before law referees, but he didn't go to trial a lot. And, anyway, his eyes this time looked enormous and brown and liquid.

Jay said, "Is it really busted, you think? The marriage?"

Jonas shrugged. "Yeah, I think, probably."

"And the kids?"

"They get hurt. You have a war, people get hurt."

"Your kids, I mean."

"Who do you think I was talking about, Jay? You think I'm doing some kind of routine here?"

"Ladies and gentlemen: take my wife. Please."

"Fuck you, Jay. Okay? Hey. I left one of my kids crying and the other one's not talking to *any*one no more. Any more. Joanne thinks every person who's a grownup, he's a, like a traitor. I'm talking like the neighborhood again, you hear me? I'm falling apart here, Jay. I'm already treating my kids like casualties. You do that and they're your kids once removed. The thing is, you end up, you have to do that. Otherwise, the pain kills you. Your heart stops from it. So you do— you turn your heart down, like a radio. Then it don't hurt so much. Doesn't. Will you listen to me? I do some divorces, you know, just for favors. Everybody's splitting up, and some of them are friends of mine. So I handle it. Every fuckin' time, you see some kid get broken, like little rocks that a truck rolls over. It's all the same parts of the kids, but it's powder. Go put that together again, right? It don't work. That's Joanne. Whatever happens, I'm afraid she's finished. She won't trust people. And—"

The big eyes ran. Jay knew that Jonas was about to speak of Joe, his son. Jay looked down at the palimpsest of white rings on his old oak dining table. He made a big brother's decision and stood to walk to the wall phone and call Manhattan to say that Jonas was here and all right.

"No," Jonas said.

"You can't just drop out of sight, you know. You have one or two responsibilities, right?"

"Oh. Excuse me. I didn't think of that, Jay. I didn't know that, about my responsibilities. I was thinking, this marriage didn't work, you could take me down to some fuckin' farm around here or something and pick me out a new one. I could marry a cow or a fuckin' pig next time. Thank you for the memo."

"Pick out a room with a bed," Jay had said on Sunday night, leaving his beer bottle half-empty on the table and going up. "Don't cut your wrists except in the bathroom, okay? I've got rounds and then I'll come home and we can talk or something. Or yell. Whatever you want. Also, fuck you too. I don't think your suffering ennobles you."

"Well, that's not why I'm doin' it, schmuck."

"Putz."

"Fuckin' asshole."

"Prick. Goodnight."

"Thank you for the bed."

Smiling, and feeling fifteen, Jay went up to bed, and he was worried that he couldn't feel more completely unhappy. Before he fell asleep, to the sounds of Jonas bumping into things in an unfamiliar house, he wondered if Jonas's dilemma pleased him. He wondered if anyone ever recovered from being a brother, especially a younger one. He was certain that being the older was far from beneficial to the soul: no matter where in the world you lived, your younger brother, on entering some place or any time, was a stranger on terrain you might already have hoisted your flag above. You could not feel such confidence about your relationship to any other person's life and still be decent, he thought. Feeling indecent, therefore, yet not so unhappy about all of it as he should, Jay fell into sleep. The whimpering woke him up almost at once. He listened hard, to be certain that Jonas was actually crying. He wasn't. It had been Jay's own noises calling him up and to the rescue. On and off, he kept himself company for long hours, or so it felt, because the sleep he fell to was so frightening, and its nature unnameable. Blinking against the dark, and rolling, rolling, he wondered whether he had taken some of Jonas's troubles onto himself. That question was the answer. Hearing the word *decent* repeated by the secret self, he finally stayed asleep.

Next day, he spent fifteen minutes in the emergency room, instead of walking his ward, in explaining to two very well-read but misinformed parents that their little girl's *herpes simplex*—the child had a lipful of cold sores—did not necessarily mean that she would come down with genital herpes and infected children and a sex life demanding a terrible precision and tact. He administered synthetic penicillin to one patient and took another off intravenous feeding. He dictated records and signed orders. He got hugged by children in pajamas and he hugged them back. He got hugged by a nurse who weighed fifty pounds more than he, and who smelled of soap, and they traded shocking stories while he helped her find the key to the drug cabinet. He fed the goldfish in the corridor of the ward and then, after checking his mail and gossiping with doctors who also drove European cars, he went toward home.

He kept going, though, and drove into Spruce Plains, which once had been a sleepy town inhabited by merchants and a few teachers from the local school and some antique dealers from New York who wanted privacy for their domestic arrangements. They all were still there, and the one or two artists who kept vacation homes. But there were also people who sold health foods, and tall bearded men who wore faded jeans and who made pots and rugs and furniture, and there was a bookstore. It had no cute name because it was Nell's. The sign outside said BOOKS. That was what she sold—no art postcards, and not even witty place-markers, and no small anthologies of religious doggerel from greeting-card companies. She sold paperback books and cloth-bound books and she made enough money, along with a modicum of assistance from her former husband who taught history at Williams, to feed herself and her daughter, whose name was Rachel, and who was sitting behind the cash register when Jay came in.

"Hi, Jay."

"Hi, Rachel. Where's your mom?"

The child smiled all of her teeth. "Nellie!" she called. "Nellie! A man's here for you."

Nell came through the curtains at the back of the shop, glared at Jay, then harder at Rachel, and she marched the length of the store. Standing in front of the register, as if she were about to pay for something, she said, "Apologize. Apologize to Jay and then to me. Now. *Now.*"

Rachel got down from her wooden stool and stood on the other side of the counter. "How do you think I feel, being humiliated like this? I'm thir*teen*." Her face frightened Jay because the eyes were like marbles in something shot and stuffed; only the lips and forehead moved.

"You're grounded. You're starving for a meal. Your goose is cooked, and I'm eating it. I mean it. Look at me: Do I mean it? Apologize."

Rachel said, "Jay, I'm humiliated right now, but I'm also sorry. I didn't mean to act like some adolescent creep. It just—Jay, when you come *after* her like that, you don't know how crappy it makes me feel."

"Didn't mean to make you feel crappy, Rachel. But it isn't entirely your problem. And you made me feel very peculiar when you said that. When you treated me that way."

"I'm sorry, Jay. I didn't mean to imply you were sniffing around Nellie's legs."

Nell squealed, swung at Rachel's face, missed most of it, but caught enough to make a plopping sound of skin and to send Rachel into a fast pallor. "Ma!"

"That's right," Nell said, panting. "Try calling me Nellie again real soon, won't you? And be a smart little shit in front of grownups again real soon. You think you will?"

"I apologize," Rachel said, not crying, "all right?"

Nell said, "I mean, do you have problems, or what?"

"I think either I'm jealous of Jay's affections for you or I'm unsettled by their implications for our family."

"Will you stop sounding so *gifted*?" Nell wailed. "Talk like the other kids. Talk like *me*."

"I do apologize," Rachel said. "I'll go into the house and chew gum and watch bowling now, if you'll excuse me."

"No," Nell said. "You'll go wash your face and fix your hair and do chores."

"Ma."

"Now." Rachel's face changed, some of the stillness and sullenness leaked out, and she left, waving casually to both of them. Nell said, "Can you tell, I made the mistake of giving her some Salinger stories? They took her hostage, I think."

"Is she going to stay a chowderhead like that?" Jay asked.

"Not if she wants to keep breathing. Hello."

"You want me to take care of your kid? I'll stay here and nurse her."

"She isn't sick. She's just an adolescent."

"Okay. You want me to stay here and take care of you?"

"What'd you have in mind?"

"I thought maybe one of us might want to sweep the other of us off of his or her feet."

The door opened and two women in identical straw hats came in. One of them wore a patch over her eye, and its delicate yellow tone precisely matched her gloves, bunched in her hand and waved at Nell in greeting. "So much for the leisure to sweep," Nell said, waving back.

"My brother showed up. He's running away from home. I meant to tell you, but I was thinking about getting *you* to run away from home. Anyway, he's here."

"He's younger than you?"

"He's thirty-seven, and he's running away from home."

"To live with you and be a kid brother?"

"To tell me some of his troubles, maybe. Maybe today. I don't know. Let's not count on tonight, though, all right?"

"I didn't know I *was* counting on tonight."

"If I can put up with your kid, can we live together?"

"No."

"Then we can get married?"

"No."

"Can I nibble your toes in the village square?"

Nell giggled, then stopped herself. She said, loudly, "I don't think there *is* a village square in Spruce Plains, Dr. Reese. Perhaps you had some other place in mind."

He said, also louder, "Where I can nibble?" Nell colored, the woman whose eyepatch echoed her gloves looked over, and Jay left the store, making the sounds of chomping.

Jay drove back to the clinic he shared, in Millerton, with two other doctors, and he saw private patients until four, when he remembered that he had been expected at home for lunch. It was an uncrowded day, and his partners took his patients when he left and drove too quickly home. His brother was wearing the wrinkled seersucker pants and the wrinkled oxford shirt. He sat outside with Jay's bottle of vodka and two glasses and a plate of rubbery egg-with-ketchup sandwiches. Without speaking, they ate and drank across the picnic table from one another, under the willow at the side of the house. Then Jay talked a little about his practice, and about the day, and, apologizing for his lateness, and gesturing with his full glass that Jonas should take his too, he led him from the table up the sloping small lawn toward the field that ran west from his house. They walked slowly, for their drinks' sakes, climbed the wooden fence and then descended, walking through cowflop and high grass, through swampy ground and dense thistle and very uneven dry field, away from the house and finally uphill, toward nothing but long meadow and bright yellow flowers that Jay couldn't name.

Then they stood, sweating slightly, but cooled by the evening wind that came up, sipping small to make the drinks last, and looking at the orange sunset that told of tomorrow's humidity. A blue jay landed very close to them and bounced twice, then flew away, nagging. "This is pretty," Jonas said.

Jay nodded.

"You still like it? Out here?"

Jay nodded again.

"You got girlfriends or something? Shit. It's probably nice, being a bachelor. I don't want it, though. That part scares me, having to date girls. Date. What a terrible word. You stamp them November twenty-ninth or something. But I'm the one who wants to be free. You understand the contradictions here, Jay?"

Jay said, "I have a friend, a woman, and when she puts a disciplinary move on me, really rags me and tells me exactly what I should do, I tell her she's conducting orthopedic conversations—like a brace, or a cast, say. Orthopedic. I don't intend to be doing that to you, Jonas. So you tell me when I start, all right? If I do, I don't want to. And not that I ever doubted that you would tell me. But I wanted to ask you something, all right? I wanted to ask you: Do you love Norma? How's that for a question?"

"It's always the first one I ask people if they come and ask me to handle a divorce for them. Same question. And what I learned, Jay, is—this's a good one for you to know. Though you're not getting any younger, and maybe it's time for you to make a move, you know? I learned, anyway, that loving the wife or husband is very often about the last problem they have when they're splitting up. Well, hell, Jay, you did this whole thing. It was so long ago, I almost forgot. You know what I'm talking about. Sure, they say, right? Sure, yeah, I love McSchmuck. Big deal, though. See: I can't *live* with him, they say. Right? Or: She eats my soul like a carrot stick, this one guy told me. So how is loving her supposed to help, he asks, and then of course he cries all over my desk. I wanted to tell him it sounded like a very spiritual kind of a blowjob, but I'm a tasteful guy. But it's amazing how little it counts for, love, when you got a marriage that's dying, dead, diseased, whatever you want to call it. You remember that from your—"

"Yes. I'm so dumb about that," Jay said. They strolled now, breathing unevenly because of the terrain, but still, Jay thought, like a couple of old Jewish guys in the neighborhood, walking and discussing issues of international importance and great local impact. They walked at the same pace and they discussed. "I always think that love is the thing," Jay said. "This is in spite of Elizabeth, who you may remember from my days as cuckold-to-a-culture in Philly, and in spite of other people I've known since then, including this friend of mine now, who's also divorced. You know someone who isn't? But I keep thinking *love*, anyway. Everybody is talking *strain* and *need* and *alienation* and the timelessly popular *self*, and this one, which is Nell's current favorite: *erosion*. She says you can get eroded, and down to bedrock, and then you have to move on or you're washed away."

"That's it," Jonas said. "She knows."

"Does Norma love you?"

Jonas nodded. He was wet-eyed again. A swallow was near them, raging in clicks behind and in front of them. Bugs flew up, and mosquitoes clung to their arms and faces and necks. Jonas kept trying to light one of his cigars, but the matches blew out. He threw the unsmoked cigar into high grass.

Jay asked, "And is everybody—faithful to everybody?"

Jonas smiled, as if this time Jay were the younger one. "Yeah. So far as I know, neither party has entered into adulterous relationships."

"You sound like Pop."

"Who, me?"

"The time they had all the trouble."

"What trouble?"

"When I was in college, away at school? You don't remember? They almost split up, Jonas. You remember."

"Never happened. That has to be your imagination. Never happened, Jay."

"Jonas, it happened."

"No way. Not them. That's a *couple*. Bullshit, Jay."

"Bullshit back, Jonas. It's true."

They had stopped again, no longer old men outside the synagogue, though, but boys in an argument. Jonas's voice went higher. "Jay," he shouted, "you don't think I woulda known if the old man and Mom nearly got a divorce?"

"Well, you did know once. You cried at night. I heard you when I came for the weekend, to study for exams, I think. I came in and I asked you what was wrong, and after you told me to drop dead, you said it was on account of them."

"Never."

"Okay. Never."

"Jay. Really?"

"No, never, I was lying."

"Jay, come on. Tell me. Really?"

"No."

"*Jay.*"

"You're a baby, Jonas, you wiped it off your mind because you didn't want it there. What the hell. You were young. That's true, you know? You were young. I was seventeen, maybe eighteen. But I think it happened in my first year of school. I was seventeen. So you were twelve? Almost thirteen? It's a disgusting age. I realized that earlier today. You were thirteen. And you wiped it out. Amazing. Domestic amnesia, you could call it."

"Hey, *doc*tor. You want me to make an appointment so you could tell me about it? All it is, it's only my parents. If it gets important, you could send me a registered letter, huh?"

"It's simple. It's so simple. You know them. They wouldn't let us hear it or see it. Which is why you probably don't remember it."

"*Def*initely don't remember it," Jonas said. "Am I a liar? *Plus* amnesia? Look at this, around here. You're practicing medicine in an office, you carpet it with cowshit. You know why?"

"All it was," Jay said, "was that Mom flew out to Aunt Anna's and Pop freaked out when she was late coming home. I mean by a *day*. He went out to the airport and she never showed up. That night—can you see her making him eat it like that all day? That night, it was in some hot month this happened, I think. That night, she telephones, and I don't know what she said, but it slams him down into his chair and keeps him there until she's done talking. I remember we were eating dinner. Horrible gray hamburgers and that peas-and-carrots mix from a can? He turned around to me. He was wearing those thin glasses with gold rims at that time. He turned while you were shoving the food in, and he said, 'Mother will probably be home tomorrow,' he said. I remember that. His eyes looked like yours do. Excuse me. They were all wet and they looked like yours. He knew something about her, or about them both, and he didn't want to. I think that was a lot of whatever he was feeling. He didn't want to have to deal with the information. Whatever the information was, he hated having to know it. And he must have hated what it meant. So out we go the next day. Kennedy was called Idlewild in those days. He took us there. He made you wear the school assembly clothes, blue pants and white shirt and red tie. He combed your hair so hard, you cried before we left. He was scared. He was *white*. We're standing there someplace at the field, and there's her plane, and people keep getting off it. For him, Pop's a mess. He's turning his Palm Beach hat around and around, he's fingering the summer silk tie from Brooks. He was wearing the brown seersucker with the stripes. Do you remember that?" Jonas shook his head. "It was a suit he wore a lot. Anyway, all of a sudden, there she is. She must have waited until the plane was empty. It was quite an appearance. She stands up there in the door of the airplane like a conquering warrior. Oh, they knew some stuff we didn't, boy. At that minute, that second, when they looked at each other, I could feel it. They *knew* stuff. After a while, she comes down the steps like a queen. Pop just stands there, and then he says—I swear this: I never forgot—he says, 'Neither party has so far precipitated an unmarried state.' I said 'What?' or something. Hell. I *still* don't know what that means. But he just shook his head and then he just waited for her. But his voice, and that poor hat rolling and rolling in his hands. Oh, was he scared. Listen, if I didn't enjoy the show so much, I think I'd have peed in my pants."

Jonas stood in the center of his big brother's countryside with a glass in his hand and dusk upon them, and he wept like a very young boy. He didn't speak of Jay's cruel relish in the telling of the story. And he didn't claim that Jay had dispossessed him of a portion of his past. He simply wept. And Jay stood a few paces from him, and then moved in to touch his brother's shoulder, hot beneath the dirty shirt. Each moved back at the contact. Jonas continued to cry, while he smiled and shook his head. Jay nodded, as if to agree with Jonas that it couldn't be helped.

TUESDAY WAS USUAL, in that no new diseases were presented in the practice, and no fevers spiked so high in the ward that children's brains were damaged, and everyone was going to get better. He stopped the aspirin for a child with stomach irritation, though he thought that the real source of irritation was the parent who dispensed the aspirin. He prescribed a seasickness medicine for the young woman who kept falling down; although he explained it as an inner-ear infection that interfered with balance, he could not persuade the child's father that she didn't suffer epilepsy, and he therefore prescribed Valium for the father, but not out loud.

To make up for the work shunted to his partners the day before, he came to his clinic early and worked without a break, and he treated plantar's wart, and he gave children allergy shots, and he tested their urine, and he swabbed at crimson throats. He stared down over tongues and under uvulae to ferret where diseases hid. The kids looked up and he looked down and, while they gagged over his tongue depressor, he made gagging noises back at them so that they watered at the eyes and retched and giggled at once. He was happy all day.

Because he'd started early, he finished early—it was too bright and pretty a day for parents to make the trek to the clinic; on a nasty day, with nothing better to do, they'd show up, he knew—so Jay decided that it was time for a drive to Spruce Plains. He needed something to read, Jay decided. He knew a bookstore, and he went there. Outside, parked in his red car, in a day so brilliantly lighted that even afternoon felt more like a start than a finish, he listed to himself what he must do. A quick joke with Rachel, if she was there, and no protracted teasing: she grew sour under scrutiny or with attention—be avuncular, but also be quiet. Be reserved. Hold back. Make no more jokes with Nell about marriage. Say: Nell, you are a secret person. I know more about the hidden places inside children's throats than I know about you. I understand that you're hiding. I respect this. I hide too—look at my high hill, my dusty road, my house of many rooms, surrounded by so much forest and field. I don't presume to say you need my comfort or that I can give it.

"Hi, Rachel."

"Nellie! Jay's here! Hi, Jay."

"I thought you were calling her Mom from now on."

The girl with large eyes and pale skin and a curly permanent—she looked to Jay like a high-fashion dog with human features—shook her head with, probably, pity. It came off as bitchiness, and all at once he felt the fatigue of his day. "That was probably what *you* wanted," she said. "Mom and I have a different relationship. We try to communicate our feelings. I have this need to be her peer. I think it has to do with my father and everything."

Jay nodded. He wondered what it would be like to give this girl an allowance and smell her shampoo and watch her sneak off to beer parties. He wondered what it would be like to become Rachel's peer.

"Oh, yes," Rachel said, snapping her fingers theatrically enough for

Jay to see—he was supposed to see—the posturing. "I forgot. Mom's at the market."

"Which one? I'll catch up with her," Jay said.

"The one in Millerton. You'd probably pass her on the road. Sorry I didn't remember, Jay."

"You're close to peerless, Rachel. Thank you for thinking of it finally."

"Would you like to buy a book, Jay? Or did you come to talk to Nellie? Or whatever you do to her, ha ha." She showed her long white teeth, and Jay decided that he'd been reminded of terriers, Scottish terriers. He turned a paperback rack around too loudly on his way out: another victory for the dogs.

Driving home, he had two thoughts that rotated in his head like the twin propellers on a pinwheel, around and around, so that neither went anyplace, and everything else got spun away. He thought that parents needn't be villains to make whacky kids, and then he wondered who ought to take the blame, and whether blame had purpose here. And then he thought that children never should be villains because their throats were so tender and, in infants, the thighs and forearms so innocent and made to be kissed; and yet they so often *were* villainous, he went on as the pinwheel spun, raping women in parking lots and running amok in subways in New York and sitting in someone's rural bookstore with twenty-one-year-old eyes and the face of a cunning small dog and the tongue of an asp. Around and around they went, and nothing came of Jay's unwisdoms, and soon he was home, and there—parent and child, villain and victim—was Jonas to greet him.

Jonas was beginning to smell bad. He was starting to rot, Jay thought. He wore no socks. He had left his scuffed loafers, wet from high grass, at the side door, and Jay could see that his feet were rimmed with dirt and had dark long nails. The anklebones showed dark patches too. His thoroughly wrinkled and matted seersucker pants carried staleness through the air, and his same blue oxford cloth shirt was stained under the arms and reminded Jay of what a high school gym locker had smelled like. Jonas had shaved on his first day there, but not today, and his dark jowls and bruised eyes, the slackness of the skin around his mouth, were challenged only by his great round heavy golden watch on its wide golden band: it proved that he wasn't a bum, that he was a prosperous man of business whose life had fallen down to stink and disarray.

They had drinks in the field again, because Jonas liked the sense of a lot of room around him, he said. This time, they carried a vacuum jug of vodka martinis, and as they strolled, like two old men in the neighborhood, they drank with the freedom of those who know there's more. Pollen blew around them, and seeds floated. The breeze that carried them carried also the smell of cows and the algae on still water and the lavender that was planted at the edge of the lawn behind the house—a combination of perfume and decay, like the merging of colors on the bushes themselves, the bright light purple in feathery clusters melting into dull brown mush. The wind took all the smells away, too, and sometimes they walked as if sheltered from the sensual world, although it lay about them, breathing.

"How was your day?" Jonas asked. But he didn't wait for Jay to tell him. He said, at once, "I feel like a housewife, asking that. Did you have a hard day at the office, dear?"

Jay nodded and sipped and kept walking. The ground was spongy here, and he wanted to get to a higher, firmer place.

Jonas also said nothing. They walked, and sometimes one or the other would sigh loudly and sniff, as if to tell his brother how fine the air felt going up the nose and past the hidden organs of taste and smell.

Finally, Jonas said, "I called home."

"Did you talk?"

"Yeah."

"Was she glad?"

"That I wasn't dead or anything. Yeah. And that I thought to call. You don't leave somebody worrying you're dead or something."

"Did you talk more, or is that the way it was?"

"We talked more."

"Good."

"Not good, Jay."

"You mean you talked tough. You told her all about the facts of life, is that what you mean?"

"I told her the truth," Jonas said. "I told her what I've come to believe. Hey: three strikes and you're out. I swung three times, she swung three times, so we're out. Everybody's out. I said that. Even Norma knows it's three swings and three misses and that's that. I took her to a Mets game once. She fell asleep in the sun."

"You instructed her about love," Jay said.

"Love, we got. That's what I told her. That's not—with us, that isn't the problem. I wanted her to know that. It's—*needs*, Jay. It's different needs, is all. Everything. But I wanted her, so she would remember it later, I wanted her to know the problem isn't love."

"So if love doesn't matter, how come you put so much time in, telling me and your wife and Christ knows who else that love isn't in short supply?"

Jonas stopped, wheeled, pointed a finger at Jay, who was panting behind him up the rise that enabled them to look at the meadow below, and then the forest surrounding the house and the clearing it hid within. "Hey, don't crow about it. Don't get swelled up like you're teachin' me something. Because I don't see *you* with twelve kids and a sweet little wife or nothin', anything. Anything. You know what I'm saying here, Jay? You're the one almost never was married, and our mother goes around saying she hopes you're not a fag."

"She does?"

"Well, she doesn't say it. She thinks it."

"Maybe you're the one who thinks it, Jonas."

"Maybe I am."

Jonas looked at his brother, and his brother looked back, and as it hadn't done when they were kids, and as he hadn't expected it now, at their age, or at this moment, Jay's stomach lurched and hot phlegm crawled in his gullet, an instant's awful taste that subsided, but that was part of a fact now. He had tasted it. And it was not because of what Jonas had said. Jonas lifted weights in health clubs. He played basketball several times a month with men who once were boys with him in the schoolyards of Flatbush. Jonas would worry about men who lived alone, and Jay had known that. But it was what he saw when he'd stared at his brother: the retreating but still heavy hairline, the broad nose that in profile was close to the face, the upper jaw's overbite, the configuration of whiskers, the size of the very dark eyes. What he looked at every morning in the mirror, early, humming to himself while the water sent up steam and the utter cleanliness of the daily shave made him glad to be awake—that was what he'd seen in Jonas. He had looked at himself. He had seen how far and proximate, and both at once, they might be.

Would he, Jay, maybe married and with kids, living, say, with a beautiful dark woman who had not gone home to a Southern city, and never mind the cultural problem and the racial garbage and the neighborhood bastards who might sit on his children's lives with deadweight buttocks—would *he* be gone from them by now? Would he have fled? Would he have traveled this far from them? And what if Nellie came there tonight and said to him: Yes. What if he then held his temper for enough years to permit Rachel to possibly grow tolerable? Would he, one day, be fleeing Nell as Nell had fled her former husband to come here and sell books to women with matching hats and gloves? Was everyone born to be separate? Was his baby brother here to tell him *that?*

He poured them each a drink, and they drank. They said nothing more. He poured them each a half of what was left in the jug. It was getting cold. It was dark. Jay said, "Cheers. Here's to what you want."

Jonas looked at Jay with Jay's face; Jay looked back with Jonas's. "To what I *need*," Jonas said.

"All right."

And then they went back down the hill, and over the meadow, through marsh and firm field, and over the fence, and along the yard and inside. Jay made an olive oil and garlic sauce for spiral noodles. He left the garlic peelings on the stove and fetched a bottle of Barolo that one of his partners had given him. They ate and drank in silence, except for Jonas's pronouncement that the food was good. They put the dishes in the sink, and Jay said that he might, at gunpoint, do them later.

In the livingroom, Jay played records—the Vaughan Williams London Symphony—and Jonas went upstairs, perhaps to telephone, Jay hoped. He didn't know why he hoped it. Surely, he wanted it for Norma and Joe and Joanne. He wanted it also, and maybe he wanted it mostly, for himself.

At the door a few minutes later was Nellie. He had been nearly asleep, slumped in the armless rocker, and he'd heard the crushing of gravel stones beneath wheels. Looking out the window, he'd seen her Jeep. So he was up and shaking himself awake and moving to the door as the knock sounded. It was constant, and Nellie didn't summon him that way. She knocked and knocked, was calling him for help, and he skipped along the floor in his stocking feet, wondering why she didn't simply walk inside. Then, opening the door, he saw why. She was holding Rachel. She was carrying her across her chest, and she had knocked with an arm under strain. Rachel's face was too white. Her eyes were open, the pupils dilated, and she looked almost shocky.

He held the door wide and Nellie staggered past, heading for the livingroom and its broad sofa. The bass of the big speaker was growling. Nell, panting, went to turn the record player off. Her eyes were huge when she came back, still gulping at the air, to stand above Rachel, who lay on the sofa with her knees curled up and her fist clenched, the right fist clenched, and dark spots on her cheek and forehead.

"Something happened," Nell said. "I was—something happened."

He turned on the lights at either end of the sofa and he kneeled to look at Rachel. He expected that Nellie would tell him what the matter was, and he waited, but she said nothing more. He smelled Rachel's breath, which was steamy and fetid, weak, and he touched her face very carefully at the sides, and then he started to feel at her bones. The face was abraded and scratched, puffy in spots where the vessels were bruised against the bone. He knew that her left arm was broken. He stood, went for scissors and a quick wash of his hands, then came back to see Nell covering her to the waist with a comforter. "There's nothing wrong with her legs?" he said. Nell shook her head. She kept blinking, he saw, and he was worried that she was going to faint. There was blood on Nell's white shirt. She looked like a meat cutter or a surgeon, there was something familiar about the white garment and about looking on it for spatters of blood. Then he bent forward and down to see what Nell had done to her daughter.

He cut Rachel's sleeve away. He wasn't talking in his easy chant—he sometimes had to use it for injured children who were frightened— because Rachel wasn't frightened. She wasn't there. She watched him from somewhere back behind her eyes, she winced as he got the sleeve off, but she was pretending not to be there. He saw that the fracture was simple, a clean green snap and nothing puncturing the skin or major blood vessels. He went for tape and some old lath he'd saved for kindling. He splinted her and then, with a flashlight, looked once more at the bruises and scrapes, looked inside her mouth and nostrils and eyes, peering down into her secrets but not finding Rachel, just her blood. He telephoned the hospital—Jonas wasn't on the line, he noted—to say that he'd need an orthopedist at the hospital in half an hour. He ordered the X-rays so there would be no delay. He got Rachel up. "We'll take the Alfa," he said. "It's faster. You can take the Jeep if you want to come. There's only room for two in the Alfa."

He heard himself pause because, he knew, what he said next would matter tonight, later on, and tomorrow, when it would be just him and Nell and what they needed to say, and what they ought to be doing. Then he saw his brother in his rotting clothes at the livingroom doorway. His brother Jonas was watching him, but with Jay's own face. Jonas looked at the battered child, but with Jay's face, except that Jonas was smiling now: a great wide smile had twitched over his mouth from right to left, like a carpet being unrolled. So Jay knew how pleased his brother was about being right.

And Jay, no better than anyone, turned his back to the cruel and frightening face that he recognized, and he said to Nell, "And I'm not sure that I give a good goddamn whether you get there finally or not."

Nell didn't answer. She was looking at his hands. They were balled into fists. He held them cocked across his chest. He realized that she expected him to punch her, just as she had punched and torn at her child. He wondered how much she wanted him to, and he wondered how far he'd be tempted to start in swiping at her frozen face. He banged his hands against his chest while his mouth made a shape he hadn't determined. Her face collapsed into its pallor, and she stiffened as if struck, hard, with a hard hand.

He saw her eyes and then he turned from her. Rachel was gray-white with pain. He put the blanket around her carefully and he leaned above her to shepherd her out, past Jonas's grin, to his car. He buckled her lap-belt carefully, and he settled the blanket about her as if she lay in bed. Nell watched them, and then she climbed up into the cab of the Jeep. Jay started the Alfa and put it in gear without waiting for the oil to heat, and they went down his road, Jay and the girl he detested.

He hadn't intended to stop his car, but he did. He said to Rachel, "A minute. Just a minute." He walked back to the Jeep that was idling with a high roar on the steep decline of his road. When he walked past the brilliance of her headlights, the air at the side of the cab seemed densely dark. He said to Nell, "Let me see your hand."

"What?"

"The hand you hit her with. Let me see your hand."

"The—what did you say?"

"I want to see if your hand's hurt. You can break bones, hitting someone like that. Your hand has twenty-seven bones. Most people don't get to meet most of their bones. Is it swollen? Does it hurt?"

"I didn't hit her," Nell said.

"You didn't?"

She looked down her headlights. They converged on the little red car, and the still shoulders and head of her daughter. "You think you know about this," she said. "You think you know all about it."

He said, "I'll see you there."

He went back to his car and when he sat behind the wheel, he saw that Rachel was crooked in the seat, her head along her own shoulder, her flesh gone clammy, her breath a kind of snuffle and wheeze. She looked like a broken stuffed dog. He drove very quickly down the rest of the hill, descending alone with what needed him, and when he raised his face to look in the rearview mirror, the great high sneering grille of the Jeep was close behind.

ABSENT FRIENDS

RALPH THE DUCK

I WOKE UP at 5:25 because the dog was vomiting. I carried seventy-five pounds of heaving golden retriever to the door and poured him onto the silver, moonlit snow. "Good boy," I said because he'd done his only trick. Outside he retched, and I went back up, passing the sofa on which Fanny lay. I tiptoed with enough weight on my toes to let her know how considerate I was while she was deserting me. She blinked her eyes. I swear I heard her blink her eyes. Whenever I tell her that I hear her blink her eyes, she tells me I'm lying; but I can hear the damp slap of lash after I have made her weep.

In bed and warm again, noting the red digital numbers (5:29) and certain that I wouldn't sleep, I didn't. I read a book about men who kill each other for pay or for their honor. I forget which, and so did they. It was 5:45, the alarm would buzz at 6:00, and I would make a pot of coffee and start the wood stove; I would call Fanny and pour her coffee into her mug; I would apologize because I always did, and then she would forgive me if I hadn't been too awful—I didn't think I'd been that bad—and we would stagger through the day, exhausted but pretty sure we were all right, and we'd sleep that night, probably after sex, and then we'd waken in the same bed to the alarm at 6:00, or the dog, if he'd returned to the frozen deer carcass he'd been eating in the forest

115

on our land. He loved what made him sick. The alarm went off, I got into jeans and woolen socks and a sweatshirt, and I went downstairs to let the dog in. He'd be hungry, of course.

I WAS THE OLDEST college student in America, I thought. But of course I wasn't. There were always ancient women with parchment for skin who graduated at seventy-nine from places like Barnard and the University of Georgia. I was only forty-two, and I hardly qualified as a student. I patrolled the college at night in a Bronco with a leaky exhaust system, and I went from room to room in the classroom buildings, kicking out students who were studying or humping in chairs—they'd do it *anywhere*—and answering emergency calls with my little blue light winking on top of the truck. I didn't carry a gun or a billy, but I had a flashlight that took six batteries and I'd used it twice on some of my over-privileged northeastern-playboy part-time classmates. On Tuesdays and Thursdays I would waken at 6:00 with my wife, and I'd do my homework, and work around the house, and go to school at 11:30 to sit there for an hour and a half while thirty-five stomachs growled with hunger and boredom, and this guy gave instruction about books. Because I was on the staff, the college let me take a course for nothing every term. I was getting educated, in a kind of slow-motion way—it would have taken me something like fifteen or sixteen years to graduate, and I would no doubt get an F in gym and have to repeat—and there were times when I respected myself for it. Fanny often did, and that was fair incentive.

I am not unintelligent. *You are not an unintelligent writer*, my professor wrote on my paper about Nathaniel Hawthorne. We had to read short stories, I and the other students, and then we had to write little essays about them. I told how I saw Kafka and Hawthorne in a similar light, and I was not unintelligent, he said. He ran into me at dusk one time, when I answered a call about a dead battery and found out it was him. I jumped his Buick from the Bronco's battery, and he was looking me over, I could tell, while I clamped onto the terminals and cranked it up. He was a tall, handsome guy who never wore a suit. He wore khakis and sweaters, loafers or sneaks, and he was always talking to the female students with the brightest hair and best builds. But he couldn't get a Buick going on an ice-cold night, and he didn't know enough to look for cells going bad. I told him he was going to need a new battery and he looked me over the way men sometimes do with other men who fix their cars for them.

"Vietnam?"

I said, "Too old."

"Not at the beginning. Not if you were an adviser. So-called. Or one of the Phoenix Project fellas?"

I was wearing a watch cap made of navy wool and an old Marine fatigue jacket. Slick characters like my professor like it if you're a killer or at least a onetime middleweight fighter. I smiled like I knew something. "Take it easy," I said, and I went back to the truck to swing around the cemetery at the top of the campus. They'd been known to screw in down-filled sleeping bags on horizontal stones up there, and the dean of students didn't want anybody dying of frostbite while joined at the hip to a matriculating fellow resident of our northeastern camp for the overindulged.

He blinked his high beams at me as I went. "You are not an unintelligent driver," I said.

FANNY HAD LEFT ME a bowl of something made with sausages and sauerkraut and potatoes, and the dog hadn't eaten too much more than his fair share. He watched me eat his leftovers and then make myself a king-sized drink composed of sourmash whiskey and ice. In our back room, which is on the northern end of the house, and cold for sitting in that close to dawn, I sat and watched the texture of the sky change. It was going to snow, and I wanted to see the storm come up the valley. I woke up that way, sitting in the rocker with its loose right arm, holding a watery drink, and thinking right away of the girl I'd convinced to go back inside. She'd been standing outside her dormitory, looking up at a window that was dark in the midst of all those lighted panes—they never turned a light off, and often let the faucets run half the night—crying onto her bathrobe. She was barefoot in shoe-pacs, the brown ones so many of them wore unlaced, and for all I know she was naked under the robe. She was beautiful, I thought, and she was somebody's red-headed daughter, standing in a quadrangle how many miles from home and weeping.

"He doesn't love anyone," the kid told me. "He doesn't love his wife—I mean his ex-wife. And he doesn't love the ex-wife before that, or the one before that. And you know what? He doesn't love me. I don't know anyone who *does*!"

"It isn't your fault if he isn't smart enough to love you," I said, steering her toward the truck.

She stopped. She turned. "You know him?"

I couldn't help it. I hugged her hard, and she let me, and then she stepped back, and of course I let her go. "Don't you *touch* me! Is this sexual harassment? Do you know the rules? Isn't this sexual harassment?"

"I'm sorry," I said at the door to the truck. "But I think I have to be able to give you a grade before it counts as harassment."

She got in. I told her we were driving to the dean of students' house. She smelled like marijuana and something very sweet, maybe one of those coffee-with-cream liqueurs you don't buy unless you hate to drink.

As the heat of the truck struck her, she started going kind of clay-gray-green, and I reached across her to open the window.

"You touched my breast!" she said.

"It's the smallest one I've touched all night, I'm afraid."

She leaned out the window and gave her rendition of my dog.

But in my rocker, waking up, at whatever time in the morning in my silent house, I thought of her as someone's child. Which made me think of ours, of course. I went for more ice, and I started on a wet breakfast. At the door of the dean of students' house, she'd turned her chalky face to me and asked, "What grade would you give me, then?"

IT WAS A WEEK composed of two teachers locked out of their offices late at night, a Toyota with a flat and no spare, an attempted rape on a senior girl walking home from the library, a major fight outside a fraternity house (broken wrist and significant concussion), and variations on breaking-and-entering. I was scolded by the director of nonacademic services for embracing a student who was drunk; I told him to keep his job, but he called me back because I was right to hug her, he said, and also wrong, but what the hell, and he'd promised to admonish me, and now he had, and would I please stay. I thought of the fringe benefits—graduation in only sixteen years—so I went back to work.

My professor assigned a story called "A Rose for Emily," and I wrote him a paper about the mechanics of corpse fucking, and how, since she clearly couldn't screw her dead boyfriend, she was keeping his rotten body in bed because she truly loved him. I called the paper "True Love." He gave me a B and wrote *See me, pls.* In his office after class, his feet up on his desk, he trimmed a cigar with a giant folding knife he kept in his drawer.

"You got to clean the hole out," he said, "or they don't draw."

"I don't smoke," I said.

"Bad habit. Real *habit*, though. I started in smoking 'em in Georgia, in the service. My C.O. smoked 'em. We collaborated on a brothel inspection one time, and we ended up smoking these with a couple of women—" He waggled his eyebrows at me, now that his malehood was established.

"Were the women smoking them too?"

He snorted laughter through his nose while the greasy smoke came curling off his thin, dry lips. "They were pretty smoky, I'll tell ya!" Then he propped his feet—he was wearing cowboy boots that day—and he sat forward. "It's a little hard to explain. But—hell. You just don't say *fuck* when you write an essay for a college prof. Okay?" Like a scoutmaster with a kid he'd caught in the outhouse jerking off: "All right? You don't wanna do that."

"Did it shock you?"

"Fuck, no, it didn't shock me. I just told you. It violates certain proprieties."

"But if I'm writing it to you, like a letter—"

"You're writing it for posterity. For some mythical reader someplace, not just me. You're making a *statement*."

"Right. My statement said how hard it must be for a woman to fuck with a corpse."

"And a point worth making. I said so. Here."

"But you said I shouldn't say it."

"No. Listen. Just because you're talking about fucking, you don't have to say *fuck*. Does that make it any clearer?"

"No."

"I wish you'd lied to me just now," he said.

I nodded. I did too.

"Where'd you do your service?" he asked.

"Baltimore. Baltimore, Maryland."

"What's in Baltimore?"

"Railroads. I liaised on freight runs of army matériel. I killed a couple of bums on the rod with my bare hands, though."

He snorted again, but I could see how disappointed he was. He'd been banking on my having been a murderer. Interesting guy in one of my classes, he must have told some terrific woman at an overpriced meal: I just *know* the guy was a rubout specialist in the Nam, he had to have said. I figured I should come to work wearing my fatigue jacket and a red bandanna tied around my head. Say "Man" to him a couple of times, hang a fist in the air for grief and solidarity, and look terribly worn, exhausted by experiences he was fairly certain that he envied me. His dungarees were ironed, I noticed.

———

ON SATURDAY WE went back to the campus because Fanny wanted
to see a movie called *The Seven Samurai*. I fell asleep, and I'm afraid I
snored. She let me sleep until the auditorium was almost empty. Then
she kissed me awake. "Who was screaming in my dream?" I asked her.

"Kurosawa," she said.

"Who?"

"Ask your professor friend."

I looked around, but he wasn't there. "Not an un-weird man," I said.

We went home and cleaned up after the dog and put him out. We
drank a little Spanish brandy and went upstairs and made love. I was
fairly premature, you might say, but one way and another by the time
we fell asleep we were glad to be there with each other, and glad that it
was Sunday coming up the valley toward us, and nobody with it. The
dog was howling at another dog someplace, or at the moon, or maybe
just his moon-thrown shadow on the snow. I did not strangle him when
I opened the back door and he limped happily past me and stumbled
up the stairs. I followed him into our bedroom and groaned for just
being satisfied as I got into bed. You'll notice I didn't say fuck.

HE STOPPED ME in the hall after class on a Thursday, and asked me
How's it goin, just one of the kickers drinking sour beer and eating
pickled eggs and watching the tube in a country bar. How's it goin. I
nodded. I wanted a grade from the man, and I did want to learn about
expressing myself. I nodded and made what I thought was a smile. He'd
let his mustache grow out and his hair grow longer. He was starting to
wear dark shirts with lighter ties. I thought he looked like someone in
The Godfather. He still wore those light little loafers or his high-heeled
cowboy boots. His corduroy pants looked baggy. I guess he wanted
them to look that way. He motioned me to the wall of the hallway, and
he looked up and said, "How about the Baltimore stuff?"

I said, "Yeah?"

"Was that really true?" He was almost blinking, he wanted so much for me to be a damaged Vietnam vet just looking for a bell tower to climb into and start firing from. The college didn't have a bell tower you could get up into, though I'd once spent an ugly hour chasing a drunken ATO down from the roof of the observatory. "You were just clocking through boxcars in Baltimore?"

I said, "Nah."

"I thought so!" He gave a kind of sigh.

"I killed people," I said.

"You know, I could have sworn you did," he said.

I nodded, and he nodded back. I'd made him so happy.

THE ASSIGNMENT WAS to write something to influence somebody. He called it Rhetoric and Persuasion. We read an essay by George Orwell and "A Modest Proposal" by Jonathan Swift. I liked the Orwell better, but I wasn't comfortable with it. He talked about "niggers," and I felt saying it two ways.

I wrote "Ralph the Duck."

Once upon a time, there was a duck named Ralph who didn't have any feathers on either wing. So when the cold wind blew, Ralph said, Brr, and shivered and shook.

What's the matter? Ralph's mommy asked.

I'm *cold*, Ralph said.

Oh, the mommy said. Here. I'll keep you warm.

So she spread her big, feathery wings, and hugged Ralph tight, and when the cold wind blew, Ralph was warm and snuggly, and fell fast asleep.

THE NEXT THURSDAY, he was wearing canvas pants and hiking boots. He mentioned kind of casually to some of the girls in the class how whenever there was a storm he wore his Lake District walking outfit. He had a big, hairy sweater on. I kept waiting for him to make a noise like a mountain goat. But the girls seemed to like it. His boots made a creaky squeak on the linoleum of the hall when he caught up with me after class.

"As I told you," he said, "it isn't unappealing. It's just—not a college theme."

"Right," I said. "Okay. You want me to do it over?"

"No," he said. "Not at all. The D will remain your grade. But I'll read something else if you want to write it."

"This'll be fine," I said.

"Did you understand the assignment?"

"Write something to influence someone—Rhetoric and Persuasion."

We were at his office door and the redheaded kid who had gotten sick in my truck was waiting for him. She looked at me like one of us was in the wrong place, which struck me as accurate enough. He was interested in getting into his office with the redhead, but he remembered to turn around and flash me a grin he seemed to think he was known for.

Instead of going on shift a few hours after class, the way I'm supposed to, I told my supervisor I was sick, and I went home. Fanny was frightened when I came in, because I don't get sick and I don't miss work. She looked at my face and she grew sad. I kissed her hello and went upstairs to change. I always used to change my clothes when I was a kid, as soon as I came home from school. I put on jeans and a flannel shirt and thick wool socks, and I made myself a dark drink of sourmash. Fanny poured herself some wine and came into the cold northern room a few minutes later. I was sitting in the rocker, looking over the valley. The wind was lining up a lot of rows of cloud so that the sky looked like a baked trout when you lift the skin off. "It'll snow," I said to her.

She sat on the old sofa and waited. After a while, she said, "I wonder why they always call it a mackerel sky?"

"Good eating, mackerel," I said.

Fanny said, "Shit! You're never that laconic unless you feel crazy. What's wrong? Who'd you punch out at the playground?"

"We had to write a composition," I said.

"Did he like it?"

"He gave me a D."

"Well, you're familiar enough with D's. I never saw you get this low over a grade."

"I wrote about Ralph the Duck."

She said, "You did?" She said, "Honey." She came over and stood beside the rocker and leaned into me and hugged my head and neck. "Honey," she said. "Honey."

It was the worst of the winter's storms, and one of the worst in years. That afternoon they closed the college, which they almost never do. But the roads were jammed with snow over ice, and now it was freezing rain on top of that, and the only people working at the school that night were the operator who took emergency calls and me. Everyone else had gone home except the students, and most of them were inside. The ones who weren't were drunk, and I kept on sending them in and telling them to act like grown-ups. A number of them said they were, and I really couldn't argue. I had the bright beams on, the defroster set high, the little blue light winking, and a thermos of sourmash and hot coffee that I sipped from every time I had to get out of the truck or every time I realized how cold all that wetness was out there.

About eight o'clock, as the rain was turning back to snow and the cold was worse, the roads impossible, just as I was done helping a county sander on the edge of the campus pull a panel truck out of a snowbank, I got the emergency call from the college operator. We had a student missing. The roommates thought the kid was headed for the quarry. This meant I had to get the Bronco up on a narrow road above the campus, above the old cemetery, into all kinds of woods and rough track that I figured would be choked with ice and snow. Any kid up there would really have to want to be there, and I couldn't go in on foot, because you'd only want to be there on account of drugs, booze, or craziness, and either way I'd be needing blankets and heat, and then a fast ride down to the hospital in town. So I dropped into four-wheel drive to get me up the hill above the campus, bucking snow and sliding on ice, putting all the heater's warmth up onto the windshield because I couldn't see much more than swarming snow. My feet were still cold from the tow job, and it didn't seem to matter that I had on heavy socks and insulated boots I'd coated with waterproofing. I shivered, and I thought of Ralph the Duck.

I had to grind the rest of the way, from the cemetery, in four-wheel low, and in spite of the cold I was smoking my gearbox by the time I was close enough to the quarry—they really did take a lot of the rocks for the campus buildings from there—to see I'd have to make my way on foot to where she was. It was a kind of scooped-out shape, maybe four or five stories high, where she stood—well, wobbled is more like it. She was as chalky as she'd been the last time, and her red hair didn't catch the light anymore. It just lay on her like something that had died on top of her head. She was in a white nightgown that was plastered to her body. She had her arms crossed as if she wanted to be warm. She swayed, kind of, in front of the big, dark, scooped-out rock face, where the trees and brush had been cleared for trucks and earthmovers. She looked tiny against all the darkness. From where I stood, I could see the snow driving down in front of the lights I'd left on, but I couldn't see it near her. All it looked like around her was dark. She was shaking with the cold, and she was crying.

I had a blanket with me, and I shoved it down the front of my coat to keep it dry for her, and because I was so cold. I waved. I stood in the lights and I waved. I don't know what she saw—a big shadow, maybe. I surely didn't reassure her, because when she saw me she backed up, until she was near the face of the quarry. She couldn't go any farther.

I called, "Hello! I brought a blanket. Are you cold? I thought you might want a blanket."

Her roommates had told the operator about pills, so I didn't bring her the coffee laced with mash. I figured I didn't have all that much time, anyway, to get her down and pumped out. The booze with whatever pills she'd taken would made her die that much faster.

I hated that word. Die. It made me furious with her. I heard myself seething when I breathed. I pulled my scarf and collar up above my mouth. I didn't want her to see how close I might come to wanting to kill her because she wanted to die.

I called, "Remember me?"

I was closer now. I could see the purple mottling of her skin. I didn't know if it was cold or dying. It probably didn't matter much to distinguish between them right now, I thought. That made me smile. I felt the smile, and I pulled the scarf down so she could look at it. She didn't seem awfully reassured.

"You're the sexual harassment guy," she said. She said it very slowly. Her lips were clumsy. It was like looking at a ventriloquist's dummy.

"I gave you an A," I said.

"When?"

"It's a joke," I said. "You don't want me making jokes. You want me to give you a nice warm blanket, though. And then you want me to take you home."

She leaned against the rock face when I approached. I pulled the blanket out, then zipped my jacket back up. The snow had stopped, I realized, and that wasn't really a very good sign. It felt like an arctic cold descending in its place. I held the blanket out to her, but she only looked at it.

"You'll just have to turn me in," I said. "I'm gonna hug you again."

She screamed, "No more! I don't want any more hugs!"

But she kept her arms on her chest, and I wrapped the blanket around her and stuffed a piece into each of her tight, small fists. I didn't know what to do for her feet. Finally, I got down on my haunches in front of her. She crouched down too, protecting herself.

"No," I said. "No. You're fine."

I took off the woolen mittens I'd been wearing. Mittens keep you warmer than gloves because they trap your hand's heat around the fingers and palms at once. Fanny had knitted them for me. I put a mitten as far onto each of her feet as I could. She let me. She was going to collapse, I thought.

"Now, let's go home," I said. "Let's get you better."

With her funny, stiff lips, she said, "I've been very self-indulgent and weird and I'm sorry. But I'd really like to die." She sounded so reasonable that I found myself nodding in agreement as she spoke.

"You can't just die," I said.

"Aren't I dying already? I took all of them, and then"—she giggled like a child, which of course is what she was—"I borrowed different ones from other people's rooms. See, this isn't some teenage cry for like *help*. Understand? I'm seriously interested in death and I have to like stay out here a little longer and fall asleep. All right?"

"You can't do that," I said. "You ever hear of Vietnam?"

"I saw that movie," she said. "With the opera in it? *Apocalypse? Whatever.*"

"I was there!" I said. "I killed people! I helped to kill them! And when they die, you see their bones later on. You dream about their bones and blood on the ends of the splintered ones, and this kind of mucous stuff coming out of their eyes. You probably heard of guys having dreams like that, didn't you? Whacked-out Vietnam vets? That's me, see? So I'm telling you, I know about dead people and their eyeballs and everything falling out. And people keep dreaming about the dead people they knew, see? You can't make people dream about you like that! It isn't fair!"

"You dream about me?" She was ready to go. She was ready to fall down, and I was going to lift her up and get her to the truck.

"I will," I said. "If you die."

"I want you to," she said. Her lips were hardly moving now. Her eyes were closed. "I want you all to."

I dropped my shoulder and put it into her waist and picked her up and carried her down to the Bronco. She was talking, but not a lot, and her voice leaked down my back. I jammed her into the truck and wrapped the blanket around her better and then put another one down around her feet. I strapped her in with the seat belt. She was shaking, and her eyes were closed and her mouth open. She was breathing. I checked that twice, once when I strapped her in, and then again when I strapped myself in and backed up hard into a sapling and took it down. I got us into first gear, held the clutch in, leaned over to listen for breathing, heard it—shallow panting, like a kid asleep on your lap for a nap—and then I put the gear in and howled down the hillside on what I thought might be the road.

We passed the cemetery. I told her that was a good sign. She didn't respond. I found myself panting too, as if we were breathing for each other. It made me dizzy, but I couldn't stop. We passed the highest dorm, and I dropped the truck into four-wheel high. The cab smelled like burnt oil and hot metal. We were past the chapel now, and the observatory, the president's house, then the bookstore. I had the blue light winking and the V-6 roaring, and I drove on the edge of out-of-control, sensing the skids just before I slid into them, and getting back out of them as I needed to. I took a little fender off once, and a bit of the corner of a classroom building, but I worked us back on course, and all I needed to do now was negotiate the sharp left turn around the Administration Building past the library, then floor it for the straight run to the town's main street and then the hospital.

I was panting into the mike, and the operator kept saying, "Say again?"

I made myself slow down some, and I said we'd need stomach pumping, and to get the names of the pills from her friends in the dorm, and I'd be there in less than five or we were crumpled up some-place and dead.

"Roger," the radio said. "Roger all that." My throat tightened and tears came into my eyes. They were helping us, they'd told me: Roger.

I said to the girl, whose head was slumped and whose face looked too blue all through its whiteness, "You know, I had a girl once. My wife, Fanny. She and I had a small girl one time."

I reached over and touched her cheek. It was cold. The truck swerved, and I got my hands on the wheel. I'd made the turn past the Ad Building using just my left. "I can do it in the dark," I sang to no tune I'd ever learned. "I can do it with one hand." I said to her, "We had a girl child, very small. Now, I do *not* want you dying."

I came to the campus gates doing fifty on the ice and snow, smoking the engine, grinding the clutch, and I bounced off a wrought iron fence to give me the curve going left that I needed. On a pool table, it would have been a bank shot worth applause. The town cop picked me up and got out ahead of me and let the street have all the lights and noise it could want. We banged up to the emergency room entrance and I was out and at the other door before the cop on duty, Elmo St. John, could loosen his seat belt. I loosened hers, and I carried her into the lobby of the ER. They had a gurney, and doctors, and they took her away from me. I tried to talk to them, but they made me sit down and do my shaking on a dirty sofa decorated with drawings of little spinning wheels. Somebody brought me hot coffee, I think it was Elmo, but I couldn't hold it.

"They won't," he kept saying to me. "They won't."

"What?"

"You just been sitting there for a minute and a half like St. Vitus dancing, telling me, 'Don't let her die. Don't let her die.'"

"Oh."

"You all *right*?"

"How about the kid?"

"They'll tell us soon."

"She better be all right."

"That's right."

"She—somebody's gonna have to tell me plenty if she isn't."

"That's right."

"She better not die this time," I guess I said.

FANNY CAME DOWNSTAIRS to look for me. I was at the northern windows, looking through the mullions down the valley to the faint red line along the mounds and little peaks of the ridge beyond the valley. The sun was going to come up, and I was looking for it.

Fanny stood behind me. I could hear her. I could smell her hair and the sleep on her. The crimson line widened, and I squinted at it. I heard the dog limp in behind her, catching up. He panted and I knew why his panting sounded familiar. She put her hands on my shoulders and arms. I made muscles to impress her with, and then I let them go, and let my head drop down until my chin was on my chest.

"I didn't think you'd be able to sleep after that," Fanny said.

"I brought enough adrenaline home to run a football team."

"But you hate being a hero, huh? You're hiding in here because somebody's going to call, or come over, and want to talk to you—her parents for shooting sure, sooner or later. Or is that supposed to be part of the service up at the playground? Saving their suicidal daughters. Almost dying to find them in the woods and driving too fast for *any* weather, much less what we had last night. Getting their babies home. The bastards." She was crying. I knew she would be, sooner or later. I could hear the soft sound of her lashes. She sniffed and I could feel her arm move as she felt for the tissues on the coffee table.

"I have them over here," I said. "On the windowsill."

"Yes." She blew her nose, and the dog thumped his tail. He seemed to think it one of Fanny's finer tricks, and he had wagged for her for thirteen years whenever she'd done it. "Well, you're going to have to talk to them."

"I will," I said. "I will." The sun was in our sky now, climbing. We had built the room so we could watch it climb. "I think that jackass with the smile, my prof? She showed up a lot at his office, the last few weeks. He called her 'my advisee,' you know? The way those guys sound about what they're achieving by getting up and shaving and going to work and saying the same thing every day? Every year? Well, she was his advisee, I bet. He was shoving home the old advice."

"She'll be okay," Fanny said. "Her parents will take her home and love her up and get her some help." She began to cry again, then she stopped. She blew her nose, and the dog's tail thumped. She kept a hand between my shoulder and my neck. "So tell me what you'll tell a waiting world. How'd you talk her out?"

"Well, I didn't, really. I got up close and picked her up and carried her is all."

"You didn't say *any*thing?"

"Sure I did. Kid's standing in the snow outside of a lot of pills, you're gonna say something."

"So what'd you *say*?"

"I told her stories," I said. "I did Rhetoric and Persuasion."

Fanny said, "Then you go in early on Thursday, you go in half an hour early, and you get that guy to jack up your grade."

ORBITS

Is visiting old parents like visiting old friends? Ginger and Charlie were talking about her mother and father while hot, wet wind poured into the car and took the sound of their voices away from one another. They kept calling, "What?" The radio was playing Haydn. They were driving up a hill and were at last in the shade for a while, were dropping into tired silence, when the station changed. Ginger looked at Charlie, but his hands were on the wheel and not the tuner. It was something in the air—radio waves or great explosions on the surface of the sun—or a secret hand in a secret place turning the dial invisibly from Haydn to an instant of rock and roll and to a voice that spat cruel syllables and then back to Haydn again, but with hissings, electrical squeaks.

Ginger said, "I'm turning it off."

They drove without speaking. Charlie waited for the radiator or the battery or all of the tires to explode. Nothing happened. He took the proper turns, and they were there when they'd said they would be.

Charlie had for twenty-five years thought of Ginger's mother as someone who strode. Now she walked slowly, with a kind of sideways hitch in her pace. She had broken a leg two years before, and though she was recovered, she also wasn't. While she had moved about, she'd been safe, he thought. But because she'd been pinned to a chair for some months, whatever it was that one fled had caught her. Her thin lips twisted as if the leg, or her sense of what Charlie was seeing, gave her pain. Ginger's father, once a tall, athletic man, now was curving at the shoulders and walked with uncertainty, as if his balance were afflicted. The hardening arteries that isolated his heart were also affecting his feet: a man filled with blood could still not get enough where it was needed, and he walked as if his feet were tender, bruised. It seemed as though a wind were blowing at him, at both of them, and that each time it gusted they were almost knocked down.

They all hugged. Ginger and Charlie reported on their daughters; one was in a dance camp for the summer, the other was a waitress at a bar near Provincetown. Ginger's father said, in his deepest professional voice—he had been a labor negotiator—that he still didn't like the idea of Sue Ellen's working in a saloon.

"It's a respectable resort, Daddy," Ginger said when they sat on the porch and drank tall drinks. Insects buzzed at the screen. The leaves hung limp on the maples. Her father opened the collar of his dark knitted sports shirt. He rubbed at the V of his pale chest as if to wipe away the heat. Charlie knew that batteries in a pacemaker underneath the chest were beating this man's heart.

Ginger's mother said, "He thinks Sue Ellen's twelve years old."

"Add seven," Charlie said. "Actually, add about twenty-five. I'm not thinking about *any*thing. I'm trusting her. She's a great kid. Trust is—"

"I can't wait for it," Ginger said.

"Overrated," Charlie said.

"I always trusted *Ginger*," her mother said.

"Yes," Charlie said, "but you learned your lesson, didn't you?"

They were laughing now, at what wasn't funny, at what was only another way of naming what scared them, and they were not talking about her parents' health or their growing burden: this large Colonial house and its twenty acres; the garden, which demanded tending; the lawn, which Charlie would mow in the morning—the general maintenance, kept up only by hiring strangers, at whose mercy they more and more were. They drank their drinks, they told each other news. Ginger and her mother left, refusing offers to help with making dinner. Ginger's father watched Charlie pour more gin, and he accepted soda water with lemon, and they sat and listened to catbirds shriek. They talked about Aida, the younger girl, who did tap, ballet, modern, and even ballroom dancing at the camp in the Berkshires. Charlie spoke of missing Aida but also of his pleasure at being alone with Ginger for a summer. Ginger's father, in turn, spoke of how they still sometimes realized all over again that Ginger didn't live with them. He said it gently, then shook his head, as if to signal how absurd he thought himself to be.

"Fathers," Charlie said.

"The softest, most demanding species of man," his wife's father said. "Nothing's worse." He adjusted a cushion at his back. Charlie watched his father-in-law's biceps and forearms under the pale skin. There was good muscle, but the skin was softening. He looked at its scabs and bruises, moles and spots and furrows, puckers.

"You did a good job," Charlie said.

"You're kind to say it. I did try to shut up a great deal."

"I wish I could learn to do that."

"Well, you will. The girls won't listen to you, and Ginger'll grow weary of hearing you say what nobody needs to hear, and you'll become a quiet man. Surprise. People will talk about how quiet you've become."

"You know," Charlie said, "nothing's *wrong*. I'm loving how they're growing up. Ginger and I are fine. There isn't anything really *wrong*."

Her father, who had more hair on top of his head than Charlie did, smoothed it over, pushed it into place, and folded his hands in his lap. The lap disappears, too, Charlie noticed: you become a stick figure drawn by a kid. Her father said, "Don't worry about it, Charlie. I'm making you nervous. Old people seem to have that effect, sometimes."

"*No*," Charlie said. He shook his head. He imitated the hair-pat gesture, but rubbed only fuzz and scalp. He said, and he heard the conviction in his voice as he said it, "No."

They ate a cold poached fish, and Ginger and Charlie drank

Sancerre, while her parents drank only water. It was a lovely wine, and Charlie drank a lot of it—almost enough to make him smack his lips and comment on the generosity of a man who, unable to drink because of his health, would provide a first-class wine for those who could enjoy it. Instead, Charlie held his glass up and beamed at the wine. His father-in-law nodded and grinned. Charlie watched Ginger's mother's face twist during the meal. Her lips almost curled. It came and went, as the voice breaking into the rock and roll breaking into the Haydn had come and gone. For dessert they ate fresh fruit. Ginger cracked nuts for everybody. She had done this, always, as a young girl, her father pointed out. Eating none, she distributed nutmeat to all. Charlie decided suddenly that her mother was suffering physically because of thoughts that danced like electrical charges through her. Her daughter, whose presence she sought, was reminding her of what she had lost and had to lose. When they spoke of the girls away for the summer, or of Ginger's going off to school so many years before, or of Ginger's second, and very difficult, pregnancy, the language set the impulse off, and a mother lost her child to time, and therefore herself, and the fact shot from her memory and hummed beneath her white hair like the insects at the porch.

There was no change of subject possible. They spoke of absent daughters, absent friends, the ailments of Presidents, and policies of nations. Ginger cracked nuts, as if she were the little child of these seventy-six-year-olds, surrounded by the house that they once had run but that now, with its demands for paint and new plumbing, its dampness in the basement, squirrels in the eaves, was running them. Around them, the grass rose to challenge their tenure, and the moths, as darkness came on, beat with big wings at the screens on the kitchen windows. Charlie watched the face of his wife's mother as it was assaulted by what he hadn't thought to possess any longer, much less to brandish: youth.

Inside, television reception was very poor. The Carol Burnett rerun broke into dots and a now familiar hissing. Public Broadcasting was a purple haze that sounded like a waterfall. They went back out to the porch. Ginger's mother reported on dead associates and distant relatives, a local sewage-tax scandal, and residential-zoning conflicts. Her father commented on Saudi Arabians who had purchased large parcels of land nearby.

They sat for a while, and then Ginger's mother said, "I hate this house."

"You love it," her father said. "You're angry because I forgot to open the cellar doors and windows this summer to air the damp out."

"I'm angry because that means *I* have to remember it."

Charlie said, "There's always something to take care of."

"Unless you live in a—in one of those *old* places," Ginger's mother said.

"No," Charlie said. "No. I wasn't saying that."

"You know how many perfectly rational, intelligent people get *dumped* into those places?" her mother said.

Ginger's father said, "Don't *worry* so much. I promise. As long as I can drawl and drool and mutter, I'll remind you that the cellar needs its airing out."

Her mother limped into the house and they sat in the memory of her tension. Ginger sighed. Then she said, "Oh, look at that *moon*!" It was full and threw a startling light, which appeared to go no distance but to burn in place. Ginger's father called for his wife to return. "The moon," he called. "Come look at the moon."

They waited, like children who had built a version of the sky, for the disgruntled elder who would come and maybe approve. She did come, with decaffeinated coffee, an offering.

Ginger's mother said, "What planets are those alongside it? Or are they stars?"

Ginger said, "Isn't one of them red? Wouldn't that be Mars?"

"It might be," her mother said. "But it might be a star."

Ginger's father said, "There are two more—I can't name them. I didn't know they clustered like that, all together."

"It's probably rare," Ginger said.

Ginger's mother said, "Probably *very* infrequent. Yes. *I* never heard of it before. I can't imagine how long it might take for them to shine together again."

Charlie said, "It probably happens once a week."

Nobody laughed. The reddish star or planet was above the moon, and they could see a larger, brighter body glowing orange-white above whatever it was that shone like rust, or terra-cotta. Something else— surely it was a planet, Charlie thought, naming it Jupiter, knowing that he would think, right or wrong, of Jupiter when he thought of tonight—seemed a great white balloon.

"Imagine," Ginger said. Charlie knew that she would say it—how would one not?—and he regretted it for her. "Sue Ellen and Aida can see this." Charlie squeezed at the bridge of his nose, hoping to shut off her speech. "And when we talk to them," she said, waving at the terra-cotta planet or star, the blue-white, brilliant maybe-Jupiter, "we can say they saw—we all saw it together. What nobody might see again for who knows *how* long."

Ginger looked up to see her mother glancing down. No one needed to say who would not be on the surface of the earth to look at the sky so many years from tonight. But no one seemed capable of saying anything diversionary. So they sat for what seemed a very long while as the darkness deepened, and as the stars and planets in their slow but fugitive formation rose in the blue-black sky.

Then Ginger's father rumbled, deep and happy, from the chaise on which her mother sat. He was still sitting on his chair, at the other side of the porch, but his voice rolled out from a bulky cassette recorder with which her mother was fiddling. He spoke of negotiating with a Taiwan national, and of how the man had outwitted him, and his voice was cheery and possessive: he clearly knew that he was being recorded, and he seemed to enjoy letting someone preserve what only he could tell.

"I've been making little tapes of some of Dad's stories," Ginger's mother said. Ginger sighed a long and shaken breath. Her mother said, "Don't worry. I won't take down anything you say, dear."

Ginger said, "I don't mind."

Her mother said, "When children grow up, they sound different. The most they can do is talk about what it was like when they were young. But they don't sound the same."

Ginger said, "No."

"That was a hell of a story," Charlie said.

"He robbed us blind," her father said, "because he was out-and-out smarter than I was. He did his job better. I couldn't help admiring him."

Charlie nodded in the dark. Ginger's mother played more tape-recorded sounds—Baltimore orioles calling, her own voice saying, "It's a soft, wet night," a neighbor saying how she had spent her day—and then Ginger's father's voice returned, sounding nothing so much as pleased. It was as if he knew that one day his voice would speak about the Taiwanese, or about the man who had tried to sell him a slum in Bedford-Stuyvesant, and that his tones would be charming, his story engaging, and his body long gone. He was winsome for the future, Charlie thought. He was speaking from the grave. And there he sat, before his wife, who mourned him already, and before his daughter, mostly absent these days, whose daughters were now mostly absent as well. Charlie's eyes ached. Jupiter glowed below the moon, and Mars above, as Ginger's mother played the cassette.

In the darkness, Charlie could barely see any of them now. Ginger's mother said, "I want you to hear something near the beginning of the tape. It's sort of funny. Dad tells about the man from the aircraft company. The fellow who couldn't tolerate dust. Did he ever tell you about that?"

"I must have bored them with that one a dozen times."

Ginger's voice said, "Tell it, Daddy."

Her mother said, "Let the tape tell it. Wait. I have to find it. It's near the beginning. Wait a minute." She clicked buttons, reversing the tape. She pushed another button that sent it forward. She clicked and pushed, making the tape whine and jump and say fragments of sound.

Ginger said, "Daddy, go ahead."

He began to talk while they sat back, invisible to one another. The hum and snick and sudden voices of the tape recorder played like a background tune in a shop while her mother searched the tape for his story. He was saying, "You see, his work involved the manufacture of instruments for fighter planes. One airplane in particular, an interceptor. They called it an all-weather interceptor. Well, you can imagine how an airplane that was supposed to fly in fog and rain might rely on its instruments. So of course the delicacy of their manufacture had to match the delicacy of the performance expected of them. Men were going to be sealed up, alone, ten miles in the air, surrounded by tons of metal alloy and wires and high explosives and kerosene, and they were going to rely exclusively on those instruments—except for their wits, of course. And who knows better than present company how little *those* can sometimes be counted on?"

As if he had rehearsed, he paused for polite laughter. Perhaps if they had sat in daylight he would have expected a smile and a nod. In the background, on the tape, Charlie heard a sound that startled him. It confused him. Ginger's father continued, "Not to mention matters of perhaps intercepting a bomber headed for the United States, or one of our military bases in Europe. So it was crucial work. He headed—this fellow I'm speaking of—he ran the team that was in charge of the final assembling of the controls display. In their lab, they wore masks and caps and gowns to keep their hair or skin off their work. They wore gloves, of course, and the lab was immaculate. One speck of dirt, as I understand it, and some gizmo might go haywire. Boom! Millions of dollars and a human life: just ashes. So he was, not surprisingly, a very nervous man. He trembled, he said, except when he was on the job. I remember saying to him, 'You had best love your work, then.' The poor guy. We were writing a contract proposal for the company, and he was among the technicians' representatives in my office one morning. We were talking about wages. It was amicable, systematic, slow. This was quite a while ago. This was almost twenty years ago, my God. He sat there, shaking and pale, watching everything. He had enormous brown eyes, I remember. He was like a great big spaniel or a retriever. He watched and he watched.

"And, all of a sudden, he sat up. He'd been slouched, looking tired, just pressing his fingers on my desk top, watching. Then he sat *straight* up and rubbed his fingertips together. The expression on his face was one of horror. I'm sure you can guess it. They don't call them dusty lawyers' offices for nothing, after all." Ginger's father paused. Charlie nodded and smiled, as if they sat in the light. "His fingers were covered with *dust*, you see. The enemy!"

Ginger's mother said, "There!" Her father's taped voice in the background paused, as the voices alive on the porch did, and then the tape-recorded voice of Ginger's father said, "The enemy!"

"This thing takes forever to rewind," Ginger's mother complained. But Charlie was thinking that the sound he had heard a few moments ago, preserved in the muted chatter and mechanical grating of the buttons, was his own voice. It had spoken a syllable, now long past in the to-ing and fro-ing of the tape—a fragment of his daughter Aida's name—and he could not avoid imagining that his daughters might listen to this same broken voice on a porch in a future night, when Ginger was absent, and he was, too, and when a rare pattern of planets would have reappeared to goggle from the dark.

A button clicked and the tape recorder stopped. They sat in the darkness. Ginger's mother cleared her throat. Charlie thought of his daughters thinking of him, and then, like a delicate moth settling, a hand that reached from the darkness stroked the back of Charlie's hand. It was a tentative touch, and the hand was very light and very little—his mother-in-law's. She offered the softest caress. Charlie waited for more. But the small hand withdrew. Ginger yawned, and her father spoke of sleep.

NAKED

RUDY MADE ME PROMISES, and they came true. He was our doctor and had always been. In his high, bright voice—a loud and happy shout no matter its announcement—he would cry, "You have the *measles*, hon!" Or: "We're gonna take your *tonsils* out, you can eat all the ice cream you *want!*" Or: "Your head will feel better when it's *exactly* twenty minutes past dinnertime!" When I was eight, I heard my mother describe him as a rascal. When I was ten or so, I knew that, according to my father, he was a presumptuous bastard. To me he was Uncle Rudy, and in the forties and fifties, he was at my bed when I was ill. If I were home from school with a flu or one of the many childhood diseases no one then was vaccinated against, I lay in my room and listened to the wood-cased radio with its golden crosshatched speaker: "Helen Trent" and "Our Gal Sunday" and, later in the afternoon, "Sky King" and "The Green Hornet." On lucky days, I heard the Dodgers play—Jackie Robinson throwing to Gil Hodges—and, despite the music about me, and the radio voices, I always heard Rudy, or always thought I did. He drove the newest, sleekest cars, Packards, I remember, and Lincolns. Their windows rose and fell when Rudy pushed buttons. He parked with impunity in front of the fire hydrant at our curb. And, although they were tuned and silent cars, I always thought, when I heard Rudy climbing the steps, that I had heard his motor cough, or his brakes mildly squeak. I liked pretending that his process up the stairs was no surprise. And so it wasn't one, for years and years.

He was light on his feet, and his step was a sort of spring. His shoes had leather heels and soles, so he clacked as he climbed, and our wooden steps made groaning noises under him. I always thought it unfair that a man who could bound like that, and click as sharply as he did, still had to walk on stairs that made him sound fat. He wasn't thin. He couldn't have been taller than five feet seven or eight, and he surely weighed over two hundred pounds. He frequently dieted, choosing faddish and unproven methods, and once, I remember, exciting my mother to complain for his safety. Once in a while he bought new suits to flatter a slenderer shape that he would own for a couple of months. But usually Rudy seemed round: his bald head was round, and it sat atop his big chest and belly, and his thick round legs, his little feet. I heard the feet, when he came to care for me with his magic, and then I saw his round, gold-rimmed glasses on his happy pale face.

He beamed when he saw me, and he stood above my bed and looked at me, then examined me with eyes and hands. He probed, he listened, he squeezed, and always he smiled the happiest smile. His breath smelled of chewing gum, and his voice carried total conviction. He might say, "This fever will break at—wait a minute. What time is it, Michael?"

I'd consult the same clock that he was looking at and, with a grand sense of drama, tell him, in my weakest voice, "Two o'clock, Uncle Rudy."

"This fever will break at seven o'clock tomorrow morning at the *latest*. Do you understand? You'll feel better by seven tonight, and by seven tomorrow morning, you'll have a normal temperature. Which is?"

"Ninety-eight point six," I would recite, as if such knowledge were wisdom.

Rudy would smile as if it were. He would nod. "Perfect!" he'd shout.

"You get yourself into college, and I'll take care of med school for you. How old are you now, Michael?"

"Seven," I would say, as if reaching past six had been a feat of art.

"Well, we've got some time," Rudy would say.

And only then would he admit my mother, home from work to care for me. He always kept her outside my door because, as he often told her, he had his time alone with me, and then he had his time with her. While Rudy talked with me, my mother paced the hall. I'd hear her high-heeled shoes. And, at seven that night, I would ask for food. At seven in the morning I would register ninety-eight point six. And Rudy would have had his time alone with my mother, after his time alone with me.

Rudy's wife, Dorothy, had always been kind to me, and though she often came with him to our house for social evenings, I didn't think of her in any special way. At dinner, when I was thirteen, my mother announced to us that Rudy had left Dorothy. "It's the way all these Jewish doctors do it," my Jewish mother said with disgust. "They marry women with money who help them pay off their debts from medical school. They buy the office equipment and pay for the nurses—and you *know* about the nurses, yes?—and then the doctor leaves them when they're ugly and old."

My father said, "I would consider calling Dorothy ugly a massive favor to her."

"She can't help what she looks like," my mother said.

"Maybe she can't help it," my father said, "but she makes Spike Jones look like Dorothy Lamour."

"That's stupid," my mother said. "All the people in the world to think about, and you pick Spike Jones? Dorothy *Lamour*? This is what you talk about all day in the office?"

"All day in the office," my father said, "we talk about numbers. We say 'six' and 'eleven.' We say 'Ninety thousand.' But we never say Lamour or Jones, unless it's a client's name. And we don't have a client named Lamour. These are names I learned after extensive reading of

the *World-Telegram & Sun*. I hope they aren't too far beneath us for me
to be saying them at the table. How was school, Mike?"

"Excuse me?"

"Without question," my father said, pulling his bow tie off and setting it beside his napkin on the table. "Absolutely. You're excused. Do
you think Spike Jones would divorce his wife just because her chin,
where she needs to shave it a little, was falling down onto her neck?"

"Huh?"

My mother's fork clanged on her plate.

My father, who was usually mild if not silent, and whose square
face rarely carried much expression unless he grew teary while listening
to Perry Como sing songs about parting, put his lips together, puffed
his smooth cheeks, and widened his eyes. He looked like a fish, and I
started to laugh, although I was puzzled—frightened, really—by these
meat loaf and baked potato antics. My father saw my expression and he
must have understood. He said, "Just wait, Michael. Wait." And I still
don't know if he meant me to wait for seconds or for years.

My mother hardly waited seconds. She pushed the yellow Fiesta
Ware pitcher so hard that water spilled from it onto a yellow, chunky
Fiesta Ware plate. I thought again of our door. "You know how old he
is? Rudy?"

My father answered her by smiling and nodding his head. He didn't
make the fish face, and I was grateful. I told my mother, "No."

"This doesn't concern you," she said, her pretty face white, her thick
lip reddening under her teeth while she waited an instant, and then
said, "Forty-four."

My father smiled broadly, then *he* reddened. Then he leaned back
in his chair and smiled at something on the ceiling. I looked up, saw
nothing, then looked down at my brown, grainy meat loaf. I waited
for more. There was silence, and then my father's voice: "I know it."

"You know his age. Yes. But hers? Do you know *hers*?"

"Oh," my father said, as if he mugged for an audience. "You mean
there's another *woman*? Well. I must say, I don't know how old *she* is.

I'll bet, though, whatever her age is, it wouldn't take too many numbers to write it or say it. And I bet you're crazy with it."

"I'm not crazy with it!"

"Michael, is she crazy with it, or what?"

"Don't you do that to him."

"*You* do it to him and it's all right. He sits here and you get crazy and it's right. I *ask* him about it and I'm wrong? What is this conversation *about*?"

Now, I was old enough to know that something more than minor was going on. I was also young enough to be tempted, for an instant, to cry out loud—for Rudy, or for everything my parents seemed to threaten to leave behind, or for what I couldn't discern in the murky innuendo of their talk. But I was old enough to succumb to none of those temptations. I took a breath, I bent to my plate, and I ate the meat loaf, pulpy as usual (my mother never thought we'd have enough) with too much torn-up bread.

My mother said, "The woman is twenty-four. Rudy is forty-four. She is twenty years younger than he is. She—"

"No," my father said. "No. You deprived me of the pleasure of announcing the *fullness* of this catastrophe. You really owe it to me to allow me to finish the cliché. Now, if I remember it—wait. Yes. Okay. I think I have it now. *She is old enough to be his daughter.* Right?"

"No. *Young* enough," I said.

My father's breath hissed. My mother said, *"Michael."*

So I said, "Excuse me," with what I thought of as dignity.

In my room, among my books and flung-about clothing and the drawings of spaceships and space suits and other apparatus of a future I saw as free of gravity and full of colorful wars, I lay on my bed and looked over the lights of our neighborhood in Brooklyn, and tried to make sense of my parents' life together, and mine with them, and ours with Rudy. It was spring, the limbs of giant high trees were whipped by winds that came up, then died, with no preamble. At one moment, the skies were quiet; at another, they softly roared. The dark blue air looked grainy, and moving branches with their new leaves sliced the light from houses on the block behind us and made the brightening moon seem to dance in its place, low above the neighborhood. After a while, I did some homework and didn't think of Rudy or my parents until I heard their footsteps as they climbed the stairs.

"There are dishes to be dried," my mother said at my closed door. "Most children your age have to wash them too."

"You all right?" my father called.

"It's all right to come in," I said.

I waited, but I heard their bedroom door close, and I knew that the fight—about *what?*—was moving to private quarters. When they'd come up the stairs together, the house had seemed to shake. I had looked from my window as they climbed, to see whether the moon seemed to vibrate more than before. The winds had slackened, the moon had looked still, and I remember that I'd smiled with gratitude. My contentment stayed with me that night, and it came down to break-fast with me in the morning; I was prepared to let their mystery be theirs. Rudy was coming to dinner that weekend with his fiancée, as my mother called her, and I would wait until then for further clues.

My father seemed apprehensive on Saturday, though as usual he worked in the garden, wearing his World War II fatigues. He'd begun to talk about how few men his age could still get into their army-issue clothes. Pausing often to catch his breath, he clipped what rarely needed cutting back, he painted a portion of the high fence that screened us from our neighbors, he mulched and raked and swept; he made time away in a place that was away, and he thought to himself about matters of which he never spoke to me. Or so I concluded. His face, when he worked, was someone else's, and I often watched him with curiosity. I never worked beside him, though: I was the usual thirteen. He was showered and dressed quite early, and he was early at his inventory of liquors and mixers and pickled onions and candied fruits and ice. I wore clean corduroys and a shirt with a starched collar that irritated my neck. I was watching wrestling on television while my father made

the living room ready for peanuts and drinks, and while my mother
slowly dressed.

I saw my father look at the ceiling only once—I was reminded of
his upward glance during their argument—and I don't know if he
was thinking of my mother upstairs. But I was. For I was listening,
over the cries of the fans of Bruno Sammartino, to her feet. She was
already in her high-heeled shoes, and I listened to their slow, lassitudi-
nous rhythm as she drifted from her bureau to her closet mirror, then
back to her bureau drawers again. Her footsteps at first seemed almost
random. She surely didn't dance on her bedroom's parquet floor. But
something under the percussion of her heels did suggest to me a kind
of dance—she moved from *here* to *here*, from *here*, then, to *there*, and
purpose changed her position, though nothing like a plan. Bruno, fighting clean while his lighter longer-haired opponent used illegal blows and
outlawed holds, persevered, then triumphed. He used his famous flying
dropkick, and he won. I watched the referee count the opponent out.
As the canvas slammed with the final count, and as Bruno sprang to
his bare feet, I understood: I had heard my mother *thinking*. The sharp
and aimless-seeming sounds of her staccato shoes had been, in fact, an
accompaniment kept by her body for the thoughts—and hadn't they
been stabbing thoughts—that were sounding inside as she picked out
earrings or brushed at her glossy brown hair. All at once, my mother's
footsteps upstairs grew purposeful. She marched across the floor. On
our groaning stairs, she came down.

My father, as if signaled, went to the hall closet for his sportcoat.
He turned to my mother and said, "You look nice."

"I look fantastic," my mother said.

I stayed with a tag-team wrestling match and didn't look up for a
while. But they'd both looked pretty good to me, and awfully nervous,
and I hoped, suddenly, that I wouldn't hear Rudy's car at the curb, and
that he wouldn't come. It was the first time I had not wanted to see
him. It was the first time I'd considered *whether* to want to see him
or not. I was enough of a child to think of grown-ups—and surely of

Uncle Rudy—as climate, neighborhood, a feature of my life, and not what I *voted* on. My own will made me itch.

And I did hear the faintest protest of brakes, I thought. And I surely heard feet that shuffled against the broad brick steps outside, and that thumped on the wooden floor of the porch, and that shushed on the mat before our door as the doorbell rang. My father answered the door, and his voice was full of bonhomie. My mother joined him—the sound of her feet across the foyer reminded me of black men who tap-danced on Ed Sullivan's show—and she was cordial, though grave. I turned the set off and went to be a cute nearly-nephew to Uncle Rudy and the woman my mother had known in advance she would hate.

I hugged Rudy; I usually did. He looked at me and, as usual, he beamed. "You look like a million bucks, fella!" he said, so clearly glad to see me that I almost hugged him again. I did put my hands on his shoulders and squeeze, and he said, "By Jesus, I love ya!" I noticed three things as he spoke—the heat of my reddening face as my field of vision included the woman with Rudy; my mother's teeth on her lip; the new woman's height and stunning beauty. "Meet Genevieve! Michael, this is Genevieve. I *completely* love her. I wanted you to meet her because I wanted the two of you to love each other. Isn't this great?"

Genevieve was taller than Rudy, taller than my mother and me. She and my mother shook hands gingerly, I noticed. My father actually took Genevieve's hand and raised it to his lips. My mother bit hers. Rudy smiled and smiled, and he pounded my father's shoulder and rubbed the back of my head and told us all how grand things were. Genevieve stood without moving, as if she were a mannequin. Her hair was the blackest I have ever seen. Her skin was so pale, it looked like the waxy yellow-white of an antique doll's. Her eyes were very large and dark in an oval face that was slightly rounded at the cheekbones, but slender nevertheless. Her figure, slim according to the standards of Hollywood in the fifties, still required my attention, and her suit, made of something white and fine, struck me as unusual. When we sat in the living room, I stared at her legs, which were very long and slender and on which she wore smoke-colored stockings. I had never seen hose like that except in magazines purchased by the fathers of my friends. I looked at her every time I thought I could study her without getting caught. She sat on our yellow sofa next to Rudy, and she said little. He touched her often, and I watched his beefy hands. When she spoke, Genevieve talked about European cities, and music I hadn't heard of. Rudy often spoke of her as though she weren't there. Looking at my mother, his old friend, he would reach out and tap my mother's knee, then say, "Isn't she a dreamboat? She's *my* dreamboat. I treated her for a sore throat! Imagine! I looked down her throat, and I wanted to climb in after the tongue depressor!"

"Rudy, you're disgusting," my mother said.

"But you're honest, Rudy, aren't you," my father said as he mixed more drinks. "You're an honest man."

I remember Rudy as a brilliant man. He seemed that way that night, in spite of his playing what I would later think of as the middle-aged fool. Light came off his glasses as he sat up higher on the sofa. His eyes grew wider, and I watched as he saw what was invisible to me. My mother was saying something patronizing to Genevieve, who nodded but didn't reply. Rudy said to my father, "You have the sound of a man with something to say."

"Oh, no," my father said, opening a bottle of club soda. "No, I'm a CPA. I just work with numbers. You know. My work involves nothing more than what adds up."

Rudy said, "As in two plus two equals four, and no latitude for interpretation?"

My father passed a tall iced drink. "Twos are twos," he said. "Fours are fours. That's it. Yes. And I've worked with those numbers."

Rudy said, "And for some time?"

"Yes, for some time."

Rudy said, "I wonder if I know what you mean."

"Oh, sure," my father said. "Yes. You do."

Rudy raised his glass and looked at my father with a smile of, I think, admiration. "Here's to your guts," Rudy said. He drank, then raised his glass again. "*Salud*. And here's to your perspicacity." He drank again, then turned to Genevieve. "Hon? You know what that means? Perspicacity?"

My father sipped his drink, then quietly left the room. My mother watched him. She said, in a voice that imitated the sounds we make when we jest, "Are you two fighting again?"

"We never fight," Rudy said, smiling. "Sometimes we disagree, but then we only argue, and just for fun. The way that old friends do." He paused, then picked up his glass. "Sweetheart," he said to my mother, "here's to old friends."

My mother raised her glass, but didn't drink. She looked at Rudy, and kept on looking. Genevieve raised her eyebrows in her otherwise immobile face. My father, returning, said, "Sorry."

Rudy drank some more and said, "Let's not be sorry."

My mother put her glass down and said, "I have to cook. Michael, tell them about school. What happened yesterday. You remember. I have to go cook." She still looked at Rudy, but he had turned toward me, so she stood and left the room with loud, quick steps.

I had always performed at my parents' evenings, and with Rudy I never had minded. But it was Genevieve, leg and thigh, breast and throat, arched thin eyebrows, long white hands, at whom I looked as I told how a fellow named Green, several years older and a foot taller and a lifetime more dangerous than the other boys in our junior high school, had been plucked from Industrial Arts by two policemen. "He shot a kid," I said. "He shot a kid in the eye with a zip gun he made. A pipe thing, lead pipe, with a bullet in it. You use a really heavy rubber band with a nail, that's the firing pin—it explodes the bullet," I explained to Genevieve. "You put a wooden handle on it with tape. He shot this kid and they had to take out his eye. The kid didn't die, though."

Genevieve asked, "What kind of school do you go to?"

"Public school," I said, assuming that creatures such as she went only to private schools in major European capitals. "Andries Hudde

Junior High School," I said, hating its provincialism. "It's on Nostrand
Avenue." I was searching for ways to make myself die, which seemed
the only appropriate response to having sat before this exotic person
to speak to her of Ralphie Green and his zip gun, and a school named
Hudde.

"I never heard of that school," she said.

"Oh," I answered, "that's all right." And, blushing sweatily, smiling goofily at Genevieve, at whom Rudy goofily smiled, I finally said,
"Will you excuse me please? I have to go help? I'll be *right* back." I fled.

And in the kitchen, which was around a corner and down a short
corridor from the living room, in a litter of black pans and wet pothold-
ers and a smoking leg of lamb, I found my parents in a sad and knotted
embrace. My father was saying, "No, no. It's all right. It's all right. No."

"I don't have any right to be comforted," my mother said.

"Sure," my father said. "Everyone does." But he moved back from
her a little.

"By you?"

"By me," he said. "Why not? Who else?"

"I don't really hate her. She's so young, though! I don't mean that.
I don't know if it has anything to *do* with her. Does it?"

"I'm a CPA," my father said. "I know about numbers. Look how
long I didn't know about you. Don't ask me that kind of a question."

"What do you know about me now?"

"Not a lot."

"When?"

He said, "What?"

"You know. When did you know?"

"I'm not talking about it," my father said, drawing farther away.
"Not when or where, not how many times. None of it. I didn't talk
about it before, and I'm not talking about it now. Let him get married to his dream girl and that's that. No more. And pay attention to
tonight. The man is moving on. He doesn't want the old parts of his
life anymore. He wants a divorce."

"*I* don't. I mean, from you."

"You should have," my father said, stepping farther back. "A long time ago. It isn't shameful. Everyone wants a divorce."

"*You?*"

"Everyone," he said. Then he said, "But what in hell do *I* know?"

I went upstairs, waving at Rudy and Genevieve as I passed the living room, smiling some sort of smile. I shut my door and walked about my room, touching objects. I heard my name in living room murmurs, and then I heard feet on the stairs. They cracked and creaked, groaning their old-wood noises. It was Rudy. He didn't knock, as my parents would have. They were enlightened parents who read the columns by psychologists in the old New York *Post*. Rudy just walked in, because he was welcome, he assumed, and because he loved me. As far as Rudy's reasoning went, I think, love gave you permission to do anything to anyone. What he did was save my life and keep my health. And make love to my mother. First he had his time with me, and then he had his time with her. I cannot remember him leaving a lot. But I remember him entering—through the front door, up the steps, or into the kitchen or living room, or swinging open the door to my room. He was always on his way in. So no wonder, then, that my mother could not imagine his departure. And his tall, pale Genevieve, so different in size, coloring, ripeness from my mother—she was Rudy's signal good-bye. Although he did love us all, I think, and even my father; and he surely wanted to share his happy news.

But he was leaving as he entered. I could tell. I started to cry. Rudy, with his sweet breath and giant chest, leaned against me and hugged me with his short, strong arms. He pulled and pulled.

"Did you ever think you were adopted, hon?"

I remember feeling my body grow cold. I couldn't bear any more news, I thought. I was always very careful about how much stress I accepted. I shook my head.

"Well, you aren't. But I always thought you were more like me than him. That's not fair to say, is it? But I thought so. I wished. I totally love ya! Remember that. Remember me. I knew your parents when we were all skinny intellectuals in the Communist Party. Did you know that? We ate lousy food and drank lousy wine and told each other lousy lies about lousy goddamned liars in Moscow. Did you know that?"

I stayed against his chest. I shook my head.

"And we were so goddamned happy! And your father and I loved your mother, and then your father won. He's—sneaky. Because he's so tough. So watch your ass with him. He's *tough*! When you see those lousy movies where the movie's always on the side of the guy who's taking the pretty girl away from the boring accountant—well, whatever. Don't believe it! The accountants always win! And I *love* ya! I'm happy as hell you could meet Genevieve. Don't you love her? Don't you *love* her?"

He pushed me back, but held on to my shoulders. I didn't look at his round white face, which I knew would be grinning while his dark little eyes studied me intently. I stared at his light brown sharkskin suit, the vest across which he always wore a gold chain that rose and fell according to his progress through dangerous diets. His tie, I remember, was maroon wool with small tan figures on it. I wonder if he was studying me the way I studied his tie. I couldn't look at his face. I only remember it from other days, because I didn't see it again.

He said, "You want to forgive them."

"Who?"

"Don't play stupid. You're the brightest boy I ever knew. You know who I mean."

"Why should I forgive them? What for?"

"For not being happy."

I pulled away, and he let my shoulders go. I was surprised, and nearly fell, but I stood my ground. I looked, still, at his turned-up cuffs, his narrow short shoes, polished to a gloss. I couldn't look farther up, but I stayed where I was and said, "No."

"No, you won't forgive them? Or no, they're not unhappy?"

"No!"

"Sweetheart," he said. He sighed. "Who am I to tell you? But I know something. Listen, when you're naked you are naked. Understand? All you are is—naked." He grunted as he moved his arms. I had closed my eyes by then. He said, "It's eight fifteen. Lie down, listen to the radio, get yourself some sleep. By the morning, by half-past seven, you're gonna feel *wonderful* about the world. I swear it!" His arms pulled me in toward him, but I resisted. I didn't know why. I don't. "You'll feel great," he said. He squeezed as much as his little arms allowed, and he went out. It is a law of brain development that you will, when grown, remember every departure by every person to whom you should have called goodbye, and whom you ought to have embraced, and on whose cheeks you could have dispensed a couple of the dammed-up tears you persist in hoarding. I heard him on the steps.

Fed and sheltered, surrounded by what I had picked for my pleasure, and sullen because the people downstairs were getting along as best they could in their sad, short lives, I decided always to live alone when I grew up. And then I turned the radio on and listened to Henry Morgan's show and laughed. At 7:30 in the morning, true to Rudy's word, I woke. I looked through glowing green leaves at a Sunday sky under which a boy played stickball or he *died*. He didn't. And he did grow up to learn how everyone, no matter who has loved him for good or for ill, no matter whom he loves, is faithful to that cruel and careless, easy childhood vow.

DOG SONG

H E ALWAYS THOUGHT of the dogs as the worst. The vet's belly heaved above his jeans, and he cursed in words of one syllable every time a deputy tugged a dog to the hypodermic, or trotted to keep up as a different one strained on its chain for its fate, or when a dog stopped moving and went stiff, splayed, and then became a loose furry bag with bones inside. The deputies and the vet and the judge, who also did his part—he watched without moving—did it twenty-six times, in the yard behind the sheriff's offices. The air stank of dirty fur and feces as though they were all locked in. The yelping and whining went on. When they were through, one deputy was weeping, and the vet's red flannel shirt was wet with sweat from his breastbone to his belt. The deputies threw the dogs into the back of a van.

They might be dangerous, Snuyder had decided. They might have been somehow perverted, trained to break some basic rules of how to live with men. So they had died. And Snuyder, doing his part, had watched them until the last lean mutt, shivering and funny-eyed, was dead. He thought, when he thought of the dogs, that their lips and tails and even their postures had signaled their devotion to the vet or to one of the deputies; they'd been waiting for a chance to give their love. And as the deputies flung them, the dogs' tongues protruded and sometimes flopped. When their bodies flew, they looked ardent.

The dogs in the yellow trailer had drawn the attention of the people in the white trailer across the unpaved rural road: their howling, their yapping, the whining that sometimes went on and on and on. Lloyd and Pris, the man and wife in the trailer with the dogs, came and went at curious hours, and that too attracted the attention of the neighbors, who had their own problems, but somehow found time—being good country Christians, they *made* time—to study the erratic behavior and possible social pathology of the couple in the bright yellow trailer edged in white, propped on cinder blocks, bolstered against upstate winters by haybales pushed between the plastic floor and the icy mud. The neighbors, one working as a janitress, the other as a part-time van driver for the county's geriatric ferrying service, finally called the sheriff when there was a February thaw, and the mud all of a sudden looked awfully like manure, and an odor came up from the yellow trailer that, according to the janitress (a woman named Ivy), was too much like things long dead to be ignored by a citizen of conscience.

But only one of the dogs was dead, and it died after the deputies had kicked the door in, and after it had attacked and had been shot. It died defending a mobile home that was alive with excrement and garbage. Turds lay on the beds and on the higher surfaces, counter and sink. Madness crawled the walls. Lloyd, the husband, had written with dung his imprecations of a county and state and nation that established laws involving human intercourse with beasts. Twenty-six dogs were impounded, and the couple was heavily fined by the judge.

The awful part, of course, had been the dogs' dull eyes and duller coats, their stink, their eagerness to please, and then their fear, and then the way they had died. Later he decided that the nurse with her hair that was thinning and her arms puffed out around the short, tight sleeves of her hissing uniform was the worst part so far. The first sight Richard Snuyder had seen, when he fell awake like a baby rolling from its crib, had been a man on crutches at his door, peering. The man had sucked on an unlit filter cigarette, adjusted his armpits on the crutches, and said, "I heard you did one *jam*-jar of a job. Just thought I'd say so. I was raised to express my appreciation of the passing joys."

Snuyder, hours later, had thought that the man on crutches, apparently a connoisseur of catastrophe, was the worst. He wasn't. The worst became the orderly who brought in a plate of mashed potatoes and open hot roast-beef sandwich in glutinous gravy, who was chased by the nurse who brought the doctor, whose odor of dark, aged sweat and stale clothing did little to dispel that of the roast beef, which lingered in the room as if the pale orderly had hurled it on the walls to punish Snuyder for being on a liquid diet.

The doctor, who had mumbled and left, Snuyder thought for a while, was really the worst part of it: his dandruff, his caustic smell, his dirty knuckles that gave the lie to the large scraped moons of fingernail above the tortured cuticles. This is the worst, Snuyder had thought, though not for long.

Because then the candy striper with her twitchy walk and bored pout had stood at his door, a clipboard in her hand and an idle finger at her ear, though carefully never in it, and had looked at him as though he weren't open-eyed, blinking, panting with pain, clearly stunned and afraid and as lost while being still as dogs are that stand at the side of the road, about to be killed because they don't know what else they should do.

After the candy striper had left, the balding nurse with great arms, and no need for such forms of address as language spoken or mimed, came in to adjust something at his head and something at his leg. His neck didn't roll, so he couldn't follow her movements except with his eyes, which began to ache and then stream. Looking at his legs, she wiped his eyes and took the tissue away. He was about to ask her questions but couldn't think of anything that didn't embarrassingly begin with *Where* or *How*.

He tried to move his legs. That was next, as soon as the nurse left. He worked at wiggling his toes and each foot and each leg. They moved, though they were restrained by something, and he called aloud—it was a relief, during the cry, to hear his own voice and to know that he knew it—because the right leg was pure pain, undifferentiated, and the left, though more flexible, hurt only a little less. His legs, and the stiffness at the neck, his aching eyes and head, a burning on the skin of his face, the waking to no memory of how he had come there, or why, or when, or in what state: *he* was the worst so far. He suspected that little would happen to challenge this triumph. He'd been born someplace, of an unknown event, and every aspect of his arrival on this naked day could be measured against the uncomforting hypothesis that, among the local discomforts he knew, he himself was the worst.

His legs could not be moved, he could not be persuaded to move them again, and he lay with all his attention on his torso, thinking *I will be just chest and balls, I will not be legs or ankles or toes.* He panicked and felt for his legs, then moved an ankle—he yelped—in response to his fear: he did have his legs, and they would move at his command, he wasn't only a chest. *And balls?* He groaned his fear, and groaned for the pain in his legs, and then he groaned with deep contentment: he had found them under his hospital gown, both of them, and everything else, including the dreadful catheter. So all he needed to know now was when he would stop hurting over most of his body, and why and how he was here. *All right. First things first. You have legs, your balls are where you left them, and a little panic is worth a handful of testes during times of trial.*

I have not gone berserk with worry for my wife, he thought.

Do I have a wife?

How do I know my name, if I don't know whether I'm married? How did I know about balls? Are you born with a full knowledge of the scrotum? So that even during amnesia, you still—

I don't want *amnesia.*

I don't want *to be a pendulum in a ward, swinging on crutches and sucking on cold cigarettes and laughing at people forever and never* remembering.

What about my kids, if I do have kids?

The same nurse, with thin dark hair and wide white arms, was at the head of his bed, looking into his eyes this time as she wiped them. She had the voice of a twelve-year-old girl, and the teeth of someone long dead. She said, "Mr. Snuyder? Do you remember you're Mr. Snuyder?"

He tried to nod. The pain made him hiss.

"We'll give you something for pain after we X-ray your head again. But could you tell me if you know your name?"

"Thank you," he said.

"Yes. And your name?"

"Woke up knowing it was Snuyder."

"Good *boy*!"

"Woke up. Found out I had my scrotum, and I never knew if I had any children or a *wife*." He was crying. He hated it.

"You'll remember," she said. "You'll probably remember. You did take out a telephone pole and a good I say at least half of a Great American Markets rig. Worcestershire sauce and mustard and beerwurst smeared over two lanes for a quarter of a mile. If you don't mind glass, you could make a hell of a sandwich out there, they said."

"Kill anybody? Did I kill anybody?"

"Not unless *you* die on us. The truck was parked. Trucker was—how do you want to put it?—banging the lady of the house? You must of pulled a stupendous skid. The troopers'll be by to talk about it."

"Did you look in my wallet?"

"Doctor'll be by too. I'm off-duty now."

"You don't want to tell me about my family? There wasn't anybody with me, was there?"

"You're supposed to remember on your own. There wasn't anybody killed. You take care now."

"Won't dance with anyone else."

"Good boy."

"Wait," he said. "Wait a minute." He winced. He lay back. He heard himself breathe.

She said, "That's right. You lie down and be good. Good boy."

———

HE WOKE AGAIN, with a thump, waiting for the nurse to speak. He saw that she was gone, the room dark, the door closed. He couldn't remember waking, ever before in his life, so abruptly, and with so much pain. And that wasn't all he couldn't remember. He thought *baby, baby, baby* to himself, as if in a rapture, and he tried to think of a lover or wife. Was he divorced? What about kids? He thought a gentler *baby* and looked within his closed eyes for children. He thought of maps—blank. He thought of cars and couldn't see the one he'd driven. He remembered that the nurse had evaded the question of who had been with him. But at least she wasn't dead.

And how had he known that his passenger was a woman? And how could he know he was right?

He was tired of questions and tired of hurting. He remembered, then, how they had rolled him through the halls for a CAT-scan and how, when he'd been rolled back, they had looked at him like magic people who could make him fall asleep, and he had fallen. He wanted more magic. He wanted to sleep some more and wake again and know one thing more. A woman in the car with him. Should she have been with him in the car? Should she have come with him to this room?

And he woke again, one more question not answered, to see a light that sliced at his eyeballs and to hear a general commotion that suggested daytime and what he had doubtless once referred to as everyday life. The door opened in, and Hilary was inside with him, and through dry lips he said, "I *remember* you!"

She said, "Can you see how little I'm cheered by that?"

No: she started to; he finished her statement in his mind, fed by memory, and he smiled so triumphantly, his face hurt. In fact, Hilary said, "Can you see—"

And he said, "Hilary. Hil."

She shook her head as if winged insects were at her, and then she wept into her wide, strong hands, walking slowly toward him, a child at a hiding game. But she was not a child and there were no children—not here, anyway, because the boys were at school, of course, and he and Hilary, Richard and Hilary Snuyder, were alone, they were each forty-seven years old, and they were working at being alone together while Warren and Hank went to school in other states. The states were *other* because this one was New York. Hilary was tall, and she wore her pea jacket, so it must be autumn, and her upper lip came down on the lower one as if she wanted to make love. Richard did, then, and his hand went down to grip himself in celebration where it had earlier prodded for loss. "Hilary," he said. The catheter guarded his loins, and his hand retreated.

She wiped at her eyes and sat on the chair beside the bed.

"Come sit on the bed," he said.

She sat back. She crossed her legs and he looked with a sideways glance to see her jeans and Wallabees. His eyes stung, so he looked up. He sniffed, expecting to smell perfume or soap. He smelled only gravy and the finger-chewing doctor. And Hilary said, "How could you decide on—going away like that?" She said, "How could you *do* that? No matter what?"

"Hil, I'm having a hell of a time remembering things. I didn't remember *you* until you came in, the boys and you and—would you tell me stuff? You know, to kind of wake me up some more? I don't remember going anyplace. They said I smacked the car up."

Hilary stood, and something on her sweet, pale face made him move. The motion made him whimper, and she smiled with genuine pleasure. Her long hand, suspended above him, was trembling. He felt her anger. His penis burned. He closed his eyes but opened them at once. He was afraid of her hand descending to seize him as if in love or recollected lust, but then to squeeze, to crush the catheter and leave him coughing up his pain and bleeding up into the blanket. He saw her playing the piano with strong bloody hands, leaving a trail of blood on the keys.

She said, "I have to go outside until I calm down. I'll go outside and then I'll be back. Because unlike you I do *not* run out on the people

I love. Loved. But I'll leave you a clue. You want to remember things? You want a little trail of bread crumbs you can follow back into your life? How about this, Richard: you drove our fucking car as hard as you could into a telephone pole so you could die. Is that a little crust of some usefulness? So you could leave me forever on purpose. Have I helped?"

THE AWFUL DOCTOR came back again, adding the insult of his breath to the injury of his armpits. He was thick, with a drooping heavy chest and shoulders that came down at a very sharp angle, so that his thick neck looked long. His fingers were large, and the knuckles looked dirtier now—this morning, tonight, whenever it was that the doctor stood at the bed, telling Richard where the orthopedic surgeon was going to insert pins of assorted sizes and alloys into the hip and femur, which the instrument panel had cracked in an interesting way. The neck was all right. The back was all right. The head seemed all right, though you never can tell with the brain. A little rancid laugh, a flicker of motion across the big jowls and their five o'clock shadow. And the ribs, of course, although CAT pictures showed no danger to the lungs. "You'll be bound."

"I'm a judge," Snuyder said.

"Good man."

"I'm a district judge with a house in the suburbs and a wife and two kids and two cars. Three cars. We have an old Volvo my son Hank fixed up. A '67 Volvo. It runs pretty well, but it's rusted out. Bound over—you say that when—"

"Yes, you're a judge. Good man. I was talking about a restraint for the ribs, is all. Two ribs. You're lucky."

"Of course, I'm lucky. And I didn't aim to hit some telephone pole."

"You remember what happened?"

"No. But I wouldn't have. People with a—people like me don't *do* that."

The doctor looked bitter and weary. "No," he said. "I can call the rescue squad, if you like, and ask them to take you back and drop you off at your car. I'd have to call the garage and tell them that it isn't telescoped. Totaled. All but small enough to use for a Matchbox toy if the grandchildren come over. Of course, you'll probably benefit by using less gas in it from now on."

Richard blushed. He couldn't shut up, though. He said, "I meant suicide."

"I know."

"I meant people like me don't *do* that."

"You want anything for pain?"

"No."

"Don't be stubborn, Your Honor. A petulant patient is still a patient in pain. Can be. Call the nurse if you hurt. I'll leave orders in case you do. I'll see you before they sedate you. It might be soon, but I think they'll wait until tomorrow, or late this afternoon. We're crowded. Sick people, you know."

"Unlike me."

The doctor let his face say that he was ignoring Richard's childishness. And Richard felt an overwhelming need to cry.

"So if you're so crowded, how come you put me in a private room. Why don't you keep a suicide watch on me? Who *says* it's suicide?"

"First of all, we didn't. Second of all: Two kids in a car, one pedestrian walking her dogs, the cop who was chasing you for DWI and reckless endangerment and all the other violations you probably pronounce on people at your place of work. I'm going. We aren't having much of a doctor-patient relationship right now."

And when he left, Richard lay back, breathless with rage. He panted with hatred for his wife and his doctor, the nurse, the orderly, the hospital, the cops behind him during the chase, and the fact that he had not slowed down when they came into his mirror, no siren on but a band of white and red light that made him blink before—he suddenly could see himself—he crouched over the wheel and then leaned back, pushing his arms straight, locked at the elbows, jamming the accelerator down until the bellow of the engine and wind and, then, the siren of the following police, were almost as loud as the howl that he howled and that he kept on howling until the impact shut him, and everything else, up.

He heard his breath shudder now, in the salmon-colored room, mostly shadows and walnut veneers. Then he heard a man say, "You wanna nurse?"

"Who?"

"It's me. You can't turn, huh? Listen, Your Honor, it's such a pain in the ass as well as the armpit, the crutches, I'm gonna stay flat for a while. I'll visit you later on, you can look at me and remember. I'm the guy said hello the other time."

"You're in here with me?"

"Yeah. Ain't it an insult? You a judge and everything. Like the doctor said, it's real crowded."

"This is *too* crowded."

"Well, listen, don't go extending any special treatment to me, Your Honor. Just pretend I'm a piece of dog shit. You'll feel better if you don't strain for the little courtesies and all. Your wife's a very attractive woman, if I may say so. Hell of a temper, though."

Richard rang for the nurse.

His roommate said, "All that pain. Dear, dear. Listen, remember this when you wake up. My name's Manwarren. Emanuel Manwarren. Manny Manwarren. It's an honor to be with a Your Honor kind of deal." Then, to the entering nurse: "His Honor is in discomfort."

Richard lay with his eyes closed until the nurse returned with water and a large capsule. He looked at her. She was young and intelligent-looking, and very tired. He said, "How shall I take this medicine without drowning? I can't sit up."

She said, "He ordered it by spansule." Her voice was flat. She was expecting a fight.

"He would," Richard said. "What if I die taking medicine?" He heard himself: he sounded worried about dying.

"Don't fret," she said. "I'll telephone for an order change, and I'll bring you a shot."

"You're a charmer, Your Honor," Manwarren said.

"Are we going to engage in class warfare, or whatever this is, for all the time we're in here? Mr. Manwarren?"

"Call me Manny. Nah. I'm a prickly personality. I hate the cops, authority figures like that, judges—you know what I mean?"

"Manny, why don't you think of me as a miscreant and not a judge."

"Can I call you Dick?"

Richard closed his eyes and listened to his breathing and the rustle of Manwarren's sheets. The pain was in Richard's bones and in his breath. He said, "There *was* someone with me, wasn't there?"

"Dick, in cases like this, there usually is."

II

THEY LIVED IN a renovated carriage house at the edge of a small country road outside Utica. Simple country living at a condominium price, Hilary liked to say. They couldn't quite afford the mortgage, college tuitions, cars, the McIntosh stereo rig—Snuyder felt like a pilot when he turned the power on—or the carpets from Iran or Iraq or India, he forgot which, that Hilary had lately come to buy as investments. He thought of them as insulation.

Looking at his lighted house at 1:25 in the morning, observing a close, clear disk of moon, a sky bluer than black, and veined with cloud—it was a dark marble mural more than sky—Richard said, "We get by."

Hilary was in the living room, at the piano. She was playing little clear crystal sounds with occasional speeded-up patterns of dissonance. He watched the tall, pale woman at the piano, her body rigid, neck tense, all pleasure residing below her moving wrists.

"Hello," Snuyder said softly, removing his jacket and then his tie, dumping them on the sofa. "I was working with the clerks on a case. It's a terrible case. Then we went out for some drinks."

The repetitions in the music came in miniature parts and were very simple. There was a name for that. He was unbuttoning his shirt and he had it off by the time she sensed him and stopped and turned on the piano bench to see him wiping the sweat on his chest with the wadded shirt.

"Ugh," she said, covering her eyes with her big hands.

"How."

"Richard, stop. It's ugly."

"It's a sweaty night," he said. He went for his welcoming kiss. She hugged his waist and kissed his belly.

"Yummy," he said.

"Salty," she said. "Phoo." But she held him, and he stayed there. "Vhere vas you so late?"

"I told you—clerks? Case? Just now?"

Richard carried his guilt and his dirty shirt toward the shower and Hilary followed. She stood in the doorway as he slid the cloudy shower door closed and made a screen of water that sealed him away. He groaned and blubbered and shook his head and shoulders and, loosening at last, dopey with comfort, shed of the sweat and oils and inner fluids of somebody else, he heard only part of what Hilary had said.

He called, "What?"

He turned the water off, and her words came over the stall. "I said you sounded especially like a whale tonight."

"Thank you. You did not. The Satie was beautiful,"

"Thank *you*. It was Villa-Lobos, a *Chôros*. I don't think it's possible to confuse the two unless you've got me at the piano, the Snuyder Variations, eh?"

"Hilary."

"Sorry. Sorry."

"A number of other performers also dislike playing to a live audience.

Glenn Gould, I remind you, for the one-millionth time, stopped playing concerts altogether. He was not, I think you'll agree, a shabby
tickler of the ivories."

"Can you see how *little* I'm cheered by that? I'm sorry Gould is
dead. I wish he'd been comfortable at concerts. But he made *recordings*,
Richard. He made wonderful recordings."

"And you will too. It'll happen." He made his voice sound matter-
of-fact, sincerely casual, casually sincere. But he knew how impatient
he must sound to her.

He had intended to leap from the shower, dangle his body before
her, and roll her into bed—and pray for performance this third time
tonight. But when he came out, tail wagging and his smile between his
teeth like a fetched stick, she was gone, his stomach was fluttering with
premonitions, and he was very, very tired. He decided to settle for a
glass of beer and some sleep. Hilary was in the kitchen when, wearing
his towel, he walked in. She was peeling plastic wrap from a sandwich,
and she had already poured him a beer. "You always want beer after a
day like this. At least I can make the meals."

Richard drank some beer and said, "Thank you. You're very kind,
though sullen and self-pitying."

"But I make a fine Genoa salami sandwich. And I look nice in
shorts."

She was crying at the sink, turning the instant boiling-water tap on
and off, on and off. The mascara ran black down her face. She looked
like a clown. He realized that she'd made herself up for him—when?
midnight? afterward?—and had worn the face she had made for him
to see. He visualized himself, proud as a strapping big boy, stepping
from the shower to greet her.

He finished chewing salami and dark bread. He said, "I hate to see
you so damned unhappy."

She turned the boiling water on and off, and steam fogged the
kitchen window. "So you make me cry to express your dismay with
my sorrow?"

"Actually, I wasn't aware that I was making you cry."

"You're such a slob, Richard."

"But well-spoken, and attractive in a towel."

"You aren't unattractive," she said. "But you're so tired, you could never make love. Could you?"

Richard sighed with fear and satisfaction as he drank his beer. "We can do some middle-class perversions if you like. Many were developed for the tired husband after work, I understand. We can—" He had by now stood and moved to her, was moving against her as they leaned at the sink. "We can do a number of exotic tricks they practice in the movies that the D.A. confiscates."

Hilary's eyes were closed. She was unfastening his towel. Her upper lip was clamped over the lower one; and he watched it when it moved. "Movie perversions?" she said. "Where would you pick up movie perversions?"

"You know those evidentiary sessions I sometimes hold? We all sit around and watch dirty flicks."

She said, "Pig."

His skin had been cool and hers hot. His body, had it been a creature with a mouth, no more, would have sung. But it was very tired, and it was crowded with his mind. He thought, now, here, in his hospital room, not about—*damn* it—whoever he had been with in a motel room in Westmoreland, New York, before he wrecked his car. He could remember that—the room, the bedspread's color, the light lavender cotton skirt on the floor, and not her face. He couldn't see her *face*.

Richard, in their house, in his memory now, had taken off his wife's clothing and had wooed her away from what was sorrowful and true. He'd loved her in their kitchen to the exclusion of everything, for a very little while. And now, in the hospital room, he couldn't see or say the name of the woman he had loved more than Hilary and whom he had washed from his body to preserve her to himself. Naked of clothes and towel and her, they had lain in a nest of Hilary's underwear and blouse and dark Bermuda shorts—skins so easily shed. And Hilary had been watching him. He'd seen her eyes rimmed with black and filling with darkness. She had figured him out, he knew. He had wondered when she would tell him. In his hospital room, he remembered hoping that she would find a way to make it hurt.

III

IT TOOK Lloyd and Pris nearly a month to arm themselves and gather their courage and rage. Then they came, through the main doors of the county office building, and past the glass information booth—"Can I help you?" the woman in beige had said to the profiles of their passing shotguns—and down one flight to the basement offices. They thought the dogs would be in the basement, Lloyd later said. "I couldn't figure on anybody keeping animals upstairs where the fancy offices was bound to be." They took eleven people hostage, including a woman who cried so long and loudly that Lloyd—"She sounded like one of the goddamned *dogs*"—hit her with the pump-gun barrel. She breathed quietly and shallowly for the rest of their visit and was hospitalized for a week. The police at first remained outside and were content to bellow over battery-powered hailers. "*I* couldn't understand 'em," Lloyd said. "It sounded like some goddamned cheerleaders on a Friday night over to the high school game. Except Pris and me wouldn't play ball."

They passed out a note that said, "26 PRIVAT STOCK CRETURS PLUS FREEDOME OF CHOICE PLUS $10,000." The money was for Pris's sex-change operation, Lloyd said in his deposition. They wanted to be legally married and live as man and wife. Pris was tired of costumes and wanted *outfits*. The police got bored and flushed them out with tear gas, then beat them badly before the arraignment. Lloyd later said, "I don't think the operation would of made that much difference, to tell you the truth. Pris, he didn't—she—whatever the hell he is. *It*. I don't think he loved me the way you want somebody to love you." Lloyd was starving himself in the county jail. Pris was defended from rape by a captured counterfeiter out of Fairfax, Virginia, and their affair was two weeks old and going strong.

And Hilary had not come back. Manwarren had paid for a television set while Snuyder had slept the sleep of the sedated, and Snuyder now lay looking at the dimpled ceiling panels, clenching his fists against the pain, and listening without wishing to. Game-show hosts with voices as sweet and insistent as the taste of grape soda cried out with delight and mortification as army sergeants and homemakers and stockbrokers selected numbers and boxes and squares marked off on walls and were awarded either bounty or a consolation prize consisting of a lifetime supply of scuff-resistant, polymer-bound linoleum clean-'n'-polisher for the busy woman who has more to do than wax, for sweet goodness' sake, her floors. Manwarren also watched soap operas that had to do with misplaced babies and frantic adulterers, always on the verge of discovery as incestuous. There were snippets of old movie, fragments of cartoon, crashingly educational disquisitions on the use of C—"C, you *see*, is also in *ka*-ristmas ta*ree!*"—and Gilligan, eternally trapped on his island with Tina Louise and constitutionally incapable of hurling himself upon her, continued to invent ways of extending his imprisonment.

Manwarren, a real critic, commented with alert smugness and an eye for the obvious. "You believe she couldn't remember who invented *noodles?*" he sang. He crowed, "Numbers are from the friggin' Arabs, dummy! No wonder he's a garbageman." Snuyder kept waiting to hear the suck-and-pour of passing traffic on the arterial highway leading into downtown Utica, but all he heard was Manwarren and the objects of his derision. "Hey," he said, "hey, Judge. You handle yourself like this 'Family Court' guy? He takes *no* crap offa nobody, you know? He's got a courtroom fulla morons, by the way. No wonder they ended up in court. They wouldn't know how to cross the *street*." A "M*A*S*H" rerun drove Manwarren into silent sniffles, but he covered well by saying, in a gravelly voice, "I don't think that's a very realistic way to talk about the Korean conflict." Of "Robin Hood," he said, for the first time approving in tone, "I never knew Glynis Johns had knockers like that, Judge."

Snuyder listened. The pain made him blink in disbelief. He looked at the ceiling panels and waited for Hilary to return. She didn't. The balding nurse, this time in a long-sleeved dress, came in with a sedative shot. He was so grateful, he felt embarrassed. His orthopedic surgeon, a tall and slender man who not only didn't smile, but who made clear both his disapproval of the patient and of having to explain to him, explained to him what he would do inside of Snuyder's hip and leg. Pins. Something about pins that would staple him together again, he remembered, after the surgeon was gone and the ceiling had dropped a few feet, and then the orderlies came to roll him away to be pinned into shape.

There was something about dogs, and their terrible odor, and somebody riding one around a muddy country lot. He said *No!* And, knowing that he dreamed while he dreamed, he awaited the dream that would tell him who had sat in the front with him while the police car chased him and he drove—by accident, he insisted to the unseen audience his dream included—into the slow breaking up of his bones. The dogs whined and whined, as if steadily, increasingly, wounded by someone patient and cruel.

The intensive care unit was dark and silent and Snuyder was in very deep pain. His hip burned, and his stomach, and the groin he ached too much to reach for. He kept seeing the skin slide open as the angry surgeon sliced. He yelped for assistance and then shuddered to show the nurse that it was he who needed her promptest sympathies. He was hooked to a drip and a monitor, she explained. Soon he would be taken back to his room. He was fine. The procedure had seemed to be effective, and now his job was to sleep. He slept, but the burning followed him, and he dreamed again of dogs whose fur was stiff with filth, whose eyes dripped mucus, and whose droppings were alive with long white worms. He heard the dogs' howling and he hated Lloyd and Pris. The television set was low, and a curtain divided him from Manwarren, but he knew, waking later, that he was back in his room, and still burning, and all right, alive, not dreaming anymore. The world was in color on the other side of the curtain where a voice electric with triumph told someone named Cecelia that the car she'd won had bucket seats. She screamed.

The woman in the car with him had screamed.

TONY ARIZONA, his senior clerk, was there in the morning to discuss adjustments of his trial calendar. He brought a cheap glass vase filled with blue flowers that Snuyder couldn't name, and a fifth of Powers' Irish Whiskey. He showed Snuyder how his cases had been distributed among the other sitting judges and that certain others—very few of them—had been postponed. Snuyder said, "No. You gave the boys with the dogs to Levinson."

"He wanted it. He hates queers."

"He *is* queer. I want that one, Tony. Hold it over as long as you can before you give it up. And try not to give it to Levinson. He'll be corn-holing them in chambers by the end of the first hour. Oh, boy."

"They cut you up some, I understand."

"Not to mention *I* cut me up."

"Judge. Dick. I have to give the dog people to Levinson. State wants your calendar cleared. You understand? I'm sorry."

"The suicide thing?"

"They think they might want to look into it."

"Tony. *You* think I tried to kill myself?"

"I think you bent your car around a telephone pole. For what it's worth, I don't care—I mean, I *care*, but only about you. You did it, you didn't do it, you'll work it out and the accident's over, that's that. It's not the suicide thing. It's the woman."

Snuyder heard himself sigh. He could see the letters coming out of his mouth and into a comic-strip bubble: Ahhhh. He waited for Arizona to tell him who she was, and whether he was in love as much as he thought he remembered he once had been.

Arizona said, "They have to do it. *I* don't know anything. And nobody else is gonna say word one. I expect a superficial investigation, announced vindication, and a prompt resumption of jurisprudence as usual."

"And then there's the matter of the law," Richard said.

Arizona, handsome and intelligent, with great brown eyes and a fondness for dark striped shirts such as the maroon one he wore, smiled a broad smile. "Absolutely," he said. "There is always the law, and the public trust, Your Honor."

Manwarren called over the curtain, "You guys believe this? They want me to believe this bimbo just won a trip around the world for two, all expenses paid, by telling grease ball over there with the microphone that Columbus didn't discover America?" The muted shrieks of the victor poured around Manwarren's voice.

The woman in the car had screamed. Arizona poured Powers' into Snuyder's glass with its plastic straw, then he held the straw low, near Snuyder's pillow, so the judge could suck it up. He emptied the glass. Arizona might know her, he thought. But he couldn't be asked. Snuyder was ashamed to remember his wife and his children, his work even down to the specifics of the cases he had tried months and years ago, when he could barely remember the presence, much less identity or necessary intimate facts, of a woman he had carried with him toward jail for certain, and possibly (if Hilary was right) toward death. But she wasn't dead. The nurse had told him that no one was dead. He thought of someone with no face who sat in a wheelchair, paralyzed. He saw her—she was like a burglar in a stocking mask, terrifying because faceless, unnatural—lying in an iron lung, crushed in a fetal sleep forever, staring through a window and drooling, staggering like a monster with hands like claws at her waist, serving the judge's sentence and locked away from his mind.

Arizona slid the Powers' into the drawer of the bedside table when he left. The pain pills and the Powers' combined, and Snuyder flinched. The doctors would have to cut and cut before they found out what was wrong with such a man as he, he told himself. He closed his eyes against the undeniable blade, as if they were cutting, as if they were at the flaccid organs and slimy bone, searching for what was the matter. For him.

It was Hilary who woke him when she sat in the visitor's chair with some effort, swearing as she fell back into the deep seat. After a silence—she breathed as if she had a cold—she said, "How's your catheter, Judge?"

"Hil. Do you know who she is?"

Manwarren turned the volume down.

Snuyder whispered: "The woman in the car?" He took a breath and then shouted, "Manwarren! Turn the sound up! Mind your own business!" He felt as though he'd been running. "Bastard," he said. He shouted it: "Bastard!"

The sound came up slightly, but Snuyder knew that Manwarren was unchastened.

Hilary said, "Why, who would that be, Your Honor? How *is* your catheter, by the way?"

"I hurt all over. Okay? I'm in a lot of pain. I'm humiliated. I'm under investigation, Hilary. They're looking into my comportment on and off the bench."

"I didn't know you'd done it on the bench. And you can't really blame them. A suicide is not always the most stable interpreter of the law, never mind his other little quirks and foibles."

"It's apparently because of the woman. That was all I could get from Arizona."

Hilary said, "I wish *I* could get more from Tony. He's really a piece."

"Please don't talk like that."

"Do I really need to tell you about the hypocrisy of this discussion?"

"No."

"You know I'm disgusted with you. That's an easy one. Disgust is easy and seeing it's easy. But what *kills* me—"

"Hil, I can't remember a lot. I remember *us*, overall, you know. And a lot of times and things. But I can't remember a lot."

"And that includes the slut in the car? *That's* what kills me. It's so *sad* for you that you can't. I feel *sorry* for you. You son of a bitch."

"Hil, she's literally a slut?"

"Oh. You boy. You infant. You expect me to keep track of your infidelities and log your bedroom transactions, don't you. You'd ask me for help. You know, knowing me, I'd probably give it. You—*boy*." She wept mascara lines down her face.

Snuyder said, "I'm promiscuous? I thought I remembered that I really loved her." Their silence widened, and a woman on the television set said, "I wouldn't dare tell them that!"

Hilary sighed. She said, "I think I'll go home. I understand they'll bring you back for therapy, and you'll use a walker. You'll be able to walk someday. I feel sorry it's so bad. Also, Richard, I'm moving. During the latter part of the week. I'll telephone you."

"Where?" he said. "Did we decide to do this?"

Hilary shook her head. "It started when you told me *you* were moving out."

"Yes," he said. He remembered at once, and as if he looked through transparent overlays: long arguments, slower and longer conversations, Hilary on the phone, Hilary weeping black lines while holding a teacup to her mouth, himself standing before her and wishing aloud that he were dead. He remembered the words about remorse that he had tried to say, and the fear of how they'd tell their sons. Hilary had told him about Warren, calling from college, in tears, because he had sensed that it all had gone wrong. Snuyder said, "I'm sorry. I don't remember women. A woman. *The* woman, I guess you'd call her."

"Yes," Hilary said.

"I apologize. If it's because of her, I apologize. I don't suppose it would make any difference now, seeing that I don't know her anymore. Is she the—"

But Hilary was up and moving. She was at the door. He heard the squelch of her crepe soles on the linoleum floor.

He said, "I suppose not."

She said, "See you, Judge." Then, too brightly, she said, "Actually, I'll see you in court." She laughed too hard, and she left.

Manwarren called over at once. "You know what, Dick? I think you shoulda hit the pole a little harder, you don't mind my saying so. You're in a pickle, to say the least, big fella."

"You think I'm in a pickle, Manwarren?"

"Call me Manny."

"I'm going to make a call, Manny. While you sleep. I'm going to have a man who runs a chain of fish stores in Syracuse—I'm going to ask him to have an employee in the Manlius packing plant come over here while you're sleeping and kill you. He's going to open your chest with his bare hands, and he's going to tear out every vital organ in your body one at a time. And he won't wear gloves. His nails will be dirty. He picks his nose. Do you understand me, Manny?"

The sound increased in volume, and bright voices clung to the ceiling tiles. She had been in the car with him. She had screamed when they'd hit. Hilary was leaving because of her, and he didn't know who the woman was. The set cried out and the voices rose. He was alleged to have attempted suicide. He would never walk normally, and his sons would not come to him. He knew that too. Hilary would take all their money and the men on the ethics committee might remove him from the bench. He thought they wouldn't, since none of them was terribly honest either, and each was equally impeachable. They would probably reprimand him, and he would suffer a trial-by-headline. But he would return to the bench, he thought. He would live alone in an apartment such as the ones near the Sangertown Mall. Or perhaps he might move into Clinton, where the old large houses east of town were divided into Victorian cells for bachelors and men such as he. He would drive alone to work and sit in his courtroom. He would say who was right in the eyes of the law. He never would know who the woman had been, or what they had been together, or why.

It was an empty mourning, he thought—abstracted, like a statement about how dreadful the starving African babies are. He wondered if the woman he loved and didn't know might have told him she was leaving. Perhaps he had aimed at killing *her.*

He heard himself whimpering, and made himself stop. He heard Manwarren's television set, and then the dogs in the trailer who'd whimpered, he'd been told by the deputies, before they heard the foot on the door; once rescued, they'd begun to bark and wail. He thought of Lloyd and Pris, armed and marching, in their terrible fetor and loss, to recover their starved, sick dogs. They were separated now. Poor Lloyd: he had taken the hostages, and only when his prisoners lay on the floor in the deeds-recording office had he realized that he wanted to insist on one more prize, the operation that would change Pris's sex. It was then, Snuyder remembered realizing, as he'd read Lloyd's deposition, that Lloyd had understood how permanently separate he had always been from Pris and probably always would be. "He don't love me," Lloyd had said. "How could he?"

It was a case he had wanted to try. They were accused of a dozen public-health violations and twenty or more violations of the civil and criminal codes. And they were so innocent, Snuyder thought. No one should be allowed to be so innocent. Shots rang out on a TV show, and wheels screamed. Snuyder jumped, remembering the sound of locked brakes. She had been there with him, in the same small space. And he had leaned back, locked his elbows and knees, and had driven at the pole. He had. And he would not know her. And even that was not the worst part.

SHE *MIGHT* RETURN. He would have to decide about trying to heal, or waiting for her next door to death. He forced himself to breathe evenly, as if he slept. The TV set made sounds. The dogs stood on the bed and chairs, they cried their pain and hunger, their fear. Manwarren cackled. The police would come soon with questions. He was held together with pins. He was going to die, but of natural causes, and many years from today. He knew it. He smelled the dark air of the trailer, and he heard the gaunt dogs whine.

RERUNS

W HEN THE State Department officer telephoned to ask if I was
the Dr. Leland Dugan whose wife, Belinda, was traveling as a
journalist in Europe and the Middle East, I answered in a manner even
I, at the time, found cagey and evasive. "Yes," I said. "I'm Dugan. But
she isn't really a journalist. Of course, she *does* journalism. But she's a
sociologist. On her tax return she calls herself a teacher."

One of our recent fights had been about income tax returns. Belinda
had wanted to be a married woman filing separately. I'd tried to show
her that such a category cost us money. She'd been resolute: "I will not
sign on some line tagged *spouse*. Underneath your name. I won't *be*
underneath you anymore."

"So I've noticed," I'd told her.

"In the Lebanon," the State Department officer said. His way of
saying it—*the* Lebanon, as if this were the thirties and we were in
Whitehall discussing Middle East chappies—made me pay attention.
I am paid to pay attention to the stories people tell. I should have done
better, but it had been a difficult morning, and one of my patients,
seeking to test and protest at once, had sat before my desk for twenty
minutes without speaking, daring me to intervene. I hadn't, and for
the thirty subsequent minutes, he'd bellowed and ranted, sweating and

heaving and, finally, leaping from his chair. "I don't feel better," he'd said, like a huge, sore child. "I don't feel better at all. So *now* what am I supposed to do?"

I said to the State Department officer, "Would you tell me again, please?"

That's how I learned that my wife, Belinda, anthropology-sociology professor on leave and part-time free-lance journalist, had gone to Beirut and was now a prisoner of some group on whom the Department of State sought further information. That was when I began to think of distances—the width of oceans, the length of borders, the prairies inside lives—as personal facts, and not just my patients' reports, or my wife's.

I said, "She's alive?"

"When they keep them there, they're alive, Dr. Dugan. Dead, they come straight home."

"She wouldn't want to come straight home, either way," I said. I chuckled, but he didn't laugh back politely. He said that someone had been sent, early that morning. I was not alone, he said.

I telephoned Kate, and then I canceled patients for the day. I thought of the man the State Department had sent. He'd have to come a winding, hesitant route. He would, as so many strangers to our cold, bleak countryside do, drift and get lost, then recover, wandering on, doubting his direction, feeling compelled to continue. He would take a route along the ground like those my patients take in time and language when they try to tell their story to me. He'd already have flown from Washington to Syracuse, or Washington to one of the New York airports, and then to Hancock in Syracuse. He'd drive the seventy-five miles in his rental car—on Route 81, then 690, then some of Route 5, then lots of 92 to 20, 20 to 12B, 12B to 12, in slow traffic through small towns, and in the wide barren spaces in between. We are so far from everyplace.

I collected Linda at the central school, and I told her. She was flushed, at first, because she'd been stared at by other adolescents as she left class early. She grew pale, then, and in the stairwell, at the main doors, she said, with dry lips clacking, "But who *wants* her?"

"Nice try," I said. We went for Melissa, who was in the elementary building. As she walked into the office, Lissa, seeing us, began to cry. "It's okay, baby," I said. I kept saying it. "Baby, it is fine."

Linda said to her, "She isn't dead."

Melissa cried harder.

"We'll talk about it," I said. "She isn't sick, and she isn't hurt."

"And she isn't coming home," Linda said.

I told her, "Thank you."

In the car, after a few blocks, after listening hard and riding silently, Melissa asked, "But who kidnaps *mothers?*"

And Linda had a question, too: "You think they'll rape her?"

I asked Melissa, "Do you know what Linda's talking about?"

"Do I like know what rape is?"

"Yes."

"Mostly," Lissa said.

I had to park across the street because the cars and trucks of the news people were in our drive and on our lawn. A sheriff's deputy led us through the onlookers and rural anchor-folk. Linda was grinning, I noticed, and she slowed against my arm as they questioned us; I pushed her home. Melissa said nothing. Her face was very pale, and her large eyes looked dark. In that way, she might have been Kate's daughter. She wasn't.

Kate arrived from her pediatrics clinic, and I nodded at the deputy who called for permission to bring her along. When Linda saw her she said, "God!" Kate dodged the same fat little man I'd pushed past; he'd told me he was a reporter from a fundamentalist Christian radio station. She stood before a fellow from our local Progressive Country and Western Sounds station as he shouted into her eyes and nose, "Dr. Karagoulis! What do you think of Mrs. Dugan being kidnaped?" She shook her head. "What are you doing here, Dr. Karagoulis, if we may inquire?"

Kate said something so low, I couldn't hear it. The deputy brought her, and we went in. Kate put her hands on my shoulders and kissed me.

"Jesus," Linda said.

Melissa said, "Hi, Kate!" Kate stooped to kiss her, and then she walked to Linda, whom she hugged, then kissed on the cheek. "I'm sorry," Kate told her.

"Tell my mother," Linda said.

"All right," Kate said.

"Sure. While she's in Lebanon."

Kate said, "Wasn't that cunning of me."

"What'd you tell the reporter?" I asked her.

"I said I was making a house call." She wore white twill slacks and a soft white man-tailored shirt, white socks, and shiny brown penny loafers. "I am," she said, opening her large medical bag and presenting a smelly brown paper sack streaked with oil. She handed it to Lissa, who unpacked long submarine sandwiches and Hostess Twinkies.

Linda, who ate nearly as much as Kate, turned away, as if sickened by food. Then she turned back. Kate took cans of cream soda from her bag. "I thought we might force ourselves," she said. We went into the back room, which was big and sloppy and filled with soft furniture. Kate took the ringing phone and unhooked it from its terminal. "I'll hook it up when I call my service," she said. "You guys go disconnect the other phones, please."

Linda said, "I might be expecting a call."

The telephone rang, and Kate stared down at Linda, who was at least six inches shorter than she. Melissa said, "I'll show you how to do it, Lin."

"I better not miss any calls," Linda said.

Kate only nodded. And when they had left, and as the other three telephones one by one stopped ringing, Kate and I stood, trying to squeeze some private talk into what would be a public day. Finally, she asked, "Do you think it has to do with us?"

"*She* has to do with us," I said. "We have to do with her. We're her symptoms. Whether or not we—"

Kate said, "Whether or not we're responsible for her situation."

"Her situation's an extension of her mind. No. I don't accept this blame."

"Well, I don't *want* to," Kate said. "But—"

"Yeah."

"Yeah, what?"

"Yeah, but."

"But what?"

"What, Daddy?" Melissa asked, behind us.

"But I don't think I'm gonna get my sandwich," I said. "If that's the man from Washington." Bernie, our 130-pound Newfoundland, was roaring in the foyer.

It was the deputy, and with him, shielded by him from the newspeople, was Mr. Pontrier from Washington, with his courteous introduction, and his letter from our senior Senator, and from the Secretary of State, and his verbal greetings from—he pronounced it as a single word—the-President-himself. Kate and the girls were gone when we went through to the kitchen. He laid his coat over a chair, and I ground coffee beans and set out mugs and milk and sugar and spoons, paper napkins. I threw away the greasy bag they'd left. It reminded me of the brown bag into which I'd put Belinda's hair two weeks before she left. I had driven with it to the hospital, where I'd found Kate on pediatrics rounds. She'd been palpating the abdomen of a struggling infant, and I'd watched her close her eyes, as if to will her senses to her fingertips. In the corridor, I showed her the bag. Looking inside, she'd recoiled. "She cut it off," I'd told her. "She left it strewn through my underwear drawer." Kate had stared and stared, and tears had run from her enormous eyes. She'd wept, I remembered thinking, because perhaps she'd thought I didn't know how to. It didn't occur to me until Belinda was kidnaped that Kate might have wept for Belinda.

When I turned around in the kitchen, Pontrier had opened his attaché case and had put on the kitchen table his pad and pen, a tape recorder, and two sets of glasses in soft leather sleeves. "Will *not* wear bifocals," he said, whinnying, showing his large teeth and pink gums. "Won't admit my age. Shouldn't say that to a shrink."

Bernie walked past Pontrier to lie beneath the table.

"Hell, we listen to anything," I said. "I once had a family—"

"You do whole families?"

"Oh, yeah. Being crazy's a family project most of the time. I had this family, and I made them bring in their dog."

Hearing "dog," Bernie banged his tail against the floor.

"How'd that work out, Doc?"

"Well, I was able to help the dog. The family stayed sick."

He whinnied again, then played back "stayed sick" on his machine. He nodded. "We're ready," he said. "Tell you what I know. Ask you for information we might want later on. We need the—" He waved his long hands.

"Overall picture," I said. "Or would you say, 'big picture'?"

"Right," he said. "Right. You know Q & A."

"Q & A?"

"Questions and answers. Part of your profession, right?"

"I have a Q," I said. "How come you're here? How come the State Department phones me up, and an official"—I gestured at him, he nodded—"leaves to fight his way through the upstate wilds? How come this attention? Were you people having her followed?"

"No," he said, "it's just your wife's the second New York State citizen they've taken. Your senator got in on this. He wants *service*."

"Politics," I said, as if that explained something.

The coffee had dripped, and I set the pot on the table atop the terra-cotta tile Belinda had bought in Peru. Kate had told me once that Belinda's affection for objects made of clay was a sign in her favor. He switched his recorder on and said, in a normal voice, "Briefing of

Leland Dugan, four thirty pee em, January sixteen, Nineteen eighty-seven. Eight! Eight. Still not up to date." I was afraid he was going to whinny again, but he was content with showing his gums.

"Now, Dr. Dugan." He took off one set of glasses and put on another. "Our people liaised with representatives of the International Red Cross and certain representatives of the Druse upon notification that a Mrs. Belinda Dugan of Sherwood, New York, a member of the faculty of the State University of, ah, New York et cetera, had been taken hostage. We assume she was taken hostage. No demands have been made. Really isn't kidnapping or hostage taking, is it, if they don't want something in return." He looked up. I nodded.

He looked displeased, then held up his little Japanese recorder. I said, "Yes. No."

"Thank you, Doctor," he told the machine, setting it down. "We have received confirmation—"

"They didn't cut any fingers off," I said. "Or ears? Anything like that?"

"Movies, Doctor. Movies. In our experience, this doesn't happen."

"It happened to Aristotle Onassis. Or Getty. One of those people. They sent him an ear."

"Guess you're not in the right tax bracket, Doctor," he said. And he did draw back his gums and whinny. I set my coffee cup down somewhat harder than I'd planned to. "But not a time for levity, so let's—" He looked at his yellow legal pad, with its green lines and red-ruled margin. I saw my name at the top of the pad, and a series of numbers arranged vertically. Beside each number were matters he'd apparently decided to set before me. As I watched, he crossed out what was next to number two. He looked up, saw me trying to read his pad, and drew it closer to him, as if we were being examined and he'd caught me trying to cheat. "No fingers or ears. Sorry you were so worried."

"Thank you. Does it matter who has her?"

"Does matter. A lot of these people don't negotiate. A lot of them, they're nuts, to put it in a, well, nutshell." Lips, then gums and teeth, then silent laughter.

"So's Belinda," I said.

"Clinically? Certifiably?"

"No. Although one definition of adjustment might be your ability to stay away from hostage situations in Lebanon. Or Lebanon itself. Belinda is a very, very intelligent woman of significant achievement and reputation. Right now, she hates who she is—her whole situation. She—"

"That include you, Doctor? Mind my asking? The big—"

"Yes. Big picture. No, I don't mind. Yes, I do. What the hell. Sure, it includes me. Remember what I said before? Being crazy's a family project. Being so sad. Disoriented. All of that. Any of that. Yes. Yes, it includes me. Yes."

"Tough one."

I said, "Are you married, Mr. Pontrier?"

"Twenty-nine years in two months."

"You work at it."

"Never had a fight."

I cocked my head as Bernie cocks his. Pontrier replied, "Work really hard at doing everything she says!" Lips again, then gums, then teeth and the long laughed whinny.

"Will they let her go?"

"From one of the West Bank settlements, this bunch, we think. They may not be trained to negotiate. Just take people. Do whatever harm they can. Full of hate. Socialism. Radical religion. You know."

"So what happens to my wife, Mr. Pontrier?"

"State is doing everything it can."

"I'm very grateful."

He crossed out two items. "Lines of communication are wide open. People out there listen hard, tell us what they hear. Friends of friends— you know what I mean?—keep asking about her. Just like the others."

"The others."

"You remember. Anglican. French guys. The other Americans. West German guys. Nobody's forgetting them. Maybe you forget them. State doesn't."

I couldn't have named one hostage. That was when I realized how politics, history, and extreme distances had taken Belinda from our three traffic lights, the hour's commute to her campus, the stores that stocked Sara Lee pound-cake and vitamin supplements, and the house where, upstairs, Kate embraced my daughters and waited for word. Soon, I thought, people in so many lives will forget that woman's name—the one who got snatched overseas. Remember?

He looked at his list, and then he looked at me, as if he had discovered my worst malfeasances. His eyes narrowed, his leathery wide mouth frowned. He seemed to reflect on what he was going to say. Then he looked at his legal pad and said, "Nobody usually takes a woman in the Middle East."

"No?"

"You're a shrink."

"They don't value women highly. Right. But they did take my wife."

"If they don't like women, except for, you know, the obvious stuff—"

"Cooking," I said. "Child rearing."

"Screwing," he said. His eyes widened, as his nostrils did: he was daring me to rebuke him.

"All right," I said. "We'll use the State Department nomenclature."

He snorted, but didn't whinny. His cold eyes remained on me. "Have to wonder, Dr. Dugan, why they snatched her. If she's just a— Don't mean to us, of course, you or me. Woman."

I shook my head.

"Who does she work for, Doctor?"

"SUNY. Sociology."

"No, I mean over there. In Greece, or Beirut, wherever the cell was. Who was she *working* for?"

"Cell? Spies? Is that what you mean? Is that what the State Department *thinks?* Belinda Hosford Dugan, middle-aged spy?"

I saw Melissa walk in slowly and quietly. Her hands hung straight at her sides. She was nine, the age of perfection in childhood. She wanted nothing more than to give her love to much of what breathed. Her hair was drawn over to one side in a crooked, rearing wave. She wore the most innocent of miniskirts over dark tights, and her dark cotton sweater hung baggily to almost the hem of her skirt. Her legs were thin and strong. She came toward us, awaiting our discovery of her. I held my arm out, and she came to it, rolled inside it as she curled it with both hands around her waist until she stood against me.

"Lissa," I said, "this is Mr. Pontrier. He's from the government. He's trying to help Mommy."

"Will they kill her? Are these the kidnappers who kill people?"

"Heavy-duty current-events awareness," Pontrier said. "You know your civics," he told her.

"No," I said. "I don't think so." I said it as reasonably as if I were telling her that a plant was not poison oak. "Where did you hear about that, sweetie?"

"On TV," she said. "Kate and Linda and me saw Mommy on Channel Two."

"Mommy?"

Pontrier bent over to his case, and when his face reappeared, he was chewing on his lip and looking at the black plastic video cassette he held. "It must have leaked," he said. "Everything does. Knew they made a couple of copies, of course. Didn't think they would leak this fast."

I held Melissa and furrowed her pompadour with my free hand. I kept my voice reasonable, pretending that I talked to an angry dog. Bernie, sleeping, was disturbed by my fake tranquility, and he grunted. "You're saying that a videotape—the kind of thing—" It was what other families saw when terrorists took one of them. We were other families now, and there was no point in saying that, or almost anything else, to Pontrier, I realized. Now, at last, after the cruel arguments and breathless dark silences, after the shattered nights, finally there was nothing to say that might matter. I spoke nonetheless. I always did. I said, "There's a tape? You people let it happen that my girls saw this tape, and I wasn't there with them?"

Lissa said, "Kate was with us, Daddy. It was mostly like surprising. Except Mommy was crying at the end."

"Yes," I said. "And you're all right?"

She nodded. She wasn't. Kate was at the kitchen door, then. She said nothing, but held her hands out to Lissa. I kissed the top of her head and propelled her toward Kate.

I said, "Dr. Karagoulis, this is Mr. Pontrier from the State Department. Mr. Pontrier, Dr. Karagoulis."

"House full of doctors," he said, taking off his glasses and standing barefaced to shake Kate's hand.

She drew Lissa to her. "Is there news?"

He shrugged. She nodded.

"She's a doctor, too," Kate said. "Mrs. Dugan. She has the doctorate from Chicago."

"Isn't that fine!" Pontrier said.

"Excuse us," Kate said.

Pontrier looked at her as she walked away, then returned to the table, where he put on a pair of glasses, removed them, put the other pair on, and said, "My own suspicion, Doctor. They'll kick her free. On account of she's a woman. Messy things, women. You know. To the Arabs. Understand?"

I shook my head.

Pontrier shrugged, then looked at his list. "So what was it?" he asked. "Greenpeace? Socialist Workers? News Alliance for Jewish-Arab Amity? Lyndon Larouche? There's so many butthead groups. Who'd she work for?"

"Work for? When she traveled? She worked for herself."

"She free-lanced?"

"Are we talking spy novels or journalism, Mr. Pontrier?"

"Isn't always a difference," he said. Whinny, tooth and gum. "It make any difference to you?"

I clasped my hands on the edge of the table. I sat up straight and looked him in the eye. I didn't like the intimacy any more than he did, and I wound up looking at the door of our refrigerator, studded with fruit-shaped magnets holding shopping lists and Lissa's drawings and Linda's reminders (all of them ending with exclamation marks); it was our accidental map. I said, "My wife—Belinda is not entirely well."

"She need medication? We can try and work something out with the Red Cross."

"Psychic well-being," I said. "Her soul isn't well."

"You a religious guy, Doctor? Is this about religion?"

"Worse than that," I said. "I'm a Freudian. He never meant to talk about the mind. Not only. He was always saying *soul*. That's what analysis is about."

"Sounds a little ripe."

"Doesn't it. Look. Belinda's unhappy. I would call her clinically depressed. She's been doing—she's looking for something else."

He was making notes. "For what?"

"She'd love to know. So would I."

"Doctor, did she walk out on you?"

"She got as many commissions from as many magazines as she could. We're not talking whacky politics, you understand. She's a pretty typical left-wing, feminist, institution-distrusting intellectual. She wanted to find a lot of serious action and write about it. She's been giving papers on women in cultures where the politics are basically life-and-death."

"Washington, D.C.," he exploded, whinnying, showing all his teeth, every wet gum, the membranes of the linings of his lips.

"Belfast," I said. "She went there first. She did a piece for *The New Republic*. Then she went to Turkey. The next thing I heard, she was going to Lebanon."

"The next thing you heard," he said. He was a better listener than I'd thought. "So she took off on you."

"We hadn't lived comfortably together for several months."

"She did move out?"

"Can I ask you: is this relevant?"

He shrugged. "Hard to know what matters," he said. "Can't know what'll make a difference sometime down the road. We can drop it."

He made a note. His pen was thin and silver, and he had turned it to make the point emerge. Now he retracted the point. "Kind of hard not to pry," he said.

"Belinda was probably asking the same kind of question when they took her. Probably some out-of-work guy with an old gun and an older rage got tired of hearing some American woman asking *his* woman about her influence on his daily political life."

"We fix it at two months she's been gone?"

"That's about right. You checked at Kennedy?"

"We got her going into London, then out and into Ireland. She was recorded entering Athens."

"She went to Greece?"

He nodded. "Good place to hook up with radical elements."

"Look she isn't a *spy*."

"That's what Julius said about Ethel."

"What?"

"Rosenberg. The atom spies."

"For Christ's sake, Pontrier, my wife is a burnt-out, sad, searching, decompensating person who used to think she struck a blow for freedom if she didn't shave her god-damned *legs*!"

"She won't be shaving her legs in Beirut," he said, showing some quick lip lining. "Maybe it'll bring some peace to town."

"Are you going to tell me what you're doing for her? What can I do? Can I see somebody?"

"Me," he said. "Unless the President or the Secretary needs a photo opportunity with bravely smiling families of hostages and the main man trying hard not to cry while he says we're doing everything we can. If that doesn't happen, I'll be your contact for our saying that."

"No one's life should come to that," I said. "A *case*. That people forget."

"Never mind going there," he said. "Get ignored for a month and come home broke. Or get yourself kicked raw, die in a collapsed house with busted legs, skull fracture. Stay here. Wait. Write letters. Listen to people tell you they're doing what they can. They *will*. We spring one, especially a woman, it's political fat city. Gold." His long hand patted my fist on the table. I recoiled from the intimacy, and he seemed surprised at what he'd done. "Doctor," he said, putting his other glasses on, "let's go to the movies."

In the living room, when I turned on a reading lamp, I saw Linda at the end of the sofa, smoking. She didn't tap nervously into an ashtray. She drew it in until the ash glowed, and she held it deep, then let it out slowly, in a long luxurious soft plume. That's when I was sure that she'd smoked dope. I wondered if she and Belinda had smoked it together in the name of the mother-daughter bond.

"That's bad for you, baby," I said.

She nodded.

"I could give you statistics about strokes. We could talk about cancer. I hope to God she didn't put you on the pill."

She stood. "Hello," she said. "I'm Linda Dugan. I don't *think* my father will be doing a Pap smear right now. If there is any personal information you don't know about me yet, he'll be happy to fill you in."

Pontrier whinnied. So did I. So did *I*. "How are you?" I asked her.

"Linda's fifteen," I said to Pontrier, as if something were explained. I seized her before she could flee. She let me hold her into me, and she hugged back. With her hot cigarette behind my neck, I thought of Joan Crawford. Linda had always reminded me of her; she had my broken-looking nose and the wide mouth that on Belinda was often cruel, but that on Linda was mean and sexy at once. She was smart, tough, and damaged by life with me and Belinda. And because she was fifteen, she lived secretly. I always missed her. It was as though she too had fled to another country. She smelled a little sour, like the sweat you sweat in nightmare-heated sleep. Into her cheek and stale hair I whispered, "Baby."

She gave in and leaned on me for an instant. Her arms tightened and then let go. She stepped back and put the cigarette in her lips. "I'll go sit with Kate and Lissa." She said to Pontrier, "Are you going to leave a copy of that videotape with us?"

"Could do," he said, nodding. "Could do."

She laughed. "Could do," she said. Over her shoulder she let "Bye, Daddy" drift with her smoke.

"A little theatrical," I told him, betraying her.

"Time of great strain," he said. "Lot of stress. Pretty girl."

"Yes."

"Little like her mother. Little like you."

"Then that worked out for us." I took the cassette from him and slid it into the VCR. When the set was on, I punched PLAY.

Apparently the camera was mounted on a tripod. It remained still throughout. People walked on- and off-camera, but Belinda stayed where she was: seated in a wooden chair with a copy of the *International Herald Tribune* on her lap. She held the paper up, and I could see the date. Then she put the paper on her lap, and sat, with her arms hanging down. I thought of Lissa's arms as she'd entered the kitchen. Belinda wore running shoes and gray, baggy, rumpled cotton pants, a dark and dirty-looking T-shirt. Her hair was chopped short, and it looked grayer. She'd lost weight, she looked exhausted. The cords in her neck were prominent when she moved or talked. Horizontal ridges on her throat were new to me. Her arms were a little puffy, and very tan. She didn't seem drugged, but she was subdued.

A small, dark man in a kind of faded khaki uniform, wearing very large and very dark sunglasses, came to stand beside her. He put his little hand on the back of her neck and squeezed. But he didn't seem to be hurting her. She straightened.

"My name is Belinda Hosford Dugan," she said. "I am an American citizen who has been interrupting—" She peered at something near the camera, and I realized that she was reading. She wore contact lenses, and I should have known from her squint that she was reading signs.

"Cue cards," I said.

"Just like Johnny Carson," Pontrier said.

"Interfering in the orderly process of the life of the people. As a lesson to such as myself, I have been seized and am a prisoner. I am safe and well. I am not being mistreated. It's true," she said and I knew she'd deviated from the lines they'd written. No one stopped her, though. "I'm all right. Please tell my girls—tell Lissa and Linda—" She began to cry. She stopped herself. "Hello. Darlings, hello. I'm all right. I can't come home yet. And this thing, really—" Then there was static, then silence, then the small man in dark glasses said, "Enough. For now, enough."

She hadn't spoken of me. She hadn't sent a message to me. For several months we'd hardly spoken, except when we traded information about the house or children. Even then, our exchanges could have been by postcard. "For now, enough." I thought of Lissa and Linda, seeing her, hearing her say, "It's true," and then the little man.

"I'm too young to be as old as you make me," she'd said one morning. She was leaving for work, and I was going to drive the girls to school. She had come up behind me to put her hand on my shoulder. She'd hissed it, so the girls wouldn't hear: "You make me so tired."

And I had leaned my head back to reply, "We know it's not from sexual exertion."

And she, almost laughing, had whispered back, "We know it's not from sex with *you*."

That was the morning of the night she chopped her hair short. It was still short, and she looked pretty on the tape—hollow-eyed, exhausted, but still pretty Belinda, my childhood bride. We had taken sixteen years to fail. In the television tape, she showed those years. I wondered if anyone else could see them.

Pontrier turned the VCR off. The TV set roared the *hush* of static, and I turned it down but not off. I don't know why. It was like sheltering under something to hear the neutral noise about me. He took the tape from the machine and handed it to me. He gave me a business card, which I didn't read. I said, "That's all?"

"You don't need medical assistance, on account of you give it. And you got that tall doctor there. You understand the situation pretty good, and you can call me. You will. They always do. Eight, ten times a week, some of them. A *day*, even. Doesn't help. Doesn't hurt anything. Built the time right into my schedule. *Families*, I call it. Write it on my calendar for the week. Liaison. You can't liaise without talking to 'em. Call if you want to. Any news, you'll hear. From us. Me. Right away. Promise. Do think they're gonna turn her loose. Woman. You know." He sounded like a machine winding down.

"You have a long drive back." I said.

"Traveling's part of it. See the country. Rather see some other part of it, no insult intended."

"It's an acquired taste."

"Like okra," he said. Whinny, gum and tooth. He took his glasses off.

He went into the kitchen and soon he was back with his case and his coat, and soon he was gone from the house. At the narrow window beside the door, I watched the journalists surround him. There were two more trucks now, large white ones with lights and antennas on top. As he stopped to speak, the air and lawn in front of the house leaped into bright intensity as television lights came on. It was like a lightning strike.

In the living room, again, I put the tape on and I bent before the set. There was Belinda, her hair, her eyes, her breasts. A prurient boy, I looked behind me, then reversed the tape and looked again—she wore no brassiere. I could see her nipples at the soft fabric of her shirt. Belinda on TV, without a bra, I told myself. I rewound and looked again: my wife on reruns, available as starkly as this, and to strangers.

I looked again, and then once more. I was her audience, now. I turned off the set and the VCR and went toward the stairs to fetch Kate and Melissa and Linda. They were descending as I reached the staircase. Linda walked past me, heading for the living room. Kate, holding Melissa's hand, stood where she was.

Then a roar came from the living room, the static of the VCR. The tape began to play, and the *hush* gave way to Belinda, speaking. The stranger on TV was talking to us, and her daughter Linda sat on the sofa before her, smoking, clicking the switch to REVIEW and then PLAY. She sought the instant when her mother stopped reading her script. We stood at the stairs and we watched her watch her mother, over and over, lost and found, the *hush* and then Belinda's voice, Belinda's breasts, Belinda's hair, and Linda sighing out smoke and making her mother say to her, "It's true," "It's true," "It's true."

NAME THE NAME

M Y WIFE isn't local. She finds it alarming that so much of where
we live is named for someplace else: Pompey, Fabius, Mara-
thon, Mycenae, Euclid, Cicero, Tripoli. Here—Syracuse and Lebanon,
Rome—in the center of the state of New York, where it often snows
in May and always in April, three hundred miles from Manhattan,
the children are entitled. Whether they are kissed for their beauty or
scalded in punishment, whipped with a belt or beaten by fists or sung
to at dawn, and in a mobile home or a three-floor Colonial with central
chimney and hand-adzed joists, they are the young and we allow for
them in the hamlets and the trailer parks, in the yellow-brick Victorian
synagogue, in the farmhouse turned by candles and chrome-plated
cross into a church.

I am the man in the unwashed dark blue truck who comes up the
snow-sealed rural road or into the street behind the boarded-over tan-
nery. If your child can't come to school, the law demands that someone bring the school to him, and I am the carrier of entitlements, with
my briefcase scuffed like cheap shoes, and my long thick overcoat and
clumsy gloves, with a white metal toolbox in the back of the truck that
I fill each day with textbooks and ruled coarse paper, and the forms I

turn in to the board every night. I am the education they must send. In Smyrna and Coventry, Lower Cincinnatus and New Berlin, I'm the chance.

At eleven in the morning, while thick wet snow fell without sticking onto crocuses and daffodils, I drank reheated coffee sweetened with condensed milk and light brown sugar by a woman too embarrassed to look at my face. She wore polyester pants with a black and white check, a man's gray sweatshirt over a heavy flannel shirt, and big slippers lined with synthetic fur; on top of each slipper was the face of a dog with a long pink tongue. She wore no socks, and the chapped rough redness of her ankles was an intimacy between us. She was feeding soft wood—scraps of lumber, chunks of pine—to a big, hot wood stove. I could smell the almost-kerosene of the creosote in her stovepipe.

Her face was wedge-shaped, and soft. Inside her fat, and under her thinning light hair, within the smell of smoke and cheap deodorant, a shy, myopic thirty-five-year-old woman was waiting for my verdict on her twelve-year-old girl. I said, "Thank you for the coffee," and while she looked at her painted-over Hoosier cabinet, I said, "Myrna's a bright girl. I'm not sure about her social studies, but I think that's only because she didn't finish the chapter. She could do it."

"I'll mind her."

"I spoke to her about it."

"I was the same age as her when I—" She pointed at her soft belly. Her fair skin was red. I saw tears behind her thick glasses.

"Not with Myrna."

She shook her head. "That would have been too young to be her. No. It was a baby bore itself early and dead. A, you know, miscarriage. I remember my grandmother—I lived with them. My mother didn't have the strength for any more kids, so she give me to them. My grandmother told me to thank Jesus it was dead. I didn't think of nothing like that, though. I cried and cried. I wanted that baby. I was like her. Twelve."

"So she'll have the baby?"

"I believe she will," she said. "Lord willing and her strength all right. She's a strong girl."

"Well," I said. "I thank you for the coffee. I'm very pleased with how Myrna's doing with her studies. Will she go back to school?"

"Oh, yes," her mother said. "I'll be helping with the baby. She has to go on and live out her life. We can afford another mouth."

"Fine," I said. "Good. And the father?"

"Myrna's?"

"Her baby's."

"No, they're too young," she said. "He'll have to live with his own mommy and daddy."

I remember how I looked at the crazy lenses of her thick glasses and then nodded. I remember being angry with myself for being surprised. I smiled my good-byes.

In the truck, I scribbled my report. I saw Myrna at the window over the long front porch. She waved like a little girl. She was a little girl. So I waved back. For the principal and the board of education, for all whose rules—and weren't they right?—required that a pregnant schoolgirl in her seventh month stay home, I waved. She would come to school with her baby anyway, and her friends would surround her, and certain teachers, even, would smile their applause. She would be heroic to them, and her trophy would be eleven years and eleven months away from a pregnancy leave and a visiting teacher like me. I wondered if one day I would teach Myrna's child and sit in my truck and wave to her like this.

When I arrived at the hospital, they were removing lunch dishes in the corridor. Outside Intensive Care, in the small lounge, people sat to wait, and they all looked as though they wanted to smoke. I hadn't smoked in a dozen years, and the NO SMOKING sign always made me wish for a cigarette. I buzzed and they asked who I was. I told them, and that I was there for Leslie DuBois—say "Du-Boyce"—and they admitted me. I always found myself wishing they wouldn't. In her room, one of eight in a large squared doughnut of such rooms surrounding the ICU nurses' station, Leslie lay. I called, above the hiss and click of her ventilator, "How's the spider?" I had told her that she looked arachnoid, nested in the IV feed lines and ventilator hose. Her tired eyes blinked several times, and the urgent O of her mouth, which was taped about the thick tube that went down her throat and breathed for her, twitched.

She wrote to me. On the Invisible Pad, with its gray pudding of undersheet, and its clear plastic topsheet that lifted to erase what she wrote with a mute pen, a pointed red wooden stick, Leslie wrote, in crooked block lines, NOT SPIDER FLY. Leslie DuBois had taken most of the pills in her parents' house. She had telephoned her doctor. So she'd lived. No one was certain when her brain would tell her lungs to breathe out carbon dioxide, or remind her legs to bear her weight, so Leslie, who had lived, lived here. And she was required to be entitled to me: they forced me at her, and she wrote to me on her Invisible Pad, and I called back above her ventilator, and then, for twenty minutes or so, we played school.

I said, "The Jersey Devils are the Cinderella team in the playoffs this year!"

She wrote, GRETZKY IS GOD.

"Wrong team," I called. She sweated long rivulets. She shuddered under the workings of the ventilator as if she were a ragged-running car. "Your metabolism needs tuning," I yelled.

Gray-blue pale, dank of hair, smelling sour and showing in her eyes how embarrassed she was when I bent close, she tore the cover up, then wrote HATE HOCKEY.

"Why didn't you tell me? I do too."

She tore and printed. LOVE U.

"I love you, Leslie," I said. "But you didn't do your homework, did you?"

HATE POEMS.

"Gotta read 'em. Gotta graduate on time."

WHY?

"Because when you get better you'll want to go to college. Stay up all night doing homework about poems. That's why."

BOLOGNA.

"Nothing wrong with your spelling," I called. I found on her crowded night table the Xeroxed sheet I had given her. We were doing Keats's sonnet "When I Have Fears That I May Cease to Be," which after that first line goes on to worry "Before my pen has glean'd my teeming brain." I said, "Leslie. *You* had fears that you might cease to be."

Her intensely dark eyes—the pupils looked all-black to me—swung up to lock with mine. LIFE NOT POEMS, she wrote.

"Poems are life. They can be. They can be *about* life. Very respectably. Very persuasively."

MY LIFE NO POEM.

She lay back as if she had declaimed. I was exhausting her. I said, "Let me. You're telling me, he, he does things like that 'glean'd' and that kind of phony-sounding 'do sink,' and you're probably saying to yourself, 'He stuck that in for the rhythm of the line. Nobody says "*do sink*."'Right?" She flapped a wrist. "Right," I said. "Well, I can't argue. The 'do sink' isn't his greatest work. It doesn't sound natural. Of course, you could argue that while poetry comes from a natural impulse—to talk!—it either sounds natural, like us, or it doesn't. He was writing in 1818. You have to be fair about that. Maybe they talked like that in 1818. I frankly don't think so. I think he gimmicked it up to make the rhythm work for him. But how about 'And when I feel, fair creature of an hour!/That I shall never look upon thee more'? Is he talking about his imagination? I mean, that's what the poem's about, right? A guy who doesn't want to die because he wants to get his writing done? Or is this part, the *thee* part, about, well, love?"

She was sleeping. While she slept, her chest shuddered and sweat poured up from her skin. And she wept. I swore—I swear—I could tell the difference between the perspiration and the tears. *Psychoanalysis of suicides induced through poetry by Doctor Farce! Romantic poetry a specialty!* I sat back, and in the low aqua-colored plastic chair beside her bed, in the rhythm of her ventilator's vacuum-and-compression, in the high-pitched *beep* her IV monitors cried as the clear solution in the sacs ran down through her, I closed my eyes and in the heat of her room I slept.

The tearing sound of her eraser sheet woke me. I leaned forward so quickly, my back hurt. "What?" I said. "What?"

Leslie looked across at me—our heads were almost on a level—and her eyes looked pleased. I reached, automatically, for her Invisible Pad. It said WHAT COLLEGE?

"Oh," I said—surely shouted—"Wellesley! Vassar! Radcliffe! Let's think *big*!"

Her fingers moved, and I replaced her pad in them. It made the tearing sound, and then she wrote.

SHAMPOO NEXT.

"You want me to wash your hair? Sure. How?"

She moved her hand, I gave her the pad, and she added, without tearing, TIME.

"I will. You have them get the stuff, and I will. I'll talk to you about colleges. I'll ask some questions, and I'll tell you. And I'll—you want me to bring in hair magazines? You know: magazines with pictures of hairdos? I'll give you a perm."

She took the pad back and pulled up the sheet. KISS.

So I leaned down into the clicking and hissing and tape and perspiration and her tears, and I kissed her on the cheek and on the eye. *Till love and fame to nothingness do sink.* I said, "You're right about the poem. You're wrong, but you're also right. Look on the Xerox sheet, and read what I wrote for you about sonnets. About the form. The fourteen lines, the rhyme scheme, you remember. Read the poem again, and we'll talk about it. All right?"

She waved good-bye with just the fingers on her left hand. Her eyes were closed.

"All right," I said.

In the corridor, a big clumsiness of briefcase and coat and gloves and forms and pens, I said to a couple of the ICU nurses, "When is she going to be okay?" They watched as I tried to put everything where it should go. I looked up from the floor where I kneeled, my back still aching, and stuffed my briefcase full.

One of them, whose name was May, a slender woman with short legs, said, "Are we talking miracles or medicine here? And would you like the fact or the fiction?"

I stood up slowly and fought my way into my coat.

"How about you?" May said. "How're you guys, you know, handling it?"

"I'm on my way to the jail right now."

"You want some leftover lunch? You look lousy."

"You never said that when we were drinking in the Solsville Hotel," I said.

She pushed her rimless glasses back up onto her nose and stepped a step closer. She smelled like chewing gum and soap. She put her fingers over the top of my trousers and her thumb around my belt buckle. "Say hello to your wife," she said, smiling, pulling once, then twice, at the top of my pants. "Take care."

I stepped back. "I'm shampooing Leslie next week, all right?"

May nodded, and the other one nodded. May let go of my pants. "You're putting on weight," she said.

I shrugged.

"Misery must agree with you." She turned, and then the other one did, and they went along the corridor. I buttoned my coat and went out through the smokeless visitors' lounge, wishing as I went.

I always kept the jail for last. It was a county jail, where prisoners waited for trials or indictment for minor offenses, or were held if they were being transported from, say, Auburn to the psychiatric hospital in Rome. The jail was in the basement of the county sheriff's offices, and was across the street from the courthouse, across another street from the parking lot of a Holiday Inn. If you stood on the steps of the elegant Victorian that housed the jail, you could see our public library and a government office building where people made arrangements for food stamps. It seemed like a rather large town, but it was really a very small city, the smallest in the state. In order to qualify for state aid in repairing the streets, our city had to file its street plan. We were found to have too few streets, according to a government rule, so we renamed certain avenues at either end. West Broughton had run, in two blocks, across the main street (a state two-lane) into (unsurprisingly) East Broughton. The town fathers renamed them, and the unsuspecting motorist now drove from West Broughton, across Route 12, and up a street called Samson Drive, never encountering East Broughton or any other Broughton. I nipped the yellow light and drove across 12 onto Samson, which was in the general direction of the jail, but which wouldn't bring me directly there.

Samson ended at a narrow lane that went up a steep hill toward a small municipal swimming pool named for a phys ed teacher who'd been thought to die in Korea. But he'd come back. The town was embarrassed by its own emotion, I suppose, and the poor fellow was punished—though everyone treated him well in person—by the neglect his pool received—clogged pool drains and a torn umbrella for the lifeguard. The road needed repaving and its potholes were his payment for the municipal embarrassment. My son had worked there in the summer of his sixteenth year. I walked around the pool and looked down into its gray slush growing like a fungus in the shaded end. I climbed up onto the chair where he'd sat and I sat in the cold air and crossed my legs, leaned forward against the weight of my overcoat as if I might declaim. There was nothing, though, to say there, just as there was little to say in jail. As the afternoon darkened, I went there.

At the desk, near the wooden staircase with the tops of its newel posts carved into giant acorns, a deputy sat to log me in and reach to pat my shoulder. I knew where to go—through the heavy wooden door beneath the stairs, and then, on metal rungs, down. Another deputy waited for me and opened the heavy barred gate so that I stood at the open end of a U made of cells. A television set high on the wall showed the cable sports channel. A local physician who doubled as the county's jail doctor was examining an Oriental man. The doctor, who smiled at me over the new prisoner's shoulder, said, "You may *think* a thing like that just heals. Let me tell you: very little 'just heals.' You get help, or you get sick. Understand?"

The deputy, who'd come in with me, was carrying his magazine as he escorted me to the cell. I said, "Bobby, I didn't know they were allowed to sell magazines like that."

He said, "Oh, yeah. The first amendment covers crotches now."

He opened the door and I went in. The smell of the disinfectant wasn't unpleasant. I discovered that each time I was there. I put my briefcase on his bunk, and then I looked at him. I think my body was confused about drawing careful breath, lest I smell something awful, and looking through hooded eyes, lest I see something cruel. I winced when our eyes met. But he was just a boy, a very tall and muscular sixteen-year-old boy who should have been attending his junior year in high school but who waited trial for vandalism. He had broken into the high school computer room twice. He'd done damage. And we all agreed, after the counseling and the tests, after the generous leniency of the school board, and after my wife and I had posted bail the first time, for larcenous behavior and several varieties of felony, that this time, awaiting hearings, Charlie—Chilly to his friends—would spend the dozen days in jail.

He was larger than I, and his hand, when I pulled at it, seemed to weigh more than I remembered hands weighing. Everything about him was large, and too big for me to move easily. His face was the same clenched thickening face of a boy I remembered as pretty. He looked at me with sharp-eyed disgust.

But I asked it anyway. "Charlie, you okay?"

His expression remained. He gestured at the one-piece toilet and the bunk bed and the metal bureau built into the wall.

"Nine days to go," I said.

He sat down on the bunk and looked away from me. I opened my coat and sat beside him. He wore a light gray one-piece boiler suit. It was unbuttoned almost to the belt line, and I saw how little hair he had on his chest, or on the arms I saw in his rolled-up sleeves, or on the smooth, hard face. I was sweating in the heat of the jail, but I wore my coat anyway. His skin looked dry.

"Mom's—"

"I don't want to talk about Mom, please."

I nodded. I was going to say *crazy* or *dying* or *praying*, and none would have been right, and none would have been fair. She was doing what I was doing: hating the decision, hating its occasion, hating our life, and hating the government that had jailed our son. She was also, as I was, approving the decision, cooperating with the sheriff and the board of education, and we were hating *us*. While we mourned our living son, we ground our teeth while we slept and in the morning shared our nightmares about punishing him.

I put my hand on his long, heavy leg, and he twitched away. I said, as he must have known I would, and as I knew he loathed hearing, "We love you, Charlie."

But he tamely nodded. So I pressed.

"You know that?"

He nodded again. He said, "Can I ever come home?"

I said, still looking ahead, "I think they want to bring it to trial."

"Prison farm," he said.

"For juveniles."

"I don't think it's as little as that word."

"No," I said. "They're tough bastards there. It's a mean, bad place. We're trying to keep you out."

"The lawyer was here," he said.

"I know. We talked to him afterward."

"He must be expensive. His suit was very far out."

"He's got a closetful. Yes."

"Does he think—"

"I don't know, honey." He looked up. I looked over. Neither of us had called him *honey* since he was small. Now, it seemed to me, in his long and heavy age, looking at his life taking shapes he had never imagined, he was small. "But we'll do everything, *everything*, we can."

"Except let me come home."

I focused on my slush-dampened shoes.

"I know," he said. "Reality."

"I didn't use that word with you, did I?"

"Isn't that what this is supposed to be about?"

It's what it *is* about, hon."

"I know. But I wish I could come home again."

"Honey, you'll come home again. That isn't—"

"Won't they take me straight from here to the prison farm after the trial?"

I couldn't look at him, because I couldn't admit to him that I had never considered his not, eventually, being home. "Reality," he'd said. I reached to throw the overcoat off my shoulders, but it felt too heavy for my hands. My chest and stomach were soaking through my shirt, but I wouldn't have been surprised to shiver.

"Here," he said. He stood, and I did too, and he went behind me and reached around, and he pulled the coat back and off.

"Thank you," I said. "I don't—"

"Yeah," he said. "That's what happens to me."

"It does?"

"A lot. All the time. That's all that happens here, except food and the bathroom, and the lights going off. TV."

"It does?"

"You want to see my homework, Dad?"

"You did it?"

"I had the time."

He handed me several sheets of the rough paper I had left with him. His handwriting, slanted acutely, yet rounded at the tops of looped letters, capitals especially, looked as it had looked when he was in the sixth or seventh grade. I was afraid to read his work. I was afraid that he had written about himself, or us. And I was afraid that he had not. "Great," I said. "Should I read this at home? Why don't I do that."

Okay," he said. "I don't care. You can bring it tomorrow. You coming tomorrow?"

"Of course I am," I said. "That's what I do."

"Okay. How about economics? The chapter quiz on inflation and unemployment, all of that."

He took a sheet from the looseleaf notebook I'd left with him, and he examined it before passing it over. I opened his text to the end-of-chapter test, and I read the questions about lowered market demands for labor in an inflationary society. I kept looking at the graphs, and at the circles with their colored pie slices.

"You gonna grade it at home?"

I thought of sitting in our kitchen and drinking coffee and reading Charlie's quiz. I could see myself checking his answers: DOWN. UP. MARKETPLACE. SPIRAL. I saw his answers as if pressed, with Leslie's leadless pencil, onto Leslie's Invisible Pad. I saw myself standing soon, as I would. I saw myself waving from the door of Charlie's cell as I had waved to Myrna from the cab of my truck. Where we live is named for someplace else. How we live is named for something else. I saw myself, the traveling teacher, sitting in our kitchen with my pale wife. I would work at my exam. The question would ask me: Name the name for what we're living now. LOVE U Leslie had written. BOLOGNA. Charlie said, "Dad?" Name the name.

TO THE HOOP

DUANE AND I didn't talk about how she killed herself or where. With us, it was as if anything to do with mothers or wives had begun two years ago. I had never told him in the first place that Jackie packed not only every suitcase she could find in the house, but cardboard boxes, brown paper bags, and plastic carryalls. It was as though we'd decided to move, and Jackie had left without me. In the bedroom was everything she'd owned—souvenir stones, creased postcards, old photo albums, discarded reading glasses, and out-of-date clothes she hadn't worn for many years. There were thirty-five shoes. I looked for half an hour for a missing stack-heeled cordovan pump that would have slid onto Jackie's left foot.

She had taken a room at the Howard Johnson's, not ten minutes from where I worked. She had eaten enough complimentary capsules, spansules, and tablets, manufactured by my firm, and had washed them down with enough complimentary cough suppressant and her own dark rum, to do the job, and stop her heart.

Nor did we discuss the women I sometimes brought home after about a year had passed. The women were good sports, and so was Duane. I would introduce them, and he would duck his head and step forward, blushing, and would shake their hand in his big fingers, then escape. He smiled at them, but not at me. And even after Cheryl stayed some months with me—with us, you'd have to say—we didn't speak too much of her. She was the last. After Cheryl, it was Duane and me.

And I stopped telling him stories of how at fifteen I had been strong and tall, though smaller than he was, and able to run all day in two- and three-man half-court games in Brooklyn's summer heat at Wingate Field. I wanted to tell him that I'd finally figured out why boys would play on blacktop courts from eight in the morning until the sun went down. It was because the other teams who challenged us would not only win the game: they'd win the court. It was winner-take-all, I wanted to say. Of course, he knew that.

I was careful to be silent about Duane's own play. I watched him, though, as he practiced outside our house in the country hills. In cold autumn winds, in thick winter snow—he'd use a shovel and a push broom to clear the old dairy ramp outside the barn on which his back-board was mounted—Duane made lay-ups, sank his smooth jump shot from fifteen feet out, leaped again and again to cradle the rebounded ball so that his feet didn't touch the ground until he'd rolled the ball over the rim. In games at his high school, against less muscular boys with fewer skills and less flexible bodies, he grew gawky, he—who could practice in a snowstorm all of an afternoon—became breathless, and then he ran with stiffening thighs and locked elbows; he would forget to set a screen for the shooting guard, he would neglect to block out opposing forwards and would yield up rebounds, he would panic when passed the ball and would shoot from too far out. And I, forgetting myself, would cry from the bleachers, "*Power* move!" I would bellow, "To the hoop! Take it to the *hoop*!"

In game after game I saw his coach let him play fewer minutes. He came to sit on the bench more bunchily, hunched in upon himself as if hiding. At home he insisted on more silence about his play, and his grades began to slide—not enough to provoke a call from school, but enough for me to notice. I saw problems coming. They were the weather I watched for as if I farmed for a living, instead of running communications at the corporate offices they'd shipped me to from headquarters in Cincinnati. During the day, I ran our house organ, writing articles on management shifts and new products, consulting about publicity and community relations, lying for a living, trying hard to make it sound as if I told pure truth about stomach settlers and decongestants and the people who lived here in the center of New York State, with its harsh long winters and splendid, suddenly concluded summers, manufacturing pharmaceuticals and mourning for the Cincinnati symphony and civic theater, the movie houses and bus lines of a *real* city, as they called it. I watched with a cruel contentment as my colleagues drew their pleasure from tales of each other's failures and malfeasances. I was a New Yorker. If I wasn't *there*, then almost anywhere would do.

I called him Dude because that is what his teammates called him, slapping high-fives with the lazy slow-motion casualness they saw among black players on television. These boys were white, and their bodies knew, if their minds didn't, or their tongues wouldn't say so, that the dark grace they imitated was the standard for the toughness of their practice habits and the courage of their play.

In the car after a Tuesday night scrimmage, as I drove us home, I yawned and made a joke of my fatigue by stretching my jaws immensely and offering the noise of what I told him was an aging hippo in heat. On the unlit snowy country roads which glowed beneath our lights, then disappeared into the general dark behind us, he turned to me and said, in a low, controlled, and sullen voice, "Would you mind not shouting at me during the game?"

"Oh. Hey, I was shouting *to* you. You know, cheering for you."

"I know. I kept looking at you. Did you see me?"

"I did. I thought you might be glad to know I was there."

"It made me nervous. I played lousy. All six minutes he had me in there."

"You looked a little tight."

"I looked a little lousy."

"Tentative, maybe."

He didn't answer.

"I meant, you didn't seem to—"

"I know what tentative means."

"Sorry. I will shut up. As long as you don't think I was *scolding* you. I hate it when parents scold their kids on the court."

"I think I'm screwing up because you're there."

I turned in at our short driveway. "You don't want me to come, Dude?"

"And would you call me Duane, please?"

"I will. And I'll stay away from games for a while. Right?"

"Thank you," he said as formally as if I'd picked up his athletic bag and handed it to him.

"You're welcome," I said.

In the cold kitchen, while Duane turned that morning's approximation of order into something shaggier, I lit a fire in the wood stove and made us sandwiches. We always ate some snack before he yawned his way through homework before going to bed. Seeing me slice ham, he said, "Nothing for me, thanks. I'm keeping my weight down."

He was on the stairs, and something like "Good night" trailed his slow and heavy-footed climb. So I was alone, with ham and good intentions, and the usual fears that ranged from drugs to teenage schizophrenia. Jackie had died alone, and in silence. She had left us no word.

I put more wood into the stove, closed its damper, took off my jacket and tie, and sat with the day's mail. Letters still, though rarely, came for Jackie and me, mostly flyers and occasional cards from people I'd forgotten. I sometimes thought of our lovemaking, or afternoons in shopping malls. But mostly, these days, I remembered Jackie's rage. Once, when she was saying she hated having to love me, she had snarled—I'd seen her even teeth. With her face red and her teeth showing, she had sat before me. And then she had walked to the stove, bearing our cups, and had poured us more coffee. And then she had taken both our cups away, before we'd sipped, before she sat again, and had emptied them into the sink. She'd stood over it, with her back to me, and had said, "When I went to bed with you on Friday nights back then, this was not my idea of Saturday mornings." She had left her Coach bags, and her printed personal stationery, and a basketball player who, when the ball was in his hands, grew wide of eye, twisted at the mouth, and leaden of limb.

I fell asleep in the kitchen, listening to the split cherry-wood sizzle and pop. It filled the air with sweetness. I could almost taste the wood, and it made me wish that Duane could. When I woke, the kitchen was cold. Duane and I were in the house, but that didn't help either of us.

The next afternoon, late, when Duane met me in the school parking lot after practice, he threw his gym bag into the back of the car, dropped into his seat as if he'd been slung there, and he said, "I want to quit."

"The team?"

He nodded.

"Why?"

"It isn't any fun anymore."

I drove us up into the hills. The sun was down, the sky was low and dirty-looking. It would snow, and the snow would stick, and in the morning we would have to dig the car out.

"We'll need firewood brought in tonight," I said.

"Will you let me?"

"Quit the team?"

"Yeah."

He was big and handsome, my gaunt boy. His hair grew low on his forehead, and it was curly, and he hated it. He was always plucking at it, as if he could force it to straighten. I noticed him doing that on the court one night, before he told me not to come anymore. I saw that the worse he failed to set a screen or pass the ball off, the more he smoothed the hair on his neck, or pushed it alongside his temples, or repeatedly pulled at the ripples of his curls. Cheryl, who was ten years younger than I, and maybe ten years tougher, had said, "He's as pretty as your wife must have been. He's got a woo-woo body like you, but he's as pretty as you are plain. Matter of fact, when I compare him to you, I wonder what it is you *do* have. You got legs," she'd said. And when I'd looked down at my feet, Cheryl had said, "I mean *legs*. You keep on going. You last. You aren't flashy, but you last. You know?"

I didn't, because I hadn't. She'd gone too, and I had heard she lived with the manager of a big sporting goods store. He drove a car that was famous among the younger chemists and junior executives at the firm because it was as tastelessly painted as any car they'd seen. Cheryl was almost stocky, but not fat, and she loved clothes too tight for her powerful thighs and thick waist. Her hair was bright blond, and she'd look you in the eye and talk to you hard, but rarely mean. She had made me feel optimistic. She had left because the feeling was a lie. "I just hate sitting around being pale," she said, "you know?"

I said to Duane in the car as the first flakes fell on the windshield, "No. You stay. You fight it."

"Fight what?"

"Whatever's getting at you. Was practice bad?"

"The two minutes I scrimmaged weren't bad."

"Are you convincing him you lost it, or did he think so in the first place?"

"I didn't lose it."

"You can play basketball?"

He nodded his head.

"So go play basketball. You don't quit."

"How can I play basketball on the bench?"

"Sit up extra straight."

I insisted that we eat together that night, and I forced him to help me cook. He carefully planted his elbows on the table and let his mouth grow slack. I heard his food grow pulpy in his teeth. I refused to react. In Brooklyn, we had called it a game face: the stony eyes and unexpressive mouth with which you showed your opponent on the court that you knew no fear, could run forever without panting, and hadn't worried about *anything* for over a year. Duane wore his, and I wore mine. We choked down our overcooked hamburgers in silence, and I washed the same six dishes over slowly, until he went up to his homework.

It was, for an instant that night, as if Jackie were away but in reach. I wanted to call her and ask what she would do if she lived with a troubled son as so many mothers do. I wanted to ask her what we, as parents, *really* thought. I'd often not known until she'd told me. Cheryl always had an opinion, and Duane had always known it, resented it, fought it, but had always been impressed. When I'd admitted to him, one weekend, that Cheryl and I were apart, he'd said, "Now you'll have to figure out my curfew on your own."

I went upstairs now to his room and I knocked. He mumbled something, and I opened his door into the hot, heavy air of caged adolescent. U-2 sang songs of social concern he played loudly, and a lifetime of underwear and long-legged jeans lay on the rug. I thought of photographs of airplane crash sites. He was on his bed, looking at a textbook page covered with diagrams. Then, as if he were timing himself, he slowly turned his head and raised his brows.

I didn't throw his jeans at him or shriek about attitudes or the impossibility of studying with such music on. I spoke softly, and he turned the tape player down and asked me to repeat myself. I did. "I said I wanted to apologize for that crack about sitting up straight. You can't play ball while you're on the bench and it feels lousy. I'm sorry you're not playing a lot. I think you're tensing up, psyching yourself out. I think it's your mother, maybe me. You can play yourself out of that, I think. You can get your form back. You want me to talk to your coach?"

"No."

"Because I will, Duane. I'll do—"

"No, thanks."

"—anything I can."

"No thanks."

I stood there and I nodded my head a lot. I said, "Well," and nodded again. He had gone back to looking at the page. His hand reached out for the volume control and I did not speak of it. I backed up, and the door swung shut, as if his thoughts had gently closed it with a slow motion, a single click.

Downstairs, I did what I always do when I have a problem to solve: I forced it into words. On a legal pad I took from my briefcase, I wrote his name at the top in capitals: DUANE. Then, beneath it, along the left-hand margin ruled in two red vertical lines, I wrote, in my finest, firmest hand:

      DRUGS?

      ILLNESS?

      JACKIE?

      CHERYL?

      ME?

      TEAMMATES?

      BEING 15?

      SEX?

      COACHING?

      CLASSMATES?

      LIFE.

I balled the list and I fed it to the wood stove. And so much for words.

Cheryl had said, "You're my first boyfriend who always wears a suit to work. Some guys wear sports jackets, you know, some kind of tweed or corduroy. But they can decide to wear a crewneck, or a sleeveless pullover. But you wear a whole suit, every day. I'm gonna be measuring people's wardrobes against you from now on."

A year before, we'd been lying in bed, wearing my pajamas. Jackie had given them to me—navy blue with red piping, shipped upstate by Brooks Brothers. Duane had gone for the weekend to a friend's house, probably to watch R-rated movies on the VCR. And Cheryl and I were drinking the wine she had brought and were talking about her favorite topic: Cheryl's future. "I'm just gathering myself," she loved to say. On the little TV screen in the bedroom, a late Friday night basketball game from L.A. was showing, and the slow motion replay of James Worthy exploding into a killer jam for two points plus the foul shot prompted Cheryl to point a stubby white finger at the black man panthering the ball. "I'm like him," she'd said. "I'm gathering myself for something like that. One of these days, brother, *wham*!" I all but tore my pajama coat off her after that. And we were together for a strong, friendly several months.

"I can't be anybody's medicine," Cheryl had finally said.

"Maybe you're mine, though," I'd told her.

"Then maybe I don't want to be. I don't like sickness."

So I couldn't call Jackie, and I couldn't call Cheryl, and what I'd called to Duane hadn't worked. It left me with myself, one-on-one.

I quit work at midday, canceling a lunch date and a conference about the new German contraceptive foam we were marketing. I asked my assistant to deliver the Christmas issue of our magazine to the printer, and I went shopping. Past ski costumes and NFL shirts, in the back, near cardiac fitness machines and free-weight rigs, I found the backboard, basket, and pole I was looking for.

Cheryl was there. I had known she would be. I told her, "I didn't come in here to pester you, Cheryl."

She shook her head and her long hair swung. "I know that. You see? You're putting yourself down. Still."

"I don't mean to."

"I guess you don't. But you do it. You're so fuckin *sad*, dammit. Now you, suppose you tell me what you want and I'll see if I can sell it to you and let's us not have this discussion ever again in our lives. All right?"

"A backboard and hoop to go on a metal pole," I said.

She pointed. "This one you were looking at already. You losing weight?"

"Nope."

"My sweet ass you're not. Are you sick? Are you in love?"

She was wearing a black turtleneck, black shorts over black tights, low, soft white boots. I didn't want to look like a man looking over a woman. So I studied the metal frame of the outdoor backboard, and I said, "No. No more love these days, Cheryl."

"You old bore. This one's got fiberglass on one side, metal on the other. It goes on this two-piece pole, which is the full ten feet, Duane'll love it for Christmas, and he deserves it, so you buy it for him. Is your life all right?"

"I hear that yours is."

"Oh, Dave? We're doing some kind of collision trip. He thinks we're heading for marriage, and I know we aren't, and he's gonna bang smack into what's what, and what's not, and then we'll be through."

"You don't make it easy," I said.

She shook her head. "Nope. I never did."

When she looked at me again, I said, "You were always very nice to me, Cheryl. You were a pal."

"A pal," she said. She inspected the cord of the basketball net. "How's the Dude doing on the team? JV, is it?"

"To tell you the truth, he wants to quit."

"Are they sitting him down, or is he playing bad? You tell him for me that coming up to JV at his age is a tough transition. He might do better on the freshman team."

"I don't think he'd hear me if I told him."

"He does sound like a teenaged boy. You won't let him quit?"

"No."

"No, you wouldn't. It must be tough at home, though, after practice and all. After the games."

"No more than any other undeclared war," I said.

She looked at me angrily. "That boy isn't in a war, and you know it. He's in his life. And that's worse, I don't wonder."

"Sure. It just makes some evenings very long."

She slapped her order pad onto the carton in which the backboard came. Then she lined her pen up alongside it. She put her hands on her waist, and then she sighed. For an instant she was silent, and then she asked, "Who do you talk about it with? You know, at the office and all."

"Nobody. You'd have guessed that."

"Well, I did," she said.

"Yes."

"Yes, yourself." She looked up, as if at the sun, or at a clock. She crossed her strong wrists in front of her and asked, "Would you like me to visit you guys sometimes?"

She was looking at me, and I couldn't look anyplace else except her broad, cheerful, muscular face with its two horizontal lines scored onto her brow that told how hard she had to work, sometimes, to smile. "I'll take the set," I said to her. "Pole, backboard, hoop. Is that a collapsible hoop? With those pins that release the hoop from the backboard if you get caught on it dunking or something?"

She looked at me a little longer, then she said, "That's right. What'd you do, get strong or something?"

I said, "Anything but that, and you know it."

She was writing down the stock numbers of the display models. "You going to hire somebody with a backhoe to come on up after Christmas and plant that pole in the hard ground?"

"You use a pickax," I said. "You keep hacking with it, and you sweat like hell, I guess, and you do it. The ground's not really frozen yet."

She looked into my eyes again. She said, "I can still make you blush."

On Christmas morning, I woke up early. I always do. I went downstairs and made a pot of coffee. I lit the bulbs on the tree that I'd brought in on Christmas Eve to decorate alone. Duane had offered to help, and the cartons of balls and hangings, and our silence, had almost defeated me. I had forgotten how much we'd bought for Christmas, the silly spidery drawings that Duane had made in class to hang on the tree, and the little dolls from her childhood that Jackie had insisted, every year, we use. I omitted them. Duane remembered them and hung each one. On Christmas morning, I declared to the tree and the dolls, "I am getting better." Then I lit the tree and called upstairs to Duane, and he came down with a sheepish expression. Anticipation, and childhood's habitual Christmas Day gladness, the pleasure of greed fulfilled—all were eroding his set, stern face. He grinned at me, and I grinned back. "Merry Christmas, Duane," I said. He stooped to lay his head near mine so I could kiss him. And from his bathrobe pocket, his gluey breath enveloping us, he took a little package and wordlessly bestowed it on me.

While I unwrapped the cassette of Linda Ronstadt singing blues songs—the card, in Duane's stringy hand, said, *For a horny old guy*— he tore open the three cartons containing his pole and backboard and hoop, as well as his lesser gifts (a Stephen King horror story, a poster of Julius Erving, a sports watch it would take a technician to start, a sultry aftershave, a Genesis tape, a terry-cloth sweatband). I went up to him, and he straightened and regarded me. I hugged him hard. He didn't hug me back, but he rested his hands on my hips and let me squeeze his ribs. "Duane, I love you," I said. I said my prayer: "We're gonna be all right."

He nodded.

I said, "You want some breakfast?"

He shook his head. "I want to practice free throws," he said. "Maybe he'll play me if I get myself fouled a lot and make my free throws."

Duane, then, was outside on his cold stone court, practicing basketball while wearing gloves and a heavy sweatshirt and a woolen watch cap, looking to me like someone else's child, a stevedore, a boxer in training, some *man*, and not my former baby. I sat inside, sneaking glimpses of him from the kitchen window when I went to fill my coffee cup.

Up the packed dirt road from the south came a long white Trans Am with purple and black stripes that ran its length. It was the ultimate expression of tastelessness in cars. It went very slowly, and I could see, as it passed the house and went in the direction of our roadside barn, that Cheryl sat in the passenger seat, pointing.

The car pulled in at the side of the road, and Cheryl emerged. The driver sat behind the wheel, and I could almost feel the motor throb over the side lawn, the cold air. She removed a postholer and a pickax from the trunk. They looked too heavy for her, but she marched with a springy step. She wore a man's oversized jacket that said *Yankees* across the back. She went up to Duane and tugged his head down to her. I watched him allow her to kiss him. Then she talked about her plans, I guess, pointing at the edge of the ramp, and Duane shrugged, then nodded. Cheryl swung the pickax, and it bit. The ground wasn't solid yet, so I knew she'd get into the earth. She did. That chunky body swung and swung, regularly, evenly, with strength I knew well. When she'd pulverized the rocky soil, she used the scissor-handled postholer to scoop up dirt. I stood near the wood stove, in my bathrobe, and watched her work away.

Duane went to help her several times, but she shook him off and, after a while, he went to stand beneath his old hoop, holding the ball against his hip. She worked at wedging some heavy rocks from the hole with the postholer. Her boyfriend sat in his idling car, and I stood in my kitchen. After a while, she had a hole I could pour cement into, then stand the pole in, propping it in place with two-by-fours until it set.

Cheryl stood by her Christmas present, leaning the head of her pickax on the pile of earth she'd made. She panted and wiped at her brow with its parallel lines. She always did know how to sweat. She wore a dark stocking cap, and her bright hair stood out around it. Then she turned to Duane, who was watching her.

I said, in my kitchen, "Oh, Duane."

As if she had said that to him, in the way I heard myself say it, he dropped his basketball, and he went to her, and he stopped to seize her clumsily by the waist, then wrap his arms around her back, then hug. He bent his face down and kissed her on the cheek. I would have bet that he closed his eyes. He stepped back. Cheryl reached up and rubbed at his cheek. He nodded, then stepped back farther. As she turned and walked toward the waiting car, Duane went to retrieve his ball. Cheryl turned her head to the kitchen window and she stared at me. I believe that she knew I'd be looking. She'd supplied the hole. I could supply the pole. "I can still make you blush."

The Trans Am pulled away, and Duane watched it go. He bounced the ball once, hard, and he caught it on the rise. He dribbled slowly from the mound of dirt that Cheryl had left to the far end of the cattle ramp, where the old backboard was bolted to the barn. He stood beneath the basket, slowly bouncing the ball. I waited for him to lay it in, or step back and shoot.

My legs tensed with a boy's thoughtless strength against a concrete court at Wingate Field. Looking at Duane, I thought: Up! Take it up! And I felt him yearn vertically.

But he stopped dribbling. He held the ball. He stared up at the old backboard and he gripped the ball as though it were almost too heavy to hold at his waist, much less toss through the air, ten feet of cold, resistant air, to the hoop.

THE CHILDREN
IN THE WOODS

———◇———

DREAM ABUSE

L OUISE HEARD the liquid click of Gerry's eyes beneath his shut lids. He lay on their living room sofa and rubbed as he talked about the cases of a long, sour day while she sat a dozen feet from him, watching his long broad fingers. Underneath them, he said, "I get them—this is the final difference in what we do—I get them at the end. They're drooling down the barrels of their guns, or they swear they sometimes think they won't be able to put on the brakes when they're coming to a school crossing. Or a cattle crossing. They don't care which, by then. Or they tremble all the time. Or keep on rubbing their eyes, heh heh. I get them, they're just one dumb, needful statement, plus a coffin, short of a funeral. You get them, they're lying down drunk in the halls, or getting knocked up by their uncle. But they're kids. They're starting out, you figure. You work with them, you keep on thinking it's sup- posed to end up like *Little Women* or something."

"But you know different," she said.

"Don't I, boy," he said, sighing into his hands as, cupped along his face, they rubbed at the lids that always looked sore.

"And then you come home, and I make you forget your worries."

He stopped rubbing. He turned on one arm, blinking, and looked at her. She ducked to sip her coffee. "Yes, Louise," he said. "That's what I do. And that's what you do."

She did not say anything. But she knew that she smiled gratefully. She knew that she had just poured too much scalding coffee into her smiling mouth because her gratitude for his assurance was as powerful as her need had been to hear it. He was the counselor for the Sheriff's Department, and she was the counselor for the senior high. And every time he called it the *final* difference, Louise refused to cry.

One of Gerry's patients, a man near retirement who drove a red and white sheriff's car and who'd been said to talk to himself in public as much as he probably did inside the car out of sight, had arrested a high school junior for hanging from a pedestrian bridge near Sidney, New York while mooning. The deputy, enraged not by the boy's risk to himself, or the thought of what his body, falling from eighteen feet, might do to windshields or the amazed people behind them, had hauled the boy up and beaten him, while he was still half naked, for his nudity. "Showing your ass like that," the deputy had said, again and again, according to the boy. Louise had worked with the boy and his parents, while Gerry had worked with the deputy. During their only conference, she had heard Gerry whistling "Moon over Miami," and she'd started to giggle.

"What?" he'd said.

In the bright room, with its smell of tobacco and something like turpentine, in the steel-colored light of the Chenango Valley in winter, she had told this man who looked as much like a deputy as his clients did—tall, thick, broad of neck, slightly stooped, as though he drove all day; handsome in the way that minor actors who end up playing clever villains must once, maybe in high school, have been called handsome— "You were whistling about a moon. It made me think of that bare bottom suspended in the air over the highway."

Gerry had looked at her—had seemed to study her—as if he aimed his high forehead and big nose and little dark eyes. He moved his head as if his neck were sore, his shoulders stiff. He'd rubbed his eyes and then, the only male she'd seen do this since her second year at Oberlin, he blushed. His prominent nose and forehead made a beacon in the grim, small steel-colored room. He closed his eyes and rubbed at the lids, and she knew he was hiding.

"It's such a wonderful expression," he blurted, *"mooning."* He laughed uncontrollably, she thought, letting his teeth show, then putting his hand to his lips as if he wished to cover them. The laughter came from his belly and his big chest so that his torso shook. He was probably a man of coarse appetites, she'd thought. She had understood, even as she'd risen to wrap her long winter coat around her and look at her watch and say excuses, that she was thinking less of this competent-looking vulnerable man than someone she had left in Rochester, a lover, dark and demanding and finally cruel, whose memory filled her with sadness about herself and what she strongly suspected, and maybe feared, was lust.

He had telephoned her that night, and she'd felt an obligation toward him, as forceful as if she'd betrayed him with the man in her memory. He had been apologetic, as if he'd gone too far. A kind of pleasant romantic duty, then, started them out, and now they had lived together, without a dog or cat or child, for almost two years, in a locked-log house on a river flat outside of Plymouth, New York. They went to work early, driving separately the twelve miles to the county seat to ply their trade; they came home late, cooked together, brought in food, and then they watched films on the VCR, or read and slept early. Louise had told him about her former lovers—a few she'd called boyfriends, and the other she had tried not to dwell on. He was the one about whom Gerry had asked the most gentle, pointed questions. She had put an end to them by telling him, "You use your mind like a penis, sometimes, you know that?"

"Sex is in the head," he'd answered at once, his tone growing hard as he looked over at her from the sofa on which he lay with the Science supplement of the *Times*. "Isn't that a tenet of the feminists?"

"I'm not a feminist," she'd answered.

"Sure you are," he'd said at once, in the new, grim voice.

"I'm me. I'm only me."

"All right," he'd said, looking at the papers, "that's plenty good enough. Be you."

They left off their lovers' archaeology until, meeting for lunch at the Howard Johnson's near the County Office Building, when Louise told Gerry about a girl who had sought her help in finding a doctor to abort her pregnancy, Gerry's face had gone smooth and expressionless, then had turned bright red.

"Only a *baby*," Louise had been saying. "And *having* a baby. And needing to *kill* it."

"Is she finding the decision difficult?"

"Oh, Gerry, she's terrified. I have to talk to her some more. I'm worried about who the father is. I mean, I wouldn't be surprised if it were her own—"

"The decision," he'd said, his lips thin and pale against his flushed face. "Is it hard for her?"

"What?" Louise said. "What, Gerry?"

"You had your Mr. Wicked Desires. I—well, a woman, of course." He gave an imitation of a smile. "I mean, there was somebody who I—whew."

And she'd said, "Loved."

Gerry was rubbing at his eyes. She had reached to hold his wrist and pull his hand away from his face, and he had held the arm rigid. *He might be someone ferocious*, she'd thought.

The waitress had come and left their iceberg lettuce, their processed turkey strips and cold French bread, and she had never seen her do it, Louise realized.

Gerry at last had let his arm fall down into her small hand, and he had looked at her to say, "The waitress thinks we're fighting over the olives, I think. She had—not the waitress, you understand." His face had lost some of its bright color, then, and his eyes had grown less reptilian. "The woman I'm referring to. Apparently I made her pregnant. I'm assuming that. I decided I'd stick with the assumption. Well, it hadn't gone well, that's all. Our being together. Our time together wasn't going well. I think I'm not easy to live with. Do you?" He'd faked his help-less smile and laugh, and Louise had found herself rubbing at her own shut lids. "She aborted the baby, but she didn't want to tell me. First she aborted, then she told me, then she put only a few of her clothes into a suitcase—two suitcases, actually, plus a carry-on bag. It was like she was *escaping*. Well, she was. She was very pale. She was sweating. I thought she'd gone infected, from the procedure. First she aborted, then she told me, then she packed, and then she left."

Looking at him in the restaurant as he moved strips of salty meat among the lettuce chunks, she'd been able to say only, "How did you live, Gerry? How did you stay alive?"

"By not loving her anymore. I took myself away from her."

"But *how?*"

"I don't want you ever to know," he'd told her, letting his fork fall and rubbing at his eyes. She had wanted to reach across the little black shiny table to stroke him. He'd looked to her like a huge boy, like a wounded creature, Gerry, her child. That night, at home, instead of suggesting drinks or mentioning dinner, she had pulled him by the same strong arm she'd held at lunch, and they had gone to bed. But what she had thought would be a consolation turned to desperate, clever sex. It was she who had wept as they turned and plunged like drowners in the sea. Her tears, she later thought, could have seemed to be her comforting.

Gerry drove off to counsel deputies who beat their wives. He gave advice to department families about child abuse, alcohol abuse, and drug abuse. And Louise talked to girls who would not eat, and to parents who refused to give their children money for meals in school, and to boys who drove long cars and came to high school only when the courts compelled them. They watched cheerful black and white films with Jean Arthur or Myrna Loy. They read fat novels about pre-historic cave women or spies who could fight with their hands without breaking them. They paid bills with checks drawn on a joint account, and they sometimes went to Montreal or New York by plane, where they stayed in good hotels and ate too much, walked through exhibitions in museums, met with professional colleagues with whom the predication was that diseases were cured, conditions improved, and frailties strengthened.

During recent nights, in their antique brass bed that squeaked and wailed with age and corrosion, Gerry began to thrash. He'd always snored. He had, from the start, sometimes muttered in his sleep. But the deep snores that echoed in his big chest, which he never dressed in pajamas, but always in a dark blue T-shirt, now became the rumbled warnings of explosions to come. He rasped and boomed, and then went on to cry aloud, in a high, tight voice she at first didn't recognize as his when it wakened her. They were always warnings—"Do that again!" or "Go try and get in here, you son of a bitch!" And he would swing big looping roundhouse punches while he lay on his back or his side, sometimes hitting the thick brass posts of the bed and waking himself enough to say, "Oh," or "Sorry," and sleep again at once, and sometimes sleeping through it all, but always waking Louise. So that she lay in a quickly subsiding panic while he muttered and swore, worked up his dreamy rage, then threw his punch, then woke or didn't, then slept at once—leaving her to feel his face, to listen to his breathing and then, again, his snores, and to grow furious at him for doing this, whatever it was, to her.

In the morning, feeling sick because sleepless, or at best, even if she'd fallen back asleep, as weary as if she'd been up half the night, she might ask, "Do you remember what you dreamed last night?"

"Did I do it again?"

"Sure did. You were hummin' and fussin' and feudin'—you're a dangerous sleeper."

"I'm so sorry, Lou. You want to sleep in another room?"

"*No.*"

And then his quick and unembarrassed smile: "Good."

They collaborated again when a deputy was reported, anonymously, for being in the back seat of a patrol car on a country road with a high school girl of sixteen. The deputy was charged with statutory rape. The Sheriff's Department brought seven internal charges against him. Once the rape was dealt with, there would be other charges, and the man was done in New York State law enforcement, although, as his union adviser made clear, he could most likely uphold the law in any of two dozen distant states. The deputy was Joe Penders, the only African-American man in the department. He was short, thin, the brown-red color of cherrywood, with high, sharp checkbones, a small slender nose, and hair going prematurely gray above his ears. In short, Louise told Gerry, Penders was a dish. So, she hastened to add, was Denise Bastone. "If they lynch him," she joked, not joking, "it'll be because most of the boys in school, and more than half of their fathers, were making plans to be more or less where Joe Penders apparently was, several times a week for three weeks. She has this very short, glossy black hair, and a kind of an expression—imagine a gorgeous nun without makeup, an Italian natural beauty, all right? Put too much makeup on her, so it's just short of cheap: the I'm-in-trouble signal, you know? And then have that sweet, sweet face almost ready to drop into a pout that tells you to go to hell. Okay. That's Denise, and she's wearing a skintight, crotch-high acid-washed denim skirt, rose-colored tights, and a sweater that's illegal in Utah. I asked her if she loved him."

"He said *he* thought so," Gerry said. "It's pretty clear he's desperate to marry her in the next fifteen minutes."

"Naturally," Louise said. "Of course. Which is why Denise's answer to the question consisted of lighting a cigarette, tossing the lit match behind her onto the floor, and telling me, 'He's a really sweet guy, don't get me wrong. What he mostly is, though,' she says, 'is a real wild piece of ass.' She looks me straight in the eye, and she smiles this *angel's* smile. Cue the celestial music. She says, 'You know what I mean.' She says, 'I can't figure out, like, why I can't go *get* some if I want to. You know what I mean,' she says."

"And you do," Gerry said.

"She's a *baby!* You're not supposed to make love to anybody when you're sixteen. Much less a sheriff's deputy in the back of a public law enforcement vehicle."

"Except most of the girls today who're sixteen do just that. The only aberration here is the kind of car, Lou."

"Gerry," she said. It sounded to her like whining. She watched him rub his eyes.

"But I'm right," he said. "And what about what she said? Isn't that a kind of feminist thing, too? Guys shouldn't be the only ones who can go after good stuff when they see it? Women have the right to it, too? Our bodies, ourselves, and so on?"

"And so on," Louise said, suddenly more depressed than angry, and curious now, puzzled, feeling as though she'd heard a song that she'd known but had forgotten.

They were making a salad at the kitchen window in the back of their house that night. It was near the riverbank, and they were looking outside more than at the scallions and carrots and green pepper and radishes, and more than at one another.

"I'll make a vinaigrette," Gerry said.

"Does she turn *you* on, Gerry?"

"The kid? Denise? I never met her, Lou."

"You know. The idea of all that hot teenager panting all over you."

"Well, she was panting all over Deputy Penders, not me."

"Imagining that she *might* be. *Could* be. What if she *were?*"

"Right on, Denise," he said, raising a fist betokening power to the people. "Right on. It *is* a revolution, Louise."

"You want to go out, in the garage, and get into the back seat?"

His face was so eager, so unguardedly excited in a new way when he turned to her, that she fell to studying the tender white scallops of the seed-choked green pepper she'd cut open. "Well, you're kidding, of course," he told her. "We're adults."

She said, "Of course."

As boys outside her office aimed their bodies toward accidental collisions with girls, as the noise in the corridors rose to the pitch of mass panic, Louise sat in her small room and turned her overheated metal desk lamp toward the old Modern Library edition of *The Interpretation of Dreams* that she had purchased at a garage sale in Rochester. She was comforted by the worn cloth of its red-brown binding: it was like an old dog's back, or a father's sport coat, a teacher's car—worn, even shabby, but an emblem of what was veteran, reliable, sage. Inside, on its bright white pages—she had to squint as she read—even the chapter headings reassured her: "The Dream as Wish-Fulfillment," "The Dream-Work," "The Material and Sources of Dreams." But when she read the familiar sections (*"Dr. M is pale; his chin is shaven, and he limps"*), she grew frustrated with the need to break the code—as if the dreamer and his mind were distant fellow spies, fearful of capture, unwilling to risk their location, needing nevertheless to broadcast their fears. But there was nothing on these pages about the lashing out, the violent reach, the heavy blow. There were only the undercover agents, incapable of silence, signaling in cipher.

That night, after dinner, in the broad low living room where they read, Louise pumped in coffee. She doctored it with milk and sugar, and she drank so much of it that by ten-fifteen, she felt sick. Gerry fell asleep on the sofa, and he snored at the newspaper over his face. She woke him to send him to bed, and he groggily obeyed. At ten-thirty, gagging as she poured the rest of the coffee into the sink, Louise turned the light out and she got into bed. The sheets were cold, the comforter warm, the pillows soft, but nothing felt good; her flannel nightgown rasped at her nipples, and the back of her neck was stiff, sore. Gerry was softly burring as he lay on his back, but the snores had not fully begun. She lay with her back to him, reading by the low yellow light of her bedside lamp: *Rolling Stone* to keep her in step with her student-clients, and then *Vogue* for real pornography. She realized, after a while, that her shoulders ached from the tension with which she held them up, behind her, like a shield against his bad dreams. She realized, too, that she was looking away from him because the realest privacy lay behind his eyelids as he slept, and she was reluctant to betray him. Of course, behind closed lids in sleep, she thought, is where you get so much betrayal *done*. Where was Gerry now? With whom?

She smelled the heat of the bulb against its frail shade, and also the printer's ink on her magazine, the morning's perfume in the air around her bureau across the room, the day's labor ripening on his body and on hers, the coldness of the air from the river-bottom land around them, and the warm rich breath he breathed at her back as he shifted positions. The bed squeaked, the pages rattled and, as they did, reflections went bouncing from the photos in *Vogue*—women who had to work to look like Denise; boys who were trained to shape a mouth like the boy or man or creature in between whom she insisted on forgetting and often did—and as reflected light shimmered on the brass pole near her head, she thought, *I am a woman inside of a life. This room is dark water, and the lights are submarine, and I am floating in my whole, entire life.* She thought, *No,* but before she could marshal her argument, or mourn it, Gerry began to snore as if a motor in his chest were pumping. *He's the aerator in the tank,* she thought; she waited to hear herself giggle; she didn't.

She dropped her magazine from the side of the bed and then, as slowly as she could, she hauled herself up against the brass headboard until she sat. In the yellow-brown light of the weak bulb, she peered down at Gerry, whose snarling snores were louder now. She looked away from his pulsing closed eyes. It was rage, she realized; his shoulders jumped, his upper arms moved; his hands, she saw, were fists. She wouldn't raise her eyes above his chest. It was time to look at him, and Louise didn't want to. When she did, the sneaky, caffeine-buzzing frightened curiosity would be reason.

She watched his fists jump, and she listened to him snore; it was, she realized, the sound that someone might make who was drowning, or being choked. And then, with a final sorrow made part of the motion itself, remembering her sad, reluctant motions with the dark, cruel man

who had worked her body so brilliantly, Louise gave in, and shifted in
the bed to lay her full attention on Gerry's face, as one might lay a palm
along a lover's cheek, connecting, caressing, taking hold.

His eyelids fluttered. His jaw worked as he ground his teeth. In
light the color of yarrow, his face seemed made of shadows. Its many
emptinesses reminded her of giant boulders dragged into fields by gla-
ciers; they were scoured, full of shallow pits, and what had sculpted
them was gone. He worked his jaws, or whatever worked him made
his jaws chew against each other. He had stopped snoring, now, and
he was breathing enormously, taking breaths so profoundly deep that,
watching the eyelids flutter, watching the bones of his face compress,
she waited with her own breath held to be certain that he would finish
one and start again.

That's love, isn't it? That kind of worrying?

When she heard herself think the question, she felt herself start to
cry. The tears came slowly and they ran down her face. She pushed at
them with the backs of her hands as she watched him in his tortured
sleep. Then his eyes rolled faster under his lids, and he clacked his
mouth open and shut a few times. "Blaw" was the sound his gravelly
voice said. "Blaw." She recognized the noise from memories of her own
scared dreams. It was what you said to ward off whatever impended
in your nightmare. "Blaw." But then, and with no warning, he back-
handed with his left arm and slammed his fist backward into her pillow.
His voice going higher even as he shouted it, he warned, "Don't assault
me." He threw his right, and he screamed, *"Blaw!"*

The wide, clumsy punch caught her left shoulder and pushed her
back on the bed. She caught his hand. She held it. She knew its weight,
and the temperature of it's skin, the dark fur on its forearm. She didn't
know whether to kiss it, or continue to hold it, or whisper to him that
he only dreamed, then kiss him on the cheek and lie beside him until
he slept without fear. *Only?*

She astonished herself by throwing his arm back against him. "Don't
you abuse *me*, you son of a bitch!" she shouted, and as she did she heard

the echo in her words of his own dreamy voice. She punched at him clumsily, *like a girl*, she thought, swinging wildly until he woke, frightened, of course, and confused, saying, "What? What?" But he traveled all the way from the borders of dreaming, through her weeping, her shouts and her blows, to find her, to fight through her punches, to clutch her against him. She knew, as he seized her, that he did so in ignorance of what had happened inside him or inside her, or in the room between them. Gerry hugged her to himself and gave what dumb and uninvited comfort he could. She knew he did. And she, now, reached to comfort in return. She felt his drenched T-shirt and thick blunt ribs, and she held herself against them, thinking *Caught*.

THE PAGE

———

THAT NIGHT I did what I had always done. It was how I'd been managing. Every morning I did what I always did, and every afternoon and night. Pooh lurched out with me while Bear slammed him into my legs and led us off the back porch. Bear was ten months old, a Labrador retriever long of muzzle and leg with vast paws. The old one, Pooh—my wife had named him—was lamed by arthritis, half blinded by cataracts, crippled by dysplasia, and still too strong to die. I placated the secrets of his physiology with Butazolidin tablets and dog biscuits. At that time, I was especially grateful when a patient or dog did not die.

It was unusually cold for early November, and the pumpkins I'd set out, because it had been the custom of the house, were settling into themselves as successive frosts softened them. No one came up our road for Halloween, but I had placed pumpkins on the front and back porches and had even fastened onto the storm doors the bunches of maize we'd always hung there. No one came to our house at Halloween because it was so remote, and because the pickings were better in town, five miles below. I had walked about, from kitchen to pantry through kitchen back to living room, waiting to give some little kids some lollipops and candy bars, but no one had come to claim them.

I had thought to console myself with Tootsie Pops, but I learned from their high, artificial sweetness that I didn't believe in consolation.

Pooh staggered around the bushes in the side yard, and I heard Bear rustling in the tall, withered grass below us. He was in the field that went down a hundred yards or so to the old apple trees on which gnarled, sour apples would gleam in the morning through winter. Pooh came back and lay down beside me with a grunt. I didn't hear the puppy and I whistled him back. He didn't come. I clapped my hands and called him. I heard slow winds and the natural sway of weeds against each other, but nothing caused by the intrepid unintelligence of a young dog rushing home. I called again, and listened, and then put Pooh inside, stuck a long-handled flashlight in the pocket of my barn coat, and, leaving the porch light on, went looking.

I walked through the fields I'd last seen him in. I walked the road parallel to the fields. I went down to the old apple trees, then past them and past the old fence and over the small creek. I followed it in the dark down through the aspen forest to where it foamed in a little waterfall. My shoes and trouser legs were soaked, and my hands ached from the cold. I had fallen a couple of times and had not, I noted, sprung lithely back up. There were creatures around me, field rats and maybe an owl, but there wasn't a stalky, imperfect Labrador retriever who knew less about handling himself in these woods than the average beginning Boy Scout.

I fell again as I bushwhacked up to the house, and, speaking of tenderfoots, this time I opened up some skin and broke my flashlight. "Bear," I shouted in the darkness, a little embarrassed by the panic I heard above the grass that insisted on making noises, in the freshening wind, as if something coursed in instant response to my call.

I found another flashlight that worked, and then I drove the car back and forth on our road. I went miles in each direction, pausing to aim the flashlight through my opened windows at the grounds of every trailer, double-wide, shack and farmhouse I passed. There weren't that many, and the dog was at none of them. At home, I locked up and, sitting in wet clothes and a shirt with blood on the right cuff, I said to the old dog that the puppy would doubtless come back in the middle of the night, that he was running a deer or ferreting in somebody's compost heap. "You wake me when he comes," I told Pooh before I went up. He hadn't made it upstairs for a couple of years.

Dogs drift. They stray. They take off because of a smell, a sound, something inside their skulls that is part of what makes them other than us. I fell asleep in our bed and not that much later I woke, as I'd been waking for a while, to the sound of my voice. I took a bathrobe downstairs with me and passed the sofa onto which Pooh, in spite of his lameness, was able to haul himself every night. I went to the other sofa and lay beneath one of the heavy old quilts.

Looking out from under it, I said to Pooh, "Any word?"

His cloudy eye glittered in the darkness of the living room and then it closed.

After hospital rounds the next morning, I drove the twenty miles home because I knew that Bear would be sitting on the porch, looking, as usual, bewildered. He was not. I drove back, and I continued to wrestle with my imagination as I'd done, fairly successfully, the night before. Every time I saw the dog cringing from headlights on a two-lane highway, or, tail down and back curved in fear, crouching over his forepaws in a dark forest that felt alien, I pulled down the wide black window shade I remembered my grade school teachers hauling on small pulleys so that we could better see a film strip on how corn grows or why the washing of one's hands is a precious errand and a high responsibility. I drew the black blind between me and the terrified Labrador, who'd been struck with a stick by a man at his trap line, or who was bleeding from the flanks where he'd been shot with a hunting bow, or who ran at a sideways angle, slower and slower, because of his kicked-in ribs.

Instead of eating lunch before my clinic hours, I drove home again, pulling the blind as I needed to, and inspected the house and the grounds. I drove with the windows open and the radio off so I could hear him, and so I could whistle for him as I drove. Past Dorney Walters

Road, past Sanitarium Road, I signaled to him, in case he was caught, or lost, or injured, that I was here, that this—toward the sound of my calling and calling—was how to come home.

After work that day, at a quarter of six, before I went back to feed Pooh, to maybe find a young black dog on my porch, I telephoned my daughter's office. I lay in the swivel chair and let my tired feet dangle. I thought I was in danger of talking about Bear, but I wanted to be certain I was calm for her, even casual, so I rehearsed. You know that dumb-ass puppy took off on me, I said. Probably got himself lost in the hills or near the river, I said. I thought about rivers, how fast and deep and cold they were. I'd never put ID collars on the dogs because I didn't want them getting snagged and drowned in rivers or streams. I said to her, I have to confess I'm getting worried, and if I *had* put them in collars then maybe someone, finding him, could call me. Maybe he wouldn't be lost or mistreated or frightened someplace. I pulled on the long white sash cord, and the broad black screen came down. She wasn't in, and I went out and drove back, climbing into the wild hills I lived in with, apparently, one less dog.

I remembered what I had actually said to myself in rehearsal for my daughter and then had chosen to dismiss: if they wore collars, I had said in my thoughts, then maybe someone could find *me*. I was reminded of something. I thought I knew what, but I drew the blind back down and, once I saw that nothing—*no one* were the words I heard in my head—was lying, all muzzle and ears and big, dark eyes, on the porch, I went through the business of the early evening without allowing myself a glimpse of what I didn't want to see. I took Pooh out and hung around the yard while he limped from bush to rock to fence post. "You do your rounds," I told him, "and I do mine. And you piss up posts a good deal better than I do." Then I fed him and thought about feeding me, but settled for some slices of cheddar somewhat spotted with blue-green mold. I chewed on one for a while and then, leaning over the garbage pail, which direly needed emptying, I spat the mouthful out. I was reminded, again, and again I drew the screen up. But I'd remembered by then. I thought to call my daughter and tell her how close I'd come that night to conversing with her mother again. But I put my coat on, instead, and went out with Pooh, the two of us crabbing our way up the road half a mile or so, Pooh marking and sniffing and glaring with his opalescent eyes, me calling with, I heard, such desperation that I sounded like a warning, not a request to please come back.

The next morning, I called the Sheriff's Department and spoke to one of the dispatchers I was friendly with. I worked in the jail as their doctor one night a week, inspecting prisoners, and I knew most of them well enough. I asked if the deputies on patrol could keep an eye out for Bear. I learned the names of the area dog wardens, and I telephoned descriptions to two of them, leaving a message for the third. I called four veterinarians to ask if anyone had brought Bear in. I called the SPCA. Now everyone knew that one more dog was missing. I let Pooh out for a final pee, then locked him in and went to work. On the way, I stopped at the offices of our newspaper and paid for a large ad. I headed it REWARD. The woman behind the counter watched the pencil, then looked up at me. She looked, and then she said, "Family pet, huh? Everybody takes it hard."

"Do they?"

"Like a child's gone, sometimes," she said.

"Really," I said. "That serious."

"Look at you," she said. "Here. Let go of the pencil. I write these all the time."

"Thank you," I said. "That's tough work."

"No," she said, studying the form she printed on, "what's tough is having dogs, I'd say."

One strep throat, one battered baby whose mother was a battered wife, a half dozen leaky sinuses, one possible appendix, one definite milk allergy, a third pneumonia for the week, and the bonus—sixteen normal, healthy kids—and I was done and driving home. I stopped at the seasonal road a quarter of a mile from the house and parked with my windows open. I whistled for him. I listened to the strengthening winds in the evergreens before me on the hillside and to the dry grass rattling on the slope below. They were so much louder and more powerful, and I stopped my little noises and sat there awhile. An airplane engine tore up the sound of the wind, and I saw a light plane banking a couple of hundred feet above, then climbing to crest the hill that overlooked the house. The plane circled in slow, widening loops. I thought—the way you laugh hysterically—of finding a way to ask the pilot to look for Bear on the fields of yellowing grass and bony weed and corn stubble that lay on the other side of the ridge.

Yes, I admitted that night, while I admitted that the screen didn't work and that I dreamed the dreams and saw the sights—the whites of the eyes of a puppy in terror, the dry protruding tongue of a dog as he died of poisoned bait, the hiss on leaves of the blood that pumped from his wounds. Yes. All right, I thought, another triumph for lovers of realism everywhere. Yes. It was like mourning again. All right?

Before I left for work the next day, after I drank coffee and turned the radio on and then off, I fetched from the back pantry, from its cubby among field guides and travel books, our gazetteer of New York State with its precise topographical drawings. I looked down at the often unconcentric indications of the sloughs and rivers. There were so many roads and hillsides above them, too many forests and steep, thicketed fields.

I picked up our newspaper on my way to the hospital and I read the ad. She had rearranged my incoherent phrases well enough. It was placed at the top of a column containing three other notices of missing dogs. I visited my patients, three of whom were improving and one, Roger Pettefoy, an infant, who was dehydrated from diarrhea. We had caught his bacterial infection, but the antibiotics, I thought, had given him diarrhea. I asked Charlene Novak to throw some electrolytes into him and asked to be telephoned late that afternoon about his progress. On the way home, I shopped. Two women who had known us asked if they could help me. I smiled at one and moved on. She let me go. The other, who fell on me in an unsteady manner, all yellowing teeth and loose flesh, was not satisfied with my thanks, and she pursued me. I stopped and turned, wheeling my cart as if it were a shield. She retreated several paces with her own cart. She wore a fur coat over what looked like pajamas, and she smelled of gin. The idea of a martini became interesting. I said, "Ms. Wiermeyer? *Widde-meyer.* Forgive me. You're being kind, I know. But I really remember, if barely, how to buy short-grain rice. My hesitation, here in aisle five, is because the store seems to carry only long-grain rice. I'd intended to make myself a spinach risotto for dinner. Hence the desirability of short grains, as I'm certain you know. So I'm considering my choice, which lies between long-grain and processed. I'm only fucked up, Ms. Widdemeyer, not stupid."

That afternoon, a boy rode up on a bicycle, rare enough on our stretch of road. Pooh let him know by yelping at the bike, even after the boy climbed off it. Pooh's rich growling bark had turned to something of a yap. A lesson for us all, I thought, as I went out the front. The boy was fourteen, probably, pimpled over a pallor he owed to canned gravies on dehydrated mashed potatoes and plenty of sweet sodas. I smelled his cigarettes and unwashed skin.

He said, not looking at my face, "You the man advertising the reward?"

"For a dog," I said stupidly.

"Dog," he said, patting Pooh's head. "Black puppy, it says, except he's pretty damned big for a puppy."

"Kind of dopey-looking ears and a little white spot on his chest?"

"Yupper," he said, breaking the word into two syllables and landing heavily on the second. "Kind of cute."

"Did you call him by his name?"

"Bear," he said. "Pretty near tore the damned chain off of him."

"Chain," I said, taking my wallet out and counting to a hundred.

He described the trailer off the road and its short gravel driveway, the long chain fastened to its riserless wooden steps and the black dog held by a collar that looked to be made of chain as well.

"A choker, maybe," I said. "It tightens up the more the dog pulls on it."

He nodded. "Could have been," he said. But I knew that he'd agree, now, to anything because he saw more money in the wallet.

"When you go home," I said, "be sure and keep one of those twenties to yourself, if you know what I mean."

"Yupper," he said, mounting the bike and looking like all these big country boys caught between handlebars and steering wheels—too long and lean for the squat kids' bicycle, and a little bit angry, as if he knew how he looked.

I checked Pooh's water dish, then locked him in and drove to the trailer. I had paused at the door of my house, wanting to heft something. This was an emergency, and it might require equipment. I thought about flashlight, ax, splitting maul, garden spade, a serrated bread slicer, or one of the French cooking knives. Finally, I took my medical bag. I wanted to know what I was doing, no matter what I had to do, and my professional tools seemed best.

I turned up a road I rarely traveled because it was not only seasonal—unplowed during the winter—but because it was unpaved and seemed to be made of potholes linked by rocks. I went slowly, rehearsing my conversation with whoever had Bear. I would have to pay another reward. I would have to have a discussion, I supposed. I would have to perhaps undergo a berating for carelessness and maybe listen to complaints about scattered garbage or the scratched-up walls of a shed or the stain on a rug. The trailer was at the edge of a state hardwood plantation. Once a year, those who'd been chosen in a lottery were permitted to log firewood. For a few weeks, the forest screamed and trees fell and pickups tottered back and forth under heavy loads. Then these woods felt dark again when I drove past the road that went through them, and there was a good silence from them—unless you had driven there to call the name of a missing dog.

I'd noticed the trailer before, its trim fence taut on pressure-treated four-by-fours, but I hadn't thought about the posts in the gravel drive, nor the very large links of chain that hung between them, nor the sign that said, in high, childish letters, *KEEP OUT.* I saw a thinner, brighter chain that was looped around the steps in front of the darkened trailer in the darkening woods. I didn't see Bear.

I was breathing too quickly for the effort involved in parking a car and walking from it to step over a thick chain and go up the little hillside to climb four steps and knock on the aluminum door of a white metal and plastic trailer with blue trim that was maybe twenty feet long. I raised my hand to rap at the storm door when someone opened the interior door a crack and said, "Get off of my property."

"Give me back my dog, and I will," My voice was so high, I hardly recognized it.

"There isn't any dog here. Get out."

"I know my damned *dog's* here. I want him back."

"He's mine."

"Bear!" I called.

"You stay right there, Buddy," the man's voice said. It had a flat dullness to it that seemed strange, since it also sounded angry. "His name's Buddy," the man said, "and my brother bought him for me over in New York. Now, you get the hell off my property."

"I guess you want to talk to the cops," I said.

He said, "I knew it was you. I knew it was you. I knew it was you. Goddamned Howard, huh? All the way over from Ohio, huh? Big undercover motherfucker Howard, huh? I *knew* it was you!"

The door opened a little wider, and I called, "Bear!"

The barrel of a rifle came out. I remember staring at the sight because it seemed to stand so high. I heard a metal sound, and I jumped off the porch and ran down the gravel drive, falling near the bottom and letting myself roll under the chain. I ran around to the far side of my car and crouched there. I thought I saw the trailer door close. I sat on the ground and shook. Everything shook. When I finally inched myself into the car and turned it around, driving almost too low in the seat to see, and when I was back in my own driveway, I thought that I could use some of my professional gear once I pulled the gravel out of the cuts and washed my hands.

I thought: The barrel of a *gun*.

I thought: I did hear him lunge inside the trailer when I called his name.

I told Arch Constantine, the deputy who arrived forty minutes later, and he wrote an incident report for me to sign.

He asked, moving his three-cell flashlight on the table, and studying his juvenile handwriting, "Did you feel menaced, Doc?"

"Menaced. Arch, you're damned right I felt menaced. I was *scared*."

"Scared's fine, but menaced is what the law's about. Menacing. Was he menacing you?"

"There's a law against it?"

"There sure is. I believe we've had him on it before, this Lester Scott guy. The sheriff knows about him. A number of us do. He's a head case. And you felt menaced, then."

I nodded. I hesitated, but he smiled. He had a sweet smile for a man who was almost seven feet tall and perhaps as heavy as two of me. It was a crooked face, as if he'd been broken and put together again with some difficulty. "Menaced," I said. "I ran."

"I understand," he said, tapping the report.

"I ran away, Arch. Like a kid."

He said, "I'd just as soon you did, Doc. I'd like to keep you alive. You take care of two of my nephews and you're the only fun we get down at the cells unless one of the prisoners gets a package of food. You let us deal with the perpetrators and you forget about them until we lock them up. That strike you as fair?" He smiled the smile I often enough used with the parents of my patients. I thought of the tiny clenched face of Roger Pettefoy in the ward and of his mother, who'd trembled when she spoke with me.

"Deal," I said.

When he was gone, I fed Pooh and then walked around the house, waiting for word. I watered the plants, many of which looked sicker than the children I'd treated that week. I let Pooh out and called the hospital. I shouted at the Head of Shift because I hadn't been called about Roger Pettefoy. She told me, stiffly, that no instructions to call had been left. I told her how wrong she was, that when Charlene Novak heard orders she wrote them into the chart. She told me how improved the baby was, and I gave her orders and insisted that she read them back. Then, of course, I apologized. I said, "My dog—" I was able to stop myself, so that when she asked me what I'd said I could reply, "It's been a long day. Forgive me. Please call me if the child's signs change." I said, "Deal?"

She didn't know what I meant, apparently, and she disconnected.

Pooh barked at Arch when he returned. He ducked as he came in and he refused to sit. There was no dog in the car and none beside him but Pooh. The deputy said, "I've dealt with him before. I was right. He's crazy."

"I believe it."

"No," he said. "He's *crazy*. He thinks your name's Howard."

"I know that."

"He thinks you work with the DEA."

"Drugs?" I said.

"He thinks you followed him from someplace in Ohio, and before that from someplace down South, and he thinks you're a spy for the DEA. You're some kind of undercover agent. I thought he was going to shoot me, sure as shit. He hates law officers. He hates uniforms. Mostly, right now, he hates *you*. That's why he's got your dog."

"He admitted it was mine?"

"Sure did. Dog came wagging to the trailer, and he just chained him there. Wants you to know it."

"Why?" I tried not to let it sound like *Why me?*

"He's not sure, he says. He says he *thinks*, maybe, he'd enjoy shooting you through the chest. He was particular about that, about the through the chest part. He says he's got a load of guns and ammunition, and he would take great pleasure in killing you and any of your cop friends."

"Jesus," I said, "you were—"

That was when he did sit down and lean over his legs and look at the clouded blue linoleum of the kitchen floor. He nodded. Then he whispered, "I did think he was ready to put me down."

"Jesus," I said, "you can't get killed because of a dog, Arch."

He looked up, suddenly. He smiled his sweet smile. "Thank you," he said. "I'd at least like a chance to talk it over with my sergeant and more than likely the sheriff. We can't have him doing whatever he's doing with guns, that's for sure. And if he's got your dog, we have to get it back. There's the drug thing, besides. The marijuana. You've heard about it. Let me talk to people about warrants or whatever, and what to do next. You do me a favor?"

"You bet."

"Don't go back there. He *will* kill you."

"That's a deal," I said.

Later, when I sat in the kitchen and wondered for some reason whether I smelled to my colleagues and nurses and patients like a sour old wooden house inhabited mostly by dogs, I thought of how noble I had been. Well, of *course*, we can't have deputies murdered for the sake of a dog.

Well, of course, I thought.

I heard from the hospital, with a dutiful report on Roger Pettefoy bouncing back. In the morning, I woke on my sofa across from Pooh, who glared from his, and I heard the sound of an airplane flying low. It was just light, it was Sunday morning, and I would have to be in the hospital to check on the kids, but not until nine or ten. I had five hours on my own, and I knew how I would spend them. Pooh lay still, pretending not to be there, until I was in the kitchen, making coffee. I heard his groan as he half slid and half fell onto the floor.

By six I was in the car, parked at the intersection of Lester Scott's road and mine. I walked through brush, keeping parallel to the road. I had my flashlight, but only used it with my hand cupped loosely over the lens. I wore a dark, heavy Irish sweater we had bought maybe fifteen years before in Clifden, and it almost fit. Putting it on, fighting my way up into its bulky sleeves, I had realized how little I'd been eating. I wore an old tan tweed cap, dark work gloves for no reason I could give, and I carried the heavy pocket knife I kept sharpened in case I had to do an emergency tracheotomy. I had carried it for years and never used it. I'd no idea why I brought it with me now. Maybe, if he shot me in the head, I would need to cut an airway in so I could breathe while dying.

Of course, I was panting. I sweated heavily, and I imagined myself as pale, as radiating my feeble heat and light through the woods like a beacon. The light plane gargled and buzzed not far above, a couple of hundred feet, maybe less. I progressed by staggering, by falling, by taking short, uneven steps, by gasping and muttering, by pulling myself ahead, this hand on that branch, this foot pushing off that unsteady rock I hadn't, anyway, seen in time to not fall on, but for all of my inability and fear, I felt something I can only describe as health.

We'd heard the stories for years, and Arch Constantine had more or less repeated them, but with more detail. Although I live on shale, clay, and bony ridges, I also live on water. The high valley that runs along the spines of hills a thousand, two thousand, feet high has water that drains off it. These mountain streams continue as creeks and brooks and branches—so they're named on the map—to the Chenango River and the Unadilla. These empty into the Susquehanna, and that runs as far as Chesapeake Bay, and there you are, from here—from this little nowhere anyone heard of—gone to everyplace else.

Farmers with moving water of any reasonable depth are attached to the rest of the world, in other words. You can bring a shallow-draft boat up into river-bottom country. What you load it with is the marijuana you've been growing half a mile back off the road, out of sight of troopers and deputies, accessible only to the harvesters, who work there while they're screened off by the harvesting of soy or corn, or the spreading of manure. So the marijuana is grown behind the grass, then it's ferried to deeper waters, and it's taken farther by lazy-day fishermen in Boston whalers through a system of rivers as complicated as a network of human nerves, or by high school dropouts in fast, converted cars who use the Onondaga reservation as a distribution hub for shipments north to Canada, south down the thruway to New York.

The plane came back over. Why Mr. Lester Scott decided I was working for some antidrug agency couldn't have had much to do with what he saw. I was a scrawny, middle-aged man who hung around with dogs. I never carried a shotgun or a rifle, never paid attention (I was told) to anyone nearby. I couldn't have the look of a narc. I felt myself smile. I was flattered.

I was also winded. I was also near the trailer. A yellow light lay around the doorway and the top outside step. I heard the jingle of the chain as Bear moved away from the trailer. I heard the click as Scott locked himself back in. Commando-Doc peering through the brush on the subject's perimeter, I needed only cork blacking to look like an unmuscular joke about films. His small lot was perfectly rectangular, I thought; all the corners were right angles. A small shed—garbage and tools, no doubt—was plumb in its relation to the trailer. His wood-pile was neat, and what he'd split of the mound of round sections was piled in face cords between studs he'd spiked into the ground. Moving around the lot, I saw at the back of the trailer a single cinder block step beneath the rear door. From it, I could see a trail. It probably went to his marijuana crop. I could follow the path, set his crop on fire, then steal back Bear while Scott was distracted. Since I didn't smoke, how-ever, and since my emergency rescue kit consisted of Agway reinforced gloves and the tracheotomy knife, I needed another plan.

I stepped out onto the back of his lot. I would like to say I glided, but in my rubber-bottomed winter boots I thumped. I walked along-side the trailer and, at the corner that would take me around to the side of his wooden front steps, I paused. I hissed. I gave the low, coded whistle that would bring my dog and, if they held him back, the steps and trailer too. He paused, I whistled again, and then he bent again to lick his loins. So much for Lassie, so much for Lad and Rin-Tin-Tin.

As I bit on my lips and tongue and cheeks, and worried what I could reach of my head for a practical thought, I found myself stepping around the corner and walking to my dog. I whispered, "Bear, goddammit." Probably, the goddammit did the trick. He looked and stiffened, he leaned forward—they are all myopic until they're blind—and then he galloped, ass high, tail corkscrewing, big jaws open in what everyone who owns a dog will call a smile.

The chain scraped as it tightened at the step, and Bear winced, a step or two short of me. Scott had put him in a choker meant for a smaller dog. I could see the furrow in his fur as it bit. I pushed into him, and back, so that the pressure eased. He burrowed into me, put his paws on my shoulders as he tried to swallow my face, and knocked me over. So there I was, one hand hooked inside a binding choker chain, flat on my back with my black dog standing on my chest, inhaling my nose and mouth.

I heard the trailer door open and a flat, thin voice: "Get away from Buddy. Get off of my land."

I lay back. Bear had gone stiff. I closed my eyes and I said, "Fuck you."

"I did grant you the sporting chance," he said.

I heard a soft sound, the closing of a little metal latch. I heard the grate of some other metal mechanism, and I opened my mouth and eyes at once. I was on my feet, and I don't remember standing. I kneeled at Bear and worked to loosen the choker. He had retreated as far as he could from the porch, so he'd tightened it, and the only way I could set him free was to push him toward his captor. There was some kind of important Zen semiautomatic large-magazine coveting-of-property message in that action, I think I thought. Scott put six, seven, eight rounds into the earth around me. Bear growled low, but also drooped with fear. He shivered, and so did I, but without the growl. I finally somehow pulled the collar off, tearing away some of Bear's ear. He screamed, and they later found a chunk ripped open where the ear meets the head.

The plane flew low above us, and I heard other engines and so did

Scott. A yellow power company truck was almost out of view where it idled, to the left of his house. I couldn't see its cherry-picker crane, but as the yellow light inside his doorway vanished, I knew they were cutting his power off. A big ambulance slid up, and so did two navy blue state police cars, and then the red and white sheriff's cars, one after another, maybe half a dozen, and then several unmarked cars pulled in. By then, I was holding Bear against my chest with his paws folded in against my arms.

I said, "I'll tell them you could have killed me and you didn't. I'll tell them how you fired into the ground."

He looked up at the plane as it returned. He raised the rifle and he fired. He said, as he shot, "A man gets a vote in this country. A man still gets a vote. Man good as niggers and DEA sneakthief undercover lawyers, keeping him from what's his due and guaranteed Constitution rights. Spics in Talladega get the vote, and so do I." He squeezed off round after round. I heard the cops calling, as if to warn, by sheer power of their cries, the unprotected pilot in his plane. I turned my back to Scott because I was afraid he was going to shoot us, and I didn't want the dog to be my shield. I couldn't move my feet. I knew I had wet my trousers, and then I felt the warm trickle as Bear took my cue. He didn't feel heavy, though he must have weighed close to eighty pounds. It wasn't his weight. It was my legs. They wouldn't move. So I crouched with my back to Lester Scott as the plane came back—this time I heard the troopers and deputies cursing the pilot—and flew in, slow and low and large above us.

Scott fired a round a second, it sounded like, and though I thought I was deafened by the noise of his rifle, I heard one of the lawmen call *Down!* at the same time that I heard Lester Scott say in his flat, uninflected voice, "I know you. I know you. I know who you are." He fired twice again, and then the rescuers fired. They must have posted snipers with military rifles because two shots, which boomed and echoed in the forest, struck him at once. Imagine swatting a side of beef with a breadboard. I heard the bullets go in. I was on my knees by then, unable to breathe. The right side of my back was numb, and I figured out, at about the time that I registered the second volley of shots—lower in register, tinnier—from everyone else firing, that one of the troopers or deputies had shot me. I figured it was a mistake, though you never know how angry someone in that situation might become at a civilian fouling their rural drug bust.

It was a high adrenaline morning, all right, with men screaming commands through bullhorns, the airplane roaring back and forth, lower and lower, it sounded to me, and everything in my body pumping head to toe and side to side. I lay on top of Bear, unable to move. The numbness on my back had been replaced by a very deep and profoundly disabling pain. I didn't think I could breathe anymore. I hadn't the breathe to tell them. I knew the Bear, beneath me, hadn't moved. So I didn't, anyway, want them to pick me up. I lay as still as I could, shaking and feeling wet all over and breathing very shallowly. I heard them gabbling and laughing and commanding one another to perform all sorts of actions.

Someone said, "Most of the motherfucker's plastered onto the trailer, and the rest of the trailer is halfway shot to shit. I believe we have lowered the resale value for his motherfucking estate." They laughed high up in their throats, and the smell of cigarette smoke poured over us.

I was going to croak a brave and wounded doctor's joke about smoking and its toll on one's health. I remember that. I remember opening my mouth, timing myself against the pulses inside my ribs and under my lungs, but I couldn't shape the big, hissing syllable I'd need to start with. The spotter plane went over, and then someone turned me. I gagged and started to cry, I'm afraid.

It sounded like Arch Constantine, a deep voice in genuine sorrow. He said "Aw," the way we said it as kids when something that seemed as important as our lives—a skate key, a baseball glove—was lost or stolen. He said "Doc." Then he said "Aw" again. I drifted out and then came back to hear him tell me, "Here's the gurney, Doc."

I timed it. "Dog," I said.

Arch didn't answer me. He said, "There you go, Doc" in a voice gone high and false. I knew not to ask them again.

Great Brook, Morris Brook, Handsome Brook. I thought of water over rocks someplace. West Branch and Canasawacta Creek, the Genegantlet. I saw them, though I had only heard their names from fishermen or patients, had only driven over them in ignorance or heard them cited by cops. I saw them as fine blue lines on a map. I saw small-eyed, pale and hungry men in skiffs, wearing gumboots, their bodies tightened, as if toward pain, against the inevitable treachery. But the rivers ran to the edge of a page, as if I held a map in a book before me on the kitchen table in our house, sitting over coffee while the old dog snored and Bear, not killed by the shots going through me, ate a shoe. The creeks and rivers dripped their wavering paths to the blank bottom margin of the gazetteer.

Only the pilot could see it all. Drifting low, hanging, he could crook his wrist and cover thousands of yards as we bent our necks back and watched him veer. He could twitch his hand and turn the page we lived on.

DON'T TELL
ANYONE

---◇---

HEADS

DID I TELL YOU SHE WAS RAPED?

And not by the man she stabbed?

If you could do ... something—I couldn't remember what—then you'd be able to do something *else*. I couldn't remember that, either. I knew it was the poem they quote at commencements and at civic-awards ceremonies in small upstate communities like mine. I remembered the rhythm of its lines, but I couldn't remember the words.

My head was a hive of half-remembered words, tatters of statement, halves of stories, the litter of alibis, confessions, supplications, and demands, the aftereffects, perhaps, of the time I spent standing beside my grown, or half-grown, ungrown, ingrown child in a courtroom. She trembled, and I tried to situate myself, standing as we were before the clerks' desk, which was before and below the bench of the judge, so that she could lean her thin, shivering body on mine, at least a shoulder or forearm, at least the comfort I could offer with the heft of my hand against the hard, cold, bony fingers of hers. But she would not accept the heat of my flesh or the weight I wished she might prop herself on. The trial for the crime had never taken place, because our lawyer convinced us—Alec, my daughter, and me—that she should plead nolo contendere: guilty, in a word. She had, as they say, copped a plea. She'd bargained down. She and the victim and the Manhattan district attorney's office had agreed to change the shape of events. We would say that Alec did *not* incise three small cuts in the skin of Victor Petrekis's face with a stainless-steel pocket knife brought to her from England by her father when she was small. She and our lawyer, Petrekis and the assistant district attorney, had constructed a language to make her crime the *attempt* of the deed she had in fact done. And we were before the judge to hear the sentence he would pass.

Petrekis and the assistant district attorney stood at our left, the judge's right. The two clerks periodically bent to write on forms. The marshals behind us, their belts creaking with the weight of their guns, their lapel radios hissing static, waited to learn if they would take her to jail. I had been warned that they put your child in handcuffs right there, as she stands beside you, and they take her off. The heavier clerk, her face a kind of mild mask, was the one who swore us in, ending her question—whether we would tell the truth before this court—with the warning that we must remember how on that *great day,* when *all* would be judged, our falsehoods would be weighed against us. It seemed to me she expected us all to lie and was trying, with her impassivity, not to show her disappointment in our dishonesty. But we all said, and in unison, "I do," as if the ceremony were about marriage and not the dissolution of whatever you might name—rest, comfort, household, and, surely, freedom.

Alec wore a suit she had bought for law school. It was too large, like everything she owned, and its eggplant color, once so interesting with her red-gold hair, now seemed to overpower her complexion. It made her look gray. Her hair was thin and muddy-looking, cropped so short I could see, from beside her, the bone of her skull behind her ear. Her head looked vulnerable to the temperature of the air, and of course to the world of cruel surfaces before which her head was naked now. Even the sleeves of the suit seemed too long, as if her body had diminished in length as well as breadth.

The judge had a wattle of chin and a thick, long nose. The flesh of

his face was pitted and loose, his scalp very broad and shiny. But his
eyes were of a rich, dark blue, and he spoke with an urgency, a sense of
concern, in which I believed. He read from sentencing guidelines and
asked the assistant district attorney and our lawyer, Sylvia Stern, if they
agreed with his understanding of the rules. The ADA, as Sylvia called
him, nodded. Sylvia said, "Yes, Judge." I found myself nodding, too,
though of course I knew nothing. I knew nothing.

The knife was about three and a half inches long when folded shut.
Its single blade was short and thin. Barry had gone to the north of
England on a buying trip. He ordered printed cottons to be sold to
dressmakers in the States, and he brought home cloth for me and a
print of Stonehenge that he said was designed by Turner though etched
and inked by someone else, and a little pocket knife for Alec, who was
going through a boy phase that year and was pining for a left-handed
first baseman's mitt, an aluminum bat, and the kind of knife that guys
carried in the pocket of their jeans.

She kept it in her purse during Barry's dying, and through the end
of college in the zipper pocket of her rucksack, and in her one semester
of law school it was in a compartment of Barry's attaché case, in which
she hauled her work between her apartment on 113th Street and the
library and classrooms of Columbia Law.

DID I SAY that she was raped?

The question's rhetorical, of course: the ploy of a woman on a back
porch alone, shielded from her neighbors by a waist-high wall, lighting
cigarettes and blowing the smoke at blackflies surrounding her head in
a cloud, thick as the words in court, as she tries to startle the black night
or circumstance itself that hovers about her. She surely, on the other
hand, was raped, and by a student she knew, and in the comfort and
convenience of her own furnished apartment. He, too, had his time in
court, he, too, pleaded guilty after first contesting her claim. He, too,
was sentenced, and Alec stood at the left of the bar, the judge's right,
and said, once more, her grievance. The man, for whom she was making

coffee as they prepared together for a test, had wept, and so had she. She should have howled her rage, though I believe, and so do her doctors, that nothing would have prevented what they came to call the break.

He raped her because he loved her, because he detested her, because he was jealous of her grade in the course, or because, when he was little, it was just this side of possible, his lawyer had claimed at first, that he was abused by a man who led the Cub Scouts. Perhaps each possibility was true. It never mattered to me. I wanted him gelded. I wanted the wound sealed with boiling pitch, with concentrated lime, and bound with barbed wire. It didn't matter to Alec either, though she spoke at first about friendship, and she wondered whether she had led him on. She soon enough stopped.

She soon enough stopped calling home. She soon enough, when I was able to catch her on the phone, spoke with no inflection. Soon, she mostly wept. And of course I should have gone at once, at the first hint of a sign of damage, to the city to rescue her. I should have stolen her. I should have fetched my baby home. But I waited, because I was leading my life, after all. I was teaching high school students how to distinguish between Babylon and Byzantium, Arafat and Attaturk, and I was failing, as were they, but that was how we were required to consume our days, and life was a storm of consequences with which one had to deal, and Alec in New York was only tense about her studies.

"It's the work, Mommy," she said. "I have too much of it."

"Maybe it's the wrong work."

"You sound so *Jewish*, Mommy."

"I think of you in New York, and I remember myself in New York, and I sound *city*," I said.

"City's Jewish."

"You're in the foothills of Harlem and you can say that?"

"I'm in the foothills of fuck up."

"Alec."

"Gotta go. Gotta go. I'm doing permutations of collateral estoppel, and I can't stop."

"Al, I think maybe you *ought* to stop."

"'Bill till you drop. Don't stop.' Bye, Mommy."

"Feel good and be careful? Please? Oh, say hello to Coriander," I said, but she'd hung up.

BARRY AND I had lived together in New York for the first few years of our marriage. He was a student at Cooper Union, and I was a dancer, and it's like watching a balloon that leaks while it zips in circles over your head, but in very slow motion, to see how those ambitions were mostly wishes and breath. But we were there when we were young, and on the afternoon of our first married day, in the room-plus-bathroom that we described as *almost* on University Place, I woke up next to my tall, hairy husband with his elegant, long, slender feet, and I didn't know which hunger banged from inside at my ribs—need for food, or need for Barry. Food won, but we hadn't very much. There were crackers and a wad of multipurpose processed cheese on the table seven feet from our bed. But there was a cake, prepared on upper Broadway to the specifications of Barry's mother, and I was assailed by a need for sweets, and the cake was, for reasons we couldn't ever remember, on the little square table from the Workbench that Barry's best man had given us. So I reached out and plucked the three-or-four-inch-high couple, made of sugar in black and white, the bride in her broad white gown, the groom in his morning coat and striped trousers, each with a genderless face of white with periods under black carats for eyes, a dash for a mouth, and I bit—without planning to, and never knowing what I'd meant to signify—at the head of the little groom.

That was how we came to spend our first married afternoon in the office of a dentist named Echaissy on Eighth Street, because the darling couple were made of plaster, and I had cracked a tooth. The groom suffered only a chip to his glossy pompadour. We carried them with us to our next apartment, on Seventeenth Street, and then to Mamaroneck, and then upstate, where Barry took over a factory and I took over a classroom, and where Barry's lungs filled with fibers of cloth, and his body devoured itself. We were married in City Hall, our witness had no camera, and the imperfect painted plaster couple are the embodiment and souvenir of what Barry and I and two witnesses had seen. We kept the bride and groom on a bookshelf in our living room, and there they remain, less the same of course, but standing watch over what you might call history.

Coriander was the name we'd given a stuffed tan cat with which Alec had slept since her second or third year. Barry told her stories about Coriander, and the saga had become the subject of Alec's first and only novel, three sheets of paper stapled together, all six sides bearing crayon drawings of adventures about which she had written in thick, tall capitals. I remember one "Aha!" in messy blue letters, and I remember Barry crooning it to Alec months earlier, one weekend night at bedtime. "Aha!" he'd called, "Aha!" she'd echoed, on a Sunday night when, to keep the next morning's class from arriving unmediated, and to demonstrate what I could not adequately say about that father and his child connected by the victorious shout of a make-believe cat, I had seduced him on a little armless rocking chair, outside on our porch, hidden from our neighbors by the porch's waist-high wall. Coriander had been washed, mended, tossed and mauled and embraced in every house we'd lived in, in each of Alec's dormitory rooms, and she had continued to be resident childhood fetish in Alec's place on Broadway and 113th. That was where I went after Alec called to wish me happy birthday.

"Darling," I said. "Al."

"What, Mommy?"

"Al, it isn't my birthday."

"Sure it is. Today's the eleventh, dingbat."

I didn't know what else to say: "But that's Daddy's birthday, remember? It isn't mine for a month, I'm afraid."

"It isn't?"

"No."

"It's Daddy's birthday? Today? But it can't be his birthday. He's dead."

"Yes," I said. "Where are you honey? Are you home?"

"What difference could that make? *When* am I is more like it. God. Daddy's dead and you don't even *have* a birthday now. When's mine?"

"Your birthday? Alec, are you in your apartment?"

"Yes. I'm here in the kitchen thing. Ette. Kitchenette. I was looking at the ingredients and everything in the cupboard to see if I could make you a cake, you know, or something, but of course that would be so stupid. I can't bake at all, as we both know perfectly well. And the cake I'd have to can't bake would have to be for Daddy, not you, and he's dead. You aren't, right? No. I really meant to ask: Am I?"

"Dead, Al?"

She said, very breezily, "What's your best bet?" Then all I heard was the sound of stoppered crying, someone's mouth and nose cupped shut while they tried not to weep and they failed.

I said, "Al."

"Oh," she said, "I don't think I'm strong enough anymore, Mommy. I don't think I can do this anymore."

"No," I said, "I'm leaving now. I'm coming. Promise me to stay in your apartment. Can you call someone?"

"Sure. What should I call them?" She laughed while she cried.

"Get some friends over, Al. Anyone you trust."

"Well, he's in jail for raping me, actually."

"Someone *else*."

"He's the one who won't see me anymore."

"I don't think I know who you mean."

"Obviously, a man I saw and I don't see him because he refuses to see *me*."

"Is he a—friend?"

"Lover."

"Ah."

"Don't 'ah' me, Mommy, all right? I'm old enough to have a lover."

"Of course. Yes. I don't remember—"

"No," she said. "I never talked about him. We didn't last long enough for me to find a short enough word that could describe how lousy it got so fast. A woman *is* allowed to want a man at the just about end of the twentieth century, may I point out. I keep waiting for a kind of sign or something, but he *will* not stand up for me. He isn't what you'd call a stand-up guy. I tried telling him that. Because *someone* will punish him. *Someone,* of course, is going to demonstrate how you're either a stand-up guy—a man, you know?—the geniune article, or you're hollow. If you're a dummy, I said, don't come around *here.* But I didn't know he'd do what I said to do or not to do. It's pretty clearcut, though, you know? *You'd* know. You got around a little when you were dancing, right? Man lets you down, you stick a pin in his balloon, right? His name is Victor Petrekis. He's Greek. He's what you would call a classical piece of ass, but hollow. Like those statues they make of the real statues, not in the museum. He can't be there when I need him to be. You know, when it's tough. It's very tough, Mommy."

IT TOOK ME four hours to drive to Manhattan. I double-parked on 113th, and at a very sloppy angle, effectively sealing off the street, I later saw. She sat on the floor, leaning against a wall. The telephone was on the floor beside her. Her legs were crossed at the ankle, and her arms were folded on her chest. She looked as if she were sleeping, but then her eyes opened undramatically, and she said, "How was the drive?" We took her purse and Barry's attaché case filled with law books, I grabbed what mail I could find, and her address book, and she put some clothing in a bag with a carrying strap. She moved slowly, as if her joints were very sore. She was pale and skinny and vacant of expression. Then she seemed to grow angry with me for having come, angry at my insisting she leave.

"Don't blame me if I flunk out," she said, walking down the single flight in front of me. Her bag rasped along the wall of the staircase, and the case clunked on the wrought-iron banister. "They don't make excuses here, understand? A little fruitcake is not an excuse, and anyway no one makes them. Can't you just leave me alone?"

We emerged to the sound of eight kinds of car horn. I set the baggage on the backseat, fastened her belt as if she were very little or very old, and I think that she was both, and I drove us away, pursued by the outraged driver of a yellow cab.

We were on the upper deck of the George Washington Bridge when I thought to say, "Alec? Have you got Coriander?"

"Oh, for Christ's sake, Mommy! Can't you think of something else besides a *doll?*"

"But have you got her?"

"Yes."

We saw a psychologist in the area, and she was worried. She said the word I expected, "depression." She used another word, "psychotic," and I chewed at the inside of my cheek to keep from crying. She referred Alec to a psychiatrist, who referred her to another one, in Cooperstown, and this one, a tall man whose hair was almost the color of Alec's hair, persuaded her to be signed into the psychiatric center. He used the word "medicate," and he said "stabilize." Alec used the word "okay," but I couldn't find one.

Then Alec used the word "no," and we went home. The doctor telephoned her, and then spoke to me, and we struck an agreement: I would bring Alec the next morning to the psychiatric unit of the Imogene Bassett Hospital in Cooperstown, New York, and she would receive "medication" and "stability" and "tests." Alec slept the rest of that day. I didn't. I looked at photographs in our albums, avoiding Barry's face when I could because I missed him when I saw him because when I looked up from the pictures I could never see him again unless I once again looked down. I was trying to find, in photos of Alec as an infant and child and young adult, a clue, in the droop of an eyelid or the tone of her skin, to what all these new words—"depression," "psychosis," "medication"—were about. I saw how often in her pictures she looked serious, or worried, or alert as if to a threat.

So we ought to have known, right?

I had asked this of the doctor, and he'd said, "No, ma'am. No.

Forget any words like 'should' and 'ought.' I have astonishing news for you. I want you to memorize what I say. You did not cause this disease and—you ready?—you can't cure it. Didn't cause, can't cure. Hug her when she lets you, and don't get mad at her. It isn't *her* fault, either. Well, you will get mad, but try and not show it."

I said, "But how can you have a problem and it isn't someone's *fault*."

He laughed. "I'm Jewish, too," he said, "but you can get used to it. No-fault disease."

I MADE COFFEE in the early morning, put the photo albums away, found my stomach too upset for coffee, and went upstairs to wake Alec for the drive to Cooperstown. She sat on her bed, her back against the wall, the covers wrapped around her as if she had just been rescued from a wreck at sea. Her face looked almost yellow, and the shadows under her eyes looked brown. She hadn't slept a lot of the night. She had wakened and, sitting before the mirror on her dressing table, she had cut off her hair. It lay on the floor around her chair. She had given herself a crew cut.

"Interesting hair," I said.

"Hair today," she answered, "gone tomorrow. It's tomorrow."

"We need to leave as soon as you shower," I said.

"I'm not going." Her eyes were dark with anger. Looking into them was like looking into the upstairs window of a high, old house. Someone, you suddenly realize with fright, is looking out of the window at you, and their expression has to do with disgust and with mockery.

I tried to say it to myself: *I didn't . . . I can't . . .* But I forgot the doctor's words.

"Sure, Alec. Yes. Absolutely. We have to go."

"Why do we have to go?"

"So you can get better."

"Better," she said.

"It's your *life*, Al. You need to do this."

"Need," she said.

"Al." I remembered his injunction against anger. I thought: Hey, *you* use your tranquility when it's *your* kid. "Goddamn it, Alec. This is for your *health*."

She said, as I knew she would, "Health."

Then I realized what I had seen. I went to her dressing table and got down on my hands and knees. Coriander lay among the long, looped shafts and shorter curls of hair, and she lay down there in two pieces. Using her shears, Alec had severed the stuffed head from its stuffed body.

I squatted there, then turned to face her. The terrible face appeared in the window and looked down the length of the room to me.

"Oh, Alec," I said.

She said, "Oh, Mommy. It's only a household pet."

The doctor had given me one more set of instructions, and I remembered them quite well.

I said, "I'm going to call the state police. They'll force you to the hospital, Alec. It'll, I don't know, go on your record. You'll be a lawyer with a note on your record: 'State Police,' it'll say."

"They can't," she said, "and don't pretend they can. You think you can put the whammy over on a *law* student? And *what* record, you Jew-mother jerk."

"I'm going to tell them I feel threatened. They'll do it."

"Threatened," she said. "Only if you're a household pet," she said, "or if you're named Petrekis."

"What about him?"

"You heard me."

"Alec, did you do something to Petrekis?"

"Who?"

"To punish him?"

"For hit-and-run foreplay? It *is* a punishable offense. For hit-and-run *soixante-neuf* compounded by simply yet absolutely Not. Being. A. Stand. Up. Guy."

"Alec, what? What happened?"

"When?"

"Okay. I'm calling the police. Have a happy morning." I went to the foot of the stairs and found the number in the phone book and dialed it. My hand was shaking, and my voice, when I spoke to a woman who called herself sergeant something, wobbled and wavered. I said, "I'm calling from outside of . . . no, it's really in the township . . . Hell. I'm a little nervous. Sorry." Take a breath, ma'am, take your time, are you all right, etc. And I was saying, "My daughter has had what I guess you'd call a nervous breakdown. I need to . . ."

Alec walked downstairs, wearing flannel pajama bottoms, a dirty white T-shirt, and slippers without socks. She shook a blanket out like a cape and wrapped it around her shoulders. She went around the corner into the living room, and I heard noises but closed my eyes and took a breath so I could tell the sergeant what I needed.

Alec reappeared. She was red-faced, and I was grateful for any relief of her pallor, even though she was the color of her anger at me.

"Whore," she said. "Candy-assed Jew whore and your pimp doctor cop friends."

She walked past me and out the back door.

"A second," I said to the sergeant.

I heard my car door slam.

"I'm sorry," I said, swallowing against what I think would have been sobs. "I think it might be all right. I'll call you back if there's a problem. Thank you. I'm very sorry for this."

I didn't and I can't.

I took a jacket and keys and my wallet and went outside to drive her to the hospital. That was where they finally came, a couple of days later, when I was in the visitor's lounge, taking a break from Alec's complaints and her anger at what she called my betrayal. It was a new word to hear from Alec about myself, and I was chewing on it, really tasting its possibilities for me. A man in a wrinkled gray uniform was directed to me in the washed-out light of the beige waiting room, and he presented me with what he called a bench warrant—I had never heard the words—for Alec's arrest, sworn out by a magistrate in Manhattan because she had fled the county to avoid prosecution for stabbing Victor Petrekis in the face.

The information about the face came from the sheriff's deputy who served the warrant. The warrant used the following words: "felonious" and "assault." Neither it nor the deputy conveyed the information that the weapon was the small stainless pocket knife imported by the assailant's father and given to her so she could be, for a little while, one of the fellows. The deputy left, and then I left. I needed to talk to lawyers, and Alec did not need to deal with one more fact served up by the world.

At home, I spent about an hour making chicken salad for a sandwich. I had no bread in the house, so I spent a while longer defrosting some rolls, then slicing and toasting one. I made myself a big sandwich with lots of lettuce, and I carried it into the living room. I wanted to sit with a book and find some language that would do me some good. I drifted along the shelves looking at titles, soon enough coming to the conclusion that I hadn't the energy to read a paragraph of anyone's book. I looked at a stack of CDs. I didn't want music either. I wanted silence, sleep, and somebody, when I woke up, who would manage the claims for health insurance, the bills from the landlord in New York, the conversation with the lawyer I would have to hire to represent Alec in court.

I realized that I was staring not at dust jackets but at the objects in front of them: the bride and groom, who had more or less outlasted Barry and me, despite the nick I'd left on the head of the groom, and who had served to demonstrate, Barry liked to say, how dangerous my appetites had always been. When he spoke about sex, he would leer, I told him, like a peasant in the countryside. And he was pleased to serve as the local life force.

I said, "Barry!"

Their heads were off. She had battered them against the edge of the shelf. Fragments lay there and on the floor, and it came to me then: the poem they recite at you during graduations and the presentation of trophies to injured athletes. It was about how if you could keep your head while all about you were losing theirs and blaming it on you, you'd own the world.

I saw that each figure had a metal rod around which it was molded, so the little couple would probably not crumble further, and would stand, adhering to their little skeletons, for as long as I left them on the shelf. I chewed at my chicken salad sandwich, looking back into their faceless stare.

I let myself pretend that Barry would walk into the living room then and ask me what I was doing.

I let myself pretend I would answer.

"Owning the world," I would say around a mouthful of sandwich.

BOB'S YOUR UNCLE

I LOVED HIS MOTHER ONCE. One time, that is, in my marriage to Jillie, I loved this boy's mother, made love to her, once, with gritted teeth, and a wet mouth, and wide eyes. When he came to our house, where his parents years before had brought him to visit with Jillie and me, I thought he carried word of his mother's death. He blinked in my doorway, he smiled with embarrassment as I did. And I started mourning Deborah. And then I was relieved. And then, of course, I grew so guilty about the sorrow and about my almost physical sense of release—freedom from the dream of her, and freedom from the secret—that I was speechless and blushing, a little breathless, while I watched his taxi back down our drive and turn toward Rhinebeck. I nodded to prompt his next words. He nodded back. I felt a tentative relief and I smiled. He smiled in return. I shrugged and held my arms out. He shrugged and we embraced.

Finally, I called, "Kevin Slater's here!"

Kevin nodded his agreement. He carried an expensive leather overnight bag on a shoulder strap, and he wore an unconstructed sportcoat of light brown linen over olive chinos. His shirt was thick, creamy cotton with olive stripes, and his loafers, over bare feet, were of a soft, tan weave. His face had grown long and lean and muscular, but he still, with his peaked eyebrows and big, brown eyes, his tan complexion and his smile you would only call wicked, looked like a boy.

Kevin said, "Hi, Uncle Bob. Hi, Aunt Gillian."

Jillie, arriving behind me, said or sang a long "Oh," and then she shouldered past me to seize Kevin and hug him.

He smiled over her shoulder at me, and I saw in his grin and in his young man's face what I saw, and had told myself I wasn't seeing, when he was a boy: a kind of menace that you call, that I had called, naughty or wicked, but that was maybe threatening—was maybe a sign of something even dangerous. The way certain autistic children can seem ordinary and then, on study, not quite, Kevin seemed in reverse— extraordinary, but then, perhaps, not quite. Maybe he was simply a tall, muscular, *café-au-lait* kid with wicked, call them naughty, eyebrows.

"How's your mother?" I said. "Your folks."

"London still. Dad's a big shot. They send for him in limousines. *American* limousines, the long ones."

Jillie said, "Your mother's all right?"

He shook his head as Jillie released him. His face grew slack and sad. "Mom has a boyfriend. He's a chemist at Glaxo. She says no, but Dad says yes."

I felt as if I'd sucked on a lemon, and as I spoke the pain remained, inside my head, beneath the ears, at the mastoid. "What's your opinion, Kevin?"

"She says no," he answered. "But some nights she doesn't come home and Dad makes breakfast for us."

"You're only as old as you think," Jillie said. Then: "Darling Kevin, come inside and stay for a while. That's why you're here, I think. To stay with us?"

"Could I? I got no place to go, I'm pretty sure. I went to my friend's house in New York, but he moved. I don't know a lot of people, Aunt Gillian." His face wrinkled in horizontal folds, and I thought he was going to cry. She hugged his arm to her, and I watched as he moved it a little to better brush her breast. She tugged him along. When he passed me, as I stood back to hold the door, I smelled again his funk of airplane travel—unwashed skin, stale air, exhaustion—and I saw that his swell shirt was dirty, as though he had worn it for a week. Grit was crushed in the nubbing of his sportcoat, and his trousers had dark spills of sauce imprinted down the front. I had sat him on my lap to drive the lawn tractor. I had held him on the dock at our pond. And here he was, wily and odd-looking, very large and a little arrested-sounding, and coated with the grime of the world.

When he was four, I remember, they had started visiting doctors and had begun to send him to private schools. Teachers called him difficult, one even called him frightening, and that sent his mother to pediatric psychologists and Kevin to more expensive schools. They had tried for six years—of taking Deborah's temperature, of consulting fertility cycle charts, of pumping Arthur into test tubes—and then they had adopted Kevin, a beautiful baby whose birth mother was Honduran, and Kevin had become the warning bird in Deborah's life. She was like a miner in a coal seam who watched the canary—a bird's health meant good air, a bird going sick meant misfortune. Deborah, always extraordinary, with her pale, oval face and her sad eyes, long pianist's fingers, ebony hair, became brilliant with Kevin. He was the dream of her life she had dreamed. When he was well, she shone like his moon. When he was becoming what the schools called *difficult,* her hair went matte, and her eyes floated over deep brown, sorrowful semicircles. Arthur, who was erect as a soldier and who never wanted children, he claimed, was a father dutiful not to the baby, but to his wife. In serving Kevin, he served her, and I thought it likely she had never forgiven that disloyalty to Kevin. He was a sales manager of switches and machine parts for all of western Europe on behalf of a British firm that also owned paper mills and bakeries. He'd grown rich and Deborah distant, at least from us, and their child with Indian and Spanish blood was here, as out of focus—no: as hard to find a focus for—as an ill-composed snapshot.

Jillie said, "Kevin, how long can you stay?"

From a distance he was a male model, and up close he was a soiled boy edging toward man. His confused, confusing smile flared, and he said, "Whatever you say, Aunt Gillian."

"I say you stay as long as you feel like."

He clenched a fist and showed it to me, as if we had both been striving for admission. I nodded back and I guess it was a smile I showed him in return. Jillie took him upstairs and I went, as if casually, to the bookshelves in the living room. I found the book, a collection of poems by Alan Dugan that his mother had given me. There was a poem in it that began, "The curtains belly in the waking room." Deborah had brought it to me, along with a wonderful antique book of flower prints for Jillie, and a bottle of Château Palmer that Arthur analyzed before he let us taste it. They were house gifts she bore, except that I knew which room the curtains had bellied in, and who had wakened with whom, and so did Deborah, and we were the only ones.

Kevin slept off his jet lag, and Jillie and I cast speculations that sank like stones in the sea.

"He might just be a little dopey from travel," she said.

"You know what weariness is, and you know it's something else."

"It couldn't be easy to march into somebody's house after, Jesus, eleven or twelve years, it must be. And say, 'Hello, my mother's sleeping around and my father's too busy, and I'm a little screwed up.'"

"No," I said, "except he didn't say or intimate or even hint *sleeping around*, Jillie."

"She always fancied your ass."

"Oh, come on."

"Didn't she."

"Jillie."

"And you were not, let's say, unalert to that exquisite face or the body that went along with it. Could we say unalert?"

"It isn't even a word, much less a smart idea. No."

"No," she said.

"That is correct."

"No is correct."

"I *said* so."

"And so you did. Except I think she did fancy you, as they say."

"Nobody says fancy you and nobody says unalert."

We were behind the house, in a field that curved like a cheek, and we were walking slowly in the bright six o'clock light of a late-spring sunset. Jillie wore her New York Knicks baseball hat over a new haircut that was so short, she said, the breezes made her cold. She wore the hat, I thought, in mourning for the Knicks, who had once again failed to make progress in the playoffs. I took her hat off and ran my hand through her hair. She held my wrist and pulled my hand down onto her head.

"You are a bit of a frog and a fogey," she said, "but I am not unalert to your cute little paunch and your much-fancied ass."

"You don't know *any* words," I said. "Paunch is out these days."

She looked at my midsection. "Out and over the belt, just about. But we can say belly if you like."

As in what a curtain will do in a bedroom window in the cool air of morning, if you like.

EARLY SUNDAY, KEVIN was up by the time I returned from Rhinebeck with newspapers and German coffee cake. I could smell the shampoo and soap, but I could smell his clothing—he was wearing what he'd worn the day before—and, for all his scent of soap, there were bands of dirt beneath his nails, and his knuckles seemed dyed a darker brown than his broad hands. Jillie was in her jeans and one of my flannel shirts and she wasn't wearing a brassiere, which I learned by following Kevin's eyes as she walked across the kitchen with coffee and plates for the cake.

"Kevin," I said, "are you all through with school?"

"I'm done with school, Uncle Bob."

"Did you go to prep school?"

"I went to the American school."

"And you graduated?"

"Sure."

"Are you out on your own?"

"Whenever I want."

"No, I mean are you *living* on your own. In an apartment, with a job and a life and all of that."

"Jobs are hard," Kevin said.

Jillie said, "Is there anything in the sports about the Knicks making a deal? So they can *silence* their critics? Bob?"

I finally said, "Ah." She rarely had to do more than hoist a cardboard sign and beat on the congas for five or ten minutes before I understood these signals. Our child had been grown and away long enough for me to have forgotten the need in a household for an alternative language. I passed her the sports section of the *Times* and pretended that I was reading the editorials.

Kevin said, "This is so nice."

I looked over the News of the Week in Review section to watch a giant tear glide out of each eye and down. It was like seeing a toddler in sorrow.

Jillie said, "Kevin, sweetheart. What? Are you homesick?"

He watched her alertly, as if she'd offered a clue. He thought. Then he said, "No, Aunt Gillian. No. We did this when I was a little boy. Remember? Breakfast? Newspapers. Cake. Everybody was happy."

"But it isn't happy at home," Jillie said.

"No more. Dad gets mad. He goes away too much. Mommy does too. I stay with Martha. I go out on Cheyne Walk. I buy things for Martha. I go home. I watch the telly. It's boring! Mostly, it's quite terribly sad."

The last five words came out in a voice that wasn't his. I imagined we were hearing Martha's intonations. He moved his neck as though his collar was tight. He scrubbed at his face with his cupped hands.

"All right, then, Kevin?" Jillie looked up. I had spoken in a kind of echo of the London I heard in his voice.

"Medicine," he said. He smiled, as though divulging something lovely. His beautiful eyes were bright and moist. "I take tablets twice a day." He opened a small gold pill box and removed something smaller than an aspirin, and white. "Once in the morning and once at night, and Bob's your uncle." He pointed at me. "And he is! Bob *is* my uncle!"

So what we had here was a seventeen- or eighteen-year-old boy who was, from time to time, about six years old, I thought. He was built like a goalie for Manchester United and he had been tied to the ground, like Gulliver, but by medicine instead of rope. And he fancied his Aunt Gillian in some fairly obvious ways. He had fled to us, or fled from them, and here he was, a young man charged with the energy of mission, of *errand,* a radiated electric sense that you might as well call purpose. He seemed to me a messenger who tarried, who chatted, who relished our anticipation of what he had come to say. But he didn't, or he wouldn't, or he couldn't, say it. We were waiting, and so, perhaps, was he. Or maybe it was the medicine, or what the medicine held in check.

Gillian asked him if he felt well, and he told her of his stomach troubles on the flight. He proved how well he now felt by eating a large bite of coffee cake. I read in the Travel section that a dollar bought .60 of a pound. I tried to calculate what that meant a pound would cost and, when I arrived at something like twenty-four dollars, I knew what I was going to do. I waggled a finger at Jillie, which meant I'd return in a minute, and, in the extra first-floor bedroom that we shared as an office, I worked out what time it was in London. My answer seemed to be thirteen dollars, so I told the phone to hell with it and dialed the international code. After the hiss and the charge of static, I heard the double ring of an English phone. It went on and on. I thought I felt like Arthur, calling home of an afternoon and wondering why my wife wasn't there to answer.

Kevin was at the sink with Jillie, leaning into her a little as they scraped and washed and dried.

I said, with the tact that won me to the hearts of deponents and courtroom adversaries, "Are you staying long in America, Kevin?"

He turned to me, smiled his smile, shrugged, then turned away and leaned back in against Jillie. He shrugged again. Jillie shrugged, as if in response, but she was signaling me. It meant: *Who knows* what *we've got here? Wait awhile and see.*

I went back to our office and dialed the call again. Thinking as Arthur, I insisted to myself, I wondered what I hadn't for years and years: Where are you now? Whom are you with? What do you feel? And, like Kevin, I was gripped in the stomach, seized that is in the ganglion there, thinking with my belly and probably my balls. Feeling, finally, like no one but me, like a lover gone into the past, I was wounded as I hadn't been for years by the thousands and thousands of miles between upstate New York and the Chelsea Embankment. The telephone chimed the distance. I could feel the hugeness of the surface of the sea between Block Island and Margate. And then the ancient but familiar furtiveness returned, so I hung up.

Kevin, in the kitchen, said, "Bob! Where'd you go?"

"Back there." I pointed with my thumb.

"What'd you do?"

"Nothing much."

"Boring, huh?"

"Kevin, you're not boring. Aunt Gillian isn't boring."

"So *you* must be!"

I said, "Exactly."

In his English voice, he told Jillie, "Bang on right, isn't he?"

She said, "Kevin, in all the years I've spent with this man, and some of them have been lollapaloozas, he has never been boring."

"Lol—"

"Lollapaloozas."

"What's that, Aunt Gillian?"

"It means he is a heavy-duty, full-time, nonstop job."

Kevin looked as though he might glow. "She really likes you, Uncle Bob."

I said, "I hope so."

Kevin gestured at the kitchen or at us. "I'm never going home," he said.

Years before, not long after London, our daughter, Tasha, had told me, "Whenever you lie, Daddy, I know it from your face. You catch yourself. You hear your own lies. I think you hate them or something, because you always look disgusted with yourself."

I'd told her, "No, I can always hedge on the facts, a little, when I'm arguing in court. It's a professional necessity. And I was even a pretty good cardplayer in the Army."

"Well, sure," she'd said, looking like Gillian's younger sister, broad-shouldered and slim-hipped, a fine swimmer, a ferret of fathers. "That's easy, lying to judges and juries and clients and shady lawyers."

"You left out hit men and child molesters."

"But with *us*," she said, "ha! You're hopeless with us."

Jillie, all those years later, said to Kevin in our kitchen, "You stay as long as you like." She sounded like she meant it.

She was coaching me, and I caught the hint. "As long as you like," I said. It sounded to me like a lie.

"I LOOKED IT UP in the big dictionary, and it means you were court-martialed," I said. "Given a dishonorable discharge."

"It means *safe*," Jillie whispered directly into my ear in bed that night. We were acting like children, I thought, or like a man and woman sneaking some time together in bed. "Bob means safe, it's an old-time English expression. I read it somewhere. I don't remember. Dickens? Thomas Hardy? Arnold Bennett?"

"The turncoat? You'd take his word? It *means* turncoat, maybe."

"No, that's Benedict Arnold." The effect of all this whispering was reminiscent of high school, the wet tongues of girls, the hard, waxy ears of their boyfriends. Her voice, hushing and warm in my ear, was making itself felt on the soles of my feet. They actually tingled. As if a wave of sensation bounced, then, back up through my body, my penis went heavy and hard, and I laid it against her thigh. "Good grief," she said, "I'll keep naming them, if I can remember any more. Oliver Goldsmith. George Gissing. *Thackeray*, oh, yum."

"So the kid's saying to me, Safe as Uncles?"

"He's saying everything's okay. All's well. He's using a piece of old-fashioned slang he heard from his nanny or housekeeper or whatever this Martha person is because she's the only one who hangs around with him now and because he's scared. He's like a child, Bob. He's like that dear little boy he was when they used to bring him here."

"When Deborah used to bring him here. Arthur dropped her off and picked her up because he was too busy in the gadget trade and because we were boring."

"I never cared. She was my friend," Jillie said. "I loved her."

"I used to think you, you know—"

"What?"

"I used to think the two of you—you know."

"Friends?"

"Lesbian?"

"Bob. You sound jealous."

"You know me. I probably was. And there's nothing wrong with—loving each other. However you did it."

"Really?"

I was halfway on top of her now, and my hand was in her pajamas. "I hope I believe it. Would you tell me?"

"What, exactly?"

"If you and she—"

"Deborah."

"Yes."

"Yes."

I said, *"Yes?"*

"I mean, yes, I would tell you. But no. We *loved* each other. We were real friends. *Real* friends. I think that's why I'm all over Kevin. I miss her really a lot. I hurt with missing her when I let myself get into it. Sink down into thinking about it."

My hand was on her stomach, edging down, and she reached in the dark and took hold of my wrist, pushing. *The curtains belly in the waking room.* I said, "Belly," working down with her, our hands moving together from her belly and together on her groin and then our fingers, pressed together, inside her, moving. We were breathing in unison, and the tone of our breathing deepened, but it was still a kind of whisper, a conversation.

Deborah had pointed out the poem for me not only because there had been a heavy white curtain that bellied in the window of the hotel in Marlow. She was also, as the four of us sat together and as Kevin played with a metal reproduction tractor I had bought him, reminding me that I had kneeled before her in the room, beside the bed, and had reached beneath her skirt to take down her pantyhose and underpants and then had climbed up inside the tent of her skirt head-first, kissing her thighs that felt cool to my lips, and working around her groin, biting on her stomach, growling, "Belly," which had made her shriek laughter, as if she were terribly ticklish.

"Idiot," she'd told me, her hand on my head through the skirt. "You're doing Cookie Monster from *Sesame Street.* God. *Coo-kie.* Idiot Bob."

"Belly," I snarled into her, forcing my face where little force was required as she spread her legs to my mouth and fell back on the bed. "Belly," I said, below it.

Jillie was bucking up at our hands, at our fingers, saying, "Bobby, come on," pulling me onto her, replacing our hands with me, filling herself with me as I loved her and cheated again with her friend.

JILLIE CALLED IN, telling them she was away for the day. She was a partner in a letterpress printing company that sold old-fashioned-looking letterhead to the publishers and antiques dealers and artists who lived in our section of Dutchess Country, a hundred miles north of New York. I was going to spend the day in the office working on a suit involving an Ethiopian national whose French-owned airplane had fallen into the Mediterranean. I was suing on behalf of the dead man's sister, who had become an American citizen. Jurisdiction wasn't undecipherable, but it was complicated, and I was going to be phoning and faxing all day. But I was also, I told Jillie, going to be worried about her at home with Kevin.

I was leaning over my coffee cup, whispering again, and resenting my need to be secret at home. Although, I reminded myself, I had surely been secret enough before and for a long time. "What if he gets violent?" I roared in a hush. "Didn't he used to get that way when he was a boy? A little boy?"

Jillie said, in less of a whisper than would have made me comfortable, "He got frightened. He got apprehensive. And he's my dear friend's child."

"Your dear friend who hasn't written or called in how long?"

"Well, she's going through some things."

"What?"

"Never *mind*." Jillie rarely sounded stern. I think she learned impatience and cruelty from me. And when she spoke like an angry me to me, I found myself, always, quailed.

"Quelled and quailed," I told her.

"What?"

"The way your eyes get big and your brows go up and your voice gets brittle and mean and your cheeks get pale. You look like a killer."

She nodded, sipped at her coffee, said, "Don't you forget it," and sipped again.

"But call me," I said. "If there's *anything*. You call me."

"And you will ride upstate in a couple of hours, once you get free of the office and out of midtown traffic and off the Henry Hudson Parkway and through the Hawthorne Circle and up the Taconic, and you will rescue me."

I said, "Damned right."

"You're a dope, Bob."

"Damned right," I said

"A middle-aged dope with delusions of heroism."

"Wrong," I said. "A middle-aged dope with a wife at home alone with a—with a troubled boy."

"Man, nearly."

"Jesus, Jillie. You never called Tasha a *woman* until she was a junior in college."

"It never upset you whether I did or not."

"And this does, so you're doing it?"

She nodded.

"You are really pissed off."

She nodded again.

"I could have sworn we were crazy and all over each other last night."

She nodded.

"And *that* makes you mad?"

She said, "In a way." Then: "No." She shook her head. She took an enormous breath. She said, "This is something to forget. To never mind. I am not pissed off. We *did* have a good time. You know that. I'm thinking, though, we're rolling around in the rack and Debbie's crazy in England and it doesn't seem *fair.*" She took another long breath.

"You'll hyperventilate," I said. "It doesn't seem fair for you to— could I say enjoy? For you to enjoy your marriage? And I suspect she *is* rolling around. In *somebody's* rack."

"If I hyperventilated and fell out of my chair and cracked my head on the floor and died, well-fucked, then that would seem to be a reasonable exchange *and* fair to Debbie. As for her sex life, don't make the mistake of thinking a random screw, or a whole matched set of them, is any substitute for, I don't know—for being happy a little." She watched me. She nodded her head very hard. "Really," she said. "Anything else, and you're dreaming."

At the office, I punched numbers on the phone. I called Deborah and hung up. I called Jillie and disconnected before it could ring. I called Tasha, who was teaching medieval history at the University of Texas in Austin. Her answering machine had no message, only a long pause and then a suddenly burped tone to prompt the speaker, but the caller needed to hear his kid's voice more than tell her anything, so he hung up. I telephoned the retired appellate court judge who was of counsel to the firm handling Air France matters in the States and soon enough was doing the equivalent of starting to try to untie a very tight knot made of soft, wet wool.

The judge and I hung up, issuing the phony quacks of business bonhomie. The telephone rang at once and my secretary, Ms. Seidman, who detested me and all lawyers—everyone, in fact, except the performance artist who pierced his body as part of his art with whom she lived in apparently something of a state of excitement—announced that my wife was on the line.

This time, she was the whisperer. I said, "I can't hear you, Jillie. Is it Kevin?"

She said, very low and muffled, as if her hand was over her lips and the telephone, "He's talking to himself."

"In a menacing way?"

"No, no. It's—it's upsetting. He's so *worried*."

"*He's* worried. He's in trouble. That's who talks to themselves, people in trouble. Is there any reason to think he's going to act out?"

"Bob, you don't know what in hell act out *means*."

"No, but I hear it a lot. Do you notice how you're always correcting my words, these days? Jillie: you think—I'm asking this, I guess—do you think he's going to do anything physical to express what's on his mind?"

"That *is* what it means."

"Jillie, for Christ's sake, you're home alone with a kid the size of a goddamned fullback who is *at least* immature and somewhat retarded and worried and frightened and more than likely he's a hell of a lot more screwed up than either of us thought, and you're *teaching* me. Are you—never mind. I'm coming home."

"You can't come home. You have to get rich people out of their responsibilities and obligations, don't you?"

"You're hunting for my *head*, Jillie."

"For your belly."

"My belly?"

In Cookie Monster's voice, she said, "Belly."

"Stay near the door or something," I said. "Go out to Millerton and hang around in crowds."

"Where do they keep them, again, in Millerton?"

I said, "Shit. Goddamn it. Jillie. Take care. I'm coming home."

"Oh, boy," she said.

In the elevator I thought it, and in the car I said it to myself: "*She* telephoned *you*. *She* picked up the phone and she called *you*." Going uptown and west, I said, "And now you're talking to yourself like Kevin, aren't you?" I was doing sixty-five on the Henry Hudson, ignoring the rearview mirror and, frankly, anything to either side. I wasn't driving the car, I was aiming it. I remembered telling clients in ticklish cases to keep their silence. People, you see them and observe their behavior, and you think: nobody talks to *any*one. But you're wrong. They do. Whenever you think they can't, or they won't, then they do. I thought about Jillie and Deborah. Oh, they do, I thought. I said, in a singsong, "She called Kevin's mom-my." Then I said, "Cookie Monster's gonna eat up all of your *ass*."

I stopped at one of the little places on Route 82 and bought hot dogs and rolls and sodas and a box of chocolate chip cookies. I went seventy miles an hour until I got to our driveway, up which I let the car waddle casually, uncle fellow, daddy guy, coming home with snacks and not a tad concerned about the safety of his wife *or* the menace of her recently discovered rage.

Kevin was outside, splitting kindling. He wore his olive slacks and basket-weave loafers and his cream-and-olive shirt. I watched his back and arms as he swung the ax, and I remembered seeing them, but smaller, and bare, brown in the summer sun, when Deborah and he had come to stay for a week. I had taken him out to our shed and showed him how to split wood. Maybe he was six or seven, broad-backed and strong, and his coordination had been excellent. Once he saw how to stand the chunks upright on the chopping block and swing without fear, letting the momentum of the head of the ax do the work, he became good at it. He was good at it now. As I got out of the car, I heard him grunt as he swung, just as he had a dozen years before. In a way, he was the same boy.

I heard the breath expelled, the woodcrack, the intake of his breath, and then the words. He said, low, "*You* can't go down there! Who ever said *you* could go down there? It isn't allowed, and you know it very well. *Yards* of bother in that, silly boy. You stay up here with me, won't you?" Then he swung, and the wood split, and he stood another piece on the block. "Of course," he said, and in a different, deeper, voice, "this isn't the kind of report we like to get. We don't *blame* you, understand. No one's *blaming* you. All we care about is if you're happy and well. Would you call yourself happy and well? Can you think of anything Mommy and I can do to *make* you happy and well? By God, we would do it, Kev. We'd do anything. You know that." He swung, but the head was canted a little and the ax skipped. He was positioned right, and he was safe. "Look the head right into the wood," he instructed himself. The voice was familiar. Of course. It was mine. He split the piece, took a breath, set up another and, looking at it and saying, "All I love is you," as if Deborah were speaking to her son in our yard, he swung the ax. All he had to do now, I thought, was imitate Jillie divorcing me, and he'd have invoked us all.

Before he could tense for another swing, I said, "Kevin. Hot dogs for lunch."

He turned to watch me walk over from the car. "How come I didn't hear you come here, Uncle Bob?"

"I guess I drove very quietly."

He laughed a little too loudly, watching me with his baby's brown eyes. He was very alert. I wondered what had made him that wary. "I was chopping wood," he said. "In case we need it for the fireplace."

"You did a good job, Kevin. Do you remember how to leave the ax?"

He turned and swung, very hard, and buried the blade in the block.

"Good man," I said with gratitude.

Jillie had been watching us from the kitchen, I thought, because she was at the door before I touched the knob. "Home for lunch, how nice," she said, as if I hadn't driven too quickly. "Kevin's been splitting kindling, and I've been trying to think of something special to eat." I handed her the paper sack, and she said, "My favorite! Hot dogs! My white knight of the sausage casing."

Kevin said, "Yay!"

"Boiled, I think. I have a package of sauerkraut and some yellow mustard and—yes, we'll grill the rolls. It'll be an all Brooklyn hot dog day. Like eating at Nathan's. Kevin—did you ever get to Nathan's at Coney Island?"

He was studying her bottom in her jeans. "No, Aunt Gillian," he told her buttocks.

She said, "We'll go there one day. With Mommy. Kevin? Your mom's coming here."

"Here? How?"

"The same way you did."

"Airplane," he said. "It was a terrible trip. It took for*ever*. They gave me an extra dinner, did I tell you that? When?"

"Jillie," I said, after a while, "Kevin wants to know when she's coming."

"Deborah is coming," Jillie said while looking at me, her brows up and her cheeks pale, "tomorrow. She's going to rent a car and drive up from New York."

"That's an ugly drive if you're jet-lagged."

"No," Jillie said, "she'll take a couple of Valium when she gets on and she'll sleep through. She always does. She'll be fresh for the trip. Will you be glad to see her, Kevin?"

"Yup."

"Will you be glad to see her, Bob?"

"It's been a while, hasn't it? Is Arthur coming?"

Jillie shrugged.

"You called her?"

Jillie, at the stove, nodded.

"How was it? The conversation?"

"Pas devant l'enfant." She added, *"Merde,"* probably because she was pleased with her rediscovered French.

I decided not to be warned off. I really needed to *know*. "I mean, after what? A real while, huh? You guys just clicked right into place and it was like no time lost? Nothing uneasy?"

Jillie said, with conviction, *"Cochon."* You can be cute when you call a man a swine, or you can mean it—the snout, the hairy tail, the four hard hooves.

I decided not to say, in French, Why, what a clever notion you had, making things safe by suggesting he play with the ax. I imagine the idea was to get him outside, away from you. But think how handy it would have been if he'd decided to get back *in* in a hurry. I did say, "I think maybe you want to let us wash your clothes for you, Kevin. I'll give you something of mine, and you let us—"

"That means Aunt Gillian," Jillie said. "Uncle Bob, with his jurisprudence degree and the *summa cum laude* from Cornell never quite got hold of the mystery of the washing machine dial."

"Quel canard," I said. "Jillie, what was Deborah's news? What's up?" What's up?"

I went to the stoveside counter and took the platter of hot dogs and the basket of rolls. Jillie brought mustard and sauerkraut and glasses of pop on a tray. Kevin seemed to have shrunk in his chair.

Jillie studied him. She said, "Mommy isn't coming because she's angry, Kevin. She's coming because she *misses* you."

He shook his head, and there seemed to be less play to his expression, less life in the muscles of his forehead and jaw. I said, "Hey, Kevin. You take your medicine every day, right?"

"Every day," he said.

"Did you take it *this* day?"

He looked at me and looked at me, and his eyes showed energy for an instant, and he shook his head. "I forgot," he said.

"Let's do it now, Kevin. You go find your medicine, your pills."

"Once in the morning and once with my tea."

"First, you can eat some hot dogs and then you can wash. And *I* will set the left-hand dial at medium, and the right at warm water wash and cold rinse. We'll have you clean as a whistle."

Kevin stuck a finger in each side of his mouth and, from stretched, unnatural-looking lips, he whistled so loudly you'd have thought someone was screaming.

We ate in a silence that wasn't peaceful. I smiled at Jillie and tried to help Kevin tend the sauerkraut that radiated from his plate in a ragged circle on his place mat and the dark wood of the table. I thought of Tasha, and I thought of Deborah. I watched Jillie's shoulders bow down, as she sat, beneath whatever she felt I had known her for so many years, and I could not have named her feelings. But I felt them gathering. I watched the lines at the sides of her eyes, the shifting muscles of her forearms, the skin of her cheeks, and the flesh at her hairline. Everything moved subtly, in ways I might have claimed once to know, but which now seemed new to me. Birds cackled near the kitchen window, and our mouths made soft noises around our food. It was gathering.

Kevin used the downstairs tub—we could hear him splash like a kid—and I loaded his clothing in the washing machine in the pantry off the kitchen while Jillie cleaned our lunch dishes. It didn't come with violence—an ax, say, wielded by the damaged son, Deborah's hope gone imperfect. It didn't come by surprise. It was the message from my life, and that should always be expected. Later in the day, later that night, alone, I told myself I'd been waiting for it for years.

Jillie came to the pantry with an obvious reluctance. But she couldn't, I saw, have stayed away. She came close to me. I could smell the bright scent of the dishwashing soap and the rich darkness of her perfume on her skin. She reached for my arm, which was poised with detergent above the machine, and she touched the back of my hand. She put her fingers gently around my wrist. She couldn't make her fingers meet although I felt the pressure of her effort. Then she let me go.

She took a deep breath. It reminded me of Kevin's breathing outside at the woodpile. I thought of myself in Marlow, years before, panting like a runner.

She said, "What was it, when you were with her, and I was taking Tasha to the British Museum—we were wearing our matching god-damned tan tourist raincoats, Bob, for heaven's sakes! And you and Deborah were laughing and doing everything together that you did. What did you think was coming to you that you deserved so much?"

Kevin stepped into the doorway behind us, a muscular man who wore a towel over grown-up cock and balls, and also a damp, happy child just out of his bath.

Jillie looked from me to Kevin and then again at me. She stood between men gone wrong, or boys who hadn't turned out right. You looked at us, I thought, and we seemed okay. You looked again and we were ruined just a little. We were your dreams come true.

JOY OF COOKING

——————

As they chewed at Cheerios in milk and drank unnaturally orange orange juice in the breakfast room off the kitchen of their house, Stephen's daughters studied him through eyes distorted by corrective lenses. Sasha seemed patiently curious, Brigitte apprehensive; neither spoke, and neither looked away. When Rosalie in their bedroom started to sing, not in words, just heavy syllables pounded atop a tune about joy—

> *Dee duh duh doe*
> *Dee da-da!*
> *Dee duh deed da*
> *Dum da-da!*

—Stephen saw his daughters watch him hurry to the kitchen, cocking his head to listen hard. Inside his face, on top of his tongue that rose as if *he* sang, and underneath a brain he thought of as boiling in his blood like an egg in water in a pot on a stove, Stephen supplied the words as Rosalie sang while she packed before leaving him:

> *Jesus loves me*
> *This I know!*

For the Bible
Tells me so!

And we're not even Christians, he thought. We aren't anything.

He had stayed home from work this morning after making sandwiches for the children's lunches. Sasha liked hard-cooked eggs in slices on mayonnaise smeared over soft white bread. Brigitte ate only smooth peanut butter with grape jelly on the same pulpy bread that Sasha liked. Both girls, nine and eleven, stared at him through dark-framed glasses that reminded him of Rosalie's (as did their eyes), and Stephen bellowed bad jokes, all but screamed *"Sure!"* when Brigitte reminded him about money for milk and an after-school snack. Rosalie, meanwhile, prowled their bedroom, blowing her nose and slamming things.

When the bus came, the children, he knew, were happy to be released. Brigitte had called from the front door, "Bye, Daddy. Bye, Mommy." But Sasha had said nothing. He'd called to them, as if deputized, "We love you!" As they fled the tension that ached in the house like flu in muscles, Stephen felt that he, too, had been set free. The feeling didn't last. He heard their bedroom door open as Rosalie marched in her fuzzy, dragging slippers to the bathroom and back. She must have left the door ajar: he heard the brass pulls on their bureau jangle, then the *thrap*, four times, of suitcase clasps, and he was certain that Rosalie was packing to leave.

He fetched a mug of coffee from the kitchen to the breakfast room and sat with it as Rosalie hummed, and as the words she didn't say echoed in his inner ear, though not in her voice but in his. She sounded, now, reassured by the song. She sounded young.

When he looked at the tile-topped breakfast table, he understood why his coffee had tasted awful. He had poured not milk but orange juice into his acid third cup. He still held the juice tumbler, which rattled on the tabletop to something like the rhythm—*dee* da-da—of Rosalie's song. Stephen kept time.

The tumbler was Sasha's. She had worn too much dark red lipstick, as usual, to counteract what she saw as the scarring effect of her braces. Of course the frame of crimson broadcast her braces, and she looked like the grille of a '49 Buick. Today she'd worn even more than he was used to, and Stephen wondered if, hearing their fight, she had laid the impasto of lipstick on as a rebuke to them. He had locked her out, though, with his porcelain grin, his morning commotion, his all-but-yodeled good cheer. He lifted her juice tumbler, and he kissed the one-lipped print that Sasha's mouth had left on the rim of the glass. It tasted like Crayola.

He left the breakfast room and walked through the kitchen, where the cat was on the counter next to the stove, eating hard-boiled eggs. He went down the small parquet corridor that connected the back of the house to the front, and he stood outside their bedroom door. It had two thin cracks that looked as though someone had tried to draw: they were stick-people, hand-in-hand, made by his kicking at the door when Rosalie had locked him out, years before. He watched her now, and he listened. She was wearing her heavy green plaid bathrobe, with a dark gray bathroom towel around her neck, tucked into the robe, like a scarf. She hummed about Jesus' love.

She looked up from her underwear drawer and her face was sullen, swollen, sliced by her glasses' dark frames. But when she took his stare and countered it with her own, she nearly smiled. He felt his eyebrows rise. "You've got lipstick on your mouth," she said.

He nodded. Leaning against the doorframe, he wiped at his lips, then licked them, then wiped once more. "Sash," he said. "I drank from her glass. She wore lipstick for two today."

Rosalie waited, then looked back into her drawer.

"You shouldn't do this," he said.

"Nope."

"Then don't."

"I shouldn't want to do this," Rosalie said. "I shouldn't feel so bad. Nobody should."

"Then don't feel bad."

"Stephen, we don't need to be as old as we are to talk like this. We could hire a couple of kids. We could get the girls to do it. God knows they hear it enough." After studying her underthings, she plunged both hands into the bureau drawer and drew out what looked like random handsful, then wheeled and went to the suitcases, and tossed some into each. She stood at the suitcases which lay on their bed and, with her back still toward him, she asked, "Why aren't you at work?"

"You really want to know?"

She went back to the bureau and began to examine pantyhose. She didn't answer him.

He said, "Because I'm scared to be. At first I stayed here to fight. But then I heard you singing that goddamned hymn. I thought: she's leaving."

"You're right."

"And I was too frightened."

He watched her shoulders slump. She pulled at the towel, settling it into the robe, around her neck.

"I'd have expected 'Onward, Christian Soldiers,'" he said.

"What was I singing?"

"You didn't know?"

She shook her head, she held up hosiery and shook her head again.

He said, "'Jesus Loves Me.'"

"I was? Really. I haven't sung that since I was a little girl. It's the song that good little girls like. They're *so* good, Jesus *has* to love them."

"Is this for real, Rosie? With taking the kids, everything? The girls go away, and you go away, and I'm supposed to live here alone?"

"No," she said. "After a while, the girls and I come back, and you've moved out. You're living in an apartment someplace. The girls and I live here. I don't know. Life goes on."

"This is really for real, then."

She slowly nodded.

"No," he said. "Rosie, we *love* each other. That's why we get so mad."

"So? You think love makes you feel better? Who said love makes you feel better? With you and me—and this is thirteen years into the mission, now, long enough for us to be out on the edge of the solar system if we're a rocket ship—"

"Wait a minute."

"Stephen, don't talk like a lawyer now. Don't you dare be smart and logical with me and tell me about facts. That's what got us here."

"No, it isn't, Rosie. What got us here was my wanting you to be my handmaiden. Dedicating your life to the Great Attorney. The thing about you as decoration in my career."

"*On* your career. You're really trying. You're trying so hard, you sound stupid. Like a kid who studied for a test and he doesn't know what all the memorized answers mean. You've been up half the night—"

"All of it."

"No. I was. I heard you snoring on the sofa."

"Wrong."

"See?"

"See what?"

"Never mind," she said, holding a knot of pantyhose away from her body, as if it were stirring and might strike. She carried it to the bed. "Just, let's say I'm acknowledging that you're really thinking about what we talked about. Except it has so little to do with the damned country club, the damned office dinner, the damned goddamned dance. Those are symptoms. It's all just a cliché. As you pointed out."

"Symptom," he said. "As in disease?"

"As in disease."

"So what's the disease? That you love me?"

She stared at him.

"Yeah," he said. "That's what it is. You love me—lawyer, no lawyer, whatever. That's what bothers the hell out of you: that you love me. *Is* that the disease? How do we treat a thing like that, Rosie?"

"I'm doing it," she said.

"No, you're not. You're taking twice as long to pack as I've ever seen you take to do anything. You could have changed all four tires on your car by now."

She turned to face him. She slowly pulled the towel out of her robe by one end, tugging on it hand over hand until the bath towel was hanging from her hand, and he could see the mottling of blue and red at her throat.

"Jesus! Rosie! I didn't do that!"

She said, "I did."

"Why?"

"Because I can't make you understand, and I can't make *me* understand." Her teeth were clenched as she spoke. "I stood in the bathroom last night, while *you slept,* damn it. You *slept.* And I looked at my stupid round face and my buck teeth—"

"They aren't buck. They're crooked. They're sexy. Your face isn't round the way you say it's round. It's oval. You're a—you're a dish, Rosie."

She shook her head. Her eyes were closed, and she kept them that way as, rolling the towel, squeezing it, she said, "I looked in the bathroom mirror and I grabbed my throat. Like this"—she put one hand around her neck; he saw the thumb slide into its bruised print above her larynx—"and I said, 'Why can't you *learn?'*"

"Rosie," he asked her, "learn what?"

"That you're going to have to keep asking that all the time we're married. That I'm going to choke myself to death or drown the cat. Or you. Choke *you,* drown *you.* Because you see a way of living. Fine. You're entitled to. But it's *yours.* Its teeth are bigger than mine are, even. It could eat me. It could swallow me." She opened her eyes at last. She put the towel around her neck. As she tucked it in, she said, "That's all. It's a goddamned cliché. I know it. Didn't I say that before?"

"I think *I* might have called it that last night. It isn't, Rosie. I really believe that: it isn't."

"No, you were right. All of it's clichés."

"Rosie, but we love each other."

She shrugged.

Stephen slid down with his back against the doorframe. He stuck his legs out so they straddled the wall on which the wide-open door was hinged.

"Are you doing that to keep me in?" Rosalie asked.

"I didn't think of it that way. I'm thinking, just, I don't want you feeling so bad."

"Because I *can* step over you."

"Rosalie, you could step *through* me."

She sat down on the bed, next to the suitcases. She nodded. "I know."

Stephen was thinking that if they made love now he would want to set the suitcases down, not sweep them aside from the bed. He didn't want her to think he was sweeping aside what she'd said. He saw Rosalie watching him, and he knew that she was thinking how aroused he always was when she fought him and told him that she didn't care about love. He didn't smile to her, and when he saw how sad her magnified eyes behind her glasses were, and her mouth, and the brutal bruises on her fragile neck, his eyes filled up.

She said, "What, Stephen?"

"I remembered when I heard that singing before. It wasn't in church."

She lay back on the bed. She pulled her glasses off and held them, folded, in one hand. She drew her legs up and curled herself down toward them so that she wasn't quite a ball, but was lying on her side in a crescent.

"You look like a half-moon," he said

"You stay there. I don't want this thing ending up in some wild screw and we forget all about it."

"I'll sit right here."

"I mean it, Stephen."

"I was little. I don't know—eight? So my mother was young."

"Your mother was never young, Stephen. She was born old and mean."

"No, she was pretty, and she was young, and my father was gone by then. She was living with Carl Boden."

"The philosopher king."

"He was an interesting guy."

"Smart enough, I'll give him that, to take off on her."

"I think she was one of those people who people leave. I don't know."

"I do. She's mean. She's skinny and mean and she has those thin lips."

"But he was there, then, and for the next ten years or so, huh? And they had a good time together. I remember all those little pats on the ass, and smooching in the kitchen. Nice stuff."

"You would."

Her eyes were closed, and Stephen then closed his. He said, "I remember Carl was wearing this seersucker shirt. And he was sitting in the kitchen, watching her do something. I think she was cooking. I was playing, I guess. Drawing at the table. The radio was on. That was before we moved out to Harrison, so it was up on Eightieth Street, and she was listening to the radio. All of a sudden, Carl says to her, 'You don't sing anymore.' She says *What,* and everybody says *What* a few times, and Carl says, 'I used to love the way you sang when you cooked. It was always so happy.' Something like that—how she sounded happy, and she made him feel happy, and now he's disappointed, something is missing. Do I have to tell you she started to cry?"

He opened his eyes to watch her lift her shoulders. She said, "And?"

"And nothing. She stopped crying. He apologized a lot, she apologized a lot. I shut up and ate my food. Something under sauce, I'm sure. Anyway, the next day's Sunday. We're going to go to Central Park, we're going to hit the streets on Sunday in New York, and the radio's playing. A very dumb, bouncy song. I absolutely cannot remember its name, but I think I still remember what it sounded like. She's making those amazingly thick, brutal flapjacks of hers, and Carl's sitting there reading a book, growling at it the way he always did. And all of a sudden my mother's humming along with the song on the radio. 'Dee duh *duh,'* she sings, all noise, no words, and *heavy,* slamming down on the syllables, as heavy as her pancakes, 'Dee duh *duh!'* She's hitting those off-key notes, she was a terrible singer—and now, because I really don't remember seeing it, but now I imagine how she's looking out of the corner of her eye, right? To see if Carl notices? I didn't figure this out for years, of course."

"You didn't figure it out until this morning."

"Yes And then Carl leaves the room." He stopped. They were silent. Rosalie turned onto her side and opened her eyes. "That's the story?"

"That's the story. He throws his book down on the kitchen table, *whammo!*, and he walks out of the room."

"What'd your mother do?"

"I don't remember."

"*That's* the story. What *she* did, *then.*"

Now Stephen lay on his stomach, his feet out in the hall and his torso in the bedroom, and he propped his chin on his forearms. "That's *their* story. My part of it is what I said. How sad she was, trying to show him all of that awful joy I suppose she wasn't feeling. She tried to give him that. I think it was remarkably generous, what she offered."

Rosalie said, "I didn't offer you anything when I was singing. You understand that?"

"I was thinking about how sad it was, somebody who couldn't sing, and who really didn't feel like singing, trying to sing for someone."

"Do not start crying for that woman."

He said, "If I cried, Rosie, it wouldn't be for her."

"Don't you dare and cry for *me.*"

"No," he said. He put his head all the way down on his hands.

Rosalie said, "This is impossible. We're impossible."

They lay in silence, he on the floor and she on the bed.

She wakened him by saying, "See? You were sleeping."

"No," he said. He didn't know why. "I wasn't."

He watched her swing her feet over the side of the bed. Her robe was hiked, and he saw her calves and knees, her lower thighs. She pressed them together and pulled the hem of her bathrobe down. She sat on the edge of the bed and said, "Now *I'm* going to sleep. You go someplace else, please."

"Where?"

"I just want to *sleep!*"

He manufactured a dignity with which to climb to his feet and leave. When he was in the kitchen, he heard their bedroom door close. He shooed the cat from the stove, then collected all the dishes and rinsed them, stowed them in the dishwasher. He couldn't remember if you were allowed to wash the iron frying pan in the machine. He scratched at it with a steel pad just in case you weren't. And when the machine was humming and hushing, when the surfaces were wiped down and the wiping rag rinsed in water nearly too hot to touch, he took off his necktie, hung it on the dish towel rack, and telephoned the office.

As he gave instructions and answered questions, he thought of the musical tones he'd punched to reach his secretary. He thought of the clients who pressed those numbers and listened to those tones, waiting for advice. He heard his voice, over so many calls, dispensing wisdoms and assurances, citing statutes, offering precedents. And he knew how he'd concluded so many times that the marital tragedies to which he'd been asked to respond were, finally to him, all alike. It struck him with a kind of disgust how banal he and Rosalie were, how quotidian their sadness would seem to some other lawyer at some other phone number who might hear Stephen complain how his mind was shaken and his heart was sore. He wondered if, when his clients telephoned, his deepest inner parts went to sleep, like an arm pressed into the same position too long, while clients wept descriptions to him of one's suffocation and the other's need for self-expression, and everyone's rage to flee. His secretary waited, and he finally heard the lengthening pause, so he finished and rang off.

Stephen walked from the kitchen to the breakfast room and back. He stood in the kitchen, frightened because he'd no idea what to do. At last, he fetched his briefcase from the hall and set it on the table in the breakfast room. He took from it a yellow ruled pad and the fountain pen that Rosalie had given him when he'd been made a partner. Then he did what he did in the office: he made notes. At the top of the page, he printed PROBLEMS. Halfway down the page he drew a horizontal line and printed SOLUTIONS. It was a letter-size pad, so he had four inches or so for problems—not enough, he thought. He tore the page from the pad and made his dividing line vertical. He headed the left side PROBLEMS. He thought he heard their door slam, and he paused. No one came, he breathed more evenly, and he headed the right-hand side SOLVE. He tore the page away.

On the next clean page, he wrote *Dear Rosalie.* He tore the page out. *Rosie,* he wrote. Looking from the breakfast room to the narrow bookshelves on which stood her cookbooks and his *Encyclopedia of Wines and Spirits,* he saw a very old, blue spine—the *Joy of Cooking* her parents, both dead now, had given them when they married. He set down his pen and went to the kitchen and, singing a song—singing Dee duh *duh!*—and not thinking of its name, he took the book, and he began. The song, he would remember later, was called "If I'd Known You Were Coming, I'd Have Baked a Cake," and his mother, he would then remember, had offered its syllables to her lover, Carl Boden.

But for now, he followed directions. He sifted flour. He found baking powder. He used nine eggs in achieving four separated yolks and whites. He set butter aside to reach room temperature. He found almonds and ground them. He slowly melted chocolate. He whipped up milk and vanilla and egg white without spattering them. And he baked the cake so that a toothpick slid unstained from its core. While it cooled, he mixed the icing, then applied it, maybe a moment too soon. But it was a chocolate fudge cake, made from scratch, and he slugged out the syllables, Dee duh *duh!*, as in the credenza in the living room he found the shoe box labeled BIRTHDAYS and took from it a single pink birthday candle. While he washed the dishes and straightened the kitchen, he thought of Sasha and Brigitte blowing candles out. He was standing near the counter, reading prefatory words on nutrition in the cookbook while the icing hardened, when Rosalie came in. She wore jeans and a soft white cotton shirt that fastened with metal snaps near its floppy collar. In her clean white running shoes she looked springy and competent as she inspected the kitchen, then him. She seemed to him frighteningly older than she'd been. He slid the pink candle into the pocket of his shirt.

She filled the kettle with water and put out instant coffee and one mug.

He heard himself offer, "I was going to do a laundry."

Before the water could be hot enough, she poured it over the coffee and walked past him to the breakfast room. He found a cup and shook some crystals into it and, without stirring the coffee, followed her. He sat and said, "Rosie."

She looked up. Her eyes behind the lenses were red and puffy. Her elbows were on the legal pad and his awful fragment of letter. She had set her cup on his salutation. Her face wasn't angry, it was solemn. She looked to him as she must have looked as a girl in church: sure of what she must do, owlish with her certainty.

He left the table again. He stuck the candle into the cake, and he brought it to her. Setting it on the table, he said, "Here."

"Very nice," she said. "Very well done."

He was going to say, "I made it for you," but then the girls came in. He heard their bus huff away, and he called to them, "Come and get it, ladies! Look at what I made for you!"

Rosalie walked past them, pausing to kiss each daughter on the top of the head. She waved and went toward the other side of the house while Sasha followed her and Brigitte waited. Stephen went to her and stooped, one knee on the floor. "How was school, baby?"

Her face was pale, her eyes narrow. She asked, "Did you make the cake so we wouldn't go away, Daddy?"

He looked down at her pink sneakers. "Yes," he said.

When Rosalie and Sasha returned, he looked up, then stood. Sasha carried two small canvas traveling bags. Rosalie carried two large bags and an over-the-shoulder carryall.

Stephen thought of the advice he gave to shattered men who called. He said something like "Wait," he thought. They came to him with this, and he said, "Wait."

"Daddy," Sasha said. He saw that she'd put lots of fresh lipstick on.

Brigitte said, "Can we have some of the cake?"

That was when Rosalie's face crumpled, but not in tears. She looked as though she fought not to laugh, and Stephen—as the counselor, now, addressing the husband—told himself not to hold that against her.

Stephen told them, "Just a minute, all right?" And he went to the drawer and found the cake server, then tore off several sheets of paper towel. He cut a wedge of chocolate cake with butter cream icing, and he handed it to Brigitte. She held it on her palm. Stephen stepped back to address them all, Sasha and Brigitte and Rosalie, their identical eyes. They paused with their baggage.

Brigitte said, "Thank you, Daddy."

Sasha smiled and shrugged.

Stephen said, "Rosie."

She said, "What?"

He tore off more towels, cut more cake, and came to offer it. He said, "For on the way."

Rosalie shrugged as if echoing Sasha. She looked down at the luggage that occupied her hands. "No room," she apologized.

"Of course," Stephen said. Like three good guests, then, they waited politely. And then, slowly, to show him how reluctantly they left, they left. When the front door closed, he bit a piece of cake and stood in the kitchen and chewed. He heard himself humming the tune he had baked to, and then he remembered its name.

THE NINTH, IN E MINOR

THE MORNING AFTER I drove to his newest town, I met my father for breakfast. He was wearing hunter's camouflage clothing and looked as if he hadn't slept for a couple of nights. He reminded me of one of those militia clowns you see on television news shows, very watchful and radiating a kind of high seriousness about imminent execution by minions of the state.

I knew he had deeper worries than execution. And I was pleased for him that he wore trousers and T-shirt, a soft, wide-brimmed cap, and hip-length jacket that would help him disappear into the stony landscape of upstate New York. He *needs* the camouflage, I thought, although where we stood—in the lobby of the James Fenimore Cooper Inn—he seemed a little out of place among the college kids and commercial travelers. The inn advertised itself as The Last of the Great Upstate Taverns. My father looked like The Last of the Great Upstate Guerrilla Fighters. Still, I thought, he's got the gear, and one of these days he will blend right in.

"Hi, Baby," he said. He tried to give me one of the old daddy-to-daughter penetrating stares, but his eyes bounced away from mine, and his glance slid down my nose to my chin, then down the front of my shirt to the oval silver belt buckle I had bought in Santa Fe.

"How are you, Daddy?"

He fired off another stare, but it ricocheted. "I have to tell you," he said, "half of the time I'm flat scared."

His shave was smooth, but he'd missed a couple of whiskers, which looked more gray than black. His face had gone all wrinkled and squinty. He looked like my father's older brother, who was shaky and possibly ill and commuting from the farthest suburbs of central mental health. He took his cap off—doffed it, you would have to say. His hair looked soft. You could see how someone would want to reach over and touch it.

"But I don't like to complain," he said.

I got hold of his arm and pulled my way along his brown-and-sand-and-olive-green sleeve until I had his hand, which I held in both of mine. He used enough muscle to keep his arm in that position, but the hand was loose and cool, a kid's.

I asked him, "Do you know what you're scared of?"

He shrugged, and, when he did, I saw a familiar expression inside his tired, frightened face. He made one of those French frowns that suggested not giving a good goddamn, and it pleased me so much, even as it disappeared into his newer face, that I brought his hand up and kissed the backs of his fingers.

"Aw," he said. I thought he was going to cry. I think he thought so too.

"Look," I said, letting go of his hand, "I saw Mommy in New York. That's where I drove up from. We had dinner two days ago. She asked me to remember her to you. She's fine."

He studied my words as if they had formed a complex thought. And then, as if I hadn't said what he was already considering, he asked, "How is she?"

"She's fine. I told you."

"And she asked to be remembered to me."

"Right."

"You're lying, Baby."

"Correct."

"She didn't mention me."

"Oh, she mentioned you."

"Not in a friendly way."

"No."

"She was hostile, then?"

"Hurt, I'd say."

He nodded. "I hate that—I didn't want to hurt anybody," he said. "I just wanted to feel better."

"I know. Do you feel better?"

"Do I look it?"

"Well, with the outfit and all . . ."

"This stuff's practical. You can wear it for weeks before you need to wash it. The rain runs off the coat. You don't need to carry a lot of clothing with you."

"Traveling light, then, is how you would describe yourself?"

"Yes," my father said. "I would say I'm traveling light. But you didn't answer me. How do I look?"

I walked past matching club chairs upholstered in maroon-and-aqua challis, and I looked out a window. A crew had taken down an old, broad maple tree. The sidewalk was buried under branches and bark, and a catwalk of plywood led from the street, around the downed tree, and into the inn. The tree was cut into round sections three or four feet across, and a man in a sweated undershirt was using a long-handled splitting maul to break up one of the sections. Behind him stood another man, who wore a yellow hard hat and an orange shirt and a yellow fluorescent safety vest. He held a long chain saw that shook as it idled. A woman wearing a man's old-fashioned undervest, work gloves, and battered boots watched them both. Occasionally, she directed the man with the splitting maul. Her hair beneath her yellow hard hat looked reddish-gold. The one with the chain saw stared at the front of her shirt. She looked up and saw me. She looked at me through her safety goggles for a while and then she smiled. I couldn't help smiling back.

"You look fine," I said. "It's a beautiful spring morning. Let's eat."

In the Natty Bumppo Room, we were served our juice and coffee by a chunky woman with a happy red face. My father ordered waffles, and I remembered how, when I was in elementary school, he heated frozen waffles in the toaster for me and spread on margarine and syrup. I remembered how broad his hands had seemed. Now, they shook as he spread the margarine. One of his camouflage cuffs had picked up some syrup, and he dripped a little as he worked at his meal. I kept sipping the black coffee, which tasted like my conception of a broth made from long-simmered laundry.

"The hardest part," he said, "it drives me nuts. The thing with the checks."

"Sure," I said, watching the margarine and maple syrup coat his lips. "Mommy has to endorse your checks, then she has to deposit them, then she has to draw a bank check, and then she has to figure out where you are so she can send it along. It's complicated."

"I'm not making it that way on purpose," he said.

"No. But it's complicated." He looked young enough to have been his son, sometimes, and then, suddenly, he looked more like his father. I understood that the man I had thought of as my father looking like himself was no longer available. He was several new selves, and I would have to think of him that way.

"I'm just trying to get better," he said.

"Daddy, do you hear from her?"

He went still. He held himself so that—in his camouflage outfit— he suggested a hunter waiting on something skittish, a wild turkey, say, said to be stupid and shy. "I don't see the point of this," he said. "Why not talk about you? That's what fathers want to hear. About their kids. Why not talk about you?"

"All right," I said. "Me. I went to Santa Fe. I had a show in a gallery in Taos, and then I drove down to Santa Fe and I hung out. I walked on the Santa Fe Trail. It goes along the streets there. I ate too much with too much chili in it, and I bought too many pots. Most of the people in the restaurants are important unknown Hollywood celebrities from outside Hollywood."

"Did you sell any pictures?"

"Yes, I did."

"Did you make a lot of money?"

"Some. You want any?"

"Because of how long it takes for your mother to cash my check and send a new one."

"Are you *allowed* to not live at home and still get money from the state?"

"I think you're supposed to stay at home," he said.

"So she's being illegal along with you? To help you out?"

He chewed on the last of his waffle. He nodded.

"Pretty good," I said.

"She's excellent to me."

"Considering," I said. "So how much money could you use?"

"Given the complications of the transmission process," he said.

"Given that," I said. "They sit outside the state office building, the Indians off the pueblos. They hate the people who come, but they all sit there all day long, showing you the silver and the pots all arranged on these beautiful blankets. I bought too much. But I felt embarrassed. One woman with a fly swatter, she kept spanking at the jewelry she was selling. She'd made it. She kept hitting it, and the earrings jumped on the blanket. The rings scattered, and she kept hitting away, pretending she was swatting flies, but she wasn't. She was furious."

"Displacement," my father said.

"It's just a story, Daddy."

"But you told it."

"Yes, but it didn't have a message or anything."

"What did it have?"

"*In situ* Native American displacement, and handmade jewelry. A tourist's usual guilt. Me, on the road, looking around. Me, on my way northeast."

"Did you drive?"

"I did."

"All by yourself?"

"Like you, Daddy."

"No," he said, fitting his mouth to the trembling cup. "We're both together here, so we aren't alone now."

"No." I heard the splitting maul, and I imagined the concussion up his fingers and along his forearm, up through the shoulder and into the top of the spine. It would make your brain shake, I thought.

"A hundred or two?" he said.

"What? Dollars?"

"Is that too much?"

"No," I said, "I have that."

"Thanks, Baby."

"But do you hear from her, Daddy?"

He slumped. He stared at the syrup on his plate. It looked like a pool of sewage where something had drowned.

He said, "Did I tell you I went to Maine?"

I shook my head and signaled for more coffee. When she brought it, I asked if I could smoke in the Natty Bumppo Room, and she said no. I lit a cigarette and when I was done, and had clicked the lighter shut, she took a deep breath of the smoke I exhaled and she grinned.

"What's in Maine?" I asked him.

"Cabins. Very cheap cabins in a place on the coast that nobody knows about. I met a man in New Hampshire—Portsmouth, New Hampshire? He was on the road, like me. He was a former dentist of some special kind. We were very similar. Taking medication, putting the pieces back together, at cetera. And he told me about these cabins. A little smelly with mildew, a little unglamorous, but cheap, and heated if you need, and near the sea. I really wanted to get to the sea."

"So you drove there, and what?"

"I slept for most of the week."

"You still need to sleep a lot."

"Always," he said. "Consciousness," he said, "is very hard work."

"So you slept. You ate lobster."

"A lot."

"And what did you do when you weren't sleeping or eating lobsters or driving?"

"I counted girls in Jeeps."

"There are that many?"

"All over New England," he said, raising a cup that shook. "They're blond, most of them, and they seem very attractive, but I think that's because of the contrast—you know, the elegant, long-legged girl and the stubby, utilitarian vehicle. I found it quite exciting."

"Exciting. Jesus, Daddy, you sound so adolescent. Exciting. Blondes in Jeeps. Well, you're a single man, for the most part. What the hell. Why not. Did you date any?"

"Come on," he said.

"You're not ancient. You could have a date."

"I've had them," he said.

"That's who I was asking you about. Do you hear from her?"

"I'm telling you about the girls in their Jeeps on the coast of Maine, and you keep asking—"

"About the woman you had an affair with who caused you to divorce my mother. Yes."

"That's wrong," he said. "We separated. That's all that I did—I moved away. It was your *mother* sued for divorce."

"I recollect. But you do understand how she felt. There you were, shacking up with a praying mantis from Fort Lee, New Jersey, and not living at home for the better part of two years."

"Do I have to talk about this?"

"Not for *my* two hundred bucks. We're just having an on-the-road visit, and I'm leaving soon enough, and probably you are too."

"I drift around. But that's a little unkind about the money. *And* about the praying mantis thing. Really, to just bring it up."

"Because all you want to do is feel better," I said, lighting another cigarette. By this time, there were several other diners in the Natty Bumppo Room, and one of them was looking over the tops of her gray-tinted lenses to indicate to me her impending death from second-ary smoke. *Oh, I'm sorry!* I mouthed to her. I held the cigarette as if I were going to crush it onto my saucer, then I raised it to my mouth and sucked in smoke.

I blew it out as I said to him, "She's the one who led you into your nosedive. She's the reason you crashed in flames when she left you."

"This is not productive for me," he said.

"You're supposed to be productive for *me*," I said. I heard the echo of my voice and, speaking more calmly, I said, "Sorry. I didn't mean to shout. This still fucks me up, though."

"Don't use that kind of language," he said, wiping his eyes.

"No."

"I thought we were going to have a *visit*. A father-and-daughter reunion."

"Well, we are," I said.

"All right. Then tell me about yourself. Tell me what's become of you."

I was working hard to keep his face in focus. He kept looking like somebody else who was related to him, but he was not the him I had known. I was twenty-eight years old, of no fixed abode, and my father, also without his own address, was wearing camouflage clothing in an upstate town a long enough drive from the New York State Thruway to be nothing more than the home of old, rotting trees, a campus in the state's junior college system, and the site of the James Fenimore Cooper Inn.

"What's become of me," I said. "All right. I have two galleries that represent me. One's in Philadelphia and one's in Columbia County, outside New York. I think the owner, who also runs what you would call a big-time gallery on Greene Street, in Manhattan, may be just around the corner from offering me a show in New York City. Which would be very good. I got some attention in Taos, and a lot of New York people were there, along with the usual Hollywood producer-*manqué* people, both has-beens and would-bes, and the editorial stars who hire agents to get their names in the gossip columns. It was very heady for me to be hit on by such upper-echelon minor leaguers."

"When you say *hit on*," he said, "what are you telling me?"

"Exactly what you think. A number of men fancied fucking me."

He let his head droop toward his plate. "That's a terrible way to live," he said. "I'm supposed to be protecting you from that."

"But why start now?"

"That's what you came for," he said. "I've been waiting, since you phoned me, to figure out why you would look me up *now*, when you might suspect I'm down on my luck and in unheroic circumstances."

"Unheroic," I said. "But you're wrong. I mean, as far as I *know*, you're wrong. I asked Mommy for your address because I hadn't seen you since I was in graduate school. And you're my father. And I guess I was missing you."

"And because you wanted to tell me the thing about men trying to—you know. Because it would hurt me. And you're angry with me."

"Well, you could say the way you left your wife was a little disappointing to me."

He'd been rubbing at his forehead with the stiffened fingers of his right hand. He stopped, and he looked around his hand, like a kid peeking through a fence, his expression merry and, suddenly, quite demented. Then the merriment left him, and then the craziness, and he looked like a man growing old very quickly. He said, "I have to tell you, the whole thing was disappointing for me as well."

"You mean, leaving your wife for the great adventure and then being dumped."

"And then being dumped," he said.

"Mommy said you were doing drugs when that happened."

"There was nothing we didn't do except heroin," he said. "If we could have bought it safely, I'd have stuffed it up my nose, shot it into my eyeballs, anything."

"Because of the sex?"

He looked right at me. "The best, the most astonishing. I haven't been able to acknowledge a physical sensation since then. Everything I've felt since then is, I don't know—as if it was *reported*. From a long way away."

"Jesus. *And* you loved her?"

"I've dealt with a therapist who says maybe I didn't. Maybe it was the danger. I seem to act self-destructively, from time to time. I seem to possibly not approve of myself. I seem to need to call it love whether that's what I feel or not. I seem to have conflated sex with love."

"A conflatable sex doll," I said. I snickered. He managed to look hurt. "I'm sorry."

"It doesn't matter much. I'm working on my health. It doesn't have to hurt to hear that kind of laughter. I suppose it's good for me. A kind of practice at coping with difficulties."

"No," I said, "I apologize. It just seemed like a very good damned pun, the conflatable sex doll. I am nobody's spokeswoman for reality. I apologize."

"Tell me how your mother is."

"She's fine. She's living a life. I'd feel uncomfortable if I gave you any details. I think she wants to keep that stuff to herself."

"So she's fine, and you've managed to endure the attentions of men with press agents."

"Mostly to evade them, as a matter of fact."

"Mostly?"

"Daddy, if anyone around here's fine, it's me. Nobody has to worry about men, nutrition, the upkeep of my car, or the management of my career. I do my own taxes, I wrote my own will, and I navigate my own cross-country trips."

"Why do you have a will? A legal last will and testament, you're saying? Why?"

"I'm not getting any younger," I said.

"Nonsense. You don't have a family to provide for."

"You know that, do you?"

"You *do?*"

I nodded. I found it difficult to say much.

"What, Baby?"

"A son. His name is Vaughan."

"Vaughan? As in the singer Vaughan Monroe?"

"As in Ralph Vaughan Williams. One of his symphonies was play-ing when, you know."

"I know nothing," he said. He was pale, and his lips trembled as his hands did, though in a few seconds his mouth calmed down. His fingers didn't.

"He's with Mommy."

"But he lives with you?"

"I'm thinking of living with someone downstate. We would stay together there."

"His father?"

"No. But a man I like. A photographer."

"Criminies," he whispered. "There are all those gaps, all those *facts* I don't know. This is like looking at the family picture album, but most of the pictures aren't in the book. Are you *happy* about this child?"

"Are you happy about me?"

"Sure," he said. "Of course I am."

"Then I'm happy about my boy. Did you really say *criminies?*"

He clasped his hands at the edge of the table, but they upset his breakfast plate. Syrup went into the air, and soggy crumbs, and his stained napkin. The waitress came over to sponge at the mess and remove our dishes. She came back with more coffee and the check.

"Criminies," my father said. "I haven't heard that word for years."

I was counting out money which I slid across the table to him. "I hope this helps," I said, "really."

"I regret needing to accept it," he said. "I regret not seeing you more. I regret your having to leave."

"That's the thing with those family albums, Daddy. People are always leaving them."

"Yes. But I'm a grandfather, right?"

"Yes. you are."

"Could I see him?"

"Ever get downstate?"

"Oh, sure," he said. "I get to plenty of places. I told you, I was all the way up in Maine just a few weeks ago."

"All those girls in Jeeps. I remember. So, sure. Yes. Of course. He's your grandson."

"Big and sloppy like me?"

"His father was a kind of fine-boned man. But he'll have my arms and my legs."

"He'll look like a spider monkey."

"You haven't called me a spider monkey for an awfully long time."

"But that's what he look like? I want to think of him with you."

"Very light brown hair, and a long, delicate neck. And great big paws, like a puppy."

"He'll be tall."

We sat, and maybe we were waiting to find some words. But then my father pulled on his camouflage cap, and tugged at the brim. He was ready, I suppose. I left the dining room and then the inn a couple of steps ahead of him. We stopped outside the front doors and watched the man, now shirtless, as he swung, working his way through a chunk of a hundred and fifty years. Splinters flew, and I heard him grunt as the wedge-shaped maul head landed. The woman in the cotton vest was watching it batter the wood.

I put my arms around his neck and hugged him. I kissed his cheek.

"Baby, when does everybody get together again?"

I hugged him again, and then I backed a couple of steps away. I could only shrug.

He said, "I was thinking roughly the same."

I heard the maul. I watched my father zip, then unzip his camouflage hunting coat.

He turned to the woman in the cotton vest and tipped his camouflage cap. She stared at him through her safety goggles.

He was giving a demonstration, I realized. With his helpless, implausible smile, he was showing me his lapsed world of women. He was broken, and he shook with medication, but he dreamed, it was clear, of one more splintered vial of amyl nitrate on the sweaty bedclothes of a praying mantis from Fort Lee, New Jersey. He had confected a ride with a leggy blonde in a black, convertible Jeep on US 1 in Maine. And if the foreman of the forestry crew would talk to him in front of her tired and resentful men, he would chat up that lady and touch, as if by accident, the flesh of her sturdy, tanned arms.

That was why I backed another pace. That was why I turned and went along the duck walk behind my father, leaving the wreckage of the maple tree and walking toward my car. I wanted to be driving away from him—locked inside with the windows shut and the radio up—before he could tip his cap, and show me his ruined, innocent face, and steal what was left of my life.

VESPERS

THIS WAS THE YEAR in which Ronald Reagan thought to honor the S S dead with a wreath in a German graveyard, and when I was in charge of funding grants to sculptors and musicians in both Dakotas, Minnesota, and Wisconsin. We had a dozen proposals on, shall we say, the theme of remembering who, from 1936 to 1945, had died the most and worst. And Bert Wragg, Jr., had brought me with him, for luck and for sex with an older woman, while he interviewed and auditioned in New York.

I rang my brother and missed him at his law firm on Clinton Street. Soon he rang back, chivvying me, at once, to recollect.

"Everything goes in a circle," he said. "Remember? Remember when Daddy said that in Prospect Park when you got lost?"

"Since when did you call him Daddy? We never called him Daddy, did we? And I was six years old, Ira."

Ira said, "Fine. Pop. Fine. Six. You remember calling him Pop?"

"Of course."

"The point is not what I happen to be calling my father in conversation with his daughter," he said.

"This is not a conversation. This is an interborough harangue."

"Now, I believe, you move on to calling it blackmail. Am I right?

As in emotional blackmail, et cetera. Or would that scare the newsboy off? Getting involed with a family where verbal cockfights, in a manner of speaking, are always taking place?"

"You want me to repeat that? So anyone who happens to be standing within six or eight feet could hear me saying newsboy?"

"Up to you," Ira said. "All *I* hear is people objecting to every other word I use."

"You're the one calling names."

"You're making me seduce my own sister."

"That, big fella, is what they call incest. It's illegal. It's immoral. It's disgusting."

"'At's amore," he sang, in not too bad an imitation of Dean Martin lightly toasted on sixties TV.

It was a routine we had used when we were in one another's company, with dates, during his years in college—Desi and Lucy, but as brother and sister, the ditzy redhead and the serious, clever, somewhat bamboozled guy. He was between Wife Two and a paunchy, sad time of dating widows and the former wives of other cuffed but not quite beaten men. I was going to remain unmarried forever, though I had no interest in solitude. I was back in New York—in Manhattan, to my brother's disappointment—while he was in Park Slope, in Brooklyn, and determined to take me and Bert Wragg, Jr., from our hotel on Central Park South back to Flatbush, where Ira and I had grown up, sometimes even together.

I said, "We'd have to go tonight. We're really booked."

Bert Wragg, Jr., sat at the foot of the bed and crossed his legs. They were bare, except for navy-blue garters with a red stripe through the center. He was putting on high navy socks that would come over his calf. I had not seen garters on a man since I was a blackboard monitor in the sixth-grade class of Miss Fredericks in P.S. 152. The man had been my father, and I had peeked around the corner of my parents' bedroom to win a bet: Ira had insisted our father—whom we did call Pop—put his horn-rimmed glasses on before his socks, and I had bet on socks before sight. I won, and I provoked a one-inch rise in my father's bushy brows. We used to wager, too, on who could bring his elastic forehead higher. Ira usually won. He won the baseball cards I bought to cause him to covert them. I didn't care to carry or collect them, though I liked the waxy taste of the gum with which they were packed, and they caused Ira to bet with me, which meant that he had to talk to me as if I was not from the Planet Jerk. So: Pop, the garters, and Bert Wragg, Jr., naked from the waist down, his penis regarding me from the nest of his folded groin, and I thought of the circle Ira said our father had described, and I agreed to subject my anchorman-in-waiting, my boyfriend from the middling market of Minneapolis–St. Paul by way of Ames, Iowa, and Syracuse University to what would at best be a sentimental journey, and to what at the very worst would be a long night with Ira Bloom.

I heard him snort into the phone and whisper, "Myrna, can he really hear you?"

"The newsboy? Yes."

"Are you in love?"

"More than likely."

"A healthy kind of love, or the dark, clammy lust you get yourself into?"

"Latter, no doubt."

"So you call one thing another? Love is lust? Or vicey versey?"

"I think there isn't a y sound, Ira. Just—"

"Could you listen without correcting me? Incorrect as I doubtless am? Could you listen, please? Just, are you coming with the newsboy or without? And I am not being raunchy, I did not *intend* to be raunchy, and don't even begin to correct my raunch. Are you or are you not. Period."

"We will both be downstairs. We will walk outside in, say forty minutes."

"Half an hour, max," he said.

"We will ride to Brooklyn. We will look. We will then take you to dinner. So you should—wait a minute. Bert? Does Ira need a tie?"

"Not for the Park Bistro," Bert said.

Ira said, "I heard him. How does a talking head on Minnesota TV, good evening, ladies and gentlemen, yawn, know what to wear in my city?"

"Maybe that's why they're trying him out in New York, Ira."

Bert had stood up, and I thought I must look like a mean bit of business in my open, pearly rayon robe to have aroused him so. Of course, I thought, it could also be the thought of his own ruggedly gorgeous face on many millions of TV screens in the greater New York metropolitan area. That's what I liked about Bert Wragg, Jr. He was not above regarding himself in the optimum light, and he was young enough to find his gaze persuasive.

IN THE LONG black car, a Buick, Ira told us, we headed downtown. When we passed Delancey, I knew Ira was taking us over the East River on the Brooklyn Bridge. It was not quite direct, but it would give him a chance to point out to Bert a landmark beloved of hayseeds.

I'd imagined myself next to Ira, with Bert hidden away from my brother in the shadows of the backseat. But Bert had gone for the front, neglecting to hold my door, almost shouldering me out of the way. His awkward posture reminded me of something I couldn't name, and it wasn't until the end of the afternoon that I remembered: a boy, my date, a Nelson Someone in a workingman's bar in Poughkeepsie, stepping in front of me to fight with someone who had expressed distate—quite rightly, I thought at the time—for college kids gone slumming.

Bert said, "Ira, I'm curious."

"Speak to me, Bert. I'm here as a—what is it, Myrna, in museums and churches?"

"Docent, dear. Little wives and widows who wear white gloves and show you the stained-glass windows."

"There we are, Ira," Bert said. "It just seemed—still seems, really—we'd have gone bit more directly by way of the Brooklyn Battery Tunnel, then the Prospect Expressway, then maybe Church Avenue up to your old neighborhood."

"Really?" Ira said. "Really and truly?"

Bert shrugged. I heard the wide wales of his tan corduroy sportcoat rasp. He wore it with jeans, a canvas off-tan shirt from Peterman, and the navy-blue socks held up by the navy-blue-and-red-striped garters.

Ira said, "I thought maybe seeing the bridge was worth the loss of six or eight seconds."

"Absolutely," Bert said. He put his left hand up on the bench seat so that it hung behind Ira. I took it. I leaned forward and put his index finger, very slowly, into my mouth. When I released it and sat back, Ira's eyes were waiting for mine in his rearview mirror.

"Hi," I said.

"Hi," each man replied, one with pleasure and one without.

I watched the back of Ira's head, now that I had seen how familiar his eyes were in their web of lines and folds and the soft flesh in gray-brown crescents beneath that testified to his insomnia. His head had become our pop's, of course, with the same untamed Howdy-Doody wings of wild fringe a few inches above the pointed ears that hung back around his skull like the folded wings of sleeping bats. His head in silhouette was long and slender, and I thought he'd lost weight because the collar of his shirt seemed not to touch his neck. His hands on the steering wheel were long, like Pop's. Unlike our father, he murmured to himself as he steered the car: "Uh-huh," as he turned, "Ah-hm" as he straightened our course again, "Uh-huh" when he checked our location by the street-corners signs. He sang his steering lightly, but with it he confirmed himself to me as a genuine eccentric. I wondered how someone saw me.

I called, "Stop!" We were on Ocean Avenue in middling spring at four o'clock. The air was gathering itself for dusk, perhaps just beginning to take on the weight of reflection of the dirty bricks on the six- and seven-story apartment buildings. Traffic was growing denser with the air that poured invisible yet thick onto Ocean Avenue in a section of

Flatbush once called Kensington, the streets of which ran to Midwood, where we'd lived. I'd used to ride my Schwinn on its ticking gears to the gas station to our right.

Ira kept the car in the street, his blinker on, traffic pouring around us. "You don't want to pull in there," he said. "They pump the gas and then they keep the car, the *schwarzim*."

"African-Americans?" Bert apparently felt required to say. His *a*, from his days in Syracuse, had the lag you could hear in Syracuse, Rochester, Buffalo, Cleveland, even Chicago: a flattened gagging that sounded as if the speaker snarled. Bert Wragg would never snarl. But I wondered if his career could be threatened by the bray of the Great Lakes.

"No, mostly Haitians, as a matter of fact," Ira said. "And, probably, most of them not citizens. But you can *call* them African-Americans if you like."

"I used to put air in my tires," I said. "And they had a cooler inside where you could get one of those stubby Cokes in the green glass bottle."

Bert said, "Myrna, those bottles are real antiques."

"So's she," Ira said.

Bert waggled his fingers at me behind Ira's back. I placed nothing in my mouth.

Two short, slender dark-skinned men stood at the office, where I'd used to pay a dime for my soda.

Bert said, "Their hands are behind their backs.

"They don't want you to be frightened," Ira said.

"They're armed," Bert said. "Is that correct?"

"Boy, are they armed," my brother said, in almost a friendly tone.

He pulled out into traffic, and I watched them watch us, alien beings in our time machine. He took a right turn quickly, and then he slowed down because soon—I could feel the car begin to turn, I thought, before Ira murmured at the wheel—we were coming to a left-hand turn, and

then the block on which we'd lived. It was as if we had gone across a
border, through a checkpoint such as the ones Bert, in his stiff tan cor-
respondent's trench coat, had passed through, once, bringing home the
bad news, for the sake of all Minneapolis–St. Paul, on the killings in
Herzegovina. If they gave him the job in New York as backup anchor,
and if I left my job and came with him, we would have to build him
closets no matter where he lived. His raincoats took up more room than
my entire wardrobe.

"No more African-Americans," I said.

"Whether of African, American, or otherwise descent," Bert told me.

"Welcome to medieval Poland," Ira said. "Lubavitchers, all you can
eat." Tall thin boys in black suits walked with heavy fathers in ditto,
while behind them on their broad hips came the girls and women.
Everyone seemed pale. No one seemed to be away at work. It felt, on
our block, as if we had parked in a village square on a market day. We
were paid little attention, although two girls in their late teens, wearing
cloth coats that seemed to have belonged to large men, stared at Bert
and giggled their embarrassment into their hands.

"They live here?" I heard myself say.

"Some of them live in our *house* here," Ira said, and I heard the
sorrow in him for the passage of time, for the dispossession he had suffered. There was the three-story stucco house, in all its broad sheltered-
ness, a fortress of the rising middle class of 1910 who had built it, and
then in the 1950s again, so that our mother had once referred to our
block, with an immigrant daughter's sense of arrival, as The Suburbs.
Ocher-colored paint had been replaced with tan, and the dark brown
paint of the screened-in porch had been replaced with forest green. A
dogwood tree that Pop had planted after a hurricane took down one
of the sycamores had in turn been taken down. The other shade tree,
across the walk on its little lawn, had been hacked and trimmed, but
was surviving. The prickly hawthorn bushes that had lined the walk
to our brick stoop were gone. I had hated them, because whenever I

played stoop ball by myself on the walk, the ball would go into the bushes and I would have to wait for Ira to show his invulnerability by plunging his hand into the scratchy hedge. Then I would have to wait while he feinted throwing it to me, and then I would have to chase it when he tossed it over my head.

We were parked next to the fire hydrant outside the house we had lived in for eighteen years of my life, and in the car, between us, it was as if someone were showing those sprockety, ratcheting 8mm silent movies that families like ours used for their grappling with time, capturing in overexposed orange the flesh of children who would one day dissolve into the silt and swamp and thinning memory of what had been East Eighteenth Street, and what had been childhood, and what had been Rasbin's Meat Market on Avenue J, or the fish store with flounder set out on ice, or the elevated tracks of the BMT on Avenue H above the candy store with its wall of ten-cent comic books. Ira, in the front, looked to his right, past Bert, who had turned, politely, to stare at large old houses on little lawns. I, in the back, regarded them both and I studied my house and waited for clues about what I ought to feel. In the leather cockpit of Ira's car, I felt our mother in her belted orange house dress, our father in his garters and his boxer shorts, our well-furnished childhood rooms, with doors we little people of privilege could shut at will against each other and, crucially, our parents. I did not, however, taste emotions. Perhaps they would come later, I thought, and then I would clutch myself against the ache.

A man had appeared to stand outside the car. He was tall and broad, and I bent to the window to see all of him. He wore a wrinkled black suit, a rumpled white shirt, and a gray straw fedora with a ribbon that reminded me of Bert's garters. The frames of his glasses were clear plastic. His smooth-shaven face looked responsive to humor. He was someone I would ask for directions in a foreign country, I thought. It was dusk in New York, and he was home from work, I figured, and here we were, parked outside his house. He was the kind of man who came down steps to defend his home. Ira turned his key to send a current through the car, and Bert pushed the switch that rolled his window down.

I waited for a torrent of Yiddish, or Hebrew. I waited for thick, guttural inquiries or demands. The householder bent, straightened, bent again to stare, and muttered.

He bent again and looked in. His face made it clear that unlikelihood had descended onto Brooklyn. He said, "Bert Wragg!"

Ira said, "Son of a *bitch*."

Bert never hesitated. "Hi, hello. Now, where do we know each other from?" As he spoke, he opened the door and stepped out and up. Ira looked at me, and I looked back. We should have laughed, and then, I thought, it would have been all right. As it was, he stared suspiciously, and I offered my expression of utter innocence, and we locked each other out.

By the time I joined them, Bert was introducing Heschie, short for Herschel I decided, who had rented from a doctor's widow for six years on Cleveland Avenue in St. Paul. Heschie, who then decided we should call him Hesch, had bought the house of our parents from the junior high school science teacher who had bought it from them.

"His wife died," he told us. "Who needs a house without a wife?"

Ira nodded his agreement. "I used to bounce a ball against those steps," he said.

"No, that was me. I'm the girl who used to live here. I used to live here when I was a girl," I said.

Heschie had a wen on his forehead and it seemed to pulse red when he was pleased. Nodding to me, he turned to Bert. He boomed, in a voice that sounded nothing like Bert's but surely was meant to be, "'Good evening, this is Bert Wragg. And I have news for you.'" He said, "Imagine, in the flesh, with behind him in tow a Jewish girl from the neighborhood, Mr. Bert Wragg, the voice of all Minnesota."

"I grew up other places, Hersch. I'm no more Minnesota than you are."

"Except," Hesch said, pulling at his jacket sleeves as if his body chafed in the dark gabardine, "my boy and my girl, so they wouldn't talk like me or Ada, this of course is the name of my wife, they listened to you when they finished with dinner before I came home. I was in Special Collections at the U: Hebraica. I'm educated, but not so religious, miss, so you're safe. Here is no barbarism or from Luddites or other refusers of progress. We own and operate two word processors, each possessing sixty-four megs of RAM, and I am tenured at Brooklyn College, just a walk from here—well, of course you know where is a walk and isn't. A walk in the jungle, perhaps, if you know what I mean, but nevertheless a walk. But—but—*ah*: the subject at hand. Raised as we were from backward and Orthodox, we could not instruct our children in acclimating to the local mores, the patterns of speech. You understand. But *you*, Mr. Bert Wragg, you were their teacher. Thanks to you, my daughter—*a girl*, and in Minnesota!—became president of her seventh-grade class."

Ira had moved away, but not in concession to Bert. I knew where he'd gone. In 1950 or so, our pop, a Marine, had come home after his outfit had taken terrible losses near Pusan. He had posed for a photograph by our mother, and he had shyly smiled, but I had come, once I knew the story of his war, to not believe the pleasure that his smile suggested. I have chosen, instead, to see sorrow in his eyes. Ira kept the picture on his bureau, at least on any bureau of his that I had seen. Pop had stood in the driveway to be photographed, and Ira had gone there, to the cracked, grainy cement with its grassy stripe down the center that was mostly packed earth and some weeds. I thought of the stripe down Heschie's hatband, and the stripe on Bert's garters and Pop's.

I took Ira's arm and smelled the starch in his shirt and the sweat underneath. He put his arm around my waist. Heschie was leading Bert into my childhood house, and I wanted to be there. It occurred to me that a moment of intimacy with Bert in my girlhood room would be priceless pleasure, or maybe treason, or the combination of both that is the heart of adolescence. But I stayed where I was, held of course by more than Ira's arm.

We stared, side by side, down the driveway toward the garage, as if we looked at someone who smiled back at us.

Ira sighed. I said, "Life biting you, Ira?"

"In the ass," he said. "Hard. But nobody suspects."

"How could they," I asked, "with you so even of temper and low of key? Are you lonely?"

"Yes."

"Sorry for yourself?"

"Of course."

"Any chance of seeing the kids?"

"Weekends," he said.

"Well, it's something. And where does she live with them?"

"Lexington."

"In Kentucky."

"That's the one," Ira said.

"Will you ever see them?"

"From, as they say, time to time." Then he asked, "Myrna, are you guys moving here?"

I pulled his arm tighter around my waist. "If he gets the job. There are a lot of men as good-looking as he is, and several women almost as good-looking, and three or four who are as smart as he is, and it's pretty iffy. He's scared. He doesn't let on."

"But if he gets the job," Ira said.

"If he does, and if we stay together, and if I want to not work for the foundation anymore, and if I can get a job with someone here, and if I want to live with him, and if he wants to live with me. If we can survive the age difference. Then, I'd say, it's a maybe."

"You got so brave," he said. "I'm at the point, now, where I get frightened from waking up frightened."

"I'm callous and cold," I said. "I'm selfish."

"I wonder if Pop was scared. I think about him every day, all of a sudden. I've begun to, I don't know, *study* him in some weird, scary fucking way. He's like a—what's the word?"

"Dead father," I suggested.

BECAUSE WE HAD promised Heschie upon leaving that Mr. Bert Wragg would see where he worked, Ira took us along Eighteenth to J, then up past Ocean to Campus Road. Near where it ran into Flatbush Avenue, we looked at the pretty campus, and at adjacent Midwood, where Ira and I had gone to high school.

"Over there," Ira said, pointing at the little building across from Midwood. I remembered lining up for first or second grade, my legs shaking with fear, outside the entrance marked GIRLS. He told Bert, "We went to grade school, P.S. 152, fully staffed by several dozen virgins over fifty plus Mr. Gottlieb with his big mustache. You had to give Heschie an autograph, right?"

Bert said, "We traded."

"Your signature," Ira said, "for what?"

"He took me up to Myrna's room."

I said, "He did?" I felt myself blush very hard as Ira started us off along Flatbush Avenue in the general direction of the river. Changing lanes, he hummed to himself. I thought of Bert in my girlhood room. It was very exciting, as I'd expected. As I hadn't, it also felt uncomfortable, unhappy, like watching the broad, hairy back of the muscular hand of a grown-up man slide up beneath the party skirt worn by a girl of eight.

"It's his son's room. It smells like old socks, with maybe a trace of sperm."

Ira said, "So it hasn't changed, Myrna, right?"

"I loved it," Bert said, hanging his hand over the back of the seat. I found myself reaching for a finger, and I stopped.

"How'd he know which room was mine?" I heard myself ask him.

"I told him," Bert said.

"How in hell did *you* know?"

"Your stories," he said. "I hear you, Myrna. The room near the stairs before the bathroom, right? I *was* listening."

I said, "I didn't realize I was telling."

"As long as one of us did," Bert said, a martyr to the gathering of news.

At Dorchester Road, humming to himself, Ira turned left, and I knew of course where we were going. A couple of blocks along, he parked, where it said *No Parking*, at the side of the Flatbush-Tompkins Congregational Church.

"I used to walk here every Saturday morning for Cub Scouts," Ira told Bert, "then every Friday night for Boy Scouts. I stayed on into my first year at NYU. I loved it. They let us use the whole upstairs. We had our own basketball court."

We followed him along the walk. Bert said, "Was he an Eagle Scout?"

"Life."

"Sorry?"

"Life Scout. Next to Eagle, but not as good."

"I never belonged to the Scouts."

"You joined the young perverts, though, didn't you?"

"I was born a pervert," he said. "Did you ever do it inside a church?"

"Not with anyone as young as you."

We followed the sound of Ira's feet up two flights of gray-painted iron steps. We came to a couple of locked doors, and one that was open. It led into the tiniest gym I had ever seen—which, when I had seen it a couple of times a year for close to ten years, had seemed no smaller than Madison Square Garden, where we attended the circus.

"Mom and Pop took me here all the time to see you march and shout orders at your little fascist patrol boys in the Alligator Patrol. It used to be so *big*."

Bert said, "The Alligator Patrol. It sounds like St. *Paul*. It's sweet, Ira. What else is worth remembering? The church giving the room over to a bunch of kids, and all those blue-haired ladies dipped in rose water with their shelves of bosom in polka-dotted dresses having coffee and cinnamon-raisin cake and mercy mild downstairs, and there you were, marching back and forth up here. And meaning it."

Ira wasn't listening, though I think Bert thought he was talking to him. Ira was standing at a basket no more than nine feet high set into the wall. Like the floors, the walls were of a treated softwood that gleamed under the ceiling lights protected by metal gridwork. In a far corner that wasn't so very far were five or six dark basketballs. I thought I could smell the electricity in the wiring, and the varnish on the wood. I remembered how on Troop Review night Pop would smile and our mother yawn, and I would inspect the older boys, Explorers they were called. They seemed closer to Pop's age than Ira's, whose bright eyes and hot, flushed face I still could see, whose belief I knew I believed as he clamped his mouth and raised three fingers of his hand to swear his fidelity to courtesy and thrift. And I remembered how they turned these lights off—they went out with a deep *thunk*—and then the boys lit up the darkness of their hall with khaki-colored Army surplus flashlights, pressing a little button to formulate dots and dashes, crying out the Morse code language in which they talked across the blackened gym about great, imagined emergencies for which, I think, Ira believed he was equipped. *Dah! Di-Dit! Dah-Dah! Dit!* they shouted. I took a deep breath, recalling the boys who used to march so grimly in ragged, wheeling failures of geometry, or practice tying knots they'd never need to know. Ira used to call off the names and then, clumsily, but with determination, he would stand before his sweaty, earnest seven-member patrol, his back to the proud, bored families who sat on folding chairs, to illustrate the tying of the sheet bend, sheepshank, bowline, clove. The knots, tied in clothesline, hung with no function from a length of dowel stained brown to represent a tree limb, or from his hand, connecting the dark-knuckled, stumpy fingers to nothing, holding tight to make-believe logs, lead pipes, mountain climbers, or fictitious fallen victims, all accepted on faith, who would one day warrant rescue by a Boy Scout with a length of line.

"We used to play dodge ball," Ira said.

"You throw it as hard as you can at someone on the other side," Bert answered. He took his corduroy sportcoat off and handed it to me.

"I no longer perform dispiriting traditional gestures like holding the guy's coat," I said.

"I wasn't a Boy Scout," Bert said, looking away and letting his coat drop onto the floor at my feet, "but I was a young pervert. We played dodge ball after junior high. They had a recreational center to keep us out of trouble. It didn't. But we did allow them to encourage us to hurt each other with basketballs."

Bert took off his tasseled loafers and trotted out toward the basketballs. He rolled two toward Ira, and then another.

Ira called, "What are the rules?"

"There are never any rules," Bert said.

I asked him. "What will you *pretend* are the rules?"

"No throwing at the head," Ira said, throwing the ball high, missing Bert's head mostly because Bert ducked.

"No throwing at the balls," Bert said, missing Ira's and hitting the wall behind him.

"It's supposed to be you're out if you get hit," I said.

"But there's only you to take somebody's place," Bert said, "and you can't keep taking everybody's place because there isn't enough of you."

"That," Ira said, in Heschie's intonations, "is the voice of all whatever."

He threw the ball and hit Bert on the hip. Bert fired back and Ira caught the ball chest high.

Bert said, "Myrna, you keep pretending you're replacing us both." He fired the ball at Ira, who giggled in the shrill way boys proclaim their exuberance, and men pretend to be boys.

I left them to it, not so much out of annoyance as because I felt stupid, trying to riddle out who was attacking whom, with what surrogate weapon because of which metaphor we all were supposed to either understand or pretend to not notice. The gym smelled of sweat, probably not theirs, I realized, as I came down into the colder air of the metal stairway, past a door leading to what clearly smelled like a kitchen used a few days before, and then out to the long walk cut through moist and tender-looking lawn. Noises came down the stairs in pursuit—the slamming of leather against wooden walls, the slapping of leather on flesh. It was uncomfortably like hearing someone beaten to the accompaniment of high, psychotic giggles. I went further down the walk, then stopped, before I knew I would, to push my finger at the soft soil. As I stood up, I put it in my mouth up to the second knuckle. I tasted all I could.

Then I went to Ira's car and leaned against the door, some woman strange to the street of high brick or wood-frame houses each behind a wall of hedge, who was wearing a skirt cut a little too short for her age, who looked like a mean bit of business. That was what Pop called me when I was undisciplined or disrespectful in mild-to-somewhat-serious ways. When I really was hard and cruel, and when he suspected me of conduct he could not bear to know about for sure, he called me no names and he listed no rebukes. He grew silent, and he tried to look thoughtful instead of confused. It was then, because I always actually did possess a conscience, I would make for my mother and beg her to interpret us to each other. And of course, since she was as dead as Pop, that was why Ira was now pursuing me.

Because I was their date, and because they were well-bred boys, Bert and Ira came quite promptly from the church where they had settled nothing. They had played a violent and harmless game, and the tails of their shirts hung out of their pants like triangular clubhouse banners. Ira's fringes of hair were aloft, and Bert's thick, glossy hairdo hung in front of his eyes. They stood to regard me. Bert snapped his head back, and his hair sat down in place like a well-trained, well-groomed dog. Ira pushed at his shirt, which in its whiteness, now that the sun was down, seemed to glow.

It was the fact of so much darkness, more than the glare of the lights, that made me blink. I supposed it was an automatic timer that suddenly lit the stumpy white steeple and the hemlocks that bristled at the walls. Bert raised an arm. Ira shrugged, then shook his head. They came along the walk toward me. Or maybe someone inside, I speculated, some cordial Christian host, with patience for the needful, or the faithless, or the faithful making their return, had thought to light us on our way.

I waited for the bells in the steeple to ring out the day. Ira came, winded and disheveled, to stand with me beside his car. Then Bert Wragg, Jr., joined us, flushed and smiling, perfect and at ease in our neighborhood, as he had been inside my home, my history, and me.

"Listen," I told them, pointing up.

The man of the world and the man bereft of it looked, expectantly, while I waited for the bells in the steeple to ring. But none, in another minute, had sounded. I checked my watch and they, in response, each looked at theirs. We waited together, looking up and then at each other.

Often, of course, there are no bells.

TIMBERLINE

A MAN RIDES INTO THE NIGHT, he meets a mysterious stranger, his life is changed or it isn't. Nobody tells him which.

For example: when he ran away from home on the eve of his forty-fifth birthday. He was at the Eleventh Street window of their apartment, trying to look through the sycamore trees, and through the nimbus-on-grit glare of the streetlight, toward Greenwich Avenue. He saw what you'd expect. He saw himself, rippling as he moved in the crazy, unclean mirror that the window made. He saw the widow's peak, or thought he did. He saw the pale, shapeless head. But he knew it was him. His guess: he'd know him almost anywhere.

Leslie, behind him in the living room, asked, "What are you looking for?"

He said, "How'd you know I wasn't looking *at?*" Then he said, "You really want to know?"

She said, "I really don't, I suppose. I suppose we're not going up to Madison tomorrow and pick out a print for your birthday."

"Why not?"

"Because you'll have thrown a scene."

"I'm not throwing a scene, Leslie."

"You're getting ready to throw a scene, Hank. And I'll end up crying. My face'll look like you beat me, so you'll be too embarrassed for us to go outside in the morning. You'll spend all Saturday sulking because we didn't get you anything for your birthday. Which you'll decide by Saturday night you do want to celebrate. So we'll go out. We'll go to a new place and you'll fall in love with our waitress, and I'll get surly and we'll hate dinner."

He inspected them in the window glass. He looked for his former lover, stunned wordless, as he had been a number of years before, in a number of borrowed and rented rooms. All he could see of his wife and former graduate student now was her face and brushy haircut floating behind him and to the left, seeming to sit on his shoulder like a second head. He smelled her breath, which was like a spicy vermouth. He smelled her soap, which reminded him of mangos.

A summer wind he thought of as oily moved the plane tree's smaller branches. He thought he could see, through himself and the streetlamp, the lights of a cab turning in toward them from Greenwich. He was thinking about the time he saw his father lifted by winds off the face of Mount Washington. He hadn't known he was recalling it, nor did he know why it should come to mind now. But he couldn't imagine, suddenly, not thinking of it all the time—how his father's dark khaki poncho had filled with the wind that had taken him off.

That had been thirty-six years ago in Franconia, New Hampshire, on the trail from Mizpah Springs up through the boulder fields below the harshest part of the ascent to the hut called Lakes of the Clouds. In the hut there had been an old upright piano, and simple food, and the tall, strong college boys and girls who had carried provisions in pack baskets up to the huts that were run by the Appalachian Mountain Club. The students raced up the trails, he remembered. He remembered hearing the thud of their cleated, heavy boots. He remembered smelling the sweat of a tall, blond woman who had seemed to him then to be almost as old as his father. He had been thrilled by her scent. You heard them coming up the trail, and you stepped aside, feeling lesser than they.

Now, in New York, still a bystander, he was smelling mangos and vermouth. "If you ask me what I was saying," she said, "I'll claim self-defense after I stab you, tonight, while you sleep."

It was time for him to turn around and smile at her and gently take hold of her upper arms, or the back of her neck, and pull her toward him and sink, somehow, through this panic, this utter ignorance of what he ought to be doing, and get to *them*. He wasn't absolutely sure, but he suspected he could always find them in her. And finding them, of course, he'd find himself.

But he kept thinking of himself, the boy at eight, in the sudden summer rainstorm on Mount Washington's lower face, standing alone, blown against a boulder five feet high by the coiling about of the same wind that had taken his father from sight. He stood at the window, and he couldn't turn around until her smeary face had moved from the reflection. Then he turned and looked at the room they had furnished. He walked through it to their little foyer, and he unlocked the door, and he left. He walked to Fourteenth Street, where their car was garaged.

As he drove uptown, proud that he'd remembered in the Seventies how to cut west with Broadway through Columbus to the Henry Hudson, he realized he had no idea how you drive to New Hampshire from New York. He was one of those Manhattanites who understood the subways and made it a matter of honor to use them, despite the hour. He knew the underground map, but he had no sense of direction, and all he understood was that he was driving uptown, the Hudson River on his left, with bunched, dense, unreadable Harlem on his right and the George Washington Bridge beyond it.

As he followed the signs to the bridge, then guessed and took the leftmost ramp that led to it, he accepted that he was driving to New Hampshire. He had believed, on leaving the house, that he was going to take a walk. Now, even while he aimed himself away, he was surprised. He wanted to look at the surface of the river, but he was made anxious by the lights and speed of the traffic. He saw a tugboat, he thought. He thought it was pushing a barge on which a mound—was it garbage?—rode low in the water. Maybe he'd expected to see it. He knew of so many error-laden first-person accounts that historians had banked on, to their grief. People rarely saw what they claimed to.

But he had seen his father on the wind, he thought. It was something he knew. He knew, too, that he would pull over when he could and telephone Leslie. He would tell her, "Don't worry." She would swear in the rhythms he knew, and he would grin. "Don't worry," he'd say. "I was in some kind of fear fantasy, heading for New England. But it's all right. I'm all right. It was nothing more than dread. I'll be home soon, and I'll tell you the whole stupid story."

He grinned in the darkness as he headed out on, apparently, the Palisades Parkway through New Jersey. When he passed a service station at Ramapo, he thought: The next place I see, I'll turn around.

He saw a sign for Route 17. He was half an hour up the Palisades Parkway, driving slowly and being steadily passed. He thought he remembered something about 17, that a lot of people he knew had driven it. He wasn't sure it went to New England, he probably should turn around if he could. He didn't. He followed a sign, after a while, that took him onto a long, subtle curve, and he had taken a ticket at a booth, and he was driving upstate on the Thruway. You can always, he thought, get off the Governor Thomas E. Dewey Thruway and go back in the opposite direction. They can tell you how to do that. But he didn't ask. He knew he was headed upstate. You could, he figured, get to New Hampshire from there, or you could always turn around.

His mother had left them. He didn't know it at the time, of course, because he was eight. You don't tell an eight-year-old with chubby legs and prominent teeth and an affection for books and games about war that his mother every once in a while takes off. Later, he understood that she had left before that summer and would leave again. She didn't leave permanently until he'd been in college for almost a semester. She kept in touch, thinking he'd need it. And he hadn't the courage, then, to tell her she was distracting him from the two great recently discovered programs of his life—falling in love with the historical narrative of anyplace in any age as told by almost anyone at all and succumbing to lust with what he later thought of as sagacity.

So Hank's father, in the summer of his boy's ninth year, left alone with the child by his wife, reread pertinent sections of the Boy Scout handbook, sought the advice of an outdoorsy friend, and took Hank by train to New Hampshire. In the motel room that smelled of wax and heat, this man—who had not camped out since basic training—showed Hank every piece of borrowed equipment in each of the borrowed rucksacks.

"We have to be careful up there," his father said. "I don't mean there's anything to be scared of. I mean we have to take precautions. It's what I do in business. It's what you should do in your life. Things are the same, di dum di dum di dum, nothing to worry about"—here, he lit a cigarette—"then all of a sudden they're different. Really changed. Understand? Weather on the mountain changes very suddenly. You feel how hot it is?"

"It's very hot," Hank had answered, eager to be right. This was an important trip, he knew. He didn't know why. "Very hot."

"But it still could snow on us once we get up there." His father pointed. "Above timberline. Do you know what that is?"

His father smoked Camels, one after another. His fingers were stained yellow, and Hank loved the harsh, dark smell of the stubby little cigarettes. He heard his father pull the smoke in. Seeing that Hank watched him, he blew a thick, steady smoke ring onto the air. He winked. Hank winked back. His father's gray-brown widow's peak was encircled, after a while, by smoke. It looked the way Mount Washington looked from the front of the motel, hidden at its top by clouds.

That night, on the metal beds with their thin mattress pads, they turned and coughed and slept to waken—Hank because of his father, his father because of one among all the secrets, Hank suspected later, that rose up around him like the smoke of his cigarettes. Early light made his father appear pale and, from the side, vulnerable as he looked through the window. A path that led to the road that would take them to the first of their trails was outside that window. His father, without his wire-rimmed glasses and with his hair pulled up by friction against his pillow, stood at the window and smoked. Seeing his father without glasses felt like seeing him naked. Hank had shut his eyes and, hearing his father taking in smoke and letting it out, he had fallen back to sleep.

They ate what to Hank was an exciting meal because it was composed of food their mother never cooked: sausages and eggs so greasy the oils soaked through the rye bread his father showed him how to fold for sunnyside-up sandwiches.

"You want coffee this morning, Hank?" His father turned a cup of coffee beige with milk and sugar. Hank half expected to be offered a Camel with it and was disappointed when, winking, his thin, sad-faced father frowned around a cigarette and lit it up, but didn't shake the pack to release the tips of one or two and offer it as Hank had seen him do for others at restaurants and parties.

When their waitress brought the check, his father, counting change and squinting against smoke from the cigarette that wobbled between his lips, said, "This man opposite me here is climbing up to Mizpah Springs Hut."

Hank remembered looking into his coffee and blushing, both because of the attention and because he disliked the taste of the coffee which his father had offered with so much sudden good cheer.

"Which one's that again?" she'd asked, taking the money.

"Well, it's just up *there*. It's our first stage. Kind of base camp, on the way to Lakes of the Clouds."

"I know where *that* is," she said, walking away.

"Hurray for you," his father said.

"Hurray for you," Hank said, passing a rest stop and reading the sign that told him he would have to wait for thirty-seven miles before the next. "A man *will* turn around when he's ready to," he said. "He will."

Hank remembered timberline. He remembered their slow, laborious, thirsty climb up a track of dirt and rocks through dense bushes and trees. He remembered the clouds of gnats and blackflies, the stink of citronella and its greasy weight on the skin of his arms and neck and face. His father's lungs made squeaking sounds as he panted, Hank remembered. And he remembered that his father forced a fast, unhappy pace, as if they were driven through discomfort and poor conditioning and the oppressive heat by an obligation that was urgent, undeniable.

When they rested, his father showed him how to sit in the harness of his rucksack with his legs pointing downhill. "Let gravity do the work," his father said. "When you get back up, it'll be easier. The pack'll fall onto your back as you stand. It's an old Boy Scout trick." He smiled as he lit his cigarette and blew the smoke up, at the gnats that hovered about them. "Isn't it great? You show 'em you can take it. You show *you*. I always wanted to do this, Hank. And you. Aren't you something? You're climbing to Mizpah Springs, you're climbing Mount *Washington*, and you're only eight years old. It might be a record. You might be posting a national record."

Hank remembered drinking too much water, and his father's gentle, breathless rebuke when they stood, facing downhill, about an hour later. "The White Mountains make emergencies. That's what I've heard. So you need to make sure there's plenty of water until we get to the Springs."

As they continued to climb, breaking free of the confines of the trail to see the widening white glare of sky unencumbered by brush, his father, struggling for breath, instructed him to note how the trees were lower, the winds steadier. Hank saw, at last, when they made the ridge that would take them to the hut, how entire evergreens, mostly bare of needles (but not dead, his father said), were no higher than his knee.

"It's the cold does it," his father said, "and the winds. They look like miniature trees, but it's all in them—they're just stunted. It's like when you, I don't know, when you just run out of it. This is what it's like." He shielded his face with cupped hands to light a cigarette. "I believe that life is a bivouac, Hank," he said as the wind took his smoke and some of the sound of his words away. "You know what a bivouac is?"

Hank certainly didn't know, but he had shrugged, imitating his father, and he had nodded. When he read the word in college, sitting in the torpor of the library late at night, he had looked up, wide-eyed, feeling in his stomach some of that day: the presence of his father, and his mother's absence.

They ate a sandwich lunch at the small, open hut with its sleeping shelf lined with evergreen branches, and then his father had moved them along, before they could grow too stiff. In the bright, hot mid-day light, hills below them were black-green under the shadows of clouds that began to mass as they walked. After a couple of hours, as his father complained about the time of day and the changing sky, Hank saw how much darker the hills were, and how clouds thickened above them. Now they were over the timberline. High cairns of rock marked the trail because there were no trees. His father kept the map, in its glassine case, in his hand.

Every January his father solemnly presented him with a wrapped gift, which he in turn gave his mother for her birthday. Every year, she added the scented oil to her bath and presented herself, in her blue silk bathrobe. Hank was aware of the heat of the water and of its perfume. He smelled it through the canvas and dust and wind. He had begun to wonder, as they labored more slowly against the pitch and the difficult, stony footing that made his calves and ankles ache, whether she might greet them, as a surprise, as a reward, when they reached the end of their climb. She came from the bathroom to find him, each year, and she presented herself, smiling, her skin a little damp. "Want a smell, sweetheart?" she would ask.

Hank remembered as he drove how his father made them stop and put on their ponchos, which were very long and which covered their packs and fastened with snaps beneath their arms. His father tugged Hank's into place and then Hank, feeling uneasy, as if he were but-toning his father's shirt, pulled the poncho over his father's rucksack.

Cold winds, then colder winds, drove at them. The field of boul-ders and cairns and scree, and sudden declines, lay all about him. He couldn't see Mount Washington. Ice-cold mist grew heavier, and the clouds, his father told him, were surrounding them. He thought in the car of his recollection of the night before they climbed—of his father, surrounded by smoke.

Hours into his drive, he saw a sign for Westmoreland. The name of a general whom he associated with the madness of the Vietnam War seemed significant, so he aimed himself there, yawning now and thinking not of a place to call from, or where he might turn around, but of someplace he could sleep.

There were the blue-gray boulders vanishing into the descending clouds, there was the invisible mountain they were partway up, there was timberline below them, and there was his father before him, breathing hard and urging Hank to keep up. "You keep me in sight," his father said, turning clumsily as his poncho was flailed by wind against the hump of his rucksack. "You see me, right?"

Hank, in the car, was going to say, "Right." He rubbed his lips and didn't. He drove the two-lane highway onto which he'd exited from the Thruway. He knew from roadside signs that he wasn't terribly far from where the battle of Oriskany had been fought. With a satisfaction he distrusted, he told himself that he was driving into a footnote.

The Oriskany Falls Hotel was closed, and he drove on for fifteen or twenty miles to Route 20, where he found a motel with an open bar, and with three other cars outside of rooms. The kid who took the imprint of his credit card and gave him a key told him he could get a sandwich and a drink in the bar until half past midnight.

"You close it at twelve-thirty?"

"This here's Oneida County," the crew-cut, harelipped boy of something like twenty intoned, "not Las Vegas, Nevada."

"Damn," Hank said, "I wanted it to be Las Vegas, Nevada."

"But it ain't," the boy said, already looking away.

"It's Oneida County," Hank said. "Am I right?"

The boy didn't answer and Hank didn't blame him.

In the bar, at eleven-fifteen, served—of course—by the harelipped boy, Hank drank bar whiskey and ate two undercooked hot dogs, garnished with yellow mustard, which the boy had purported to roast in a microwave oven on the short counter of the small room. Hank sat at the end of the counter. The red plastic-covered stool to his right was empty, and so was the next one. On the one after that, a man wearing a dirty sling over his suit jacket drank shots with beer. On the stool beside him, a woman with a black hat that was like a turban drank coffee.

He was looking at the hat or at her head, and he didn't know why. Then he did. She was bald, he realized, and she was disguising it with the turban. She looked up, past the man's shoulder, and caught him studying her. She stared back and slowly adjusted her hat, letting it shift enough to confirm her hairlessness. He felt as though she had taken off her shirt.

"Sorry," he had to say.

"Dickie," she said, "I'm going to discuss my life with this man over here, all right?"

The man beside her looked Hank over and shrugged. That says it all, Hank thought: dismissed by a man in a sling who is getting drunk on boilermakers at the outskirts of a footnote.

She was very, very thin, and she was jaundiced-looking. Her mouth, which was broad with a full lower lip, had a jaunty curve despite her pursing it, maybe in pain. She looked like a supporting actress—the one who isn't pursued by Franchot Tone in a movie that Leslie might watch after he had fallen asleep. Hank often woke to find that she'd turned the bedroom TV set low and was sitting on the floor before it, wrapped in a blanket. She reminded him of his father, smoking at the window, studying the White Mountains. Or perhaps he had fashioned the memory of his father after Leslie, he thought. Maybe none of it was true, whatever *true* meant.

She said, "You were looking at me like you knew me." She adjusted her wrinkled ecru shirt in the waistband of her loose cotton slacks, as if expecting him to study her. "But we don't know each other, do we?"

"No, we don't."

"And you're not the kind of man to be rude."

"Not on purpose, usually," he said.

"So you must have been transfixed by my hairdo."

Her eyes were the kind of clear blue that was almost gray. They were large, and so, he realized, was her nose. She was a woman whose bold features could probably compete with even her smooth, broad head for your attention, he thought. He wished he could tell her so.

"I apologize," he said.

She sat beside him. When she leaned closer, he could smell her coffee and a kind of sweetness that he later realized was the corruption in her body. He had come to know that smell in his father, not so many years before. "You're a gentleman, then?" Her voice was low and tired. A couple of hundred miles from home and almost forty-five, he had met someone who made him feel young, someone older than his young wife. He smiled.

"Yeah," she said, accepting the coffee passed over by the boy, "you're a gentleman. You have a gentleman's smile. You're the kind of man who thinks the world is tougher than he is. And you're right. And you smile so maybe it'll be easy on you. Why not?"

"It's my birthday. Thank you. You—"

"What'd I do for you that you're so grateful for? I'm giving you me with cancer so you can enjoy your life while you haven't got it? The cancer, I mean. I don't know if you've got your life. Have you?"

"Like a very, very bad cold," he said.

She shrugged.

He was emboldened to say, "I know. It beats cancer."

She said, "I'll be the judge of that." She looked into his face. He saw the hesitation at the corners of her mouth, and he smiled to signal that he'd laugh if she would, and they both began at once.

After a while he took a pull of his drink and raised his finger to ask for another. The boy looked at the clock, then slowly moved to the shelf of bottles.

"This isn't Las Vegas, Nevada," he told the woman.

"This here's Oneida County," she replied.

He said, "I'm Henry Borden."

"Mine's Lorna Wolf. One *f*—like the animal. The other inmate over there's my brother. We're going to Sayre, Pennsylvania. You know where it is?"

"I don't even know where Oneida County is."

"There's a hospital there," she said.

"Good luck in it, Lorna."

"Oh, no," she said. "We're going there for him. There's a bone guy there. My brother, Dickie, he has to have his arm reset. We did me, in Utica. Now we do him in Sayre. Then we come back and do me. What we do is we drive back and forth. He's got a wonderfully comfortable car—I read a book, and Dickie drives. He's excellent with just the one arm."

He nodded.

"Wait a minute," she said. "Borden? I've heard of you."

He shrugged.

"I heard you on the radio. Henry Borden."

"Hank."

"Hank. I heard you talking about—a crooked President? But which one? A general—was it Grant?"

"Restoring the tomb, yes. It was one of the morning—"

"Sure," she said. "Isn't that something. And we meet up here in the faux Las Vegas of upstate New York. Isn't that something."

She bent to the coffee. The boy poured a shot for Dickie. Lorna took a deep breath, and Hank heard her work to do it. He thought she was going to shout, and he turned to her. She said, looking at her cup, "Oh *God*, I hate decaffeinated coffee." Her voice shook as she straightened to speak. She slowly blew air out between her lips, and it sounded to Hank like his father's cigarette smoke. He sniffed, expecting to smell it.

Then she said, making an effort, letting her anger sink again, "The most powerful stimulant I'm allowed these days is the Prince Valiant cartoon on Sunday. Sometimes, on TV, that fat fascist, what's his name, with the wardrobe. And the occasional cup of decaf." She sipped. "God. So what're you doing in Not Las Vegas?"

"Oh," he said.

"A lecture? Something exciting? Though, if you don't mind my pointing it out, you look—what's the word? You look like you feel a little shady. What's your story, Hank?"

He paid for the drink and her coffee. The boy emphatically snapped switches that shut off outside lights. "You can finish whenever you finish," the boy said, "I don't mind waiting. But I can't sell you no more, 'cause we're closed."

"Closed is closed," Lorna said. "It's apparently twelve-thirty in here when it's not quite midnight in the world."

"This *is* Oneida County," Hank said. Then he said, "I'm sorry, Lorna. I guess I don't really have a story."

"Well, that's all right with me," she said.

He saw his father, who had turned to instruct him about the trail of cairns or the weather, get struck by the wind, which slammed noisily into the mountainside. His father spread his arms for balance and opened his mouth. No sound came out, or the wind suppressed it. In the thick dirty white mist about them, his father, poncho taut with wind, was lifted into the air and taken from sight.

The wind died and the cloud eddied. Rain had made the stones slick and shiny black. A dozen or so feet from the ledge over which his father had flown, Hank had stood in place, his back against rock face. He remembered standing with his legs together, the heels of his boots touching, leaning forward under the weight of his rucksack, his arms folded across his chest for balance or warmth. The wind came up again, and he stood still in it, leaning into the icy rain and waiting.

He didn't know—and he hadn't known then, he was sure—what might have waited for. But he stood in place and looked at the ledge. Now he wished that this woman, Lorna Wolf, knew about his waiting there. He'd have enjoyed asking her whether she thought he was wait-ing for instructions.

He suspected she might agree with him—that he was waiting with utterly no hope for his father to reappear and tell him what to do about his father's disappearance. Hank would have stressed, if he'd told her, that he had no confidence at all his father might return. Now it sounded to him like some kind of allegory, and he was almost—almost—grateful that she didn't know.

Slowly, his grinning father, bleeding along one temple and holding his body stiffly, climbed to his feet from the far side of the ledge. He had not been blown off the mountain, only over an apparently undangerous shelf of stone. Holding on to the rock now for balance, his father nod-ded. Hank wondered whether he had winked. And, walking alongside his son instead of before him, Hank's father told him over and again, until Hank took his turn in telling *him*, how the winds had rolled him over rocks until he'd fetched up hard against some that had broken what would have turned into a fall.

"Only the fall got broken," his father said. "Who'd believe it? Only the fall got broken."

His father held Hank's shoulder, though he didn't lean his weight on him. At one point, they held each other's hands, reaching automati-cally to balance themselves on a slippery, rounded face.

"I was afraid we'd have to bivouac here," his father said, heaving soon for breath but talking, talking. "You can get benighted and end up frozen dead on this mountain. And this is the *gradual* part. But don't you let anyone tell you it's easy. We'll come back here—I'll get hold of ropes and axes and pitons and whatever else they use, and we'll practice, and we'll come up here another time and climb straight up a different trail. *Route*, they call it. But this is how you start. You start this way, and then you take the more dangerous route."

A few minutes later, his father said, "And my glasses didn't even break."

Hank said, "Only the fall."

His father pounded on his shoulder in response.

They went to the top. His father stopped to light a cigarette where sun broke through the cloud cover. Big athletic hut boys and boyish New England blondes like those he would pursue in college—like Leslie, in fact—worked outside the low wooden building he and his father would enter, making shy, effortful, casual conversation, like people used to adventure.

His mother would not be there to greet them, of course. They would eat and they would listen to a hut boy play the piano, and they would sleep in a dormitory for men. Then they would go home. His mother would have returned. He would become nine and ten and forty-four. And where, in the logs of a thousand centuries' navigation through oceans of blood, would the tiny moment of a father's lifting into the air be entered?

"No story, Lorna," he said. "I wish there was."

She patted his arm.

He thought how, when Leslie slept and he came late to bed, he patted her arm as he lay down. She said she knew in her sleep that he was there, so he did that. She slept with a leg protruding from the comforter, often in the coldest weather. Usually bare, her leg lay on top of the cover, its slender calf and extended foot an elegance he admired.

Lorna leaned over as if she were going to kiss him good night, and he held steady, hoping she would.

"Catch you later," she said, in her hoarse, dark voice.

"Catch you later," he said. "Good luck."

She said, "That's right." Then, louder, she said, "Dickie boy. Early day."

Early day, Hank thought. As soon as he woke, he would telephone Leslie. Lorna's brother slid from the stool, wobbled an instant, braced himself against her with his undamaged arm, and they left. Maybe he would make the call tonight. The glass door closed behind them. Hank looked through it, waiting, but not with hope.

You're right, he told himself. But he heard the words in Leslie's voice, as if his wife were not in Manhattan, as if she were here in Oneida County, bearing all of the rest of his life in her strong hands, in her powerful voice. *You're right*, Leslie said in him: *If you don't have a story, there isn't an end. You don't get punctuation.*

Lorna must have agreed. She did not turn to look at him. She did not wave.

STILL THE SAME OLD STORY

O NCE UPON A TIME, I was dissatisfied with how I used my brains and with how Sam used his. He was what they call—and still, in upstate New York, with respect—a banker. I was the banker's wife. And I had grown bored with my candor, weary of my brittleness, bruised by my own dissatisfactions. So, driving from a canal town that since the late nineteenth century had been thrashing about to survive, I went to bed with a man named Max who practiced medicine and who had no heart.

I met him at a party and I met him at the hospital—need I say that I worked for the Auxiliary?—and I met him at a motel outside of Syracuse. He was stocky, and his soft skin gleamed over bunchy muscles. He was the sort of man who exercised not for his health but so that women would admire him. He wasn't, so I'd heard, a good doctor; he wasn't a happy one, and he was close to leaving the area when we met. Perhaps his imminent departure gave us a feeling of license. We made love three times on a Saturday in November, the second time while the Florida–Notre Dame game was showing on the television set. He wasn't so cruel as selfish. He used me hard. I was stimulated by his lack of generosity, I'm sorry to say. And as men must, I've learned, he told his colleagues at the hospital. It seems that doctors, especially, need to talk like boys about sex. Maybe I knew he would. Maybe that foreknowledge was also a stimulant. Maybe I knew when it began that Sam must finally learn of it too.

As is Sam's way, he didn't tell me directly. I knew that something of it was in the wind when he told a story at dinner, after Joanna had gone upstairs to her homework, ending it with these words: "And he said it was the best blow job he ever had."

I knew what Max was saying. I knew that Sam was hearing rumors or reports. I blushed over my chicken with rosemary, and if Max had been at the table instead of Sam, I could not tell—nor can I now—whether I'd have gone around to burrow into his lap or slug him with an herbed paillard.

I said, "Nice language."

Sam looked lean and fit, tired, uninterested in food, and a little dangerous. As he'd aged, as he'd lost hair, his bony forehead and prominent nose made him look like something with keen vision and cruel abilities and the habit of hunting.

He said, "Sharon, a blow job is a blow job. You want to call it, you know—"

"Fellatio?"

"That's right. You want to call it that? It's still what she did with her mouth."

I said, "You know, I think you're right." I cut a square of chicken with considerable care.

"We *agree*," he said to the ceiling. "But I didn't mean"—his smile looked nasty—"to be dis*taste*ful. If you know what I mean." He looked at me with his eyebrows raised, his eyes unblinking. I looked into them. I wanted to find something of our fifteen years together. We watched each other like that, and his eyes filled with tears that ran onto his face. His mouth collapsed, and he said, "Pardon me, please." I remember that I nodded as he left the table. I remember thinking that I should have wept too.

We didn't talk that way again. We meshed our social calendars, as we customarily did, and we attended dinners and cocktail parties at which doctors looked meaningfully over my body and sometimes met my eyes. I suppose they were waiting to be selected for the best-ever sex of their lives. In a provincial big town or small city, sex and thievery and numbers of dollars constitute the curriculum, and apparently reasonable adults grow hypertensive about them. So I was their hot topic. I find it of interest even now that I didn't care.

I knew that Sam and I had foundered. I knew that Joanna could be drowned along with us. I knew, I insisted to myself, that she *might* survive. I worried only about how, I told myself. Everything else, I decided, would take care of itself. I gave up my local newspaper column, slid from the Auxiliary, and signed up for all the substitute teaching of French and Spanish I could, preparing myself for full-time employment as a single parent.

Gene McClatchey telephoned on an April afternoon to say, "This is Gene."

"Gene?"

"At the bank, Sharon? I work for your fucking husband?"

I said, "Not that happily, I guess."

"We need to meet."

And of course I thought he was a tardy quester after the world's best etc. I said, "Why ever, Gene?"

"On account of your husband is dicking my wife? Would that be a good enough why-ever?"

"My husband? Your wife? Valerie?"

He said, "Name someplace, will you? That's private?"

"That's secret, you mean."

He said, "Please?"

We ended up a dozen miles to the north, at a conservation training center run by the state, a little park of nature trails and wooden blinds from which to peer at waterfowl. I don't know why I felt compelled to bring a loaf of bread to feed to the ducks. I tore the pulpy slices into bits and hurled them at mallards while Gene McClatchey, a red-faced man with curly brown hair and a hard, black double-breasted suit, studied the tearing of the bread and its arc toward the water and the wheeling of the ducks as they fed.

He said, impatiently, "You don't seem upset, Sharon."

"I'm not surprised that something happened, Gene. I didn't think of your wife, to tell you the truth. She's so glamorous and Sam's—well, I don't know, I guess. You want me upset? How upset do you want me?"

"What *I* am," he barked.

"You're jealous," I said. "Or angry. Because the beautiful woman who's supposed to be yours—"

"No! I don't want to hear any of that feminist horseshit about freedom and owning people and whatever. She's my *wife*."

"And hurt," I said.

"Yeah?"

"Yeah, Gene. Wounded."

"Bitch," he said. He flinched, stepped back from the fence at the duck pond, and scrubbed with his wide hands at his face. He said, "Sorry. I apologize. I'm so *disgusted*. Look at what I found that she left around by accident on purpose. Disgusted'll do it."

He held a small notebook with thick covers. The paper was heavy and the binding looked like the inside covers of a fancy antique book. She had written in aqua ink, of course. She wore mostly pinks and limes and aquas in soft cloth that emphasized her breasts and hips. She was the best-built woman over twenty-five in town. Gene struck her, so they said at our parties. Looking at his big hands and red face, I believed that he might. I recalled her long, solitary walks through a town in which you drove everywhere, in part to show off your car. I remembered marveling at the erectness of her carriage. I remembered watching men who marveled at what she carried with such pride. She might well have enjoyed provoking him, I thought.

"You can borrow it," he said.

"What?"

"You can keep the diary awhile. I have xeroxes. I figured you'd want to see the real thing."

"Oh. Thank you, Gene. But why?"

"They can't get away with it," he said.

"For the sake of argument," I said, "why not?"

"Because it's wrong. That's why I wanted you to know. I want it stopped, Sharon."

"You're asking me to stop Sam from—"

He said, *"Please?"*

I can't believe S! Silly-billy lover! Put the tube of jelly in his hand and he just held it. Asked me what it was for. Looked at me the way he does. I think I got wetter. He said O Boy. My boy lover. O Boy.

S says Sh frigid for months. How about those stories about her? Backseats and motels and quickies in cars? S says S wouldn't know where to put a cock without the instruction book. Here's what I told him—Lie down. He knew what I meant.

S thinks his daughter smokes pot. Got to talking, asked if he ever tried it, S surprised. Said I heard a good high gives great orgasms. We'll try it together if we can get some. Stay *young*. It's the ticket. Keep your body good and your lover crazy.

Gene growling like a dog these days. He smells it. Dogs can smell it on you.

You *can't* belong to other people. You have to belong to yourself. You have to love yourself. Then other people.

When S comes, his balls jump. Mexican Jumping Balls. S phones up and says Cucaracha! Makes me think of his balls. My lover's balls.

When I showed him the page after page of round, uncertain hand-writing, Sam slapped the book from my fingers. I thought of Gene beating on Valerie and wondered if it was my turn. I said, "If you hit me, I might end up killing you, Sam."

He said, "I'll bear that contingency in mind."

"You understand, of course, that she's using you—this thing—affair—relationship—"

"Don't smirk, Sharon. Or I *will* hit you. And then you'll have to kill me, remember. And your mother will raise Joanna in Cleveland while you're a gray-haired convict. And for Christ's sake don't tell me about any *other* woman using adultery against her husband!"

"You think this is about 'adultery,' Sam? Your balls are jumping so high, they're blocking your vision."

"My *balls?*"

I retrieved the diary and painstakingly found the page for him.

Which brings me to Joanna, whom I had to hold and talk to after Sam, that night, took a room at the Valley Rest Motel, which is on the southern end of town. She let me talk, but she had no mercy for my need to hold. She twitched away from me that night. She paced the living room, touched the lampshades, prodded at books, moved records and discs on their shelves. She plucked at her hair and bunched her lips in disgust.

"You know what they'll say about Daddy? Big banker-man Daddy? They'll say, 'Old Sam Edel's been punching the town bag.'" She looked at me pointedly and then she looked away. "You know how humiliating this is?" She looked at me again and cried, "Oh, of *course* you do!" Her pale, imperious face went soft, and she ran to me like a fugitive from *Giselle*. We hugged. By the time I decided it was safe to close my eyes and enjoy what I could, her lean body had gone hard. "That *bitch*," she whispered.

She endured my rubbing at her hair, and even my kisses. When I explained that her father might really be gone, she simply nodded. "He's angry," I said. "He's not a happy man. But he *adores* you, Joanna."

"That's nice," she said. "A guy'll tell you love all you want. They say it a lot. It's like at a hockey match. They sing 'The Star-Spangled Banner,' they look like nice kids, and then they beat the shit out of each other. It's a guy thing. I'm just not that terribly impressed. I love you. Right. Thanks ever so much."

"Oh, he means it, darling."

"Ma," my fourteen-year-old daughter instructed me, "they all mean it."

"Oh."

"We'll be all right," she said, like an older aunt, embracing me again. It was later, after the buttered popcorn, that she asked me to confirm the requirement under law that her father, once divorced from me, had to help pay her way through college. On behalf of the lawyer I hadn't consulted yet, I guaranteed. It was really then, as I promised Joanna her future, that I began to feel the fractures of our collapse.

S makes me feel worshipped. Says all women before me were girls. Kneels and kisses his way up my legs. Chews at me. I am my lover's food and he is mine. We were starving, but now we nourish each other.

Sam was still away two days later. We spoke coldly on the telephone. I said I'd be out of the house one morning so he could come for clothes. He agreed to a transfer of money from the joint account to my household account. I suggested that we get in touch with lawyers. He was silent for an instant, and then he hung up.

As I walked from the phone, it rang, and I formulated something chilly and not too intimate with which to greet him. But it wasn't Sam. It was the aqua-colored voice.

She said, "Mrs. Edel?"

"This is Sharon, Valerie. I recognize your voice. How are you?"

"Mrs. Edel—"

"Honey," I said, "you're screwing a man who's been married to me for fifteen years, so you can get your nutritious ass down off of your high horse and talk straight a little. You don't want to go around sounding like the district manager for Amway, do you?"

"I want your little snot bitch of a daughter to stop it. Now. And I mean it. That straight enough for you? Honey?"

"If my daughter—you better watch your mouth about her, Valerie. If there is a problem concerning my daughter, please feel as free as possibly only you can feel to tell me all about it."

"You're a possessive, dried-up prude, Sharon. So if he wanders to the warmer climates—"

"I'd call you a tropical rain forest in that case, Valerie. What about my daughter?"

"Tell her to stop stuffing every mailbox she can reach with her letter about *me*. That's what about her."

She hung up. I wondered if she and Sam had decided jointly to hang up on me that day. I went to our empty mailbox and looked across the street, then down our side of the block, and I saw the little white protrusions. As if I were entitled to, I went to my neighbors' house, withdrew the single white page from the box on their porch, and carried it home in clear view, not like a thief but as a citizen bearing the news.

Dear Occupant,

As you may have heard, my father, Mr. Samuel Edel and my mother, Ms. Sharon Hilsinger Edel have separated. Whether that is temporary or permanent, is not yet known. I'm sure the ever reliable town grapevine will let you know as soon as we do.

This is to set the record straight and do away with the rumors and innuendos. My father, Samuel Edel has been having an "affair" with a brainless slut named Ms. Valerie McClatchey. Otherwise known as "The Town Bag." I hear that men of Mr. Edel's age often do things like this e.i. getting oversexed and horny if their wives are getting somewhat mature. That is no excuse. However, I've been hearing vicious gossip that my mother, Ms. Edel pushed him into this type of "activity" by something she did. That is a lie. Mr. Edel went "sex mad" as many men do and broke his sacred marriage vows. He did it on his own e.i. leaving our bed and board. Ms. Edel is a right on woman. She did nothing wrong in this. I gladly put my reputation on the line to say this.

Mr. Edel will have to answer to heaven along with Ms. McClatchey.

Thank you for your time and attention.

Sincerely,

Joanna B. Edel

When I came home, I had Joanna's letter from the Lewis house, from Feimster and Murray and the crazy people on the corner with all the cats. I didn't have it from the Lutheran Home or the Noels'. Mrs. Montemora had beaten me to her mailbox. I had it from Hilsenrath and Boynton and Hendricks. I had turned the corner onto Canal Street, which is also the old north-south highway, and the street had suddenly seemed unnaturally bright, the cars too terribly loud, the people outside the gas-and-electric and the drugstore like a surging mob in a movie— say, *King Kong.* There were too many mail slots in too many doors, too many postboxes, too many streets off Canal, and too many houses on each of the streets. I knew Joanna. Now I knew why I had heard the printer next to our word processor—it had sounded like a little electrical saw during the night. She had printed enough letters for a lot of the boxes in town. And she would have tried to reach them, stalking on her stiff, long legs, her chin up to signify her dignity, her story—Joanna's story about the story—in her backpack and in each of her small hands.

She was late from school. Or maybe her deliveries had taken the entire day. It was almost six, and I was sitting in the perfumed squalor of her room. There were more of the letters in a pile on her desk. Dear Occupant.

I reread one, the line about Ms. Edel, who was a right on woman.

Joanna, from her doorway, said, "Why are you in my room? Why are you reading my stuff?"

I said, "I'm an occupant. And how private is a letter you've delivered to every address in the ZIP code? Is that your *hair*, darling?"

It was short, ear-level on one side, a little shorter on the other. It was the color of yellow cough drops, and it looked as though it would glow in the dark. Her lips looked rigid, and her eyes were very wide. She pulled the wiry bunched hair that heaped the top of her head and she flushed as, pulling more hair, she exposed what was a quarter of a shaved scalp. "*This* is my hair," she said.

I thought for an instant that if I dyed my hair the color of hers, she would somehow be less alone in the midst of our lives. But I knew promptly that I wasn't cut out for a cough drop. I said her name a few times.

"It just looked cool when I did it," she said. "Nothing else. It's not the biggest deal in the world. I *like* it like this, Mommy, so don't start, all right?"

I said her name again. And then we were both wailing, and assuring each other that it was only *hair* for Godsakes and, after all, it was going to grow back.

That's the story. It straggles off into Gene McClatchey's swollen, masked, and splinted nose—broken, according to the usual sources, by his wife, who stayed awhile and then left. Sam left, too, to run a bank branch in Sidney, New York, where he lives alone and dates young secretaries and is said to look seedy. Joanna and I came to Cleveland, where her hair grew in as black and thick and springy as before. Everyone in the story thought they were going to die of it, but of course they didn't. Once you're in a story, you must live forever. You must choose again and again. You always do it the same.

ARE WE PLEASING
YOU TONIGHT?

—————

WE WERE VERY BUSY, and the rooms were loud. Even the kitchen was loud, though our chef never stood for noise that wasn't necessary. I kept thinking I could hear the barman whistle through his teeth—Comin round the mountain when she *comes*—which he often did when he made mixed drinks. We had two seven-fifteens, a party of three, and a party of two, and the three came early. The old lady led them, then came the son, and then his wife. I looked away from the wife because she was the same bad news I'd been receiving all day.

The old lady was very small, maybe under five feet tall, and her skin was that pale, tender white you only see on the extremely old. Her wraparound skirt and rayon blouse were too large, and I expected her to walk out of her scuffed, low-heeled pumps, like a kid playing Mommy in her parents' bedroom. She didn't shuffle, though. She had a kind of stride, although she wobbled as if the bottoms of her feet were tender. Or maybe it was balance, I remember thinking. The world was spinning a little too fast, or gravity wasn't working right on her, and something kept pulling her slightly sideways. The son walked with his head down, as if she embarrassed him, or as if he embarrassed himself. That's a choice, right there, isn't it? How you call it is who you are.

"How are you?" she asked me before I could say it to her. And she asked as if she knew me. Of course, a lot of people out there thought I was someone to know. It wasn't quite Rick's Place, but it was a good restaurant. I ran it tight, the food was Provençal, we cooked it well and served good wines. I cultivated my tall, tough manner, and my clientele worked to make me smile. People who spend a lot when they dine out consider their money better spent when the people who sell it to them make believe they're friends. As for my famous service, I had learned to run a squad while attached to Graves Registration, and my career had taken me from dishing out the dead to *daube Aixoise.*

"Ah, *and you!*" I said, as if with sudden pleasure.

"Peter," she said, "this is my son, Kent, and his wife, Linda. This is Peter," she said to them. "He owns this lovely place."

It was the way she said Peter. She rounded off the *r* just a little, and I heard New York or New Jersey—she'd say *ah* instead of *are*—and not Southport, Connecticut. I thought I recalled that she'd come, once or twice, with a handsome old man. He was burly the first time, then waxy and thin several months later. I'd forgotten them. Her son was broad and sunburned, his brown hair was bright with highlights of red and light brown from saltwater sailing.

As I seated them, his mother said, "Peter, I wonder if you would instruct our waiter to leave the fourth place setting. It's my husband's birthday. He died."

"I was very sorry to hear about it."

"You heard?"

I bowed my neck and shut my eyes an instant. I didn't want to have to lie again.

She frowned, and her skin, I thought, might crack. Her teeth were dingy with a kind of heavy film. Her dark hair was thinning. And still, she was a pretty thing. She must have been one of those small Austrian cuties with her narrow nose and prominent cheekbones. "Tonight is my husband's birthday," she said. "Kent and Linda and I are having dinner with him." She said it as though the husband had forced his way to dinner with them. He was dead, and she was sorrowful, and he'd been hers, and she was dining in his honor, but he still, according to some definition I hadn't yet heard, was uninvited.

I turned toward the empty chair and nodded deeply. I said, "Happy birthday." I'd fed stranger tables. I had supervised the emptying of cargo planes filled with the horribly dead, the routinely dead, the accidentally dead, and the dead who'd been murdered by people under their command. Service is service.

"Isn't he lovely?" she asked her son and daughter-in-law about me. I tried to avoid the daughter-in-law's eyes. Linda's eyes. She wasn't the twin of the kid in the papers, but she looked enough like her. I had trouble with that. I was having a bad night, and I'd had a bad day.

"He's wonderful," Linda said. Her voice was edgy and entertained at once. It didn't make my night any easier. I refused to meet her eyes.

"I'll take drink orders, and your waiter, Luc, will be over shortly," I said. There was a line at the reservations desk, Luc for Lucien was tripping on something he was managing well enough, but I thought he might be ready to fly, there was a new kid making salads, and it had been a very bad day. In light of which, after taking their orders for Johnnie Walker Black straight up, Beefeater martini rocks, and the house white, a Chalone from Monterey, I turned to the old lady—I thought I could see through the skin of her jaw—and asked her, "Are you going all the way?"

She had brown-green eyes that looked faded, as bleached as her son's thick hair. They smiled when her thin, chapped lips did. "I imagine that I am," she said.

"I meant—" I gestured toward the empty chair.

"No," her son said.

The sound came up as the kitchen opened. My chef was probably getting on the kid. And I needed to get to the desk.

"What a wonderful idea," she said.

Linda, who was tan and not red, and whose blond-brown hair was in those thick, wavy strands, said, "You must have a wonderful imagination, Peter."

That's right. That's right.

"Bourbon?" she asked her son.

"Maker's Mark," he told me, "rocks, water back."

I said, "Thank you. And a happy birthday to—to—" I smiled to finish. I had looked. Now I couldn't stop looking at the daughter-in-law's dark eyes. She was the ghost of the ghost I had seen. It was a terrible night.

By the time I left their drinks order at the service bar and seated people who'd been waiting, the noise level in both rooms was high enough to drown out the shouting in the kitchen. I was on my way there when a yachtsman decided that he and his companion would not wait any longer. He didn't wear socks, and I could see that even his ankles were sunburned. His shirt was open to show the sunburned flesh beneath the coarse gray hair of his chest, though all three of his blazer buttons were fastened. He wanted none of us to miss the golden Bill Blass emblems.

I said, "Let me bring you another round of drinks. I know you and your daughter have been waiting for a while."

"Daughter?" he said.

"Oh," I said, but with a little too much relish in my voice. "Sorry. My mistake."

"You're damned right," he said, taking her hand and aiming them at the door. "*Damned* right."

I smiled at the guests who entered across their bow and told them with the correct hint of regret about their ten-minute wait. I took their order for drinks to the service bar and noted that a tray of cocktails was ready to be delivered. It was the water chaser, in the squat Italian tumbler we used for those purposes, that told me whose order it was. I took the tray to them and apologized for the delay.

The daughter-in-law said nothing, the son thanked me, his mother shrugged as if to signal that, among us working folk, such matters are understood. Definitely a Jew from New York, I thought. We all seemed to fancy ourselves, once in a while, Marxists once removed. When I leaned to set down the bourbon and then the chaser, I saw they'd placed two photographs on the appetizer plate of the fourth place setting.

I looked, I moved a step away, and then, as if to arrange the drinks better, I stepped back. Linda said, "Help yourself." Her voice was as dark as her eyes. Ghost bitch, I thought. I stepped alongside her into the musky cinnamon of her perfume, and I looked down at the pictures. One was of the son, Kent, in happy, animated conversation with a bald, broad-shouldered man an inch or so taller than he. The man, apparently the father who had died, was facing Kent and therefore not the camera. And, in the other, on some path near a lake or pond, carrying a rucksack over one shoulder, this same man was striding from whatever held the camera. When I looked up, his widow was frowning in real distress.

I saw Lucien floating up behind her. Oh, he was on something, I thought. He had a goofy smile on his thin, handsome face, and his lids were flapping as if to keep his eyeballs in his head.

"Luc will take your order. The wine list you see. We have a Domaine du Pesquier Gigondas I like, and it's a good price. The Cahors is inky and full of fruit, unusually good body. The Puligny-Montrachet is *not* a good price, but it's a gorgeous wine. So's the Arneis. If you select the duck special, which Lucien will discuss with you, the Diamond Creek, a fairly dark cabby, would be a happy marriage."

"What a lovely and unusual expression," Linda said. "You really enjoy your work." She said it the way you might tell a child what a big, strong boy he is. Thank you, bitch of a ghost, I didn't say.

"Ladies," I said. And then I couldn't resist it: "Gentlemen. Enjoy." To Luc, bearing down on their table like a fireman on call, I whispered, "A special celebration. A—kind of birthday. You will be alert, please, to their requirements?"

In the kitchen, one of the exhaust fans was faltering. I apologized to Abbie, my chef. She was the tallest person in the room, and that included the kid doing salads, who was over six feet tall. She was also, except for the daughter-in-law in the party of three or, counting dead people, four, the handsomest woman in the restaurant that night. Her long oval face was unhappy now, but not because of the heat. She was orchestrating dinners, and she danced, concentrating. It gave her a displeased expression. Fires flared as she or the sous-chef, Caroline, poured wine into pans. I asked if we had enough duck. Abbie strode like an athlete, spun like a chorus girl, scattered shallots, dipped out gold-green oil and ignored me. Caroline, her deputy, nodded that we did.

To the college boy composing endive, radicchio, scallions, and red-leaf lettuce, I said, "You're doing fine. Don't let the greens get soupy with the vinaigrette. Better to give them too little than too much. In the case of dressing, anyway. *Ça va?*"

He looked up.

"Okay?"

He said, "Sure."

"When it's *your* place, it's sure. In my place, when I ask, you *make* sure and then you tell me, so I *feel* sure. Correct?"

"Yes, sir," he said.

"That's what *ça va* means. Good man."

I went out the kitchen back door, and I stood behind the place, between the stuttering exhaust fan and the one that worked, and I looked down the dark slope of the hill. I lit up and leaned against the wall. At eight in the morning, in the kitchen of my house, four miles away, while mist blew in from the sea and it was chilly enough to make me consider using the fireplace, I'd made the *café filtré* and opened *The New York Times*. It was a stab at discipline, and of course it was a sham, but I never lit the first cigarette until I had read the sports and was ready to look at the business pages. To get there, I turned past the wedding announcements while I lit up, sighing it in, and I saw the face of Tamara Wynn, the girl I had loved in college, and when I was unloading corpses at Dover Air Force Base during the war, and when I was in the first and second graduate schools I'd tried. By the time I was at the Cornell management program, I was past talking about her with the women with whom I tried hard to fall in love, one of whom I'd married.

We'd been the usual story. I was unreconciled to her departure for other men and then marriage to a surgeon. I didn't die of it, but she had died of something about which I hadn't heard. I read in the *Times* how her daughter, Courtney—wasn't there a year when every female born east of the Mississippi received that name?—had been given in marriage by the widowed father, who had been a premed in the class ahead of mine. There was the picture of Courtney, except it looked like her mother. Tamara, with her high brow and wide mouth and reserved, quizzical smile, looked out of the *Times* and up over thirty years.

All I could think to say that morning—I heard my voice; it sounded like a kind of wounded groan—was "Oh. Hello."

Dottie, on her way into the kitchen, said, "Hello to *you*. That was pretty enthusiastic for first thing in the morning."

It wasn't you, Dot. It was the one I loved. It was the daughter of the one I loved. It was dead people. That's my job: meet 'em and greet 'em. Hello.

I put the cigarette out against the wall of my restaurant and stripped it, letting the tobacco and paper fly in the wind. I put the filter in my pocket. I wondered how many ash marks pocked the wall outside the kitchen. I went back in, tucked and groomed in the men's room, wiped the sink clean, and rearranged the white cotton washcloths we folded on a table to be used as towels. Then I went to visit my customers. I managed, by striking off at odd angles, to save until the last the table of three or, depending on how you feel about it, four, one of whom was a woman who could have been the twin of the picture I had seen in the paper. Note this: she was not Courtney or a sister. I could see the differences—a dimpling of chin, a fullness at the neck, the closeness of this woman's eyes compared to Courtney's and Tamara's.

Nevertheless, how *is* that for extracorporeal life? Most nights, you sell food and drink and it's deposited in verifiable flesh. Here, in twelve hours, I had seen two ghosts, and one of them ate a steak of swordfish marinated in oil, white wine, thyme, marjoram, salt, and red pepper flake, accompanied by a scallion risotto and roasted carrots along with a glass of house white at a table one quarter of which was occupied by somebody dead.

The pictures had been moved. The one of the dead fellow walking with his rucksack was, despite the absence of his face, facedown. The other lay near the son, Kent, who was finishing the last of a Black Angus steak we sear on a grill over hardwood and dried grapevines. A good bottle of Châteauneuf-du-Pape, the Vieux Telegraphe, was close to his plate. His mother had given up on her grilled fresh sardines. She was drinking mineral water. Her Scotch was unfinished. She looked to be tasting something spiny and corrosive. As I came up, and Linda's face assumed its look of amusement, I heard the old woman say, "And then, every time, in spite of my best efforts, I remember the dishonesty and disloyalty. How can I forgive them? And I *try*. You compartmentalize your life, and soon you get locked in one of the compartments. And I was locked in another. And guess who'd kept the key?" She raised the mineral water, then put it down. "Still," she said.

Luc hurried past. He was sweating through his shirt and his face ran slick. His eyes were huge, and I couldn't imagine his being able to see for the constant batting of his eyelids. I held a finger in the air, which was normally a sufficient signal for my waiters. It meant they must meet me at the back corner of the service bar *now*.

Linda said, "Is everything all right, Peter?"

"Aren't you kind to ask, madame," I said. "It's a busy night. I must seem preoccupied. Forgive me. Are you pleased? Are we pleasing you tonight?" I had to look at her—I don't know. Yes: I had to look at her encyclopedically. I did. I looked at the way her throat creased when she moved her head. I looked at the folding of flesh at her wrists when she moved her flatware. I looked at the width of her shoulders, the size of her muscled upper arms, the flatness of her barely arched brows.

She said, "What?"

I fled the question. "And you, madame?" I asked her mother-in-law. "Sir?" I said to the son.

Most of a bottle of wine was in his answer: "Ask him."

"Pardon?"

"You didn't ask him." He pointed with his fork at the photographs on the table. Luc went past again, and I raised my finger. He nodded, raised his finger in reply, and all but loped for the kitchen. Tonight, Luc was the amphetamine king, I thought. Tomorrow, he was on probation or canned, I didn't yet know which. I carefully did not look at the woman who smelled so good, who smiled so cruelly, and who bore the face of the woman whose face on her daughter had greeted my day.

The old lady's lips were pursed. It was as if she fought a pain. She looked at her son and then at the photographs. She shook her head. The son gestured again with his fork. I looked at the unused place setting. He was there, of course, though I didn't see him. The son did. So did the widow. I didn't watch to see where the daughter-in-law looked. Though the rest of them couldn't see who sat in Linda's place, I knew, and I didn't want to know, and I stood in silence, my hands clasped before the waist of my lightweight midnight-blue tuxedo, a man of admittedly studied elegance who tried to smile for the clients. Who couldn't, though.

"Cat's got his whatever," the son said.

From out of the kitchen came Luc. He seemed to roll, as if on casters, across the floor. He moved with grace, the burden of his upper body cradled on stiff muscles, while his hips and thighs moved flexibly to cushion his cargo's ride. I saw another waiter, Charles, and the barman, Raymond, as they watched Luc move. They were timing it, as they so often did. I had trained my staff well. By the time he'd arrived behind the old woman, then had moved around her and into her line of sight, the kid from the kitchen, Raymond and Charles had stepped forward.

Luc had listened well to my parting instructions. "We would like, 'sieurs-dames, to present, for the celebration of your birthday, this token of our absolutely happiest wishes." His voice sounded ever so slightly as if he'd been sucking helium. His eyes goggled as his mouth moved. He bowed, sweating and red-faced, over the small gâteau made with no flour and crushed almonds and imported apricot preserve on which five token candles flared. "And may I ask whose birthday it is?"

The old woman looked at the cake. I saw again how thin and stretched her pale, frayed skin was. Her mouth was open. Her son, lying back in his chair, slowly lifted his soiled white napkin. I thought he might drape it over his face, but he carefully wiped his lips and pointed to the empty chair. I did not look at the daughter-in-law.

Luc strode to stand between the daughter-in-law and the photographs. He looked at me. I shook my head. He didn't know what I meant. Neither did I. He sang, in his drug-enriched tenor, "Happy birthday to you—" And Charles and Raymond joined him, and so did the boy who made the salads, and so did several diners at tables nearby.

Luc mumbled some sounds as he realized he didn't know the birthday celebrant's name. He bestowed the cake on the table, he bowed, and he left to offer service to hungry people who awaited him. The other men went back to their work.

"I am so sorry," I told the old woman. For she had been betrayed again. "It was a misunderstanding."

"Yes," she said. I tried to meet her faded, angry eyes.

The son cleared his throat. He held the photographs. He looked at them with a sorrow I found familiar.

The daughter-in-law's expression was only a little puzzled. I realized she'd seen how susceptible I was to her. She wondered why, but not too much. She didn't mind my appetite. She said to me, "Misunderstanding?"

"Yes," the old woman said, "it always is."

THE BABY IN THE BOX

T WASN'T HIS JOB, it *wasn't* his job, but there he went, in the only
vehicle left, a blown-out Suburban with a hundred thousand miles
on it and the seat pushed so far forward his belly rubbed against the
wheel. He was fighting with the wheel instead of loving it. His father
said that when he taught him to drive twenty-five years ago. Love the
wheel, be gentle on the wheel, keep your hands on the wheel like you're
touching the tits on a girl you're scared that will make you stop.

"Fucking *dwarf*," he shouted as he pushed the truck around the
long, uneasy loop of dark, slick county road between the cutoff to Si
Bingham Road and the farm track called Cemetery Road in spite of
its sign saying Upper Ravine. He was cursing the mechanic, a nephew
of the sheriff, who changed the oil and filters on the deputies' cars and
who claimed he could change a timing belt and who couldn't. His legs
were short. At the station they called him Chicken Man because he
walked with his neck stretched and his shoulders back and his knees
stiff, thinking it made him look taller. It made him look like a grease-
stained, white-faced freak with those dead white eyelashes and knees
that didn't work. He pushed the seats all the way up when he test-drove
the vehicles so his legs would reach the pedals, and he was a chicken-
legged runt.

Pumping the brakes with not much hope because the pedal was almost on the floor to begin with, he remembered the Suburban was in the garage because of a master cylinder leak. So he was going to die, probably burning, when the truck went off the road into trees or those big rocks at the entrance to the snowmobile trail at the mouth of the state forest when the brakes failed and he rolled, and sprayed gas onto the manifold, and exploded.

He didn't pretend that he knew what was happening to the county or his job in it or the world. But he knew nothing much worked right, and on his night shift, often alone at the station, he smoked so much that his tongue felt burned and his chest ached and he recognized he was scared as much as he'd ever been in his life, including his months on patrol in South Korea with an Army platoon of psychopaths, illiterates, and whore dogs.

The rear end of the Suburban swung out as the county road dropped into the valley that ran up to Sheridan Hill Road, where he thought he had to turn. He considered trying to reach someone on the radio. He grabbed the transmitter, then pushed it back hard into its clamp. There wasn't anyone to reach. He was the dispatcher. His chair was empty. His illegal public work place cigarette was probably just going out, his coffee maybe wasn't quite ice-cold. He had left a note in the station logbook. He had traced over his letters several times with the county ballpoint pen, darkening the words until he'd torn through the page, so there would be no mistaking the emergency that had sent him away from his post. He blinked when he remembered what he had written: *Baby in box.* That was because he couldn't remember whether you spell dumpster with a *p* and it embarrassed him to look uneducated. He snorted and almost blew his nose onto his uniform. He was always finding something, his father pointed out, to get embarrassed by. "You might be better off not thinking," his father had said, making the face he made when he swallowed some of his drink.

"I could follow in your footsteps," he hadn't answered his father.

So they were down to four patrols at night, with the backup

emergency vehicle still without a transmission because of course the chicken-legged white-faced son of a bitch was a liar as well as incompetent and he could no sooner change a timing belt than do a hip joint transplant.

And there was no one on overtime clerical work at night to help them catch up because they were cut down on clerical help during *days* as it was. And the sheriff himself was in Albany with a dozen other sheriffs to lobby against the new budget cuts. And the state police were all on call in Oxford, where the deputies had also gone, because a maintenance man laid off by the sheriff's department had been turned down by Wal-Mart for a clerking job and had purchased a rifle at Wal-Mart's excellent discount and had taken hostage several hundred thousand square feet filled with appliances, bright-colored dishes, pet food, plastic toys, and cheap clothes.

"We're biting our tails here," he'd said to the woman on the phone. "We're turned around in a complete circle, three hundred and sixty-five degrees, and we're shooting each other in Oxford, lady. I don't have anyone to *send*."

"Who is this?" Like she had a right to know and maybe she was going to dock him two weeks' pay or something. "What's your name?"

"My name is not the point, ma'am." He tried to be polite because everything you said on the line was recorded.

She said, "It's three hundred and sixty degrees. You got it mixed up with three hundred and sixty-five days in a year. Anyway, it's really a hundred and *eighty* degrees, if that's what you mean."

"If what's what I mean, ma'am?"

"The turning-around thing. Look. We found a *baby* in the dumpster and you have to send somebody. A nurse. EMTs and the ambulance—"

"You found a baby in a dumpster, you say."

"I don't *say*. I mean, we really found it. We heard it crying."

"Jesus," he had said.

"Amen," she said.

"What I'm telling you, there isn't anybody *here*."

"How can there not be anybody there? Isn't the sheriff's depart-ment one of those places there *is* somebody there? Isn't that—what's it called—government?"

"Restructuring, ma'am. The new budget thing, the contract, I believe they've been calling it?"

"We're doing that here? In this county? *Tonight?*"

"I believe we are, ma'am. We can't even use the copier without permission now."

"This is a very small baby and she doesn't seem to be healthy. Of course, a little time in a dumpster in November can cure you of being healthy."

"Yes, ma'am," he had said. Now, as he turned off, and the Suburban wobbled, and he headed uphill toward where he thought their house might be, he wondered whose baby it could be, and how you threw one away. Did you pitch it up and into the dumpster on the run? Would you climb inside the dumpster's high walls and lay it there? What did you say when the time came to climb back over it and get out and onto the road?

He had said to her, "I'll find you someone."

"I knew you would," she'd said.

"How come?"

"You sounded slightly human is why."

So there he was, slightly human and slightly in control of a huge Suburban that was slightly losing brake fluid and slightly on the way to rescuing a baby that a person had put in a dumpster filled with maybe green garbage and cat vomit or, say, furring strips with nails sticking out and busted Sheetrock and old insulation with mouse turds all over it like raisins in a cake.

He finally did switch the radio on and turn it to the tactical band. He heard the state cops in Oxford and a voice he thought he recog-nized as the day shift supervisor for the sheriff's department. No one was asleep, and they were all about forty miles south and more than busy. And he was here. They would talk about him failing to man his position. They would talk about the calls coming in that he was not there to answer. Maybe one of the off-duty clerks would decide to come by. Maybe Chicken Man would walk stiff-legged in his sleep and come take the calls. Maybe no one would call.

"My name—you asked me for my name," he'd said.

"All right," she'd said, "but that was when I was going to try and get you fired."

"It's Ivan. It's Ivanhoe, but I don't use it. Ivan Krisp."

"But really Ivanhoe," she'd said. "It's a very unusual name. Do you spell the crispy part with a *c?*"

HE RAN OFF the road about half a mile away from her house. He'd been driving fast on Sheridan Hill Road when the surface curved and dipped at once. He'd seen moonlight on wet shale and had pushed the brake pedal down to the floor, figuring he wouldn't get much pressure because of the leak. It had been perfectly amateur maneuvering, and he'd slewed right and gone nose down a few dozen yards past the shoulder into a young stand of hardwood, taking some trees down and whacking his chin on the wheel.

"Okay," he said. "You're not hurt."

His knees did hurt, though, and he was afraid he was going to walk like Chicken Man for the rest of his life. His head was beating, and his chin was bleeding, his hands were wet with his own blood from cupping his face and rubbing it. Probably he looked like somebody shot in the brains. Good way to be sure of keeping Ivan Krisp alive, he thought, is you shoot him in the brains.

Bigger-bellied than when he was young, if you said it kindly, and lard-assed and gut-hung if you talked like a sheriff's deputy commenting on the department night dispatcher's physique, he fought his way out of the door and up, on his hands and very sore knees, to Sheridan Hill Road. He continued to answer a sheriff's department emergency call by responding, as it happened, at one. A.M. of a very bright night in November, on foot. He called out *Whoooooo!* Which was his rendition of a siren, but it hurt his face and he shut up.

He sped on call, a public servant responding to the public's need, by trundling on his banged-up legs so fast his belly wobbled and his chest ached. He couldn't quite catch his breath, and he had to stop and open his coat to bend over, heaving for air. This will be the way we do it in the new restructuring, he thought: chubby men with funny names would go out on foot to answer calls for assistance. They could carry whistles, and every time they panted they could blow the whistle so vehicular traffic would know to pull over and wait on the side of the road until they were past. You call them, and you could lose a family member, convert to a new religion, develop a hobby, move to another county and leave the empty house for sale before the sheriff's department showed up, he thought. He stopped and caught his breath, or some of it, and lit a cigarette, and coughed so hard on the first hard hook of smoke into his lungs he almost threw up. That's government, he thought.

It was almost two by the time he reached the house. It was a low farmhouse with yellow aluminum siding and a dark green dumpster, one of the long ones, outside on the side of the road, hard against the front of the garage. The outside lights on the house and garage lit the road up, along with the pale blue of the moon. Lights were on in the house. He waited at the door to wipe his face and catch his breath. He listened for the cries of an infant.

The woman who came to the door said, "My God, what happened to your face, Deputy?"

He looked at the blood on his hands. "I had a little fender-bender a ways down there, toward County 29? Cracked my chin on the wheel, and it might not have stopped yet."

"I'd say not," she said.

"Chins and foreheads," he said. "They look worse than they feel. Though I have to admit it feels terrible."

She was as tall as he was and a little heavy-thighed in tight, fade blue jeans. Her face was long and bony, though, and she had hollows at the eyes. She looked like she never slept enough. Her skin was dark, and it looked as though it would feel soft if you put your hand out gently and just touched it under the cheekbone or at the corner of the eye.

She said, "Yes?"

"I'm not a deputy, strictly speaking," he said.

"What *are* you, strictly speaking?" She looked at his gray uniform, his black tie, and he knew she'd been hoping for someone a little more capable-looking. Maybe she'd settle for secretly competent, he thought. He knew *he* would. And he knew he wasn't.

"Well, ma'am, I'm what you call the dispatcher."

"Ivanhoe!"

"Yes, ma'am."

"You're all they had left?"

"I'm the entire available people on call and in the station and on the air. It's terrible night. There isn't anyone. I'm not supposed to be here. I *can't* be here. Because if I am, I'm not manning the telephone and radio. And I am. So I'm not. I'm in really terrible trouble."

"And you racked the squad car up," she said. "Your fender-bender."

"Blew it off the road," he said. "Might have cracked the block or an axle. It wasn't *really* my fault," he said, hearing his voice skid into the beginning of a whine. "The brake cylinder was leaking, and this guy was supposed—"

"It's not your fault."

"Strictly speaking, since I was at the wheel, I guess it was."

"But it wasn't. It *also* wasn't."

"No."

"No," she said. "It isn't anybody's fault. They just ran out of sheriffs and deputies and cars."

He shrugged. "Where's the baby, ma'am?"

She let him in. The heat in the house was high, and he thought he smelled tomatoes and peppery spices and the dampness of gypsum board and old wood. He was dizzy again, and he caught at her shoulder. She stepped away and he stumbled and then she stepped in again, holding his arm and easing him into a kitchen chair.

"Smells good," he said.

"You got hurt, Ivanhoe."

"No," he said, "only my head and my brains." He put his arms on the table and rested his forehead against them. "Just let me catch my whatever here a minute," he told her.

"I sure can't think of anyone else we can call who'd come out," she said.

"Local services are stretched a little thin," he said.

She said, "How nice to know they're keeping busy. Can we—as soon as you get over your concussion and your fractured skull," she said, "do you think we can load the baby into your arms and wave while you speed the little foundling child away on foot to get rescued? Is that how you see the shape of the evening?"

"Is there a car here, ma'am?" He said it into his hands or onto the tabletop.

"There is a car here," she said. "There is a 1989 Chevrolet Blazer with about an eighth of a tank of gas and something wrong with the battery. As in dead."

He decided that he had to sit up. He did it slowly and was horrified when tears filled his eyes. He blinked, looking away from her, and saw the bare ceiling joists they had pried the Sheetrock from. New sheets of it were stacked against a papered wall that someone had started to strip. "I can walk back to where I went off the road and take the battery out," he said. "There'll be jumper cables in my vehicle, and we can start your Blazer right up, if all it is is a weak cell in the battery or something."

"Does that sound complicated to you too?" she asked. She ran water into a kettle and lit a burner on the stove.

"No, ma'am, it's something I believe I can do." Then he asked her, "Is there a young woman here, ma'am?"

"You're thinking of me as old."

He tried to shake his head. "Oh, no. But I meant somebody of child-bearing age."

"I'm thirty-nine years old," she said. "I have an ample pelvis and I still have my fallopian tubes and both my ovaries."

"Yes, ma'am."

"I could have had a baby and dumped it there."

He thought it was time to be something like an officer of the law, so he made his head stay upright, and he felt in his pockets. "I wonder," he said. "Have you got any pencil and paper I could borrow?"

She was making tea. She pointed at the telephone on the counter near the refrigerator. He found a pad beside it, and a ballpoint pen. She gave him the tea. It was very sweet and very hot. He leaned against the counter. "You told me your name," he said, "but I forget."

She was at the stove again, across the room, with her back to him. "Carole Duchesney." She spelled it, and he wrote it down. As he did, he saw how bloody his fingers were.

"Miz Duchesney."

"Miss."

"Oh," he said, "I would have thought you might sooner call yourself Miz."

"My partner calls herself Miz," she said. "I call myself Miss. I'm an antiquarian."

"Yes, ma'am." He looked at the pad as if there were instructions on it. He reached for a cigarette, but stopped because he knew better. Finally, he heard his mouth say, "What's *her* name, please? Your partner?"

"Frances. Frances Leary. She's one of those redheaded, freckle-faced Learys. *She's* only twenty-seven. With a hell of a pelvis and ovaries on her. It could have been her. That would be interesting as all get out."

"Is she around, ma'am?"

"She is around. Upstairs. With the kid."

"You said the baby isn't healthy?"

"I did, but Frances said I was wrong. She said the little girl was just doing what the situation warranted. Crying really hard and turning red. Frances is from a large family."

He was looking at her, at her tan chamois shirt and her jeans tucked into high black rubber farm boots, her small hands and round fingers, the dark skin of her throat and face. He was trying to see what was different about her.

She raised her chin a little and she said, "What?"

"I don't know quite what I should do next," he said.

"Let's get my Blazer started and drive to the hospital and donate the baby."

"I think we have to get social services into it."

"Orphanages," Miss Duchesney said.

He said, "Well—"

A short, skinny woman with a pale face and cropped red hair and freckles on her nose came into the kitchen. She held the baby across her chest and she was smiling, the way a mother smiles when she presents her child.

Miss Duchesney said, "Frances, this is Ivanhoe Krisp. He's all they had left at the station house, and he abandoned his post to come out here and rescue us from the baby someone left off in the dumpster. On the way, he wrecked his car. He forgot his pencil and paper, so he borrowed some. You can tell from the way his teacup shakes that he is somewhat fucked up. He was wondering what to do next."

Frances didn't speak. Her face reddened, and she smiled the widest smile he remembered seeing.

"Yes," Miss Duchesney said. "It's that wonderful."

"The baby's asleep," he said.

"Or dead," Muss Duchesney said.

"Aw, no."

She said, "No." She walked to him and patted his arm and moved him to the chair. When he was in it, she went to the sink and returned with a brown bowl filled with steaming water. She handed him a folded dish towel. "You might clean the blood away," she said.

He looked into the bowl. He could see a dark shape that he thought might be his reflected face. Looking down, he said, "I found out my daughter, she's a little over sixteen, she's having sex with this boyfriend of hers."

"She probably loves him dearly," Miss Duchesney said.

"Is isn't funny to *me*," he said.

"Of course not. You're right. But that's what we all of us said, is what I mean. You're making a total mess of everything, and you naturally resort to blaming it on love. It's been known to be the name of almost everything wrong," she said, behind him.

Frances Leary said, "Cue the violins."

"I hit her tonight," he said without meaning to. "Before I went to work. I slapped her face."

"And yours ends up bleeding," Miss Duchesney said.

"It comes around three hundred and sixty-five degrees," he said, nodding at the shape of the bowl.

"Sixty," she said. "I told you, remember?"

"Right," he said. "And supposed to be one-eighty." She took the towel from him and dipped the end in the water. "My wife is very upset," he said. Miss Duchesney worked the warm cloth on his chin and around his mouth. The baby began to cry, and he jumped. Miss Duchesney took hold of his face and kept working the cloth on it. He said, against the warm towel, "And now the baby's crying."

He saw himself, though he didn't carry a weapon, holding one of the big, black Beretta 9mms that were issued to the deputies. He was kicking at the door of a scuffed white trailer on the side of Sheridan Hill Road. Against the cries of the baby he heard his own voice: "Sheriff's department!" He saw the door swing in and he demanded to know if someone on the premises had driven to the Leary-Duchesney farmhouse to leave a baby off in the stink of garbage and the giggle of rats.

He said, "Should I go back and get the battery?"

"I think that's what you ought to do next," Miss Duchesney said.

Frances Leary said, "That's a girl. That's a girl." From the sound of her voice, she was rocking the baby a little.

"Maybe some milk," he said.

"I think they need formula," Frances Leary said. "A special kind of formula. I don't think they can tolerate milk right away."

"You wouldn't have any formula," he said.

"No," Miss Duchesney said, "we don't use it. And, worse luck, neither of us is lactating tonight."

"No, ma'am," he said. Then he said, "Could I look at the baby?"

Miss Duchesney said, "You've been sitting there with your eyes closed."

He opened them. He stood and leaned on the back of the chair. He felt as short as Chicken Man when Frances Leary bent toward him. He saw a crushed and furrowed face inside a harsh-looking gray woolen blanket. She was red, and dark with crying, and her blunt nose and her eyelids looked like they were made of wax. He saw her fists beside her face. He thought the miniature fingers were perfect.

"Everybody looks like that," he said.

"You're too sentimental for your work," Frances Leary told him.

Miss Duchesney said, "How can you tell what he *does?*"

He had something to ask. Before they fetched the cables and battery to start up her Blazer, and before he drove like hell to the hospital where he would summon social workers and doctors, if the hospital could find them, and call the sheriff at his Albany hotel and begin to lose his job, he had to ask someone his question.

He saw himself kicking in another door in a trailer half a mile down on Sheridan Hill Road. Miss Duchesney and Ms. Leary sat in the Blazer with the child, and he was kicking in the doors of trailers, of shake-shingled one-story houses, of shacks with no siding, of clapboard cabins with rusted tin roofs. Doors slammed in and he followed, assuming the shooter's stance, legs planted wide and Beretta cupped in both hands before him, demanding the surrender of whoever had disposed of a baby.

"Who," he needed to ask, "would throw a person away?"

He broke another lock with two powerful kicks and he was inside, menacing the doughy couple at their television set.

No, he wasn't.

He made his eyes open. He stood in the kitchen of these women and he fastened his jacket. His knees were sore, and he must look, he thought, like a wounded rooster among his willful hens. He went toward the front door, and he didn't speak. He was embarrassed by Miss Duchesney. She made him feel incompetent. She reminded him of his father, a little. And he was afraid that if he asked his question she would answer it.

DOMICILE

_____

IT MADE ME THINK OF FAIRY TALES—stories of children who drop from the sky or roll from the cupped petals of a silky flower—because he simply appeared one morning and was picked up by a yellow van, a small school bus, which meant that an actual adult had made arrangements for him, and that school authorities acknowledged his existence, and that he was an authentic child, not a product of my second-rate education or of what I considered then, with what I'll now call theatrics, as my third-rate mind.

Wearing a blue hip-length jacket that was streaked with a faded white or yellow stain along both arms and down its back, from underneath the fleece-lined hood to its hem, he did this every day: walked out the door of the white wood motel cabin, pulled the door shut with both hands, then climbed down two steps and walked around to the side of the cabin that faced the direction from which the little bus came. He stood very still, always, as if his khaki knapsack were heavy and pinned him in place. When the bus appeared, he hiked with long, measured steps to the edge of the road, cutting across the ice and snow over the gravel drive that led to the closed offices of the shut-down motel. He arrived as the bus did, and he climbed into it as he had walked, with a nonchalance that seemed important to project.

He was gone until around four o'clock in the afternoon, when the bus paused to let him emerge, and he hiked to the cabin, climbed its steps, and, using a bright, brass-colored key attached to a long, oval tag—the sort you're issued as you sign the register and show them a credit card or dare them to turn down cash—opened the door of the cabin, the one closest of all eight to the one with OFFICE on its door, and he went inside. He had been doing this for a week, since the February thaw had hardened back into mud frozen in twists and ruts and permanent pockmarks into which new snow had fallen in a thin, icy crust through which the mud glared up in weak sunlight like sewage.

The bus, then, would move from view, and so would the kid. Except for the usual squirrels and the usual birds, and the usual March winds that came up the Hudson Valley bearing moisture, all that was left on the one-lane blacktop county road was me, moving snow and ice off stones with a stiff brown whisk broom and my canvas-gloved fingers, sorting the ones I would use to repair the roadside wall which, among other chores, provided me with cramped shelter and, sometimes, food. I was in a good deal of trouble that year, and I knew it, though I didn't worry. I think that I did not. I was fit, and too stupid to be frightened for long, and more concerned about the kid of eight or nine who lived at the nameless motel—its square sign was missing from a rusted roadside frame on top of two scuffed four-by-fours—than I was about the long-range prospect. I actually didn't have one, I now believe. I had decided, as I remember it, to think a couple of hours ahead—the next few pages of a book I tried to read, the next few lines of a sketch I tried to make, the next meal of the day.

I had broken my last dollar to buy a can of supermarket-brand creamed corn, and when I wasn't speculating about the kid, as I built my pile of fieldstones, I was tantalizing myself with alternate visions of dinner cooked on the two-burner gas stove in the trailer: corn chowder made with water and some frozen potatoes I had found in their garden, or plain creamed corn spooned hot onto slices of stiff but not yet moldy Wonder Bread, and with potatoes reserved for the next night's meal.

The light in the window of the cabin across the road was a yellow that verged on palest amber, and it wavered almost as a candle would. I'd have bet that he was using kerosene, and I worried for him, thinking of the fumes, thinking of the flame. I had seen a car there once, its long, scarred hood half hidden behind the cabin, but I had never seen who drove it, nor had I never witnessed an adult who waved him goodbye or who greeted him. There he was at his place, and there I was at mine—a graduated senior who had spent an extra semester making up credits, living in a trailer I had to hunch in unless I sat in my canvas director's chair of glossy red wood and black cloth that I had salvaged from behind a dorm. I could of course lie in the built-in bed too short for me. The toilet wasn't hooked up to a septic system, though my landladies had assured me that flushing would come with spring. I cooked with bottled water they supplied, and I took showers at the main house. I used the pine forest behind the trailer for my john unless I made it to town and the burger palace bathrooms. The battery in my Datsun was absolutely dead now, so I stayed at home and I shat in the woods like a bear.

I probably looked like one. I had a lot of dark hair in those days, and no mirror. I shaved and combed myself in the fugitive reflections of the few framed pictures I owned, one of them—an etching of a woman's footprint, long and narrow and perfect (you could tell) in its arch, pressed into bright sand—by a person named Julia, the owner of the foot, who had left the area and me and who had not looked, nor written, nor telephoned, back. I had no phone, but the landladies did, and they'd have come for me if she had called the house. She knew where it was, and where the trailer was. She had wakened in it with me, had answered its small door when one of them—the mother, Mrs. Peete—had knocked, on an autumn morning, with a chore for me. Julia was now in Central America, and she wasn't alone, while I was here, cutting knobby, icy potatoes into an aluminum saucepan, slashing in some onion to fry with them, opening a can of creamed corn, pouring in water, and pronouncing myself competent as I bent in the trailer,

shuffled in my crouch, and worried about the temperature—it was diving again—and about my landladies, and about the boy across the road.

Not a night to be a kid and living alone, I thought.

It did not take a genius like Julia to make the point. I knew which
kid I was feeling sorrier for. And the night would get worse. It was the
night I broke my policy and, as my father had asked me to, I did, on a
trial basis, consider the future. I stood at the stove and fanned my fingers out, one at a time, to indicate to myself that I was being concrete
and realistic.

No Julia now, nor tomorrow, nor ever: one.

Given my academic record, no vocation-with-coat-and-tie plus prospects of a sleek-apartment-in-a-bigtime-city: two.

Noplace to live except here, in trade for too much work, or at home,
in exchange for enduring desperate lessons about life plus the long,
silent evenings of a faltering marriage that ought to have died some
time ago: three.

Present prospects had dimmed for me with the rise, you would
have to say, in immediate pleasures—landlady problems, you could
call them: four.

I apparently could not paint a picture unless I worked in a bright,
heated studio, supplied like a locker room for the gifted and talented
children of the managerial class, by a high-tuition college, and that
was a kind of truth you had to face, I was beginning to think, or you
might end up teaching design in community colleges and overdos-
ing on whatever it was you could—now that you had some kind of
salary—afford: five.

She knocked five times, it seemed to me, and I am not kidding. I
knew who it was, and I was spooked because she was there and because
it felt as though she was reading my mind.

She came in, as I expected her to, and, as I expected her to, she said,
"Oh, Jesus Christ. How can we let you live like this?" I wasn't surprised
that she was a little tipsy.

She wore a red wool mackinaw with black designs, the kind of

hunting coat somebody would have used twenty-five years before. She
wore a long-billed red woolen hat with earflaps, and old black woolen
gloves. Her face was shiny and flushed, her crinkly, bright brown hair
had bits of ice in it, and her eyes were wide and light. When she took
the hat off and beat it against the side of her leg, ice flew up into the
light and disappeared, and her hair sprang out, giving her face a wild
look, as if she reacted with shock to something nobody else could see.
I smelled the sweetness of the Manhattans she drank, and the smoke
from their kitchen woodstove and from her cigarettes.

"You mind if I drop in?" she said, unbuttoning the coat.

"Want some soup?"

"Is *that* what that is."

"I dug the potatoes up in your garden," I said, staring into the pot.
"You don't mind, right?"

"You must be strong as an ox to get to them. Well, you are. The
ground's so damned hard, David. You know, we'd have given you potatoes. And—whatever. Soup. Dinner whenever you want it. I keep telling you that."

I nodded. "Would you like some?"

She kept her coat on. "It's awfully damned cold in here."

"There isn't any heat."

"We'll get electric baseboard heating installed. Come spring. The
land will sell by then. Property sells better in the spring. We'll have
some money, and we'll make you comfortable. We promised that."

I nodded.

"But you'll have left by then, you're saying."

I said, "You know, Rebecca, I don't have any idea. I don't have plans
for anything except the wall, and maybe building you some raised beds
for the garden."

She was standing closer, then, directly behind me, and then she
was leaning in on me, first against my back and then against the rest,
holding on from behind with an arm around my waist. It made me
uncomfortable that a woman who once had been married and who

wore an antique coat like that would feel the need to hug me. I guess you would say I felt unworthy.

"Tell me more about raised beds. They sound fascinating," she said, running her hand up under my shirt. I felt her cold nose at the back of my neck and I felt the words against my nape as she said them. "Whatever they are," she said, "you build us some."

"Your mother won't shell out for the lumber. She won't ever fix this place. She hates me. She thinks I'm a wastrel and the last of the hippies and the seducer of her kid," I said.

"Don't be insulting," she said. "You never seduced me. Yes, you did. But I knew you didn't mean to. You were respectful. You pay your respects, and you stand there being shaggy and a little shy, and people sometimes, anyway, no matter their intentions or any of that, they fall in—whatchamacallit."

"Did you ever think of that as scary?"

"It's the word you're scared of," she said. "You're saving it for Miss Plexiglas Maidenhead of the Short Attention Span. But that's fine. Really. Let's say fall into . . . flesh. That's what happens when people get to be postgraduates."

"You always talk about how old you are," I said.

"Postgraduate, I said. Who said anything about old?"

"No, you're afraid that you're the scary older woman."

"I'd just as soon you do not predict my intentions or supply me with meanings. What happens," she said against the back of my neck, "is that people fall into flesh."

I turned off the stove. She was pulling on me and my leg went back for support, and she pushed her groin against it as she dragged me by the waist, and I started to fall. She straightened and caught me, big as I was, because she was a strong woman and she liked to prove her strength. I pushed off, turned, and we were standing straight again. I put my hands inside her jacket.

She hissed because I had touched bare skin. I said, "No wonder you're cold." She pulled me toward the built-in bed a few feet from the stove.

"You aren't resisting," she asked. "We could cancel the rest of the badinage and just enjoy ourselves. Do you think?"

"I'm not resisting," I said.

"I'm not resisting either," she said.

I tried to say how grateful I was, and how worried about my gratitude, and how she turned my temperature up like an oven. But the idea of saying it and of knowing she had heard it would make me sad. What happened a lot, that year, was that I worried about making myself sad and then about permitting myself too much pleasure. It was like taking care of a sick roommate, or a patient, except that he was me. The lights were on, but we closed our eyes. You always want a little darkness when you go to bed with someone who's a stranger you will probably never know much better but who you like a lot. You end up watching yourself and each other, which is what you need, together, to get past. And I knew her well enough to know that the end of anything at all could make her sad—of her marriage some years ago, of her father's life last year, of her twenties this year, of her mother's money, of whatever she and I were caught in, and probably, I thought, of what she would describe as the end of her happiness or sanity or something immense and dreadful to conclude.

"You don't need to call Julia those Miss Whatever names," I said, "do you?"

"Yes," she said. "Very much. Absolutely very much. She's got training-bra spring in her tits, and she's got you forlorn. Yes, I do."

"You don't even need a bra, Rebecca. Look at you."

When she looked down at herself, as I looked up her chest, beneath me, where we lay, her eyes nearly crossed. She put her hands on herself and said, "They're hard as ice."

"It's the cold."

"So, David," she said, "let's be practical. Get me warm here, will you?"

It was Rebecca in the darkness I wanted, so I pulled the covers up over us, and I also closed my eyes. I lay inside her, and she lay beneath me inside her dead father's hunting coat. Later on, I thought that we hadn't solved very much between us, and then, still later, after she had gone to the house, as I stood at the stove in the smell of natural gas and of her whiskey and vermouth and cigarettes and soap while the soup slowly cooked, I thought that we hadn't done so badly at what it is you do when the weather is bad, and prospects are slim, and it is best to not be wholly on your own.

The next morning, there was some kind of dazzle in the sky. The clouds were milky and low in a blanket, and little flecks of sun broke through. They made me think of the flecks of ice in Rebecca's hair as she shook them off in the dull light of the trailer. They also made me think of the gray-white plastic walls of the trailer, which were flecked with a gold-colored paint. I noticed the sky, and then the low gray car that was parked behind the kid's cabin at the motel. It looked as though it had been in a fire, or as though whitewash had been dumped all over it and badly cleaned off. I wondered if the stains on his jacket had something to do with the charred look of the car, an old Pontiac with busted springing in the back which suggested that someone had used it for hauling heavy freight over long distances.

I lugged and wrestled a long, flat rock that would serve as a kind of keystone for the wall, at what was once, years before, the beginning of their driveway, when they kept it paved and when anyone drove on it to visit them. The wall would be about three feet high and would separate their land from the road for a hundred feet, ending at the other end of their former driveway, near the stone house where Rebecca and Mrs. Josephine Peete managed a very small estate, mostly by selling off parcels of their property. They were in a corner of what had been hundreds of acres. They were the only year-round residents, and in winter, without the protection of foliage and brush, they could see the A-frames and faux-Victorian cottages of their neighbors.

The kid backed from the door of his cabin as I loaded a wheelbarrow with rocks to set out in a bottom layer leading from the keystone. He didn't come down the steps to wait for the bus, and he didn't wear his backpack. That was how I knew it was Saturday morning.

"Hey," I called across the road.

He looked at me, but his face showed no expression and he didn't reply.

"I live over here," I said. "In the little trailer in there." I pointed in the general direction of the pine trees. "How's it going?" I asked, trying to sound like an all-right person.

He studied me, and then he took his hands out of his coat pockets and lifted them a little way into the air before him and, with no expression, shrugged. He looked like a miniature man who indicated that fate would have its say.

"I'm David," I said. "I work at this place."

His hands were back in his pockets and his pointed, pale face gave me nothing.

"Okay," I said. "It's time to work."

I fitted the stones together right. I knew how to do that because all I ever did right as a kid was build. I'd constructed a fortress near my parents' place in South Jersey, narrow but tall, maybe fourteen feet high, made of wood on a stone foundation—not drypoint, like this one, but made solid with mortar—and it still was there. My mother reported on it when she and my father came to see me, after I had finally graduated. She'd been kneeling at the little refrigerator in my trailer, putting packets of food inside, and she had just told me how my fort still stood, when she began to cry. I thought she was crying about the size of the trailer, the smell of it, the pretty powerful sense it radiated that, living in it, you had given up on acquiring a future. I didn't ask her, though. I sat back at the little fold-up table and let her pretend not to cry while she, down at the refrigerator, pretended not to know that I observed her weeping. Giving that kind of privacy to each other can be almost as good as a set of walls, or a door you can close behind you. My father had never learned about it, and pretty soon he was standing behind her, almost shouting down onto her head. "Lily! What? What's wrong?" He turned to look at me, and something about my face—maybe the nothing I tried to compose on it—made him think about shooting me, or slugging me, or shouting. "Lil," he said, "*tell* me."

When I looked up from the second barrow load, the kid was on the Peetes' side of the county road, and he was watching me.

"I guess you're allowed to cross the road," I said. "Your mother lets you do that? Your father?"

He said, "Traffic here is surprisingly light."

"Yes, it is."

"Surprisingly light."

"Yes. There isn't very much of it at all."

"No," he said, moving his arms, "and you don't see a great deal of commercial traffic, do you? I would say it's mostly residential."

"That's what I would say too," I said. I was on my knees, and they were growing cold, but I was afraid that I would startle him if I rose. "So how's school?"

"School is a responsibility," he said. "Some things—you just soldier on. Do you know that expression?"

"I think I've heard it used," I said. "And that's what you do on schooldays? You soldier on?"

He nodded.

"You don't like it, though."

"Oh, I don't mind," he said. "It's what I'm supposed to do, so I do it. School's all right. Are you a college student?"

"No," I said, "but I used to be."

"What exactly are you?"

"I'm the handyman," I said. "I do the chores for Mrs. Peete."

"Like building a fence," he said.

"This is going to be a wall, actually. You can *use* it as a fence, but it's a wall."

"How do you know the difference?"

"Well, *I* know because I'm building it. You'll know because I told you."

"And I might tell someone else," he said. "So *they* would know." His lips looked swollen, his skin seemed almost blue beneath its pallor. His hands were broad, with long fingers, and he kept returning them to the pockets of his coat. "So if it keeps a person out, it acts like a fence. But it's a wall."

"This baby is nothing but wall," I said. "So I told you, right? And I told you my name?"

"David."

"So now you can tell me yours."

"All right." He looked at the ground before him, and I wondered if he was making one up. Finally, he said, "Artie."

"Artie what?"

"Artie Arthur."

"Glad to meet you, Artie."

He said, "Hi."

"I hope you don't mind my noticing," I said, "but I really couldn't help it. There being so little traffic around here to look at. I've seen you leave for school."

"Bus 26."

"And I've seen you come home on it."

"Well, it's my bus," he said. "Number 26."

"Yeah. No, I was wondering, when you get home from school is there anyone around to say hello? Or goodbye when you, you know, start to soldier on?"

His face was almost purple, the blush coming in over that milky skin with blue beneath it. "Nobody's neglecting me," he said.

"No," I said, "I didn't think so. Absolutely not. I don't need to hear *anything*," I said. "Zero is good enough for me."

"Zero probability," he said.

"Pardon?"

"Zero as a base."

"All right." But he had nothing more to say except, after a while, "I have to go."

"I'll cross you," I said.

"The traffic here is surprisingly light," he said, "so there's no need to bother."

"Surprisingly light," I said. "Catch you later."

He removed his right hand from his pocket and he waved it as an infant would, holding it before him and opening and closing his fist.

"Bye-bye," I said.

He looked to his right, then to his left, and he dashed for the motel grounds and his cabin, admitting himself with the brass key on the oval tag. At the door, he turned to look across the road. "Domicile," he called, sweeping his arm about him, and then he went in.

I arranged a few more barrow loads, and Mrs. Peete drove past as I worked, her face set and her eyes wide with panic. She would not have agreed with Artie Arthur about the traffic on our road. Even the memory of traffic was enough to undo her. And my presence didn't help. I worked for a while longer, then got myself away from the vicinity of the house, now that Mrs. Peete was gone. If I didn't, I would drift up the driveway and finally I would knock at the door, hoping that Rebecca would be in. And then I would have to admit to myself what I had done, and I would be forced to guess why, and then I would be stuck with my answer, either making up lies to contradict it, or agreeing with myself about my needs. At that time of my life, I was bent on the conquest of many of my needs, among them the falling into anything, even, sometimes, what Rebecca referred to as the flesh. It was what I had decided to aim for—speaking of fences and walls—after Julia secured her passport and cried the night before she left, and didn't cry in the morning, and then was gone.

I took myself down the road, away from their house, and into the hummocky field, through which I walked to the swamp behind it. Hundreds of trees had come down over the years, leaving only dozens

standing, and most of them dying or dead. Everything there was a
kind of icy gray—the surface of the water, the vegetation on top of and
around it; even the gigantic flying dinosaur, the blue heron who roosted
in one of the trees, was gray. The air coming over the water was steady
and cold. I had never been to Central America, but when I thought of
Julia living with some kind of not-quite-royal person who was dedicated to aiding the orphans of war-torn states, I thought of this kind of
damp wind and this kind of desolate countryside. She would be brave
and beautiful in it, and he would be earnest, and at night they would
drink some kind of brandy and list their good deeds and then devour
each other's body in some bullet-pocked hotel room. The heron was at
the far side of the swamp now, in the top limbs of a dead aspen. He
looked to be about a million years old.

I went a little closer to the swamp, ducking under evergreen branches
and the leafless branches of oaks. Closer, I could see something green
in the water, and I wondered if spring was really so close. I was very
tired, I realized, of clenching myself against the cold. It was not vegetation, though I thought I could smell some. It seemed to be cloth. I
went as close as I could, with the toes of my boots almost in water, and
I saw that the cloth was in layers, green and bright blue, red and white
stripes, a good deal of white. Near a tamarack still without needles, but
with black-green buds on it, I saw a large oblong green garbage pail.
I squatted at the edge and studied the cloth. It might be clothing. It
might be someone *wearing* it. I thought, of course, about Artie Arthur
and whoever he might no longer live with. I thought, too, of the burnt
car that had parked near his cabin. Julia would lead me to the cabin
and knock on the door and make inquiries. Rebecca would insist on
our conferring in bed, or at least in a clinch. I would have done either,
I suspected, with either of them.

I squatted there, looking at the cloth, most of which was underwater,
though some of it lay along the surface. I saw myself returning to the
Peetes' garage and fetching a long square-headed rake and returning
to the swamp. I saw myself dragging at the offshore cloth, pulling it in

to me, and then seeing how, very slowly, the corpse beneath it rolled over and came to the surface to bob there, swollen and eaten away, with maybe no nose or lips or fingers.

Of course I was seeing only cloth, no corpse, and even if there *were* a corpse it did not have to be Artie Arthur's mother, or some young aunt, his mother's kid sister, say, who had tried to rescue him or who had been the only relative left in the world to take care of him on a daily basis. I had no idea why he might require rescuing, or why he had ended up in the mortgage-vortex motel. And I could not account, bloated body in the swamp or none, for the car behind his cabin this morning or its absence on the other mornings.

Otherwise, I thought, I had pretty much caught up on events at the swamp. I stood, and the great blue heron, in all his leathery grayness, jumped slowly into the air and flapped away on wings I would have sworn I heard creaking. I looked at the cloth again and thought again about the rake. This is what can happen, I thought in my father's tones, when you succumb. You let yourself fall into flesh, and then you see what you get.

After Mrs. Peete's car had lurched past, returning from the market, I brushed and brushed at my hair with the set of military brushes my father had given me when I went away to school. He had bought me a gray three-piece suit at Brooks in Manhattan, and a leather toilet kit he'd called a Dopp bag, and a set of stubby, wood-handled hairbrushes. He dressed very well, if your taste runs to clean shirts and shined shoes and good suits. He ran his own consulting firm, and he was brilliant, my mother said, and I knew him to be very sharp about numbers and strategy. He was always making plans with me, over the phone, when I was in school, to come up with strategies for dealing with my teachers. I remember how during one of those calls I insisted that all they wanted was for me to read my fucking *textbooks*. I was almost in tears. After quite a long silence, he breathed out hard, and the noise flooded the receiver and my head. "Strange, how I never thought of that," he said. "I kept thinking you'd gone stupid," he said, "but all we're confronted with here is you're lazy. Is that right? Or you're busy curing cancer, and you don't have time to waste on what the mortals are supposed to do?"

I took a towel and my toilet kit, and I walked across the frozen but softening ruts and wrinkles to the Peetes'. Rebecca's very old Saab wasn't parked beside her mother's sedan, and I was relieved and disappointed. Mrs. Peete, in fawn-colored slacks and a black turtleneck, her slacks tucked into high, black boots—a kind of joke about country manors and those who struggled to maintain them—seemed not to be relieved, and, actually, she appeared to be very disappointed when she opened her door to find me on the old stone stoop.

"Oh," is all she said.

"Hi. I was wondering if I could use the shower today. Now, actually. If that would be all right."

"You look like you could use one."

So much for the military brush.

"I thought you were here for your wages," she said.

"You don't pay me wages, Mrs. Peete."

"Yes," she said, "that's right."

"Though you *could*, if you really wanted to."

Her glare was not what you would call the expression of someone receptive to humor. The only time I saw her face in a friendly expression is when she reminded Rebecca, in front of me, of a habit of Rebecca's former husband, a viola player in Albany. He seemed to like to crack his knuckles, and Mrs. Peete's square face, with its bulging blue eyes, framed by a coppery color so fake it made the color of Rebecca's hair look phony, had broken into three sections: the creased forehead notched vertically above the nose, and then the cheeks which dimpled and went red, and then the mouth, lips parted to show her thick yellow teeth in a glaze of saliva.

She waddled ahead of me, as small and chunky as Rebecca was tall and thin. She led me upstairs, on creaking steps, although she knew I knew the way. She pointed to the guest room, where I would change, and from which I would walk, in only a towel, to the adjacent bathroom. She would sit in her own bedroom, down the hall, and would listen. I assumed that's what she did—listen to the pad of my bare feet, to the sound of the shower or the flushing of the toilet or the scratching of the towel against my back as I dried off. When I was done, she would listen to my return to the guest room and, when she heard my boots on the floor, she would emerge from her room to frown at my cleatmarks—though she'd never asked me to take off my boots—and then she would lead me down the stairs.

The guest room was painted pink, with white woodwork. The bathroom was tiled in white with pink woodwork. The soap was pink, and so was the bath mat, and so were the towels that I was not allowed to use. I tried to think of Mrs. Peete's pink skin, yards of it, against pink sheets, beneath a pink Mr. Peete, employed, to the moment of his death, as an insurance adjuster. Talk about falling into flesh, I thought. I realized that I'd been singing in the shower about how I was going to board a passenger plane and not come back again. Suspecting that it might be true, and living in hope that it was, Mrs. Peete would have the three-story smile on her face again, I figured.

Downstairs, she led me into the kitchen. I caught a glimpse of the living room, its dark antique furniture, its maroon sofa long enough to use as a lifeboat, and I could see the signs of them both—the scattered magazines and papers of Rebecca, and the basket filled with twine balls on a neat stack of what I knew to be *Reader's Digest* condensed novels (all of William Gaddis's *The Recognitions*, I thought, but in seven pages). I sat at the kitchen table as she expected me to, with my damp towel and toilet kit on the floor beside my feet, hands folded on the table's edge, and Mrs. Peete served out—not once engaging my eyes or, so far as I could tell, looking directly at me—a plate of homemade beans and little pork chunks, all of it baked in molasses, and a large glass of milk. I despised milk, but I always drank it at her table.

"I got the wall started," I said.

"I saw it."

"It's a good idea. You'll like it. You get a feeling of separation, but you still can see what's going on."

"Yes. That's how Rebecca said it. Just exactly like that."

So she had found a way to make it clear precisely why she hated me. Not only did I look a little alien to her—not quite Martian, but not assuredly not, either—but I was her daughter's choice of recreational drug. Which was not entirely true, since Rebecca also brought with her, from time to time, for recreational purposes, a little packet of grass that she purchased in Poughkeepsie. At those times, looking at it from Mrs. Peete's point of view, Rebecca was compounding the crime.

She always poured me a second glass of milk and gave me a plate of her buttery cookies to eat with it. In silence, then, I finished the cookies as she watched me. As she always did when I said my thanks, she replied, "You're entirely welcome." This time, she added, "Have a nice week."

I said, "You can feel a little spring out there."

"I'm not so sure," she said.

I nodded, as if to signal that I'd reconsider, and I gathered my bag and towel, and she walked me to the door, perhaps to make certain that I left.

I paused in the foyer and said, "Could I ask you something about the neighborhood?"

"Neighborhood? There's this and there's that, across the road."

"That's the that I wanted to know about, Mrs. Peete."

"That's the that. You went to college to learn how to talk this way?"

I hung my head, because she was gifted in her production of the sound of sneering and facial furrows of disgust. I could not imagine anyone whose pride she wouldn't erode.

"You know the way to Poughkeepsie? When your car is working?"

"It needs a new battery. It can't hold a charge."

"What does that say about you?" she asked.

"I'm afraid to guess."

Her face writhed and then composed. "This little road, once upon a time, could get you to Poughkeepsie. Parts they don't keep up anymore, and parts they shut down. But in the 1930s, the 1940s, this was a good road. The motel people lived in this house. One of them's a ghost. I have seen him, but never mind. I don't argue about ghosts."

"A little boy?"

She looked pale now, and I understood how much of an effort she was making to be civil, much less give her knowledge away to the hired man. I was stealing her magic and, because of her daughter, she was abetting the theft.

"A man," she said.

"The motel owner?"

She said, "Enough. Enough. Shower, lunch, the guided tour... enough. Have a nice week."

"Just—do you remember his name, Mrs. Peete?"

But she had closed the door as I stepped across the threshold. My mouth tasted gluey, and I smelled the heavy, sour smell of milk drifting up my face as I sang the song about leaving while I walked. Before I forced myself back into the trailer, I went around to the front and looked across the road at the motel: eight cabins, empty sign frame, and no charred car.

Inside the trailer, I took my jacket off and put a sweater on. It might have been close to spring, but it was very cold, and I was quite sorry for myself.

"Give us a smile, ducky," I said, looking at my reflection on the glass that sealed in Julia's print. "Oh, I see. You're just *not* gonna smile, are you?" I said to the bushy, shape.

"Eat my ass," the shape replied. I did hate cheerleaders. I also hated my poverty and almost any exchange with Mrs. Peete. I detested my insistence on living here the way I did. In addition, I was violently allergic to feeling that I had no choice. And I was down to only one, which I despised: go to my parents' home, watch my mother weep, listen to my father, sounding like a badly played slide trombone, perform his solo from The Lost Time But Lesson Learned Don't Stray Again Now Get Back Prodigal Blues.

Fortunately, the beans began to have their effect, and I was driven from my profitless metaphysics to considerations of the actual: the state of my digestive system, and the cold winds in the woods. I lay down on the little bed and closed my eyes and, every once in a while, sent up a hiss of gastric distress. I actually fell asleep. It was the only other place I knew to go, this side of suicide or military service. I woke with a little stirring of pleasure, for I had come to realize that I had three choices instead of one. Though in truth I could not imagine myself shouting in unison with a bunch of eighteen-year-olds and then running in step for miles to the cadences called by a drill instructor. I think it never occurred to me that I might try to be an officer. Officer Bear. So, I thought, waking, beginning to lose what had passed, an instant before, as an insight, there is always suicide. But maybe this *is* suicide, I thought. It seemed pretty likely. On the other hand, I thought, if you aren't killing yourself tonight, you had better head for the woods.

So I put my jacket on, took toilet paper and flashlight, and went from the trailer in what was now a porous darkness, and I walked into the woods. The winds had died, and I could hear creatures in the underbrush—voles and mice and rats, I thought—and stirrings in the high branches of trees—maybe owls beginning to hunt. I also heard a car gear down, then crunch its way along the gravel of their drive. I cut toward the house and got closer, then stopped behind a Norway maple to listen to Rebecca in the dark. I heard her turn the radio off, and saw the lights go out, before she turned off the motor, which meant that she was sober. When she was drunk enough, she'd leave the Saab in the driveway, engine running, radio loud, and all lit up. I backed away and headed for a far corner of the pine plantation, where I was as useful as I'd been for weeks. Rebecca would eat supper with her mother, and her mother would doubtless describe my provocations. Rebecca would smile her nervous smile—it came and went, like a tic—and I would crouch in the trailer, as I was doing at that moment, and, rather than try to make a sketch or read a book, I would lie in my clothing on the bed, waiting to sleep and, as usual, waking the next day with a kind of alarm as I noted that I had slept the deep, easy sleep of a man possessed of reason who was weary from his many accomplishments.

I was out and working on the wall by seven on Sunday morning, hauling stones, cleaning them off, setting them in. I used the back of a hatchet I had found in their garage for chipping off lumps so the stones would fit together. I whistled a medley of tunes from musicals that had flopped. I was working my way through *Anyone Can Whistle*, which was about crazy people being the only ones who are sane. The sun wasn't strong, but I could feel it, and I sensed the turning of the seasons as, all of a sudden, a fact. I was getting ready. I was going to make a move. I had no idea what it would be, but a move, I would have sworn to you, was forthcoming. I got pretty loud and sparky as I chirped a number that Harry Guardino had bellowed, and then the toes of Rebecca's tan work shoes were between me and the rocks at which I worked.

"Well," I said. "You caught me."

"Working?"

"Whistling."

"Working and whistling," she said. "Isn't this where Sneezy and Dopey and Sleepy come in?"

I did a few bars of "Whistle While You Work" and then stood up. She was hatless, but she wore her father's old mackinaw. I reached for the part where the lapels crossed and I looked inside.

"You have clothes on," I said.

She went red. "Sorry," she said.

"For having, or for not having had?"

She shook her head, looked away, into the sunlight, then back to me. "I need to leave here," she said.

"Me too, Rebecca."

"I can't live with my mother."

"I'm pretty sure that no one can live with your mother. If you don't mind my saying so."

"Nobody can," she said, "you're right. Anyway, *I* can't. I'm signing a lease on a place in Hudson. It's just off the main drag, near all those antique stores. I figure my mother and I might know each other longer if we don't live in the same house. But I *am*—" She closed her mouth and pressed her lips together before she said, "I was about to make one of those miss-your-good-company declamations," she said, looking away again, then looking back. "But I am. What's your thinking on it—about missing me and all?"

I stood there with her, feeling shaggier, and dirtier, and less than familiar with English-language conversations, apprehensive, lightheaded, proud as well as embarrassed.

"I will guaranteed be missing you," I said.

She nodded. She looked across at the motel, she looked down the road, as if she thought of crossing it. "So come along," she said.

"To Hudson?"

"To my *place* in Hudson."

I mustered an "Oh!"

"It wouldn't be the same as, you know, moving *in* with me," she said, as the first car of the day passed, an immense Land Rover inhabited by three yellow Labradors and their driver. "You could rent a room from me," she said. "I have a guest bedroom. You could rent it, or you could have it for nothing. You could also use the nonguest bedroom. You know I'm a good copywriter. You know that I write okay ad copy for the third-rate news shows up here. And you know that I'm the voice of upstate HMO. I can afford it. I don't need to take money from you."

"You and your mother need every dime for this place," I said. "You can't even afford to keep it up, much less renovate. And I'd be uncomfortable, staying home while you went to work."

"You could get a job," she said, spreading her legs as if to set herself for warding off my excuses. Her frizzy hair was lit from behind by the sun, and she looked as if she glowed.

"Let's see," I said. "A job, an apartment. Rebecca, I'd be a—excuse me for this. I'd be a husband, wouldn't I?"

"The last of the pagans," she said. She shook her head, though she didn't smile her fast, flickering smile, and I knew for certain that the invitation had been a great deal more serious than I'd guessed. "I am trusting you to *not* bring up the age thing, all right?"

There was nothing else to do, so I stepped up and put my hands on her shoulders and I leaned in and kissed her. It was a long kiss, and at the end she gently bit my lip.

"Pack your things," she said.

"They're in my pockets. There isn't much to pack."

"No," she said. "Charcoal, pencils, brushes, paint, your sketchbooks—you know. You can even bring Miss Patootie's etching."

It seemed to me that we were both too embarrassed to understand what we were doing. When you get to that point, I knew then and know better now, you will take steps or draw conclusions you end up regretting. I could offer my four and a half years of college and much of my life with my parents as examples. We stood at the wheelbarrow filled with stones, and then Rebecca turned, the way you do when you're dancing, and she went back toward the house. Then she stopped herself and slowly walked back.

"Look," she said, and her face was full of sorrow for me, "nobody's forcing you to live inside that terrible trailer. Or my apartment. Or anyplace else." Her voice was thick with feeling. "It's pretty much you, David. Whatever place you're inside of, you're the one who turned the lock."

She looked at me very directly, and she nodded her head. She wanted me to know how certain she was of what she had said, and I nodded back with respect. She walked toward the house again, and this time she kept going, waving goodbye over her shoulder. The movement of her fingers reminded me of Artie Arthur's wave. When Rebecca was out of sight, I looked at Artie's cabin: still no car. When, I wondered, would someone come and rescue us?

I finished several yards of wall, and it was a shape now. There were chickadees buzzing back and forth, and there were a few more cars.

Surprisingly light traffic, Artie. The sun had a little weight. And to all
of it I could now add the stone wall along the edge of Mrs. Peete and
Rebecca's property. I had made something pretty true, I thought, looking at the brilliant flecks of mica, the voluptuous whiteness of limestone
veins, the hundred shadows and hollows, the sense of bulk and perma-
nence, the undeniable function it served of tying down their land and
holding it in place.

Julia would not have hung around even if she knew I was going
to build this wall so well. I knew that. And she had seen me at work
before. I trusted that she remembered I could build with stone or stud
up a house or put up wallboard so well you'd not find the seams. I knew
that, and I knew that a sudden reminder would not sweep her back to
me. Still, I did wish I could show her what I'd made. I thought of tracking her down by telephone by using a fudged pidgin Spanish, calling
with the announcement that I had built another good wall. I thought
of hearing, from behind her, around her, the wails of wounded children she was tending as the sniper fire sang off packed earthen streets
outside the clinic. I propped the wheelbarrow, standing it on the nose
of its wooden frame, against the wall. I collected the discarded stones
in a mound. I had been preparing to do it, though I hadn't suspected
I was. I know it now. I had awakened with a sense of purpose and,
though working on the wall had satisfied much of it, the need to cross
the road remained strong.

So I went—across the road, and across the dead lawn, across the
pebble walk, directly to Artie Arthur's cabin. I knocked, too driven to
be frightened, though I had no idea what to say or do when someone
opened the door. But no one did. And the key, its oval tag hanging
down from it, was in the lock. So I knew I could turn the knob and
go inside, and I did.

I smelled something that reminded me of the milky, pyramidal
bottle that Frank the barber would tip over my head when I was a kid.
It helped keep my hair in place for a while, though, soon enough, it
sprang back up. I realized that I was running my fingers through my

hair. I sometimes did that when I was upset. I did it for all three months that Julia and I were together. "It's like you're petting an animal," she had said, "except the animal is you."

There weren't any towels in the bathroom and there weren't sheets on the large bed. Nor was there a television set, a radio, or a clock. The rug was covered with dried mud. An open bureau drawer was stuffed with plastic and cellophane and cardboard wrappers of snack food. Someone had eaten most of two pizzas and a little bit of Chinese food. The wrappers and the top of the bureau were sprinkled with mouse turds. Near the small window, on an oval table, I found burnt matches, perhaps from lighting the lantern by which he had done his homework. The matches were in a neat grouping in a stained, slimy-looking soap-dish. The one piece of paper on the table, from a two-ring looseleaf notebook, had numbers written in an adult hand. Someone had added the same set of figures about a dozen times. They always started out with 39,000 of something and then concluded with a meticulous minus sign, and a final 1,100. On the other side of the page was handwriting practice, or practice in remembering a name: ARTIE ARTHUR ARTIE ARTHUR ARTIE ARTHUR ARTIE ARTHUR. The big characters filled up the page. He was there, but noplace else. Although there was one more place to look.

When I went outside, I walked around to the back of the cabin and saw the tracks of the long, charred car pressed into the wet soil. I was pleased to learn that the vehicle in Artie Arthur's life was actual, and that I had truly seen it. But I was not pleased with where I had to look. I crossed the road and went back to their garage, walking along the side of the stone colonial house, and I fetched the long-handled rake, which I carried on my shoulder like a man a long time ago off to rake hay. It was damper and cooler in the field I cut through, and it was outright cold at the swamp. Little sun seemed to get through to warm the water, and it radiated cold like a freezer left open. I squatted at the edge, listening to ducks squabble, and then I straightened and walked to the water, took a breath, and went in up to my knees. The deep chill

went up my legs and through my chest, and my head suddenly ached
as if I'd eaten ice cream too quickly.

I cried out and the ducks, several dozen yards away, took off, making
their wheezy noises. I waded further in, balancing myself with the rake,
and then I began to look for the horrible news behind Artie Arthur's
story. I let the rake, which I held at the end on its haft, flop down,
and then I pulled it back to me as if it were a rope, and most of the
time something came with it: bath towels, horribly smeared, and then
a big green towel such as you'd use at the beach, I thought, and then a
shower curtain with figures of seagulls on it. I let the cloth eddy about
me where I stood, and I went back with the rake to free whatever was
trapped beneath the remaining clothes. The reds and oranges of T-shirts
and underwear came up, and then fancy-looking pajamas that perhaps
a small woman had worn. Up, too, came bubbles of gas, the broccoli
smell of trapped vegetation, and the cheap white dress shirt of a man
with unusually long arms.

I was prepared, or I thought I was, for little Artie, blue and open-
eyed, to come rocking up. And I suspected that his mother or aunt
might be down there with him. It would be a sudden surfacing, I
thought, and then the vandalized body would arrive to float before
me, and I would have to figure a way of getting it on shore. But no
one came up from exile back to the world. I was surrounded by cheap
clothing and filthy towels. I heard his wings before I saw him as the
heron clumsily angled for the top of the tree across the swamp. He saw
or heard me, then, and he curved off and out of sight. Wading in further, so that the water was above my waist, balancing myself with the
rake, I tried once more, but I drew up only weeds and a bit of rotted
tree that caught between the tines of the rake.

It was difficult to lift my feet from the floor of the swamp, and it was
tricky to escape from its edge. But I finally stood in the field, a failure
at rescue and disinterment. I was the robber of graves, and I was the
rescuer, with nothing to show for the work and with no evidence of my
good intentions except for the odor of rot that I wore.

I went back to their garage and replaced the rake. Rebecca was looking out their kitchen window and when she saw me—I figure I was
green from the swamp and red with shame because of my failure—her
eyebrows rose. I shrugged in reply. We had slept together a couple of
dozen times. We knew each other, I guessed, but I thought then of my
parents and I doubted I was right. I didn't know whether to want to
know someone or not. I had a suspicion that it was good for the loneliness, but maybe after that you knew in ways you'd rather not.

I went back to the trailer and used some bottled water for a sponge
bath at my sink. Then I changed into khakis I ought to have washed
some weeks before and a dark green sweatshirt that I rarely wore because
it said, across the front, CAMP NOK-A-MIX-ON, which was where I'd
worked as a waiter in the summer between my freshman and sophomore years. I put on sneakers and went out to continue at the wall. I
kept seeing the door swing in at the motel cabin. I kept thinking of the
little kid who wrote his name so many times. And of course I thought
about the car. Someone had come to take care of him, I thought—I
wished—who wasn't always able to. They were broke and fleeing credi-
tors, I thought. Or they were fleeing the Cosa Nostra, to which the
driver of the car owed an allegiance he had violated. Or the father
robbed banks. It really didn't matter to me, except that they not be
captured, and that Artie have somebody on the other side of his door
as he went off to school and returned.

I hauled the stones and cleaned them and set them in. I could feel
the cold of them as well as their weight through my rawhide work
gloves, and I didn't mind, because what I felt was the first reward of
this kind of work. The second was that it stood and you had made
it. I caught my breath and stood beside the wall when Rebecca came
out to me, wearing her father's coat open. I went back to work as she
approached, and she stood there awhile. I felt suddenly very shy with
her, and I focused on the wall and on the quality of my work. I was
acutely conscious of her bright, crinkly hair, and of her small mouth,
her large, smart eyes, and of her body too, hidden within the jeans and

coat, but familiar to me—a hipbone I had held to, a breast at which I'd nuzzled. I admired the urgency with which she dived into bed, and with which she drank cocktails made of bourbon and sweet vermouth, and with which she pulled on her cigarettes, or drove the narrow roads, or argued about politics or the cost of hotels in Monopoly. She watched me admire her, and she gestured me up and onto my feet. She had a canvas bag with her, and it contained steaks and the makings of Manhattans. We had a long, drunken evening in the trailer, and we were so far gone, so fervent in pursuit of our anesthetic stupor, that I cannot remember much of what we said, or what we did together, but I remember our saying a lot, and doing a lot. If we were valedictory or sentimental, I have gratefully managed to forget.

A few days later, she moved away, returning irregularly on week-ends, when she remained with her mother in the house. On a Saturday in April, when Rebecca hadn't come home, I went over for my shower and my meal. Instead of her beans, Mrs. Peete served up casserole of potatoes and cheese.

I didn't drink the glass of milk that came with it, and she said, "You hate that milk, huh?"

"I'm afraid so," I said. "I never liked it, even when I was a kid."

"You are still a kid," she said, "but you should have told me. I wouldn't have wasted good milk. It's money down the drain, you understand." She looked at me with a kind of softness I was unac-customed to. Her face went into those three parts I rarely saw, and I understood that she was relenting. I wondered if Rebecca had put in a good word on my behalf. "You were trying to be polite," she said.

I nodded, tried a smile, didn't get one in return, and kept a serious face on.

"That is what I would call a good sign," she said.

"Mrs. Peete"—I was flooded with courage, desperate with a need to escape, and very glad to feel, and to act on, the need—"would you say you're pleased with what I've built around here? With the repairs I did?"

"You want wages," she said. "They are not a part of our arrangement."

"If you could lend me enough for a new battery," I said, "and maybe a battery cable, I could be on the road. I'd mail you the money. Really, I would."

"Leave?" she said. Her eyes were wet. "You are leaving too? But for where? Doing what?" She paused briefly for the answer I could not begin to give her, and then, moving as her daughter did, she turned to leave the room. I thought of taking a sip of milk to please her, but I couldn't. She came back in with a large brown reptile-hide purse, and she searched in it for her wallet and counted out what I told her I thought a battery would cost.

She nodded in agreement. "Rebecca said about that much."

"She knew I would ask you for this?"

"Oh," she said, "David. You are not as much of a mystery as you would like to think."

RESCUE MISSIONS

GOOD TO GO

————

"Y
OUR FATHER SAYS you bought a gun. He says you bought a surplus army gun."

"We used the M16A2. This one, they call it AR15. It won't fire auto."

"What's that, Patrick?"

"Automatic, Momma." From the mattress where he sat, wearing
camouflage trousers and a khaki T-shirt, his back bisected by the corner
of the room, he said, "You know. *Blam-blam-blam-blam-blam-blam-
blam.* That's semiauto. You need to squeeze off one round at a time, but
the rate of fire's good enough. Anyway, I didn't buy enough ammo to
fire full auto for long. I don't need that much."

"For what, dearie? Why do you need a gun?"

"You talked to Pop?"

"He telephoned." She took her raincoat off and set it on the back of a
short wooden chair. "Les answered the phone and of course they jawed."

"Jawed?"

"That's what Les calls it. He says it's like a couple of bull moose
with their antlers locked and their forelegs set. All they can do is make
noises."

"Now, what would Les know about two mooses?"

"Oh, dearie, he's a traveler. He's been to places. He's more like you."

"Travel. Here to Hawaii, and then Kuwait, then fucking paradise. Goats and camels and sheep and sand. And then I never barely came home."

"Dearie, yes. Yes, you did. Here you *are*."

"Here I am," he said. "That's right." Then he said, "That's right." His eyes were closed. She took one step nearer the mattress on the floor where he sat in his scuffed, sand-colored boots and his camouflage pants, his hands knotted around his knees, pulling them up against his chest.

He opened his eyes. What's the 'more like' supposed to mean?" he asked her. "More like me than he's like Pop? Except Pop's your *husband*. Legally, he still is, right?"

"Yes."

"But you want that part of it over," he said.

"Yes."

"Your life's moving along," he said.

"It is, yes."

"Mine isn't, anymore."

"You've just come back from a terrible time," she said. "You were in *danger*. You got *hurt*. You didn't have a shower for weeks and weeks. Those moistened baby wipes—I must have sent you a hundred."

"I didn't get them. I told you that."

"I'm sorry, Patrick."

"The mail was fucked. Everything was fucked."

"Would you like to come over to my—to where I'm living?"

"With Les and the mooses?"

"You could sleep on a sofa bed on clean sheets. We'd leave you be. Maybe you'd feel safe there."

"Oh, I'm safe, Momma. I'm safe. It's other people in danger." His face looked bony. He rubbed his cheek with the tips of four fingers of his left hand as if he wore a mitten. "I'm good to go."

She sat on the chair where she'd put her coat. She watched him look at her legs the way men look at a woman's legs. His etched, thin face was different, and so was his close-cropped hair. She realized that some of it was gray. He wasn't twenty-five yet, and his hair had gray in it and he wore a stranger's face, she thought. And he sized her up when he looked at her. She knew he wasn't her baby anymore, but now she wondered whether he was still her son. Her husband, Bernard, had said, "He's in trouble. I can't get hold of him anymore. He's out there. Have you *seen* him?"

She'd said, "You know how angry he got with me when he came back."

"He's loyal to me," Bernard had said.

"If that's the way you want to put it."

"I don't want to fight with you anymore. You're out of my life, and I'm out of yours. We're getting on with it. You wanted your freedom, you got your freedom, and now I'm—I'm shut of the whole damned thing."

"Aren't we all free," she'd said. At that moment, she had felt inventive and full of effective words she had every right to call after her husband as he vanished from her life. "But here you are on the telephone," she'd said. "You didn't vanish, after all."

"What vanish? What are you *talking* about? Patrick's in an awful lot of trouble, and we need to be useful, or something. I don't know what to *do*."

"No," she'd said, still feeling wiser than Bernard. "Tell me how to find his place."

"It's a slum," he'd said. "I didn't know they let people live in those places. Down where the Earlville feed mill used to be, where the train station was in the old days. Somebody bought up all the old buildings down there. I wonder did they even bother to *look* at the wiring."

"I'll get down there. It'll take me an hour or two. I'll go in the morning. Is he sick? Did he come home, I mean, with some kind of illness? A lot of them had fevers when they came back. A lot of them had dysentery."

"'Saddam's Revenge,' he said the troops called it."

"And what did he say about the gun?"

"He said he felt the need of a weapon," Bernard had said. "I asked him why he did, and he mocked me. He said, 'Danger lurks.'"

"'Danger lurks'?"

"It's what he said. I can only tell you what I heard and that's what I heard." Then Bernard had said, "So, your new life's agreeable to you."

"It is, thank you. How are things for you?"

"Well, considering. My wife leaving me, and the lawyer's bills, and of course I've got the sleep apnea thing. I keep waking myself up."

"I remember it well."

"Dr. Bittman says it can sometimes be fatal."

"Let's hope it isn't."

"You could sound a little concerned."

"Well, I am a little concerned. I'm sorry you don't like how it sounds. And this is about Patrick right now, isn't it?"

"Yes," he'd said. She said *sullenly* to herself, and the description pleased her. She had felt, when they hung up, as if she had won a small contest. And then the fear for her son had poured in, like the sudden sound of the nurses laying out instruments when the orderly pushes your gurney through the OR doors.

Patrick lit another cigarette. He looked so much older than when he'd left. And she couldn't find recognition in his eyes. She couldn't find herself. Before she thought she'd speak, she was saying, "It's *me*, dearie."

He looked her over, the way a man looks over a strange woman, and he blew out smoke as he said, "Hi, Momma."

Although his shoulders were wedged against the walls, she wanted to find a way to get her arms around him. But how could you protect a man this large and hard, in his terrible, dim room that smelled of rotted vegetation, when he looked like a stranger made of only angles and skull?

He smiled, and she saw how white his teeth were. She thought of trips to the dentist when he was eight or nine, of the coupon book for payments that the orthodontist had issued them when Patrick was thirteen. "We're paying the son of a bitch to buy a goddamned *boat*," Bernard had said. Each month, as he tore out the coupon and wrote out the check, he had said, "Here's for the goddamned boat."

"I thought of you," Patrick said. "I did. I thought about you and Les in your new house and you in your new job. I thought about Pop all alone. He'd be so bad at that, I thought. And I was right. He eats bologna on white bread with mayonnaise. That's his dinner, some nights. With a can of light beer to wash it down in front of the TV."

"He knows how to eat intelligently. He knows how to cook. I'm not his mother."

"No. You're mine."

"Yes, I am."

"And that's why you're here."

"Yes, it is."

"Because I own a Colt Arms AR15. If I didn't own it, you wouldn't be here, right?"

"I'd have waited until you invited me."

"You're always welcome, Momma." He looked to her like someone else, and she wanted to cry out a warning to him, tell him that he was disappearing, that he needed to return. "Just like I should know I'm always welcome in your house in your new life with Les, who is such an experienced traveler and he knows about mooses."

There was one window in the room, a beautiful twelve-over-twelve with crazed glass and mullions probably gone to pulp. She imagined that it would sell for more than a month's rent if the wood, through some miracle, hadn't completely rotted. The light that came in was like the water you look up through when you open your eyes at the bottom of the pond. She could see him by it, and, turning, she could see a knapsack and a duffel bag hung from nails spiked into the walls. Behind them and across the wide room was an old, dark veneer closet with no doors, and, in a corner of the closet, as she looked over her shoulder, she saw the weapon's ugly mechanisms, dull but a little lit by what was left of the window light that spilled into her son's room.

"Do they give you a bathroom here?"

"Downstairs, in the back corner. You want me to show you?"

She shook her head. "I'm all right."

"Momma, you are always all right. You land on your feet."

"Dearie, no, I didn't fall. I just kept living my life is all."

"Pop said you fell in love. That's falling."

"It wasn't falling, though, so much—what I'm saying about the next thing? That's what it was. That's what it felt like. 'Oh! We're *here* now. We aren't *there* anymore.' It wasn't about your father, all of a sudden. It was Les. I even tried to not let it be, but it was. And it couldn't be Bernard. It couldn't be your father. No matter how I wanted things to work."

"Shit just happens and have a nice day. The kid used to say that, PFC Hopkins, the one that I lost. He used to say that when he fired his weapon or when they opened up on us. 'Have a nice day, motherfucker.' He was the boy that I lost in Falluja, doing house-to-house."

"No, *you* didn't lose him, dearie. *They* shot him. The officers told you what to do and you did it and he got wounded."

"No, he was plain damned killed. He bled out while he kept on moving his feet. Never stopped until, you know, he *stopped*. I was fire team leader and he was my SAW gunner and they just hollowed him out. I tried to stop the bleeding with my hand, but there wasn't any-place to put it. You're supposed to apply pressure. Right. Apply pres-sure. But on *what*?"

She knew that tears ran down her face. She wished that Patrick could cry, too, though she had her suspicions that crying might not do all the good she used to think. It did help you realize that you were mis-erable, she knew. Maybe that was useful information. But she wanted to stop crying because she didn't know what tears might goad him to do.

This was new between them, part of the so much unfamiliarity. That, she thought, was also something worth weeping about.

"Patrick, what's the danger?"

He motioned with one hand, sweeping it before him. He smiled, but his dark eyes told her nothing.

"Really. You told your father there was danger lurking."

"And he told you?"

"Well, we're *worried*, dearie. Guns make people worry. And you came home troubled. So naturally we'd talk about that. As your parents. As—because we love you."

"But you didn't send Les," he said, "your new next thing, with his travel experience, and knowing a lot about life."

"This is about us," she said, thinking that the words had come out in a whine.

Patrick said, "Wrong us. This is about reservist PFC Arthur M. Hopkins of Rome, New York. And rifleman Sweeney Sweeney of Madison, and PFC Danny Levine out of Gloversville, the ones who were not KIA. And me. I was the corporal let us get separated from the squad. I was the one directed our fire onto a little square sheep-shit hut, and I was the one got us shot to wet fucking rags. That's the us."

She said, "And that's the danger? Why you needed to buy the gun?"

"Why not? It's a reason. It'll do. That better not be Les," he said, his emptied face lifting as slow, heavy footfalls sounded on the raw lumber stairs.

But she knew the weight and pace of the sound of the steps, and she knew that Bernard would appear at the door, a little out of breath, a little wide-eyed because he stared so hard when he was worried—a tall, broad, decent man she had tried to live with after losing every reason except gratitude, regret, and this lean, sad man who was their boy once.

"Hi," Bernard said. "I had to come. I couldn't not come. Is that okay?"

She stood and went to the doorway and kissed his cheek. She knew that he'd close his eyes. "You smell nice," she said.

"A different soap is all."

"Well, good," she said, patting his chest, then stepping back. "Patrick was talking about Falluja."

"Terrible," Bernard said.

"That's because of the sweeps they had to send us on," Patrick said. "House-to-house is terrible in any place. The hajis are good at ambush. You get your unit isolated, and you are pretty fast all fucked up. They smell how all alone you get to feel. Not PFC Hopkins. He just said, 'Have a nice day, motherfucker,' and he sent over one long burst of 5.56 and then he died, all scooped out, that kid." Patrick lit a cigarette and said, "I wish I had another chair for all the parents that are here."

"We're good," Bernard said.

She said, "It's fine, dearie."

"Okay," Patrick said, "good and fine, then. But you don't have to hover here, you know. I think I know what I must sound like. I think I sound like I'm blaming you for not being there, in Falluja. I'm not. Really. I wouldn't *want* you there, all scared and doing your duty and shit. I don't want anything bad to happen to you. This is—I must be scary enough." She heard his throat close down and she watched him blink and blink, his dark eyes suddenly as wide as his father's.

Bernard said, "Is this the post-traumatic—"

"Private First Class Hopkins didn't mention any open-sphincter stress syndrome while he was getting dead," Patrick said, "so I would just as soon skip it, Pop. Nothing personal. I didn't mean to insult you, right? You're my man. Only . . ." He crushed the butt into the coffee cup with the other butts and he lit a new one. "I apologize, Pop."

"No," Bernard said, "I'm good."

"And Momma's fine. And I am good to go. What?"

Bernard had walked across to the veneer clothing cupboard. He squatted, and she heard his ligaments take the strain. "This is it," he said. "I don't see the clip. This does take a clip, am I right?"

"We call them magazines," Patrick said. "Mags. I've got a couple."

"It's safety precautions, keeping them separate from the weapon," Bernard told her.

"I don't see anything safe about it," she said. "It's ugly. It's frightening."

"It's efficient," Patrick said. He drew in smoke, then said, "You're thinking I'm going to open that window and set a pillow on the sill, then insert a mag and lean the weapon on the pillow and do some wild-ass-vet-on-a-rampage deal with people out there suddenly all falling down. But no way. Do you know where we *are*? Greater downtown Earlville, New York, folks. There's nobody *out* there."

"But Patrick," she said, "you wouldn't do it anywhere. You wouldn't do it anyway. It isn't *you*."

"No, Momma."

"Patrick, boy," Bernard said, "you bought it. You went someplace on purpose and you bought it for plenty of money that you had to set down onto some gun dealer's table."

"You're right, Pop. I have to admit that."

She remembered them standing side by side and looking up at Patrick as he leaned over a rifle that he aimed at them. They were in the side yard of their first place, a tall Victorian farmhouse on a half an acre of land in a little hamlet that wasn't very far from Earlville. It was summer, and Patrick had been working for weeks on his fort. As an eleventh birthday gift, they had opened an account in his name at the lumberyard, and Patrick had purchased small lots of planking and studs, an expensive framing hammer, galvanized nails. He had built himself a fort in the crotch of a young sugar maple outside the dining room, and he was up in his safe place after dinner in June, she thought, or early July—the sun was still high, and no one ever talked about autumn coming on—and she and Bernard looked up at their son. He looked down over the sights of his wooden scale-model Garand M1 rifle.

"You didn't see the ambush," he'd said.

"No, we didn't," Bernard had answered.

"You don't need to worry, though, on account of I won't shoot."

"You know, I knew you wouldn't," she remembered telling him. She remembered, now, in the old feed mill, looking at her grown and damaged, dangerous son, how disappointing to the boy her confidence had been.

"You knew?" he'd said.

"I mean I was hoping," she'd told him.

"We hoped you wouldn't shoot," Bernard had said.

"Please don't shoot," she'd called to him in the shadows of his fort.

"No," he'd said, "I won't."

Across the room from their boy who was now grown up, Bernard stood slowly. He leaned against the wall and put his hands in the pockets of his khakis. He always wore khakis and a blue button-down shirt under the white medical coat he put on when he was in his pharmacy, filling prescriptions. He said, "I'm worried about you. You can understand that."

"And I'm sorry," Patrick said. "I am. But now I think you need to go. You did what you could." He'd gone onto one knee, his forearm leaning on the opposite thigh.

"What does that mean?"

"You said what you thought you should say, Momma. And it was nice to see you and Pop be friendly with each other."

"And does something happen now?" she asked him. "Is that what you're saying? Because I won't leave here if it is. I won't."

Bernard said, "Me either."

Patrick flushed very dark. His lips were set in a bitter line. In the underwater light of his awful room, with his gray-flecked hair and his unfamiliar eyes, he seemed to her to be a new creature she must care for. She knew that she didn't know how. But she walked slowly to the cupboard, expecting each time she stepped that he would order her to stop, and she was breathless when she stood near Bernard and the gun she was afraid to look at.

Patrick said, "Please." His voice was flat, as expressionless as his face.

Bernard shrugged. She watched him take a deep breath. She squared her shoulders and waited.

"I *am* warning you," Patrick said in the flat voice.

"Dearie," she called to her son, seeking a level, low voice with which to address him.

"No more conversation now," Patrick said. "I warned you."

After twenty-five years, she thought, all they knew was this: standing in their separateness to hold their ground against their son. And what kind of achievement did that amount to?

"I warned you," Patrick said. He said, "Here I come."

He leaned forward, but he was far less graceful than she'd expected. He tripped off the mattress and then he caught himself. And she remembered this. She remembered standing in a room on an overcast day. It had to have been in their first house at the start of a long winter. Patrick was little and grinning. His chin was covered with drool. He'd raised his arms to the level of his shoulders. Then he reached higher. He lurched and then he righted himself and he made his way across the room in a wobbly march. She remembered how they'd clapped their hands to celebrate their boy's first step. She remembered thinking that there, stumbling across the room, came the rest of her life.

THE SMALL SALVATION

HE SAW HER at the start and finish of playschool mornings as the children gusted about her like blown leaves. She seemed to him to smile like an actress playing a part. He thought of her as the pretty girl in high school and college who had starred in every play but who hadn't gone on to anything but earnest, sweaty civic little theater since she'd been condemned to grow up.

Her large dark brown eyes looked merry. He couldn't tell if she was pleased or feeling ironic. She sat on the small, low child's wooden chair in the center of the preschool playroom and indicated a little chair opposite. Her bent knees, parallel and pale, struck him as graceful. His long legs were locked, and he tried leaning back while he extended them.

She hiccupped a laugh and said, in a bright and ringing voice, "Poor man. Should we stand?"

"I've forgotten my preschool skills," he said. "But I'll be fine. This is fine." He took a deep breath. He found himself staring at the silk scarf of cream and gold and black that was tied at her throat. He thought of it, or maybe he thought of her thinking of it, as a brave little scarf.

She nodded. She clasped her hands on the hem of her dark, figured jumper. She raised her brows, and he realized that he was supposed to begin.

He said, "My grandson—"

"Jeremy's lovely."

"Jeremy is," he said. "But he's shy."

"Don't worry. Look at you: *you're* shy."

He felt himself flush as he said, "I am?"

"And you're a fully functioning grandfather. Shy's all right." She smiled as if he were Jeremy's age. She might not have intended to, he thought. But what did it mean if she had?

"Yes."

"Was that the problem you called about? I mean, that's utterly swell, if it is. I'm happy to address it with you."

He shifted his legs and felt that his knees had come to the height of his face. In the basement of the village's Baptist church, on an errand that was sad and even ridiculous, but inescapably important, he addressed this younger woman on behalf of his daughter's child and he was certain that he was a fool.

He said, "Someone took Jeremy's cape."

Her face creased in sorrow. She shook her head. "Oh, it *saves* him," she whispered.

Jeremy's mother, his only child, had cut the cape from a piece of white corduroy. She had stitched a red *J* on it and sewed the grosgrain ties with which she fastened it around him. He wore it every day. He had stood, solemn and invulnerable—less vulnerable, anyway—as Nora tied it on.

"And somebody took it," he said.

The teacher responded as if to the child. "Do we *know* that someone actually stole it? Could we have mis*placed* it?"

"Mrs. Preston, he came home without it. He was as pale as a piece of paper. He couldn't talk. He went to his room, he threw up his lunch—"

"Ill? Perhaps he's ill."

"Illness doesn't jettison a cape. Getting the cape swiped made him feel sick."

They sat too far apart for her to reach him, but she leaned in his direction with her arm out. "Of course. I understand," she said. "You're a good grandfather. Is Jeremy's father back?"

"This is such a small place, this village," he said. "No. No, he isn't. I think that he won't be."

"It's good you're here visiting, then."

"It's why," he said.

"You're Pop-Pop, yes? He talks about his Pop-Pop. Your daughter, Nora, she's lucky to have you. I understand the place she's in."

He wondered if he was supposed, now, to ask her for details.

She looked at the linoleum between them, then she looked at him from underneath her brow. His eyes skittered from hers but he forced himself to look again at her resigned, sad face. He thought, frighteningly, of slapping her to punish this theatricality. He thought next of holding her face between his palms. Looked away again.

She said, "Both my parents were dead when *my* husband left. My sister visited a brief little while, but of course she had a life to return to. What do *you* return to—ah, is there something to call you besides Pop-Pop? Do you prefer Mr. Royce?"

"Bing."

"As in Crosby?"

"I'm afraid so."

"It's an upbeat name. You inspirit us all, Bing."

He said, "You've been wonderful to Jeremy, Mrs. Preston."

"Muriel?"

"Thank you."

"Thank *you*," she said, smiling what he thought of as a gracious smile. He wished she would simply *talk* to him instead of demonstrating what she intended her words to mean. But he also liked looking at her, and she clearly wished him to.

"The cape's gone. Nora and I looked at home. You didn't find it here, or you'd have said so."

"Poor man. And poor, poor Jeremy."

"Muriel, would you mind terribly if I stood up? My knees are strangling."

She made the hiccup of laughter again and put a hand over her mouth. She stood, saying, "Here." She extended her cool, small hand and he took it and she tugged. When he was up, she slowly let go of his hand and said, "There's so much of you. You just kept coming. Unfolding, I meant—you know."

Her eyes met his. She was pleased to have said it that way, he was sure.

"Thank you," he said. He looked away, at the walls decorated with pasted constructions on rough paper, at crayon drawings of towering stick-figure parents and little sheltered stick-figure kids. He was afraid of seeing Jeremy's. He wanted Muriel Preston to find another reason for taking hold of his hand.

"You said that you understand Nora's ah . . ."

"Plight?"

"Yes. Plight. Did you mean you're a single parent?"

"Whose husband left. I raised the boys myself. Tim's in the navy and Barry goes to Hobart. He—my husband—said that he felt like all the air in the house was gone. After *that*, he told me about his girlfriend in Syracuse. She was salesperson of the year that year for the Stickley furniture showroom. Yeah. So I know how Nora feels, more or less. How is she about it?"

He closed his eyes and spoke slowly, but still his voice was unsteady when he talked about his child. "Not confident."

"Getting left will create that effect," she said in a dry monotone. "And not just on Mommy. Behold: Jeremy's cape."

He looked at the chairs against the near wall and at the clothes closet, open to display its low, bare hooks. "Oh," he said. "You meant—"

"*Voilà*, I meant. They both need a cape."

"And his is gone."

"And so is hers," she said. "Does Mrs. Bing Royce visit our perhaps claustrophobic municipality? Jeremy never mentions her."

He thought again of striking and of cradling the sweet, insincere face. He shook his head: acting *could* still be sincere, he thought. And he thought that he was hoping so. He said, "No. Not for some years. She died."

"I'm sorry."

"Yes. Thank you. Well, it sounds like we're all pretty damned sorry, Muriel."

"It sounds like we all need a measure of comfort," she said. She looked directly into his face. She seemed sad, not bold, but her voice was even and determined when she asked, "Should I tell you the way to my house?"

He knew the village well and didn't want to. He thought of Nora as trapped here. He thought, often, of insisting that she come to live with him in New York, and he knew that he was afraid she might give in. He believed—it might, he thought, be all he believed—that he could not share his bereavement yet. His sadness seemed all that was left of Anna, his wife. So here he was, fugitive comfort to his child, driving through the village large enough to contain several churches, one of them fundamentalist Protestant, one Roman Catholic, one the traditional Baptist that housed the nursery school, a small Presbyterian church of elegant white clapboard, and no synagogue, of course, or mosque. The Methodists had established themselves in the next village to the north, five miles up on the commuting road to Syracuse. People here drove to Syracuse or Utica, or they repaired computers locally, or staffed the insurance company or hospital, cut cordwood, ran a snowplow, and a few on the outskirts still farmed.

He thought a lot about churches these days. He wished he could believe in leaving his sorriest thoughts in the dim, comforting coolness of one. But he couldn't. All he left, in the basement of a church, was his worried grandson, and all that Jeremy had left behind was his cape. His daughter's husband was an architect in Syracuse. He lived, now, with an interior designer who had worked on one of his homes. They went to church every week, Nora had told him with scorn.

"But maybe it's not supposed to be like taking out the pails for the weekly trash pickup," he snarled as he drove. "You're supposed to be a pilgrim in church. You're supposed to *love* something. Or somebody. *Acknowledge* the damned cosmic whatever-it-is." He didn't know whether he was disgusted with himself, or Nora, or her nearly former husband, or this theatrical woman whose limbs he thought of, whose jumper and sweater he described to himself as he drove the village, taking far longer than he needed to reach her house. He thought about her brave little scarf and was confused by the cruelty of his thoughts about her since, obviously, he was also drawn—through these well-tended streets—to Muriel Preston. He went past one after another Greek Revival, Cape Cod, and Queen Anne house, most very well kept and all of them brightened, now, by the orange maples and copper oaks and yellow poplars that flared as the year swung around October and dropped toward another upstate winter in which Nora would worry about Jeremy's health and Jeremy would worry about everything. And Bing, he knew, would think not only of them, as the snows sealed the village in again, but also of Muriel Preston, no matter what happened.

It was about to happen now, he thought, parking in front of the narrow gray shake-shingled house with its small porch littered with wind-blown, bright leaves. It was going to happen now.

Her living room was small and shadowed. She still wore the jumper, but had removed her white cotton turtleneck sweater, and her chest above the bib of her dress was red with warmth. The scarf was knotted loosely about her neck. It was a grown-up woman's neck, with some less-than-taut flesh beneath the smoothness of the scarf. He thought he could smell her bare shoulders and arm when she brought him his wine.

"I like red wine," she said. "Is that all right? It's a big, rich Pommard that I can't afford. Except I love it. I've saved it for a special occasion.

So here we are inside of it. In the occasion, that is, not the wine. You understood that."

"I understood that." He would have sipped laundry bleach or buttermilk. He'd felt a little drunk while parking the car. Make that unsteady, he amended.

She was barefoot now. Her toes were stubby on small feet. She sat on the sofa, two white linen cushions to his left. There were muddy-looking canvases in gilt frames, and photographs of boys and the young men they'd become. Lemon peel, he thought, and the almond soap they give you in the bathroom of the Georges V in Paris, that was what the skin of her shoulders smelled like.

She sipped her wine and smiled. "It'll open out plenty more," she said. "Give it a while."

He looked at his watch but didn't note the time.

"Bing," she said, "give it a while."

He nodded. He smiled. He drank the wine. As if he were about to sign a document that was the engine of great consequence, he wondered what was going to become of Nora and Jeremy. What was in store for him?

She poured more wine for them, reaching to the coffee table and scenting the air of her living room. Her eyes moved sideways at him as he breathed her. He couldn't tell whether he was intended to see her observing him or whether she had merely looked. She smiled as if to herself when she sat back. She was careful, in the adjustment of her hem, to cover her knees.

"Does Jeremy talk to you?" she asked.

"About—you mean about his feelings?"

"He says you're wise. That's his word for you: 'wise.'"

"We talk a lot. When he asks about his father, it destroys me. It's like watching a sick puppy, or a wounded bird. Words don't work when they're devastated like that."

"No," she said, "you're wrong. You do give him comfort."

"The goddamned cape gave him comfort. I beg your pardon."

"Oh," she said, "I've heard that locution before." She sipped wine. "I survived it."

They sat, they drank, and then she stood to pour a little wine they didn't need yet.

He said, "You think of yourself as strong, then."

"Bold, I think you mean. Licentious, even. Do you feel . . . rushed?"

"No," he said. "I didn't mean that."

"It's all right if you did, because it's possible I am a little forward with you. Anyway, I do feel competent, I'd say."

"Yes," he said. "That's what I'd say, too."

"At what, would you say?"

"Living your life, I guess." He moved his arm, and it touched her jumper, for she still stood, holding the wine bottle. "Making your way."

"Try me," she said. "See for yourself." She set the bottle on the table's dusty wood beside their glasses, and later he remembered his concern that the bottle might have made a permanent ring. He put his arm about her thighs and pulled her against him, pressing his face into her jumper. Her hands, on his shoulders, drew him in, but then she said, "Upstairs, all right? Come up."

In her room, on the maple bed that groaned as they shifted and slid and bucked, she actually said—he would repeat the words in his thoughts of the afternoon—"Oh, my darling." He thought it as arch, as premeditated, as stickily poetic as anything he'd heard. He wanted romance, he thought with pity for himself. He wanted this to be as fresh and just invented as her words turned it scripted and somehow untrue.

He thrust very hard to stop her from saying it again. And he felt, at the time and later, that his motive betrayed her even as she made their passion seem a little ludicrous. Neither her words, nor his response, nor her tears, nor his wondering whether she truly wept, prevented them from marching on together, with strength and with what struck him as a comradely regard for what felt best for each of them. He realized that he wanted her to say those saccharine words again. He wanted her to mean them. He asked, with his body, whether she did. He demanded that she did. He held her down on top of him as he slammed up. He closed his eyes and heard her grunt and maybe, then, whisper a protest once, though she moved and moved and moved with him. He demanded, with his body, to know what she had meant. But it was Bing who gave in first, surrendering to his angry pleasure, knowing only a little of what he had intended and knowing nothing more about her own intentions, to lie beneath her like a victim, emptied of himself.

He didn't know if he had slept and dreamed in the chilly, dark room when she moved on him and then climbed out of the bed. "I would like to wear your shirt," she said.

"Please do. But it's a little big for you."

She stood beside the bed to pull it on. Its tails hung to her knees. "I know," she said. "That's why I wanted to wear it. Stay there, please."

She returned with their glasses and the bottle of Pommard. "I think you'll find it's opened more than generously," she said, smiling what he thought she might think of as a wicked grin. She sat on the bed, touching him, still wearing his shirt, as they drank.

"I flushed it down the toilet," he finally said.

"Yes. And you're noting, when you say that, how I kept a condom in the drawer of my bedside table."

"No," he said. "Yes."

"Is this the first time since—"

"No," he said. "There was another time. An earlier time. Well, of course it was earlier. I was awful at it."

"How did you think you did here? Just now?"

"Could we talk about the World Series?" he asked her. "Or how you like the Knicks for the upcoming year?"

"You are the rare man I would talk with about the World Series if he asked me to," she said. "So that should tell you how we did here together. If you'd like to know. How would you say we're doing?"

"Muriel," he said, "I got lost in you. I didn't mean to say anything like that—about the apparatus."

"Apparatus! That's wonderful. I wish I could be indiscreet about it and tell someone." Her voice sounded sad when she said, "I don't trust anyone that much. Maybe one day I'll tell it to you. Do you think?" She drank and settled back against him. She said, "I believe these things are meant to happen as they insist on happening, and it isn't given to us to necessarily understand why. Do you agree?"

Her hand moved over his belly and groin, and he moved to be available to her. What she said seemed absurd to him, like the flabby talk that disappointed him in churches. But he said, "Yes."

"Yes," she said, leaning to kiss his mouth. She sat back and said, "I wasn't just left with my boys. I was left when I didn't have a job, when there wasn't money in the bank for us, when it was a brutal winter and I ended up selling shoes in Utica. The store went out of business. The strip mall it was in went bust. One of my kids, Timmy, was caught for shoplifting, but I begged and begged for him, and they let him go. That's why he had a clean record when it was time to try for Annapolis. Do I think of myself as strong? Yes. Do you?"

"Yes. You raised your sons," he said, "and they're all right."

"Oh, yes. They are."

"And you're young."

"Young enough, I suppose." And then she said, "For what?"

"A life? I don't know."

"Well, I always had one, Bing. *That's* the being-strong part."

"Of course."

"No. Please don't *of course* me. It's a little complicated for that."

"Yes," he said. "Muriel, for what? I'm confused."

"Yes, you are, I'm sorry to say." She set her glass on the floor and stood, removing his shirt. He wondered if she indicated by shrugging it off that his obtuseness was ending the day for them. But she stood before him an instant and then climbed into the bed, pulling the comforter over them and climbing onto him again. Then she raised herself up, with her hands on either side of his face. "I want to look at you," she said. He closed his eyes in embarrassment. "No," she said. "Bing." He forced his eyes open, and she gave him a rueful smile which, he thought, was precisely how she had intended, hours ago, to complete their afternoon.

Then he saw her eyes flicker and close halfway. She made a surrendering sound, and she kissed him deeply—as, he speculated, she might possibly *not* have planned.

Downstairs, in jeans and a baggy T-shirt, she held the cream-colored scarf as if she meant to knot it on her neck. She raised her face to be kissed goodbye.

"I'll see you tomorrow," he said. "You know—with Jeremy."

She said, "Darling." She held the scarf against her cheek as if he had just presented it to her.

As he parked in the driveway behind Nora's old Volvo station wagon, his legs felt tired, as if he had walked great distances. His body hadn't ached like this since before Anna died. He was only past the middle of fifty and she was in her forties, but he thought of her as young. He thought of her, too, as confusing. Yes, he thought, but remember the sounds she couldn't help making. Those were not, he thought, the noises she planned for him to hear. He snorted. He shook his head. He tried to feel only experienced about the flesh, and not excited, but he couldn't pretend. He still smelled her, and he felt her in his shoulders and thighs. He thought he still smelled the mixture of them. He paused at the back door, wondering whether Nora would smell them, too. He crackled his chewing gum to cover the excellent wine with artificial cinnamon scent, then spat the gum away and went inside.

It seemed a normal early evening. Jeremy assembled unbrilliant constructions of locking plastic bricks while not watching the television set that brayed bad news in the little breakfast room. Nora, he could see, was listening to the news and sorrowing for the fall of mutual funds, for dying rivers, for soldiers wounded, for migrant families pursued through a southwestern desert by federal officers armed as heavily as soldiers sent off to war. Her thick eyebrows sloped down, her lids were low, and her narrow lips frowned. She looked like Anna, he thought. And what help was that to anyone?

"So where were you?" she asked, not listening, he thought, for an answer. He waved to Jeremy and the boy waved back, his fingers together so that his hand looked like the paw of a cub. Jeremy's smile was real but disappearing, and he looked as usual: worried, small, and slumped against the end of a harrowing day.

Facing Nora in the kitchen and murmuring into the sizzle of the small chicken she'd just lifted up from the oven, he said, "I spoke to Jeremy's teacher. The nursery school woman."

"Muriel Preston."

"Yes. She didn't see the cape. I think she thinks maybe one of the children stole it."

She said, "They don't need it."

"No."

"Jeremy does."

"Yes, he does."

"I mean he *really* needs it."

He nodded, then went to the counter on the far wall for the hardwood cutting board and the carving knife and fork that he and Anna had given to them when Nora's husband, Jeremy's father, was home. He dripped juice from the bird on his shirt and along the floor.

"Sorry," he said.

Nora said, "That's all right." She tore off pieces of paper towel so that she could clean up the juice, but she held the paper, watching him, and she finally set the crumpled squares near the sink. Bing told himself to remember to wipe the floor after dinner.

"I'll let the chicken sit awhile," he said.

She said, "I should have bought some cloth someplace."

"For what? A new cape?"

"Maybe I could have persuaded him. I asked, but he flew into a rage. He said it wouldn't be—Hey, Jeremy, honey. Hi."

He held something like a white, yellow, and red pistol made of the locking plastic bricks. He solemnly offered it to his grandfather.

"Look at that," Nora shouted.

"Good job," Bing said, holding it as you'd hold a handgun.

Jeremy said, "It's a angle iron."

"Of course it is," he said. "What do you do with it, honey?"

Jeremy took it from him and held it against the side of the refrigerator. With the eraser end of a pencil, he made measuring motions. "You get it straight," he said.

Bing said, "Yes, you do."

"I love how you didn't mark the fridge up," Nora said too loudly. "Thank you."

"It was pretend. Arnie does it real."

"God, doesn't he," Nora said. Arnie Holland was the country man in his thirties who was as celebrated among the women of the village for the effects of his shirtlessness while he worked as he was for his achievements at rough carpentry.

Bing, slicing a drumstick and going to work on the thigh, said, "Arnie was here, then?"

"At Lindsay Delano's."

Bing had dropped Jeremy there after school so that Nora could stay on at work in the hospital admitting office, where a flu had cut into the staffing. He had driven from Lindsay's back to school, then from school to Muriel's house, and from there to the Quik-Mart for his guilty cinnamon gum, and from there to his daughter's. He was becoming a local, he thought. It was time to go home. It was time to get back to work. He hadn't checked for messages, he hadn't called the office, he hadn't even opened his briefcase in nearly a week. He was moving with his usual long-legged, slow-motion lope—that had been Anna's description of his progress through the world—but he was really on the run.

Nora said, "What, Daddy?"

He looked up to see Jeremy staring at Nora as Nora stared at Bing. He had separated drumstick from thigh and thigh from the carcass. He had cut off the wing. He had carved the breast meat into semicircular slices, and he stood above this orderly disposition as if he had come upon an accident, a wreck.

"No," he said, "I was thinking."

Jeremy said, "You looked sad."

"Sir," he sang at the boy, "I was *glad*. I was glad to know you and in a transport of delight to be carving up this great big slice of bologna for your platter. *That's* the matter."

He waited for a smile. He had hoped for laughter, but a little smile across the dull white cheeks, pushing at the dark pink bags beneath the eyes, would have satisfied him. Jeremy only watched him with his usual care, and Pop-Pop served up breast meat. Then he talked to Nora about a textbook they had to revise, for school board adoptions in Texas and Arkansas, because the sections on evolution referred to the *immutable cycles of mutation*. "Far be it from me to deny a biology professor his zippy little pun, his toothsome academic oxymoron," Bing said. "But that Texas guy with the bullwhip on his office table in Congress— truly, a big black bullwhip—summoned us to Washington. I didn't go. I refused to. But I did have to send two of the kid editors. Adoption means huge sums. Do you care about this, honey?"

Nora's eyes, as dark and liquid as Anna's, looked miserable. "Like you said before," she said, "I was thinking."

"About what—besides textbook adoptions?"

"How you're telling what somebody else ought to be hearing. But that can't be, can it? And how I'm listening to you while I ought to be hearing a different somebody else."

"Somebody else," he said.

Nora said, "Somebodies. The case of the missing somebodies."

"But that can't happen," he said.

"Apparently not."

He said, "Apparently not. *But*," he said, "do I *not* get to gobble Jeremy's dessert?"

His grandson looked up expectantly, but not with resistance in his eyes, or a willingness to joke that moved on his chapped, bitten lips. He was waiting, Bing understood, to find out whether the world intended to take away his wedge of pineapple upside-down cake.

"Oh, baby boy," Bing said.

Nora sat with Jeremy while Bing cleaned up dishes. He worked in a trance of hushing hot water and the simple process of scrubbing at pots and the roasting pan while the dishwasher made a grating noise behind which he sheltered the way someone is private behind a high hedge. He thought he understood everything about his loss of Anna— the complaints, the physical exam, the tests, the results, and then the roaring speed of it. He knew what he thought and felt about every grim inch of the cornering, the pinning-down, every day, into a smaller and smaller space, of the tall, tough Englishwoman he had known for so many decades. Whatever he understood about his life was through what she'd seen in him and how she had told him of what she had seen.

But something had happened, and no one but he and Anna had witnessed it, and he thought he would never understand. It filled his chest, it pressed him breathless, to realize that he could ask only his forever-vanished wife what she had meant in the artificial dusk of their bedroom as she, on their bed, opened her eyes to find him in a chair beside her, weeping.

He sighed, now, in Nora's kitchen, as he recalled the discovery. Anna's mouth had tightened, and her dark eyes had scratched like fingers at his face. He remembered straightening in the chair as if expecting a blow. And he'd received it.

Her weak whisper spat from the yellow crepiness of her face. "Jesus, Bing," she'd said in the darkness, "can you give me a *break* here. Give me a *hand*, old boy, and push me off."

So why not think of synagogues and mosques? he thought, turning his hands beneath the water. Why not wonder about churches? Besides the nighttime hauntings at home, were those not where the truths of the dead were said to reside? No one but Anna could tell him what she had wanted of him, and what it was that he couldn't provide. She hadn't asked him to kill her, he thought. Or had she? If he had understood that, would he have agreed? Had he tried, out of fear, not to understand? Was that the way he had let her, in her agony, down? Or was it something different, maybe even something, somehow, more?

He had never told Nora. He wouldn't, he knew. Jeremy knew the most, he thought, about feeling failed. His hands opened in surrender under the hot, rushing water. If he and Jeremy made it another twenty years, he thought, he might try asking his grandson the meaning of the loneliest moment of his life.

On the way to the car with Jeremy, each of them wearing a sweater in the chill of the morning, he saw the pink, shining offal, like a tiny brain, that he had spat out before entering the house the night before. He kicked it aside, saying, "Yuck," to Jeremy, who hadn't noticed because, Bing suspected, he could see only the bleak patterns of the morning ahead at school. Whatever they were, they were unspeakable, and Jeremy didn't try to describe them.

As Bing buckled him in, Jeremy echoed, "Yuck."

"Yuck what, old sock?"

"New sock," Jeremy replied, dutifully socking his Pop-Pop's arm.

"Yowch!" Bing howled, but Jeremy didn't smile. He would return tomorrow, he thought, and he would see—while he drove, or while he added fares to his Metro card at a subway station, or while he looked at proofs—the ivory cheeks, chewed lips, and anxious eyes of his child's child. There he sat, pinioned by buckles and straps. Bing thought of last night's roasted chicken, now a half-stripped carcass. He thought as he started the engine that its flavor filled his mouth, as if a sour bubble of grease had come up his throat to burst behind his teeth.

"You are my hero," he sang to the tune of "You Are My Sunshine," "my lovely hero—" He said, "Did you know you were my hero?"

"No."

"Do you know what a hero is?"

"No," Jeremy said. Then he said, "Yes."

"What, honey?"

"They have blue pants and boots and a red shirt," the boy recited.

Bing prayed: Oh, don't.

But Jeremy continued. "And they have a cape," he said.

All that Bing could say, then, was, "I love you, honey. Pop-Pop loves you to bits."

Jeremy whispered, "Yuck," and then they were silent for the rest of the ride through the tidy village, and then while Bing found someplace to park, and then while he lifted his grandson out and onto the pavement, and then while they joined their hands and walked to school.

Muriel greeted her students outside the basement entrance of the Baptist church. She wore an unbuttoned navy blue raincoat over her shoulders. He saw white tights and a short, dark skirt, and he thought— as he had so often during the evening and the long night—of the smoothness of her thighs. She smiled at them, and Bing felt himself smile back goofily, as happily as adolescent boys can smile at adolescent girls who have been kind to them. She wore a raspberry-colored silk scarf, he noticed, that was held in place with a cameo pin. He thought of it as little and brave, but he felt only pleasure—his, but also hers—in the observation.

She said, "Good morning, Jeremy. Good morning, Pop-Pop."

Jeremy looked at Bing before saying, "Morning."

"Yes, ma'am," Bing replied.

"Yes," she said. She said, "I have something, Jeremy. I think you might need a new cape. This one is very powerful." She drew a bundle from under her coat and shook it loose. A cape unfolded, a different shade of blue from her coat or skirt, but clearly part of an outfit she had planned while she planned this moment. She held it out, and Jeremy, after looking it over—Bing saw its *J* in white and lavender paisley— silently turned his back toward his teacher so that she could fasten its paisley ties about his neck.

When she turned him back around and kissed his nose, he looked at Bing.

"Looks good, old sock," Bing said.

"New sock," Jeremy told him and punched him with power on his offered upper arm. Bing winced and yelped, and Jeremy grinned very broadly.

"Thank you, Mrs. Preston," Bing insisted.

"Thank you," Jeremy said, moving away from them and toward a cluster of children who had been watching.

Bing said, "That was a great—I don't know. Courtesy. Favor. Small salvation, for goodness' sakes. Nora asked him if she should make another one, and he said no. He cried. He was angry, I think. Because the magic of the original was gone. But there you were with this—"

"A different magic is all," she said.

He knew that he had to return to his car and drive to Nora's and then leave. But he also had to stand among the copper and the orange leaves with his grandson's teacher. "It was generous," he said, "and a beautiful gesture in friendship. And it was gorgeous in and of itself."

He felt himself reddening as she flushed up from the knot of her scarf along her cheeks and then her forehead. Her eyes were full. A father and his child were half a block away, followed by a mother who wheeled a stroller, and he sensed that they were aimed toward Muriel. Bing felt a desperation about being forced away from this final intimacy with her.

"Gorgeous," he repeated.

"It's when someone decides that the difference in the magic is acceptable," she said. "And by the way: an action isn't always a gesture." She looked at the approaching father and she said, "A person needs to know the difference."

And he didn't. Maybe she knew that hesitation in him. Maybe it was why she was, apparently, alone—because others also didn't know the difference in her. He saw his grandson's long blue cape as the boy, under its protection, dared the dangers of his peers.

She turned from him. She turned back. "You might take some time and decide," she suggested.

He said, "Yes."

She smiled a sunny, theatrical smile. She said, "Teachers. They're always giving homework assignments."

"Nora's coming to get him after school," Bing said. "I have to get back."

"Back," she said.

"To New York. I have a job."

Yes," she said. "We never talked about our jobs very much. We were in a hurry."

"Yes."

"Too much of a hurry, do you think?"

"Not too much of a hurry," he said. "No. I wish—I wish we could start in a hurry all over again."

"We could continue in a hurry," she said.

"Maybe I could phone you during the week," he said, with a thick-tongued dullness he hated.

"Dear man," she said, "I think you could do anything to me." The spasm of anger he felt for the theater in her voice was frightening. He stepped back. He looked away and he waved at Jeremy, who moved his cocked arm back and forth—all he dared, in front of his friends, to display of farewell. "But you're already gone," she said. Her face grew serious and it seemed smaller. He thought he saw what she might look like, grown older.

Even he, Bing thought, could hear the sorrow in his voice. "Not that far," he said, because he wanted her to smile. "Not as far as you'd think."

Waving goodbye to her across perhaps ten inches as Jeremy had waved to him over a dozen yards, he turned away from the school. He prayed. He addressed no heavenly father stitched from children's dreams. And he didn't believe that his prayer could be heard. Still, he prayed, because now, he thought, just possibly, he understood some of what his wife might have meant in the rigors of her dying.

Anna, he said to her as he walked through the leaves to his car, could you do me a favor, dear girl, and give me a bit of a push?

THE BOTTOM OF THE GLASS

T HE COUSINS MADE a rough crossing, they'd have said, if they had
thought to complain. They mentioned but didn't lament the time
in the air, the late arrival at de Gaulle, the bus ride to catch the train
at the Gare Montparnasse, or the long wait for the Très Grand Vitesse
to Bordeaux. They did joke about the man in the car rental agency at
the Bordeaux terminal who spoke no English and who resented that
they spoke some French. He cost them a half an hour of futile searching for the car he pretended to direct them toward, nearly shouting
his exasperation: "*Les voitures, il restent la, à droit—la, monsieur! La!*"

Eleanor could imagine them, with their several heavy bags, their
sacks from the duty-free, their great, damp slabs and mounds of muscle
and fat shifting and trembling as they panted in and about the station
and, finally, through the darkness of the garage beneath it where the
rentals, *les voitures*, were parked. She imagined Eugene's French, with
its awful accent and its wonderful vocabulary, as he breathlessly sought
to entertain the traveling salesman who, speaking French with native
fluency and English with a transatlantic businessman's ease, had offered
to lead them to their car.

Now Eugene sat at the table in the kitchen of the rental house,
which he called, quite properly, a *gîte*. They had never met, and her

husband had never spoken of these enormous creatures who, it seemed, were kin. Eugene had embraced her on arriving in their sporty convertible, climbing out from behind the wheel with slow, laborious motions to hold her neck in a yoke of moist, thick fingers, kissing her head with the greatest delicacy until Bertha had pulled her away to smother Eleanor's bowed face in those enormous breasts that shifted as if they were independent creatures trapped beneath the baggy tan traveling dress she matched with tan strap pumps and a tan leather handbag that looked as though it were weighted with stones.

"No la, no la-di-da, and surely no parked vultures, dear girl," the cousin of Eleanor's dead husband chanted. "The fellow knew we'd never find them. The Sino-French gentleman, a manufacturer's agent for *plastics*, if you can believe it, unless he meant explosive *plastique*, now that you mention it, finally showed us where to go. He'd been there before, of course, and he was waiting in the corner of the rental office with that polite tranquility of theirs—"

"Not that my dear husband wishes to be mistaken for a racialist," Bertha warned.

Eugene smiled damply at the table in the kitchen they had planned, she and Sid, to use during the rest of June and all of July. While Madame Panifiette, their landlady, took the advice of her husband and several friends in the area to consider whether—here she had made a number of faces involving downturned lips, raised brows, and a half a shake of the head—given the legalities involved, she could release Eleanor from the remainder, as she said it, of "your obligation to me."

Eleanor had said to the tiny Madame Panifiette, with her alabaster complexion, in front of Eugene and Bertha, "You never liked me, did you?"

"Well, now," Bertha had said, in sweet, slippery syllables, "we don't want to necessarily accuse anyone of anything, do we?"

Between them, Bertha and Eugene weighed seven hundred and fifty pounds, Eleanor would have bet. On a better day, she'd have guessed it at six-fifty. But this was only a few days after Sid had looked up from

the little corner table on which he leaned toward his white, lined pad
with his fine-point fountain pen. She had been sitting at the pine dining table in the tile-paneled kitchen, writing postcards home at maybe
eight in the morning. She looked up as Sid did. They caught each other's
eyes. She thought he was going to say something rueful about his work.
She was ready to smile and cluck and go back to the cards that told
what a fine time they were enjoying. But it stopped, inside his eyes,
and they went out. He fell sideways from his chair. She went to him,
she called to him, she blew her breath past his teeth and felt it going
nowhere except back up at her mouth. That night, after following the
ambulance to the regional hospital and after talking to a man from the
gendarmerie who seemed too young to drive, much less take charge of
her husband's death, she used Sid's address book and her own to call
home and speak to eight or nine people. She did not call her daughter,
Margo, and every day that she failed to, it seemed like a more impossible task. It was an overdue account, accruing a terrible interest. Of
the people she did call, Sid's cousins, whom she'd never met, insisted
that they come to her. They flew from Baltimore to Roissy–Charles de
Gaulle, they took the train to Bordeaux, and they navigated their rental
car over the small roads of the wine country of southwestern France,
and here they were, managing, among other elements, her grief. Over
some days, the details of their journey emerged, and she came to think
of them as her big, fat heroes.

They were probably sixty, she thought. Bertha was as tall as Eugene,
with beefy shoulders and thick, rounded arms. She dyed her hair black
as if to match it to the hair of her shaved moustache. She wore either
dresses or skirts with matching tops, nothing tucked in, which was a
vanity that Eleanor found moving. She could see the breadth of Bertha's vast thighs as she walked briskly, in dressy high heels, through
the echoing, cool, white or white-and-rose tiles of the floors and walls
of the *gîte*. She "straightened things up," she said. "Not that it isn't as
neat as a pin. But one tries," she said, "to help. The best, the most useful help, they say, is order. So one picks up."

Eugene, who ran a rare-books business in Baltimore, on one of the streets near the revived waterfront area, looked every day at the few French books Madame Panifiette had supplied, as well as the couple of stacks that had taken up too much of the space in Sam's and Eleanor's rolling duffel cases. When he wasn't reading in books he clearly didn't like, or looking at titles he didn't want to open, Eugene spoke on the telephone, using his credit card, to arrange in his blatting but quite correct French for the passage home of three vertical Americans and one who would, as soon as his body was released by the authorities, travel prone.

"Assuming," Eleanor told him as he hung up and sighed, "that Fifi LaPue over there lets me out of the lease. She had a little hankering for Sid, by the way, would have been my bet. What the drug people call a jones? Though I don't know her position vis-à-vis the African-American dead."

"Perhaps, then, she'll be glad to see you go, now that you're on your own. I *am* so sorry," he said. "Forgive me. Sidney—"

Eleanor nodded. She didn't know what else to do with her face, so she put her hands over it. Sidney and I, she nearly said to his cousin, would not have made it from the June we are in to the start of autumn. They'd been a middle-aged couple in a second marriage for each that was going as sour as the wine their landlady's husband produced in what was little more than a very large old stone garage. Now Eleanor was a middle-aged widow whose husband had died of what the very sweet young doctor, who smelled of a citrus soap Eleanor had thought clean and sexy at once, called *une attaque*—a stroke.

Then the doctor had added, not hesitantly at all, for she was a sophisticated woman of France, after all, "*Les neiges* . . ." She did pause on Eleanor's behalf to say "Do you know this word of ours for, er, the Negroes, madame?"

Eleanor took a deep breath in order to shout at her, to screech, she realized, about her experience as a teacher of French at the sixth-snootiest prep school for girls in the city of New York. She was going to scream in impeccable French. But the woman's kind, tired light green eyes, her obvious concern for the dead man's wife, silenced her. She touched the doctor's forearm with the fingers of her right hand, and she nodded.

She let her breath out, and she said, "*D'accord.*"

"*Eh, bien,*" the doctor said. "*Donc. Les nègres, il sont tres vulnérable des attaques. Je regrette, madame.*"

It had seemed to her before he died, and it seemed to her afterward, that they had remained in love. The sorriest part, she was beginning to believe, was that love did not necessarily make it possible to live, together or alone. And a desire to live, something beyond the animal drive to not be killed off, she had reluctantly come to think, was the most necessary and most elusive of feelings. Thinking of the size of Sid's mistake and hers in marrying, she wondered if Eugene suspected something of the great error in which Sidney and she had courted and married and traveled abroad. Here he was, because he thought it right to come to the aid of his nephew's white wife, this gentle, vast, and elegant pear-shaped cousin from Baltimore, sweating through his white duck trousers and his dark blue long-sleeved shirt, waving his white, broad-brimmed straw hat as a fan between them while they sat at the kitchen table and checked their little list of what to do after a husband's death in a rural rental house among the rows of the Panifiettes' sauvignon blanc vines at the end of a very warm June. She knew that Bertha's whiteness could be all or some of an explanation, but she doubted it. His hairless café-au-lait head shone from the heat, and she thought she could feel it, like his decency, radiate from him across the yard or so of polished pine.

"I'm sorry the weather's so uncomfortable," Eleanor said. "And I'm so glad you're here, you and Bertha, that I feel *treacherous* about my relief—on account of your discomfort. But thank goodness."

"You're a cousin. A cousin-in-law. I do not know *what* you are, in legal definitions, Eleanor. You are our family. If you want to be. If you do, then you are. If you don't, consider us a very, very large pain in the ass until we see you safely home."

She took his beefy, moist hand, the one that rested on the table near his coffee cup, and she set it against the side of her head.

"Dear girl," he said.

Bertha walked in, moving as gracefully in spite of her size as Eugene did, whether it was to lift a cup of coffee or cross a room. Eleanor could imagine them as they somehow, helping each other quite cordially, made their slow, breathless way up the stairs of the Très Grand Vitesse and stowed the bags at the end of the first-class carriage. She could imagine them murmuring to one another—"Are you all right, dear? If you'd give me your hand..."—and could envision them as they faced each other across the little table of their compartment, stomachs folded doughily over the table's edge, great arms flattening on its top, arranging bottles of Evian and sandwiches, wedges of cheese, perhaps, and chunks of fruit that Eugene cut for them with a folding wooden-handled picnic knife while the train gathered speed. She saw his vast hands manage with delicacy the division of a Cavaillon melon or a crescent of Brie, saw hers distribute napkins and plastic cups.

"I have just been having another word with Madame Panifiette," Bertha said. "She was most accommodating of my accent." Her smile might have excused Madame or indicted her own French, but it was kind, somehow. "She expects to 'achieve a resolution' quite rapidly."

"I'll bet you money," Eleanor said, "that it costs us extra money."

"I will expect her to do better on our behalf," Eugene said, with a little steel in his voice. "But some money might pleasantly change the equation. I *could* see that."

Bertha asked, "Did Eugene tell you that we were cooking tonight?"

Eleanor shook her head.

"Well, we're cooking," Bertha said, "so you might prepare yourself."

"Is that a stressful situation?"

"No, dear," Eugene said. "It's noisy, a little, and sometimes quite messy, but I wouldn't call it stressful. You are in one of the superb culinary districts of the world, and not at all far from St. Émilion, such a great wine center, as I'm sure you know. We're off to shop, and then, when we return with food and drink, you are invited to a meal prepared by relatives. Are we your in-laws?"

Eleanor shrugged. She tried to smile brightly.

"Outlaws, then," Bertha said, and she laughed like a girl, though her eyes seemed sad as they slid toward Eleanor and then away.

"Outlaws it will be," Eugene said.

Begging her pardon for seeming intrusive, they moved about the room, opening cupboards and inspecting the refrigerator, each naming items for a list while Eugene wrote down, on one of Sid's green-lined white legal pads, what they would need to buy at the open-air stalls in the square of St. Macaire and at the supermarket in Langon.

Eleanor, who was tall and broad-shouldered and, according to Sid, "the slightly repressed all-American lifeguard at the country club pool," was thinking of Margo, also tall, slender, and broad-shouldered, who suddenly, it seemed, was in graduate school for the study of some kind of cell physiology that her father, a medical doctor, seemed to understand while Eleanor could only decipher the meaning of "cell" and "physiology," without formulating an intelligent sentence that used both words. She was remembering how, early that winter, Margo had come home from Madison, Wisconsin, to Eleanor's place on West Ninth Street to stay the night and register her opinion about Sid and her mother before spending the weekend at their old apartment, now her father's, uptown.

She said, "Mother, for Christ's sake. Have an *affair*. It's an itch, so scratch it. Get over the thrill of it. Then learn how to live alone like the rest of us, for Christ's sake."

"And have you considered that it could possibly be more than sex?"

"When a forty-five-year-old divorced white woman gets a jones for a slightly younger, fairly hot black man who writes books, one of which she happened to read *before* he picked her up at the Metropolitan

Museum show of those Vienna Whoevers who did the highly sexual-
ized paintings? Ma: *duh-uh*."

"I don't know where to begin," Eleanor had said. She remembered
stumping back and forth on the broad, painted planks of her little Village living room. "I don't know whether to shout terrible things about
your not knowing the Vienna Secession, or calling their paintings 'sexu-
alized,' like you're the Dean of Correctness at a second-rate college, or
portraying me as this over-stimulated matron who just wants to get *laid*
by the nearest black man, who, like all the rest of them, you know, *you
know*, is a phallic engine who cannot stay away from dumb and oversexed white women. Margo: *duh-uh*. How could you? And why are *you*
so lonely, handing out that living-alone stuff? And since whenever do
you say I have a *jones*? I don't know where to begin."

"Don't say anything I can't forgive, Mother."

Margo had called her Mother since the divorce, which they had
conducted like a small war while their civilian casualty was in the
eleventh grade. Eleanor said, "Margo? Are you really that alone? Are
you saying that *I* am? Are you accusing me of being in despair? How
desperate do you think I *am*?"

"How much do you weigh, Mother?"

"How much—"

"How much do you weigh?"

"One thirty-three."

"I thought it was, like, a hundred and forty-five?"

"No comment."

"Right. So I'd call you roughly a hundred and forty-five pounds of
desperate. That's how desperate I think you are."

Margo sat in silence, then, and watched her wander in the living
room, from the wall of bookshelves to the long sofa to one of the windows onto Ninth Street. Finally, Eleanor let a long sigh slide between
her lips and she said, "I've been holding my breath. I've gotten so strung
out by you, I forgot to breathe."

"Then you know the principle of blowing dope. Hold it and hold it and then let it go. I could roll us a joint."

"Of marijuana?"

"What did you think it involved, Mother?"

"I don't want to know."

"All right."

"Do you smoke it a lot?"

Margo looked at her with the pity of the young. Eleanor had seen it on her students' faces. That it was undisguised made it cruel, as if they had never considered the possibility of an elder understanding the gulf between them. You decayed before their eyes, it said, and you didn't know how close to dead you were.

"I think you're learning to value yourself is all," Eleanor had said when they told each other goodnight. "It's not easy. I know."

"And do you?"

"Do I what?"

"Mother, do *you* value yourself?"

"Of course. And I know that Sid values me. Oh," Eleanor had said, "not a great answer, is it?"

"You're still learning, too."

"Life is long," Eleanor remembered telling her.

"It better be," Margo had said, about to go inside the guest room, "because you are one slow learner."

Which apparently was true, Eleanor thought as, in the French rental, Sid's great cousins prepared to drive into St. Macaire to purchase butter and cream and duck breasts and two kinds of mushrooms. "We can bake in those little ramekins instead of metal molds," he said. "Absolutely no harm done. And that's a reminder," he instructed Bertha, "about milk for the timbales. We cannot forget the milk."

"You're making the list, dear."

"Yes, I am," he said. He told Eleanor, "The preparation of food, you will not be surprised to learn, excites me. I get forgetful."

"He can also be dictatorial and quite like a master chef—decidedly cruel," Bertha said, smiling. "It gets quite dangerous when we cook."

"The danger," Eugene chanted, as if from memory, "lies in running short of reliable duck confit, not in any slightly bruised feelings among the sous-chefs."

"Who said that?" Bertha asked.

"I did, of course."

"You can see," she told Eleanor, "he grows brutal."

There was a rustling of linen clothing, a seizing of lists, and a counting of currency, and then they were off in their black convertible, down the stony drive to turn left onto the little connector road, then right onto the paved secondary, and then to wander the turns past vineyards and the sheds that sheltered stainless steel storage tanks and the descent into St. Macaire with its ramparts and its small, plain cathedral, and its narrow streets. She thought for a moment of the cousins as they loomed over the small, taut French while they inspected the wares of the seller of Basque sausages and cheeses, or the local man so proud of his harsh Armagnac, and the butcher who always seemed to sneer over his duck legs, his unplucked chickens, his thick loins of pork. She could hear their murmurs to each other and their charmed, polite replies.

In the master bedroom, which like the dining area opened into the vineyard, she moved folded clothing about and tried to pack. There were two large bags and two small ones for carrying books and bottles of water onto the plane; they hadn't brought more than thin summer clothing and a cotton sweater apiece for a cool night, but there seemed to her to be too little room in their luggage. It felt important that she leave nothing of his behind, although she suspected that, eventually, she would give it all away in New York. For now, though, she wanted to bring him home with everything he'd carried abroad.

Did that include her? She wondered if they would have returned together, assuming the small matter of his not having died of an explosion of blood in the brain.

"Probably," she said to the chugging of insects outside, the slow droning of fat bees in the waist-high pots of rosemary next to the house.

"Of course," she said.

Looking at the herbs and thinking of the cousins at their list-making, she thought of the preparation of food. She remembered the first formal date with Sid, who had taken her for dinner to Jarnac, the restaurant in the West Village. He had insisted that they order the cassoulet, which was better, he said, than the cassoulet, with white beans and duck and pork sausage, that he had eaten in the Fifth Arrondissement of Paris the previous year. A stocky, jolly, but tough-looking woman came out of the kitchen while they ate, and she circulated through the small room. She and Sid embraced, she patted Eleanor on the shoulder, and she moved on.

"The chef," Sid said.

"I can't help it," she told him. "I'm impressed."

"That was the idea."

"It was?"

"Oh, yes. You're who I'm determined to impress."

His thin face, which she thought had as many muscles in it as an athlete's arm, was a little darker, with a little more putty color, she thought now, than Eugene's. Sid kept his coarse hair short, and she had enjoyed inspecting the beautiful shape of his head. She could imagine a mother holding her hand around the back of that head. She could imagine her own hand there. He saw her speculating, and he suddenly grinned, a big and boyish, happy smile.

"What?" he said.

"Never mind. Although I suspect you can figure it out."

"I hope so," he said.

"I'm considering matters," she said. "So tell me something."

"About what?"

"About anything besides me. Tell me something about your work."

"You said you know my work. Now I'm disappointed."

"What you are is like a boy about it."

"I'm like a boy about everything else, too," he said.

"Never mind. Tell me about what you do. I read the one about the women who robbed banks. Very cool, as my daughter might say. A bunch of right-on women, she'd say, except for the part about shooting people. Your detective cries. People seem to like that."

"Margo. Your daughter."

"Yes, Margo. So what are you working on now?"

"Why, you."

He had never mentioned any relative except his mother. He had certainly never referred to his cousins, the vast Caucasian Bertha and Eugene, the giant brown purveyor of rare books who would return chirping to the house to prepare something involving magret de canard in order to nourish the widow. And here was the widow, trying to fit too many clothes into too few cubic inches of luggage that, a couple of weeks ago, had accommodated everything.

Eleanor slept among the stacks of neatly folded undershorts and T-shirts and olive-green cargo pants and the socks she had bought him at Brooks Brothers. She had been frightened while she slept. She had awakened herself by calling out, had looked about the room and closed her eyes and gone to sleep again. Now her mouth was gummy and foul, her face felt greasy, her left hand hurt from clenching it. She showered but put on the same clothing she'd worn—khaki shorts, a wrinkled white camp shirt. She brushed her teeth and worked her hair into a ragged bun. She went barefoot into the kitchen, where she drank iced spring water while watching the sun hang huge and orange over the hills at the far edge of the grape vines cultivated by Monsieur and Madame Panifiette. The sun appeared not to move, though the insects chirred louder, she thought, and the bees worked harder now, and the hills began to go dark, almost as if they were a silhouette, even though the brilliant orange sun appeared to be directly over them. You would think it would light them up, she thought.

"Stand by, Eleanor," Eugene called. She heard the throbbing of the engine of their Saab, and then she heard the slamming of doors, the rustling of plastic sacks, and the panting of very fat people moving across the hot slate walk at the back of the house.

She and Sid had not slept together during the week before he died. They had agreed, though they'd said nothing aloud, to continue to sleep in the same bed, to kiss each other good morning and goodnight, to walk naked from the shower to their bedroom, to use the toilet without hesitation or shame, and to in every other way manifest their intimacy. The making love had stopped as though a mechanism had broken without any other symptoms. They had malfunctioned without a fight, only slightly acknowledging the increment of tension between them. Sid was making some progress with the book, his fourth, about a black detective of the upper middle class who solved crimes out of his affection for the victims, but never quite learned how to love the woman who, by the end of each book, loved him.

On the night of her learning about the breaking down, they lay in the dark in bed, he in pajama bottoms and she in sleeping shorts and a sleeveless, scoop-necked top, not touching, at the start of their sleeping this way every night.

"I keep wondering," she said. "I mean, about how, where you are— at the start of it—you could go off to France for a couple of months and work on a book that depends on being in New York, where your people are—"

"My *people*?"

"Now, you know what I mean. Your *characters*. You couldn't have meant—you didn't think that *I* meant anything about race."

"No, El, of course not."

"It doesn't sound like us," she said, "talking that way. I mean, making that kind of mistake about each other."

"No."

"We don't do that."

He shifted. He sighed. "We surely didn't used to," he said. He tee-tered on his side, and then rolled onto his back again. "We didn't. We mustn't." He turned toward her and kissed her upper arm, letting his teeth gently close on her flesh.

"You're trying to turn me on," she said.

"I am."

"So that—so that what, Sid?"

"So that you know."

"It's part of the argument, then?"

"We aren't having one."

"What are we having?"

"I don't know."

"A power struggle," she said.

"El, come on."

"Well, I'm not hard to get," she said.

"That's not what I meant."

"I don't know quite what you meant," she said. "But I do think we're a little old to be wasting our time on so much talk about what we aren't doing when what we *could* be doing is making each other happy."

He lay beside her, he didn't move, and the orange sun hung in the early nighttime sky.

"Except we aren't," she said. "Am I guessing it right? Happy, I mean. I mean, we're *not* happy." Here they were, she thought, two adults who functioned in terms of language carefully chosen, and it was as if neither spoke the other's native tongue. But the attitude of his body, his distance though he lay so close, his silence, now cut through the words they didn't or couldn't select. It's as simple as that, she thought. We are not. "What we've been doing, maybe," she said, "has been hoping. Maybe what we did was mostly hope."

"Mostly hope," he said. "Nothing ignoble in that."

"We tried."

He said, "We did our best."

"Oh, Sid," she said.

After a while, he said, "That's right. Oh."

And finally, she had returned his kiss, on the hard curve of the top of his shoulder, letting her lips come away slowly from his bronze-tan skin that always smelled to her like spices—and she thought of their names, although she never cooked with them and really didn't know one from the other: mace and cloves and nutmeg—because it seemed likely, she thought, before she turned over to face away from Sid and from the enormous, ragged sun, that they had just kissed goodbye.

Bertha and Eugene cooked, and they did their best to entertain her. They made drinks of Campari and soda over ice, and Eugene warbled bad renditions of tragic French arias while Bertha complained about the mysteries of the stove mechanisms.

"I am using dried cèpes," she told Eleanor, "along with chopped shallots and milk and no more than one-half a cup of heavy cream to make a kind of gateau of mushrooms. They're really called timbales. You know the term? After we combine over heat, we'll bake. You'll find it echoed in the heavy cream, the port, and the shallots of the woodland sauce that my husband, the fascist chef, is coercing together for what will, after all, be simply sautéed duck breasts. Are you hungry, dear?"

Eugene was gliding from the sink to the table to the stove, wiping at his sweaty forehead with a dish towel hung about his neck. The evening breezes came in over the grapes while the air of the kitchen took on the aroma of the reducing canned chicken stock he apologized for using. "We bought it at the hypermarché outside Langon," he said. "It's a travesty, of course, but there hasn't been time to make real stock. And we had better hope, by the way, that the co-fascist to my left"—and here Bertha actually performed a half a bow, her huge breasts falling against her dress—"knows that I require some of those cèpes for my sauce. And, darling," he said to her, "can you scoop me five tablespoons of butter?"

She said, "Eleanor, would you mind awfully grating some nutmeg?"

Eleanor said, "Why?"

Eugene stopped washing parsley at the sink. Bertha, panting as she sautéed mushroom strips and chopped cèpes, with a knife in one hand and a tub of butter in the other, paused, then turned to Eleanor, looked at her face, and said, "An unpleasant association?"

She almost spoke, but only shook her head.

"It's hardly necessary, dear," Bertha said.

Eugene danced, immense over his relatively narrow, small feet, toward the table where she sat. "I must make you another Campari-soda," he said.

"No," she said. "No, thank you."

"Some of the dinner wine? If you know me, then you know I brought enough. I have Chateau St.-Georges-Côte-Pavie, which is a St. Émilion from nearly up the road. It's supposed to be very fleshy and full of blackberries. It's breathing on the counter, let me pour you a glass."

"I can grate the nutmeg," she told him. "That's all right."

"And I can pour you a glass of wine," he said. "And *that's* all right."

She held her palm out and Bertha deposited the little tin grater with its small compartment that held the nuts. Eleanor leaned to sniff at the compartment. That was the smell of nutmeg. She said, "I wonder if you could excuse me?"

"Dear girl," Eugene said, "it's all too, somehow, celebratory, isn't it? We were afraid it might feel that way. Although one *could* celebrate Sidney. Perhaps one ought to, even. My brother's boy. And aren't genes *so* treacherous? Arthur, my brother, also died too young. And he was healthy. Anyway, he was slim. Broad at the chest, but slender all the same. He was a dancer for a couple of years, a professional chorus-boy hoofer in Philadelphia and New York. You'd have thought that one of us was adopted, my mother used to say, because we were made so differently. Of course, I happened to them twelve, nearly thirteen years after my poor mother thought she was done with bearing babies. Arthur believed I was this pick-me-up-off-the-street creature, but I wasn't. I was born to them, and we were brothers, the poor soul. We both of us adored Sidney. He was more like a brother to me than Arthur, now that you mention it, who was, if you'll forgive the psychology, a little bit more of a *father*, if you can believe it, as we got older. So maybe the meal's for him. But it's also for you, Eleanor, because Sidney loved you and you loved him. God bless you both."

Bertha said, "She's all done in, Eugene. She's exhausted. She should sleep. Eleanor," she said, "you must have a nap. At once. We can worry later about food. Do you hear?"

Bertha insisted on shepherding her from the kitchen table and past Eugene, who leaned to kiss the air beside her face, around the corner, and down the short corridor that separated her bedroom and Sid's from the room in which the cousins slept. She smelled the nutmeg, she believed. And she smelled Bertha's heated skin, and a floral talc, and the astringency of a deodorant. Bertha held a vast, round, heavy arm about Eleanor's shoulder and she murmured to her, making noises but not whole words, little cooing sounds of encouragement, as she saw her through the bedroom door. Inside the bedroom, as she lay on the bed beside the open French doors, Eleanor heard them moving across the tiled floor of the kitchen, heard the sputtering of sautéed food, the clatter of implements against crockery and pots, the thump of the oven door, the gurgle of liquids measured out. It all calmed her, and she let herself listen to the sounds of their cooking as, when she was a child, she heard, from her room, the noises made by her parents as they cleaned up in the kitchen at the end of a dinner party, her father's voice tired and grainy and deep, her mother's voice rich with satisfaction as she gossiped about her guests.

Eleanor woke to the sweet smell of grapes outside the bedroom, and the creamy, thick odor of the chalky soil in which they grew. Over those smells lay the dark richness of roasted vegetables and seared, sauced duck. She was lying on Sid's side of the bed, among his scattered clothes, closer to the open doors onto the fields, in the darkness of a cloudy sky lit coldly now by the pale, small moon. It would rain in the morning, she thought, and the day would be humid. Eugene and Bertha would be uncomfortable in high humidity, and they would soak through their traveling clothes. They would suffer, and so might she, she thought, but none of them would look up, like Sid, and then, like a lamp extinguished, go out.

She put on clogs and went into the kitchen, passing the closed door to the silent extra bedroom. A bottle half filled with the St.-Georges-Côte-Pavie glowed in the low light the cousins had left on. She tugged at the cork and poured some into a kitchen tumbler. In the refrigerator she found sliced duck wrapped in plastic, and she sat at the table and ate. The wine was fruity and rich, and the taste of the duck made her hungry for more. But when she thought of the smell of nutmeg, although she couldn't make out its taste in the duck, she removed the partly chewed meat from her mouth and threw it into the garbage pail under the sink. She took a swig of St. Émilion and spat it down into the drain.

Walking past the great pot of rosemary, and among lavender bushes, she slowly carried her wine down a row of grapevines. Something flew close to her head, but when she looked up she saw only the rows of cloud, like the serried layers of flesh on a fish, lit from above by the dim moon. She squatted, suddenly, and coughed, waiting to be sick. Nothing happened, though. It was as if they had eaten the corpse, she told herself, and she gagged again. But nothing more happened except a strangled cough, and she turned from what she thought of as her theatrics, sipped at the tumbler, and then walked the short distance back to the French doors of the bedroom, where she sat cross-legged on their bed and emptied her glass and thought of the sorry sweetness of their confession to each other that, at barely their beginning, they were failed.

A night bird at the far edge of the grapevines called, another answered, and then she heard Bertha's rich voice. It had made a kind of whinny in the bedroom across the corridor. She moved from the bed without thinking, and she crouched at her closed door. Breathing raggedly, shallowly, she pressed the empty glass to the door and her ear to the bottom of the glass. She heard the whining of what she knew were bedsprings in the extra room. She heard the shuffle and brush of bedclothes, and she heard their skin. They were probably running with sweat, she thought. They were naked and their bodies were wet and they were making love. She had never thought of them this way. She had considered them delicate of feeling, gentle of motive, bound inside themselves by their fat and the difficulty with which such large creatures moved, no matter how graceful they might appear. But now she heard them whisper with pleasure, she heard the smack of lolloping, floppy skin, the suction of their flesh as they moved together and apart and then together again.

Eugene said, low, "Oh, for God's sake, my *dearest* girl."

Bertha made a sound of pleasure at her wickedness.

"God," he said.

She thought of the hundreds of pounds of flesh that shifted and slid, of the way a mounded stomach was stuck by fluid and friction to the loose, damp canyon of a crotch. She was excited by what she heard, but she was also suddenly aware that what she ached with now was not the grief of this morning or of the days and nights before. It was envy, she thought. She didn't breathe out, and didn't breathe out. She knelt at her door, one hand closed on the knob and the other holding her eavesdropper's glass as she listened to the long silence in the room across the hall. Then one of the sweat-slicked, gargantuan lovers held by death at bay whispered words she couldn't distinguish. Then one of them shifted great weight, the guest bed groaned, and Eleanor began to breathe.

METAL FATIGUE

W HAT YOU MIGHT notice first is how dirty they are. It probably isn't from not bathing, though you have to wonder how they could have the energy to shower or wash their hair. I think that's what it was, with my daughter and the others. They all had the look, all over their skin, that you see on somebody's hair who doesn't shampoo. There was a dullness to them. They couldn't catch the light.

But coming there to see someone, you still can hope. There are doctors and nurses. There are dirty pink walls and almost-wheat-colored linoleum floors and ash furniture with yellow plastic cushions. There are closed-circuit television cameras in the corners of rooms where pink wall meets bright white ceiling. There is someone in a security office dressed in jeans and a Gold's Gym T-shirt who oversees the little screens of the monitors and supervises as many of the patients as he can. There are bedrooms without interior door locks that can be sealed from the outside and there are several sets of steel doors on each floor that open only with a staff member's card. There is a gray-carpeted room with dark gray chairs and sofas on the street level, inside the locked glass doors, where family members sit until the ward doctor or nurse or psychiatric social worker sends word that they should ride the elevator up. So you can wait there or go up or sit in the ward cafeteria or the television room with its chained cigarette lighter and ceramic red ash-tray and the laugh track of the rerun that seems always to be on and, if you want to, you can hope.

Linda and I sat at one of the cafeteria tables and watched a small young woman with matte-finish dark blonde hair writing with a foun-tain pen in a leatherbound journal. She bent close to the pages and wrote very slowly, pausing to look up, sometimes at us and sometimes at the other patients with their visitors, then leaning to the journal again.

"She's playing tic-tac-toe," Linda said. "Over and over. X and then O, X and then O."

"No," I said.

"Oh, yes. What—you think we're in here because we very sanely write in our journal all day? 'Dear Journal: Today, I took my meds on time. I didn't spit out the mood enhancer or the antipsychotic. Not once did I try to gnaw through the vein in my wrist with my unbrushed teeth.' Dad, we're nuts. Remember?"

"You're tired. You aren't nuts. God, Linda. If you're nuts, we're all nuts."

"And is that a consolation? No, I mean it was nice of you to tell me. What I'm saying is I can't remember whether I feel good because of it or not."

I got hold of both her hands, which were clasped in front of her, and covered them with mine. The backs of her hands were cold and a little damp. The skin of her face was very dry, and it looked as if she'd been standing in strong winds for days. She was wearing fleece-lined moccasins from which the staff had unlaced the rawhide cords so she couldn't use them to hang herself. They flopped when she walked, but at least she couldn't commit suicide with her shoes.

"What's so funny, Dad? What's the joke?" She pulled her hands away.

I shook my head. "I think I'm getting a little strange, myself," I said.

"They did wonder if it was genetic, the depression."

"Do you think it is?"

"Mom never tried to kill herself and neither did you, right?"

"Well," I said, "no."

She smiled a great, toothy, unfunny smile and said, "Well, there's *time*, you know? There's still time for both of you. Be patient." She furrowed at the skin under her thumbnail. "Mom couldn't handle coming today?"

"She's with Max and Allison, sweetheart."

The wit that made her look lively went out. Her skin looked only wind-scoured again, and sore. Her eyes were as dull as her hair. "The kids are fine," she said. "Yes? The children are fine? They're fine."

"They are. They like it that we're staying with them. They aren't frightened."

"What do they believe?"

"I'm not sure. We told them you were in the hospital and you'd be home in a while."

"Not soon?" she asked. "Not 'imminently'? Well, you wouldn't say 'imminently' to a kid, would you? You would say 'soon,' I think. *I* would. I'd say 'soon.' Could you have told them 'soon,' but remember it as 'in a while'?"

"Yes. Absolutely."

"So you did say 'soon.' 'Mommy will be home soon,' you said."

"Yes."

"Even though you told *me* 'in a while,' you told my children I'd be coming home 'soon.'"

"Yes. Yes, I did."

"And what'd they say back?"

"When I told them 'soon'?"

"Yes. 'Mommy's coming home soon.'"

"Max nodded, you know, like a judge granting a motion. Allison looked at me, squinched her eyes together, and then she smiled."

"Yes," Linda said. "Good. Good." She got hold of soft flesh under her thumbnail and worked it up and out. She put her thumb in her mouth as if it stung, then said something around it.

"I couldn't hear you, Lin."

"I said I was glad to be getting out of here soon. These people are all nuts. Whereas I," she said, "am only tired. Ask my dad. And what should I know about Matthew?"

"He calls and talks to the kids."

"Do they cry afterwards?"

"No. It's always a very short call, and I think he keeps it light. They seem fine with it."

"Do they ask when *he's* coming home?"

"Not so far."

"You're lying, Dad. Lie, lie, lie. You're telling me what you think I should hear. You know, I didn't get terminally stupid to get myself locked away in here. I got crazy is all. I'm still smart enough to tell when you lie to me about the children, et cetera."

"You're not locked away, Lin. You admitted yourself—you know: you asked them to let you in. You wanted to be safe. You wanted to feel better. Nobody's locking you in here."

"Every door you go inside of, *they* can lock. It's up to *them*."

"That's the paradox of psychiatric hospitals, I guess. People volunteer so they can feel safe. I imagine—"

"What is it that you imagine about me and my overdose and my children and my husband who left me and them and us and everybody else except some *guy*—"

"Oh, Lin, the guy couldn't help it. Matthew couldn't help it. He didn't know who he was when you got married."

"He knew. People know. They're all too goddamned glad to tell you how they always knew and always felt and always wondered and always hoped. And then they met the guy, who was always knowing and feeling and whatevering and praying to meet my absolutely heterosexual husband and *convert* him." She stopped and looked at me the way you would make an apologetic face to a stranger and ask if they knew the time. "Am I making any sense, Dad? Am I being logical?" She smiled a smile I knew from her childhood. "Did I just say it *was* Matthew's fault or it wasn't? I can't remember. Was it he knew or he didn't and the guy converted him? I mean, I know I'm making sense about possibly not making sense, but I'm not sure, at this juncture, whether Matthew volunteered to leave his wife and children and room and board and the meal plan plus activities fee, or whether he had this *attack* of not-heterosexual that kind of set fire to existence. At least as we know that we know it."

She set her face close to the thumb tissue she was tearing. Two lunch tables over, the sad girl with dull blonde hair was leaning over her journal. A smiling man in aqua pajama bottoms, T-shirt, double-breasted blue suit coat, and aquamarine hospital slip-ons came into the room adjusting his dark blue beret. What had looked like a moustache seemed, as he passed our table, to be a double line of scab from deep cuts. Across the room, a very fat woman in a bright red bathrobe was using a hole puncher on the pages of a glossy magazine.

When she saw me watching, she waved. "Don't worry," she called, "I know to clean up after myself. I'm responsible."

I waved back. Linda watched me. I shrugged at her. She said, "You didn't answer."

I almost muffled my sigh. I said, "To tell you the truth, Lin, I can't remember the question."

"Right," she said. "Me, too. It's the meds. They try and keep you stupid with pills here. It makes you more tractable. Was I a tractable child? Do you think I was a tractable wife?"

"I'm sure you were a fine wife."

"And the other category I mentioned?"

"You were my beloved child. You still are."

"Do you think I'd try and kill you, Dad?"

"No."

"Do you think a child would ever try and kill her parents? His parents? You know: general, all-inclusive whoever the parents are the parents of? Do you think *they'd* try?"

My throat closed down and I shook my head.

She said, "Depressives or women whose husbands get converted to gay will often get very, very down on the anniversary of something bad that happened to them. You probably knew that."

"No," I said, "I didn't. But it makes sense."

"Oh, it all makes sense," she said, "if you renounce the logic you're used to and accept either the word of your doctor or the policemen who took you away."

"No one took you away, sweetheart. Remember? I came here with you."

"And who's to say you aren't the cop?"

"Oh."

"'Oh,'" she said, in a deep tone. Then, in her own voice, she said, "Now, what could have happened five years ago to the day I was arrested and locked up?"

"You weren't arrested, sweetheart."

"No. All right. If not five years, then maybe three. Maybe it was only the one-year anniversary of the event. Who's to say? Except your doctor or the cops. But in either case, what was it the anniversary of that flipped me out and I drank all that horrible whiskey—what was it, Dad?"

"Lagavulin."

"Matthew's favorite Scotch. Plus Ambien plus Darvocet plus precious, pure, and dependable Bayer baby aspirin. Puke City, huh? So: what was the question? Ah! Anniversaries. Well, the group and I have been pondering the matter. Did you know that it turns out I *like* group? I bore the asses off of them all, but I talk and talk and talk. And they're so crazy, they'll join in about anything after a while. So they pondered my pondering. And they decided it's you, Dad."

All I could say was, "Me?"

She gave me the toothy, unfelt grin. "I predicted you'd say that. Well, to be fair, I thought you'd say, 'Who? Me?' But that was close enough."

"Linda," I said, "me?"

The man with the beret and the suit coat was bleeding from the upper lip and it had dripped onto his T-shirt and the table he leaned over. A tall, fat nurse in a pink uniform held a little green towel to his face and helped him to stand. She led him out of the room. "Don't you be dripping blood all over *me*," she told him.

Linda came around the table. She sat on the chair beside mine. I could smell her sweat and something salty and sweet at once. I was so tired, then, that I almost put my head on her shoulder. "Dad," she said. "Daddy."

"Sweetheart," I said.

"You looked so bewildered."

I nodded.

"I am, too," she said.

"I know."

"You do know."

"I think I do, Lin. Matthew, and the children, and plain damned fatigue. It tears the wings off airplanes, you know. Metal stress fatigue. The plane looks fine and unless you examine it very, very closely, and often they don't, it takes off and then a piece of the wing tears away."

"The plane comes down," she said.

"Yes."

"And everyone on board is killed."

I didn't answer.

"And they reassemble all the little pieces they collected on the floor of some huge airplane hangar in Queens or Texas. They put it back together."

"But not to fly it. Just to know."

"Like here," she said.

"No. Here they help you get back up in the air."

She leaned in close. Her breath had something like iodine on it, and the phlegm you smell on a sick, small child. "I don't want to fly anymore," she said.

"Sweetheart, they're going to help you do whatever you want."

"Can I still be married to Matthew? And he'll love me," she said.
I said, "I don't know."

"That's not what you told your father."

"What about my father?"

"You know. Shh." She looked behind her, at the girl with the journal. She looked across the table toward the woman with the hole puncher, and the others, at farther tables with their visitors. She whispered, "When they cut off his leg."

"That was diabetes, Lin. It was very bad, and he was old by then. His heart was in awful shape."

She sat back. "And he asked you to help him."

"Yes, he did."

"And you said you thought he should die. He told me," she said in very reasonable tones. "I know about it."

"It was the night before the procedure—the amputation. He was very frightened, very upset. He hadn't much hope. He told me he had already discussed it with his doctor. He'd told his doctor he didn't think he wanted to live like that anymore. 'Like this,' he told me, and he pointed at the leg they were going to take. It caused him terrible pain. He was in pain all the time that we talked. And he had angina very badly, his heart was pretty much shot. He told me his doctor said, 'All you have to do is stop taking the medication. I'll write it up as heart failure.' And he looked at me, Lin."

She said, "Like this?" She stared with a cowlike innocence, and she looked silly. I shook my head. "Then like this?" She looked pointedly at me, just as my father had. I looked away. "Got you," she said.

"So I told him I would help."

"Help what?"

"Help take the medicines away, or pour them out into the sink, or whatever he wanted. I really didn't have much of an idea. I just thought he was asking me for help, and I wanted him to know I would give it. Even if it meant I'd go to jail."

"They'd have put you in jail?"

"If somebody wanted to accuse me of euthanasia, yes. It's murder, or manslaughter, or something terrible. It means years and years in jail."

"I am not staying here for years and years."

"No. But you aren't in jail, Lin. You're in a hospital and you're getting out soon to be with Max and Allison. You never told me you talked to my father about this."

"After they cut off his leg and he didn't stop taking his medicine. When he was alive until he died of old age." Then her face was alight again, and she said, "But maybe he didn't. Maybe he finally died of *you*."

"We never talked about it again. I thought he'd forgotten."

"Yes, but how can anybody really know you didn't talk about it again and then what if you *did* it, Dad? You see?"

"Well, because I didn't do it and he didn't do it and he lived for several more months, almost a year."

"Except he told me."

"Told you what, Lin?"

"He said, 'Harold wants me to die. Harold told me to stop taking my pills. My son Harold said he wants me to die.'"

"No."

"He did. He told me. I was there with him and the nurse went out and he told me. I was his only grandchild, remember. He and I always talked."

"Yes. He loved you plenty. But he couldn't have said I wanted to kill him."

"Wanted him to die, he said."

"Yes. But I mean *no*, Lin. God. Sweetheart, once a person hears something like that about himself and somebody dead, he can't fix it. I can't fix that anymore."

"Well, you heard it, Dad. So I guess it's broken now because that's what he said. And every time you think about Grandpa, you'll think about him telling me how you wanted him to die. Maybe you weren't clear when you and he had that conversation."

"No," I said, "maybe I didn't make myself clear."

The girl with the journal walked past us, reading her pages. She said, "Bye."

"Bye-bye," I said. "Good luck."

"I guess maybe you wish I didn't tell you about it," Linda said.

"You told your group therapy session about it."

"Oh, sure. We were wondering if it was the anniversary thing that could have flipped me out. Only, I couldn't remember when Grandpa died. Whenever it was you did or didn't kill him."

"So why did you think it might have been some kind of anniversary, since you had no idea when it happened?"

She leaned in closer, until her shoulder fitted under my arm. She pushed up with her shoulder and I put my arm around her and hugged. "It's a simple enough mistake to make," she said. "Don't you think?"

"About me wanting to kill my father."

"Right."

"Right," I said. "But it wasn't an anniversary."

"Good," she said. "It would have been easier, if we could have blamed it on that. But good anyway."

"Good," I said. I looked at the hole puncher punching and the little scattering of glossy dots that lay across the woman's table. She waved and nodded, and I waved back. I said, "I really think it was fatigue, Lin."

"You're saying my wings got tired."

"It's hard, staying up in the air."

"Sometimes you have to come down," she said. She said, "Okay." She sat against me and then moved off to sit in a different chair at our table. She said, "Okay."

"Yes," I said.

"Buy Allison something pretty, Dad. Would you do that? I don't know what. Just so it comes from me."

"Yes," I said, "I'll find something."

"And get Max something about ball. Any kind of ball. If it rolls or bounces, he wants to do it."

"He's a bouncer," I said.

She yawned and shivered. "It's late out, isn't it?"

"Probably it feels like that," I said, "because you're tired."

She closed her eyes and I remembered reading bedtime stories to her. Suddenly, her lids went up. She caught me looking. She said hoarsely, "We'll find out for sure."

"Find out what, Lin?"

"If you're the one who goes to hospitals and visits people, then they die."

"No," I said, "I'm not."

"Well, we'll see," she said.

PATROLS

H E KEPT HIS EYES closed because if he opened them he would see Murphy's mad, bright stare. Since Marty Mason had been there, the bunchy, gleaming black dog had left his owner's bedroom late each night to patrol the hallway outside the guest room and then the room itself, his claws ticking on the wooden floors while he investigated corners and spaces under furniture, his snuffling inspection punctuated by soft panting, as if he breathed in whispered tones on account of the hour. Then he would settle beside Mason's bed and, head erect or laid on top of his extended paws, he would watch. He was ready, Mason knew, to slap his tail concussively against the bedroom floor if his owner's guest should meet his devoted glare. Closing the guest bedroom door meant only that Murphy would scratch for admittance, whining softly until Mason opened the door so that the dog could check the room, then settle down to watch the guest.

After tonight's long period of stillness, Mason lay between waking and sleep. He'd begun to think of himself as buoyed, like kelp or driftwood or a boat of shallow draft, on top of the waters of the cove. Now, at dawn, the radios of the lobster boats broke the rhythmic night noises—the regular panting of the dog interrupted by its small, strangled squirts of body gas, the rising tide and the slap of ocean on stone, the winds off the sea washing hard against the house—that had carried him out of nighttime and into the day.

He wasn't surprised that he thought he could feel the greasy grit of sand on his fingertips and in the corners of his eyes, over his teeth. He wanted to get to the bathroom and drink from the tap to wash his sandy mouth out, but the dog farted and winked in the brightening room, so he played dead. He thought, of course, about the dead Marines and the dead hajis, as the live Marines called them, and the one Iranian, a bearded man in Western clothes, driving north and west over the Iranian border in a white Toyota long-bed truck into Checkpoint Eight One, established and commanded by Captain Jerome Goldsworthy with whose Alpha Platoon, five light armored reconnaissance vehicles, Mason traveled as journalistic baggage because Major Harvey Fathers, commanding Fox Company, had told Goldsworthy to carry him along for the sake of public relations.

Captain Goldsworthy was a slight, slender man who struck Mason as being made entirely of hard leather. His South Carolina accent was musical, Mason wrote in his notes, and he never raised his voice, even if he swore with conviction. He never chided Mason or complained about having him in tow. In fact, he never addressed him. He referred to Mason exclusively as *he* or *him*, as when, standing before Mason, looking sourly at his Orvis-catalogue traveler's vest and L. L. Bean khakis, he told one of the rifleman scouts to make certain *he* knew how to fasten the rear scout compartment hatches of the captain's vehicle when they needed to swing the turret cannon to the rear. Mason rode in that small scout compartment with three Marine infantry, sweating and sucking warm water from plastic bottles and banging against the walls. "Make sure *he* stays inside the pig until you know for certain we're in a safe environment," the captain told his scouts.

Now, before dawn, at Checkpoint Eight One, Goldsworthy had opened his turret hatch and positioned the vehicles, establishing his firing lanes. Mason heard the hatch go up forward of the turret just after a short, thick PFC, William Pontelecorvo, from Rahway, New Jersey, had pushed their hatches, behind the turret, up and out. About a half an hour later, they heard the driver of the truck gear down, either because he meant to, or to feign stopping. It was apparently a feint, because he began to go up through the gears, gathering speed, and they pinned him with the lights.

The captain said, "This is irksome."

Mason heard the driver say, "Sir."

In his soft, low voice, the captain said, "There's a cure for irksome." He said, "Button the forward hatch." He said, "Gunner. Battle sight. Truck in the open."

The gunner called back, "Identified."

Pontelecorvo said, "He armed with the HE."

The captain gently said, "Fire."

"On the way, sir," the gunner said.

The 25mm turret cannon fired three times. Mason was deafened at once. Pontelecorvo must have been right about the high explosive shells, Mason thought, because although their hatches faced away from the action, he saw the air of the nighttime desert go whiter than their lights had made it, and then he saw bright fragments, blown vertically, raining down around them. He heard voices as if from a distance, and he couldn't hear the fragments strike the ground. When Pontelecorvo permitted him to leave the vehicle, Mason stood with some of the platoon a few dozen yards from the burning truck. The Marines edged closer, he noted, and then closer, as if to prove that they were unafraid of secondary explosions. Then they moved even closer, flinching from the heat but needing the risk, and he joined them because he was afraid to stay behind and seem to be afraid. What was left of the driver lay partway between the truck and the Marines: some beard on some of the cooked face with one wide eye in it, strips of burned gristle, a section of clean, white rib cage, the halved corpse sprinkled with powdered windshield glass that caught their lights and reminded Mason—he faced away from the Marines to write it shakily in his notebook—of ice droplets in the air on a very cold night in St. Paul.

As he thought of the roasted, torn face and its eye, Mason thought of Murphy's ecstatic glare. He remembered the sand in their mouths, and how the night winds carried grit to them as it filled the hairy nostrils of what was left of the driver. Mason raised his fingers to rub at his gums, as if he were still there, watching the corpse's nose fill up. The dog slammed his tail and Mason set his arms down, trying to breathe like someone asleep.

The lobster boats were coming in, some with small outboard motors and some on throbbing, big diesels. He had seen them over the last several days as they drove at a buoy, the lobsterman somehow knowing, out of all those hundreds of bright, bobbing markers, which were his. Then, alongside, he cut his engine and while the boat wallowed on the tide he hauled his trap by hand or by machine, withdrew a lobster if he found one, baited with the chum that drew the prowling gulls to circle the boats, dropped the trap overboard, and took off full-bore for the next nearby buoy. Some of the boats broadcast ship-to-shore CB chatter, while most of them played country music on their radios, nasal complaints about death and passion and diminished prospects.

The cooperatives made money by shipping the lobsters downstate to the resort restaurants and into Boston and New York. The lobstermen, after they bought fuel and paid for repairs, made little profit, he imagined. And he suspected that it was all they knew to do. He wondered if they depended on federal food subsidies during the winter if they couldn't find work repairing vacation houses or salting roads for the highway department. He wondered how many silent, angry children, how many battered wives, that life produced. He wanted Ada Shields, his editor, to tell him about this coast, about saltwater fogs and who ran the lighthouses and how you knew which pound to buy the lobsters from and what the lobstermen's families ate—frozen Salisbury steak, he'd have bet, and artificial gravy on packaged mashed potatoes, all of it washed down with pop poured from plastic two-liter jugs. He knew himself to be a freelance hack with a need to dodge steady work and the habit of asking questions in order to deflect attention from himself.

Ada's purpose, which he was coming to regret, was to prod him into studying the self he had tried to omit from what, together, they were working on. She had inherited the house from her parents, and it was where she hid out, she said. According to her assistant, Mason ought to be flattered to be invited for a working week. He knew, as he played dead for Ada's ardent dog, that he wanted their conversations to be local and not about his time with Alpha Platoon because then, he thought, he might not lie under the winking stare of Murphy, unable to sleep because he was selling out, as if by the pound, the Marines live and dead with whom he had patrolled the southeastern deserts of Iraq in order to compile the book he'd once believed it was important to write.

It had begun well enough. The first chapter opened with a character called Mason, who was mostly not him—a vehicle, as he thought, for conveying the strategies of the old men who made this war, and the courage of the young ones taking fire for them—who was on his way, after his time over there, back to the States. This Mason sat in a dark, icy Frankfurt bar, drinking too much and therefore talking too much to Leon Rosenthal, an Israeli businessman who was, of course, not in business. Mason didn't know whether he was a civilian, but he was certainly in some aspect of intelligence. It could have been as high-powered as vetting for assassinations—he was that secret, and that rock-hard confident—or he might have conducted random harvests of raw data from big-mouthed sources, Mason thought, like himself. Rosenthal was a small, muscular man with gold-rimmed glasses that rode over big, dark, angry eyes under a high forehead. He wore a blue blazer with three horn buttons that he kept fastened over an open-necked shirt. He sat straight on his barstool as if a child at school. Mason had recited some of his adventures although he was embarrassed, even as he spoke, because he believed that the little man knew more than enough about wars on his own. In the book, uncleverly exchanging one brand of dinnerware for another, he called the little man Spode.

Mason was telling about Captain Goldsworthy's outrage when his orders were reversed. In Badra, Major Harvey Fathers had spent a night organizing checkpoints and patrols and Captain Goldsworthy and his Alpha Platoon had run Checkpoint Eight One, Mason in the compartment of the pig, feeling like a child in grown-ups' clothing under the heavy flak jacket and the oversized, chin-strapped battle helmet. At 0400 they had killed the driver and blown up his truck. The captain had reported the kill, and Major Fathers had instructed them to patrol to the north for two hours at a leisurely pace, then descend at high speed back to the Eight One checkpoint and see if their departure had lulled some bombers, posing as religious pilgrims, into trying to cross over.

At 0530 new signals came in from the major. Division had instructed Battalion to instruct Fox that priorities were reversed. Standing outside their vehicles they listened to Captain Goldsworthy say, "The situation is now officially a clusterfuck. You will *not* be looking to capture or kill. We *will* interrogate all incoming personnel. Those that we have no choice except to deem true pilgrims, we will respect their faith and permit them to cross over from Iran"—he said it *Eye*-ran—"in the hope that the message will go out that U.S. guys are good guys. We will permit the pilgrims to find whatever it is they are looking for. Salvation, I believe. Salvation is all right, and they are welcome to try and find it. You will not fire unless you are fired upon or deem yourselves in peril. In which case, you will kill with efficiency. You will try to check with me on any peril factor. But you will stay smart and therefore *live* Marines. And *he* fucking well had better not be putting any salty language in my mouth when he writes his tale of Alpha's derring-do."

At that point, watched by the platoon, Mason stowed his notebook away. The captain consulted his own notebook and then he pulled down on the hem of his flak jacket as Mason had seen him do a couple of dozen times a day. He made himself remember the gesture to record when he could.

"All right," the captain said. "We will carry out the mission. No questions? No answers? Let's get back to the goat rodeo."

Rosenthal, now named Spode, said, "My friend, you enjoy the colorful captain, and he is doubtless a brave man and a bold leader. Goat rodeo: colorful American vernacular. With the occasional fucking this or that. Of course: American. But what you *should* be remembering is the real importance of that particular moment. In two or three years from now, and probably less, you will think of the goats and the fucking and our chance encounter, yours and mine." He poured more Pilsner. "You will know, because I am lecturing you about it, that the captain's address marks the moment when the cancer cells began to grow. And not only inside of the goats. This is the gospel according to Rosenthal, commercial traveler, you ran into him in the Getrunken Pferdchen saloon in Frankfurt in the benign, well-ordered German republic. You'll remember, yes? That they brought the money in, those so-called pilgrims your patrols suddenly permitted to cross. They purchased the information and assistance and of course the weapons that will punch the bloody holes in your soldiers, who will be pinned in place in Iraq, dead Hussein or live Hussein, for a decade. This is minimum, I'm talking about. Boys will grow up expecting that part of their young manhood must be wasted in Iraq. They will become sullen and probably brutal, like our children serving in Palestine in what is finally an occupation, not a war. Those pilgrims from Iran who your President forgot to fight, they assembled the resistance cells, they organized the terrorists. And Iran"—he made a show of pulling back his sleeve to check his watch—"Iran as of this moment has won your little off-the-cuff war."

Thinking of the bottles of Czech beer they drank, and of all the water that Alpha Platoon consumed under orders to hydrate themselves, Mason knew that he would have to dare the dog and get to the bathroom.

"Murphy," he said, "I give up."

The dog's tail banged on the bedroom floor as if a dedicated child were slamming a hunk of hawser rope down, again and again.

The house remained silent. Murphy banged another volley, and Ada, from her upstairs bedroom, called, "Oh, Murphy, you goofy boy." The squat Labrador froze and then, with his nails scrabbling on the slippery floor, he ran out of the bedroom, past the bathroom down the hall, and then up the steps as Mason walked into the shower. He turned his face to receive the warm water in his open mouth. After the early days with Alpha of Fox, when matériel convoys bypassed them in order to get to Baghdad and north of it and there wasn't enough water for showers, when the heat swung between 125 and 135 Fahrenheit, he had vowed never to be ungrateful for water, whether it came in the form of ocean, thunderstorm, or droplets from a leaky pipe. He still felt the grit that had caked the inside of his lips and that sat on his teeth no matter how often he drank to rinse it off.

He had forced himself to make entries in his journal as Alpha fought, patrolled, and bounced between contradictory directives from Battalion. He'd written paragraphs to later be stitched onto what narratives he could generate on his word processor. And he had managed to file several stories, one dictated over a military phone in Badra to an intern at the magazine who patted his every word into a word processor, making him feel as important as one of the real war correspondents. This was the material that he and Ada Shields were turning into a book, she assured him. "It's all here," she said several times a day. "You wrote it. This is just one of those wine racks or bookcases or children's toys you order from a catalogue. 'Some Assembly Required'? I'm the Some-Assembly person. Though I do not know boo about the children's toys part of it."

She was taller than he, very slender, very pale, a little stoop-shouldered, and long of arm and leg. She wore scuffed brown penny loafers over bare feet and usually denim shorts and a work shirt. Twenty times a day, for three days, she had opened the barrette that held her thick, dark hair behind her neck and gathered handfuls to fasten again. The intimacy—the bareness of the back of her bent neck, the opportunity to stare at her unseen because she closed her eyes to fix her hair—had compelled him and embarrassed him. And he had wakened this morning to think not only of the heat, the sand, the eye of the torn, burnt truck driver, and the lunatic eyes of the dog, but also of the tall, slouching editor who read herself to sleep at night by going over what he had said to himself in the intimacies of fright, discomfort, and even despair during six weeks of Operation Enduring Freedom.

They sat now in her breakfast room in the old house that smelled of mildew and salt and resin. A few lobstermen worked their traps farther out, but the gulls had given up on them, stalking instead the broad, flat granite sheets between the back of the house and the sea, while crows made the noises of argument in the evergreens around them. Mason had heard a half of the phone call while he was drying himself after his shower. He hadn't been able to discern her words, but he had listened to her tones, which began sulkily enough and quickly declined into bitter single syllables.

While they chewed English muffins in silence, Ada stood to bring more coffee to the table and, pouring, announced, "I believe that I am starting to smoke again. Would you like to file any objections?"

"It sounds like you'd slug me if I did."

"I might."

"No, then, I think. No objections."

"No, tell me straight. Never mind, don't bother. I know it's stupid and suicidal and obnoxious. But I mean, *aside* from the usual arguments."

"Strikes me as a terrific plan."

"I'll stop again. You aren't, I don't know, allergic to it or something?"

"Just to the cancer part."

She said, "Well, I'll stop again. Before you leave, I'll stop smoking."

"Is it time for me to go?"

"Is this a tolerable process for you? Doing the work like this?"

He nodded.

"It is not time for you to go. We almost have the shape. Structure is the concern for us, because you know how to tell stories. It's—it's like your dead Iranian. He's all over the book. It's like the book's his body. He's all blown up, so how would you put him back together? Same for us with the book. We're reassembling a body of experience. It's going to be different from what happened outside you, in the desert and while they were driving all over, but we have to find the shape it took *inside*. What your memories made it, what your emotions—well, you understand. You know what we're doing. And you know we aren't done."

"You paid me a pretty good penny," he said.

"One hell of a lot more than a penny."

"It doesn't seem entirely fair that I get the more-than-a-penny, and you still have to do all this work."

"That's what I do," she said. "I buy broken, and I fix."

"But meanwhile," he said, "I can't help noticing you've got stuff going on. . . ."

"Stuff."

"Stuff in your life. Private stuff." She left the table to open and close drawers in the pantry. Then she was back, sitting opposite him, looking unhappily at him over the cigarette she lit, sighing. He waited, as if he were the one who drew in the smoke. "It makes you sad," he said. "It makes you smoke."

"Thank you," she said, "but don't worry. The private stuff is just one more—what did your Marine Corps rifleman call it? 'One more shit storm in paradise'?"

Murphy took the half of buttered English muffin she handed down to him, and he fastened his thick black muzzle carefully around it, as if the muffin were alive, and then he carried it off to the doorway of the breakfast room with his head up. He lay and licked it, watching them, then closed his mouth around it, raised his head, and worked at the bread while butter and crumbs leaked down from his leathery lips.

"So I should mind my own business," Mason said.

"I appreciate the attentiveness," she said. "You're a man who has feelings. That's a nice part of the book—your honesty about being afraid, your sweetness about the younger men in combat, and the children you observed in the villages. And—listen. Listen, this is just the killing each other part you're overhearing when I'm on the phone. It's natural, it's part of the cycle, and when you go looking to be happy, if that's what this is about, then you have to do it. There's the smiling part—first shy, then plain damned glad, then the way people smile right after they finish sexing each other tired. There's the happy habit part—you know, how you get to understand each other's arriving early or arriving late, ordering drinks for each other because you know what the other one likes, all of that. Then there's the no longer working smoothly part, and that runs into the let's just shoot each other part. I more or less happen to be in that particular aspect of the human misery sometimes called a relationship. I've been there before. As a matter of fact, it's one of my specialties. Look," she said, "I'm already chain-smoking. See how fast it all comes back? So could you tell me what that was about the Spanish Gate?"

The dog banged his tail against the floorboards and made a sound that was half growl and half yap. Mason knew by now that it signaled his desire to go outside. Ada went to the back porch door and held it for him. She stood at the door, her cigarette in her mouth, while she bent, blinking her eyes against the smoke, and loosened her barrette to gather her hair and fasten it again. Then she held the cigarette and looked out through the screen.

"Do you remember?" she asked.

"Where did that come from?"

"One of your notebooks. Some day in September, October. Just before you went over to Kuwait to join up with the Marines. I could find it. You wrote something about mussels in white wine with brown bread."

"Oh," he said. "I did? I don't remember doing that. But it has to be about Galway, and this little restaurant near the Spanish Gate. We were—I was—there was somebody with me, and we were drinking a lot of white wine and eating mussels, and these thick slices of coarse brown bread. We got pretty drunk, as a matter of fact, and very fast."

"So it wasn't just the wine that did it," Ada said, sitting again now that Murphy had returned.

"It wasn't, no. I was with a friend, as I said."

"A man or a woman? Can I ask? Has to be a woman."

"Woman, yes," he said. "Her name is Marianne Neal. We were in the smiling part of it, according to your breakdown."

"Excellent word," she said, "breakdown."

"I was thinking that something terrific might possibly happen. And of course, a few days later it did. Just, it was terrifically unhappy. We were drinking and eating, we'd just come from some antiquarian fair in a great hall someplace in the city. Terrific city, Galway. Being there made me happy. I'd bought a brass jam pot for her that she thought was beautiful. Marianne's a poet," he said.

"Oh, now, never even approach the outskirts of a poet," Ada said. "Didn't you know that by then in your life? They *love* pain. For you if it can't be helped, but for *them* if they have any say in it. They specialize in the five stages of misery. First, get some love going. Second, find a way to want to kill yourself because of it. Third, polish it and polish it. Fourth, insert it in a vital organ. Anyone else gets snuffed, it's a shame. If the poet, however—this is Number Five—if the poet manages to sustain a dreadful, agonizing, not quite totally fatal wound, then there you have it: a long cycle of poems at the least, and quite possibly a book of them. Never go *near* a poet. Of course, you know that now, don't you?"

They went to work. Each of them took notes, and Ada managed the papers, arranging pages and renumbering them. She indicated with glued memorandum slips where he would have to provide new material or insert old. She asked him, over and over, to tell her the meaning of what he had thought were clear, simple sentences. It was a history of unworthiness, he believed, the story of a man without courage who traveled with young men and their officers who went only toward trouble, whereas he constantly wanted to run away.

"I was always making believe," he told Ada during their lunch break. They ate chicken salad sandwiches and drank rosé under the steady stare of Murphy, whose panting, Mason found, established the rhythm to which he chewed. "I was scared. I was ashamed of being so scared. I made noises like somebody who hadn't ever *heard* of being scared. I kept wishing they would just, goddamn it, turn *around*, go back."

"You suggest it plenty," she said, "but maybe you want to talk about it directly. Give examples—what they did automatically, compared to what you wanted to do or would have done if nobody else was watching. Fear's a great topic. Everybody wants to hear about it. You know: how to fail."

"I'm waiting for you to give me the eleven stages of fearfulness. You have this wonderful habit—"

"Yeah. I know. I break everything down into sequences. I could number the stages of bleeding to death while I was bleeding to death. I'm a comedienne, of course, right?" She drank off her rosé and licked her lips. "Pure amateur."

He said, around the chicken salad, "I find it a little exciting, to tell you the truth."

She moved her head slowly while elongating her neck, and it was as if she were peering down at him from a significant height. "Why would that be?"

"I've always wished I could be chipper and bitter and tough like that, maybe. I don't know. It attracts me."

"I attract you?"

"Yes. It does, and you do."

She nibbled at a piece of chicken protruding from the edge of her sandwich. She poured them more wine. She shook her head. "Well," she said. "And I'm sitting here, telling you how compelling I find your being so scared. Aren't we just a meant-to-be couple? As in, who needs sex when you can have failure?"

He thought that if he said something about sex *and* failure, they might end up in bed. But he was afraid to talk about failure and sex, because then—he was certain—the sex would fail. He wished he could tell her, because it would be a fine joke about his fear, which she seemed to find so valuable.

"Well, well," she said, feeding a piece of sandwich to the dog. She learned back, removed the barrette, leaned forward to gather her hair, then fastened the clip again. Mason pretended not to watch. "I'm running errands, in town," she said, "mail, and dental floss at the IGA. You take a nap so we can do a session of work before low tide. All right?"

"Why low tide?"

"Because of your pleasure in mussels," she told him. Then she and Murphy left.

Obediently, he took off his shoes and socks, he opened his bedroom window, and he lay under the powerful light off the sea and the winds that waxed and waned as if they were a tide. He sensed a giant shadow passing, but opened his eyes to see nothing except fir trees and the ocean off the rocks below the house. He wondered if a condor or an eagle had flown over. After a while, when he'd closed his eyes again, he saw different structures of rock and in different colors. He knew at once: the strand off the bay in County Sligo. He and Marianne Neal were walking on the coarse tan sand after their time in Galway, where they'd seemed to him so easy with each other. Outside of Sligo town, in Marianne's little stucco house that was several miles northeast of the crowded road to Donegal, he'd felt her grow watchful, as if she had begun to worry about his fragility. And her care made him know that he ought to expect misfortune.

She had driven them in her small, apple-green, misfiring secondhand Ford to a little sandy track that went down to the beach. She pulled up the hand brake and sat, looking out the windshield at other parked cars and the gleam of water farther down. Her lips looked tattered, and he had seen her biting them. When she worried, she nibbled at herself— edges of her lips, her cuticles, a wisp of her frizzy, light hair. His stomach bucked, and he was certain now of unhappiness ahead. There were few people about, perhaps because cool winds had come up. He and Marianne had walked, saying little, along the curve of the bay. A small, white-hulled boat with an orange sail was turning into the wind.

"Can you see her?" Marianne asked.

He shook his head.

"She's got ahold of a rope, she's standing at the mast there."

"Is it a nun?"

"It is, Martin. A nun in her blue robe on a sailboat. She's grand, I think. Martin, there's a man I'm going to see again that I wanted you to know about?"

"Ah."

"Ah. Poor man. What else could you say, then? I'm so sorry. He's the father of my dead child. The infant boy born dead. He's asked to return again to my life. I don't know. I don't. But I don't think I can sustain the two sets of emotions at once. And here you are, off to the deserts over there, and I'm giving you something like the shove."

"This is the shove?"

"I wouldn't feel it inappropriate if you gave expression to some *anger*, Martin."

He knew her powerful poems about the baby. He wanted to say that he would rather cry, just then.

He remembered that he gave her no reply. He looked away from her, at the nun standing against the background of the orange sail on Sligo Bay, and he put his arm around her. She tensed. Then she very slowly relaxed against him for the space of a breath or two. All this time, he thought, and what you carry out of it for certain is how she fought an embrace and then gave in. She would probably write something about that instant of fighting, he thought. Marianne was a revelation about inventing ways to use words, unlike him with his timid notations on how others behaved. He remembered the citrus scent that she wore, and the smell, like crushed ferns, of the Sligo sand that the afternoon's sunlight had warmed before the winds came up—the smell so different from the animal rankness of the tawny sand patrolled by Alpha in its reconnaissance vehicles—and he remembered that her skin was cool to the touch, at the strand at Sligo and in their bed at the Galway Great Southern, or anyplace else. His skin cooked while hers grew cold, and she produced sorrowful poems, and he grew sentimental over mussels steamed with shallots in white wine.

When Ada woke him, she seemed to be wearing sneakers and a long denim shirt and nothing else.

"You slept all afternoon," she said.

"I was running away from work. It's a great tradition of the trade."

"We can work tonight," she said, "or tomorrow. We're doing all right. Listen. Wear some shorts, or a bathing suit if you brought it. I can't lend you one, I'm afraid, unless you're comfortable in a red maillot. And you'd best wear something on your feet."

Ada left, but Murphy stayed, to pant and fart and wink as Mason put on a pair of shorts he wore when he played basketball with his friends, and then tennis shoes and a T-shirt. Murphy went to stand before the back door, his blunt, spade-shaped head leaning on the jamb. Mason let him out and then walked down the narrow path of dark, mossy soil along which Murphy had already run out of sight, past wind-stunted evergreens, then driftwood crushed against the huge rocks lying on top of the great stone sheets that radiated black and pink-gray layers into the sea. Ada was there, halfway down to the turning of the cove. She carried two plastic buckets, one of which she handed him.

"Your hands will probably get sore," she said. "The more you try and hang on to the rocks, the more you'll get those very pale knees and shins chopped up on the barnacles and all. But it's worth it, because they're so sweet here. It's pretty much a secret place, so far."

"What's the secret about? Did you say?"

"Mussels, for goodness' sakes. That's what I've been telling you. This place, when the tide is low, is a gorgeous mussel bed."

She and Murphy went farther out, climbing over or around immense glacial rocks that lay on top of the pink and gray stone sheets. At low tide, which was now, he imagined, you must be able to reach ten feet or more below the level of the high tide of six hours before. She had disappeared over the edge, and so had Murphy, and he went to find her. She was in ocean to her waist and thighs, and Murphy was swimming away from her, threading his slow, powerful way through the bright plastic buoys of the lobster traps, his head low on the water, breathing in groans that were carried back on the wind.

The rocks seemed steep to Mason, and slippery, and he sensed that, trying to climb down, he would slide along them into the sea, striking his head and shoulders and spine against the sharp white barnacles and—he watched her pry one loose—the hundreds of long black mussels that she faced. The water had painted her shirt against her stomach and groin, and he could see the shadow of a bathing suit beneath the shirt and the movement of her stomach muscles under the suit as she pulled and twisted until a mussel she was harvesting came loose, to be dropped into the white plastic bucket that she held in her other hand.

She looked up with a concentration that struck him as ferocious. Then a pleasure seemed to come over her, and she said, "Come on, all right? Come here."

He held a finger up. It was supposed to say that he would be there soon, though from a different direction. She looked away, as if disappointed, and then she returned to plucking. Mason headed back twenty yards or more, then climbed down a more gradual decline of rocks nearer the house. He made his way along low stone outcroppings that gradually circled toward the curve of the point, where he thought she would be.

He couldn't hear Murphy now. Mason held on to the rock, chopping his fingers on bright white little shells that adhered to it, prodding for the beard hairs of mussels. The pail he held was floating on the tide, and the icy water was soon above his knees as he foraged where the rocks declined. He had worked two small mussels loose, with great effort, and tossed them into the bucket. Now the freezing sea was at his waist. He came around the point to see Ada, tall, spread-legged, and at her ease, with one hand through the wire handle of her pail to hold the rock face, and the other hand working to her right, tearing mussels loose and dumping them. When she saw him, she gave him a look of inspection and then smiled as if all at once, after a time of confusion, she understood him.

He held on to the rock against the bucking of the sea. He was watching the small Labrador attack one of the foamed plastic buoys painted white on top and red on the bottom and fastened to a lobster trap that held to the floor of the sea.

Ada cocked her head as dogs do when they're puzzled. "Murphy!" she called. "Murph! Come here!"

The dog made as if to swim to her, but then he stayed where he was, with his jaws clamped around the buoy. He made paddling motions but didn't come away.

"Get his ass shot up by a pissed-off lobsterman or the conservation patrol," she said, "and nobody would question it. Murphy, damn it!"

"Ada," Mason said.

"Murph!"

"Ada, he's stuck. Isn't he? He can't get his teeth out of it."

"He can't? Oh, he *can't*. Murphy!"

They started at the same time. Ada let go of her bucket and pushed off from the rock face to swim a long-stroked crawl. Mason tried to think of himself as doing the same, though he knew that what he really did was make a little yipping noise, push his head down into the water, and, spitting ocean out, set forward with the only stroke he could swim—if, he thought, you could really call this swimming—a despairing sidestroke that sent him in slants not quite straight at what he alleged to be heading for. He stroked, looked about, corrected his direction, then stroked some more. He had no real breathing rhythm, but he did have strong arms and legs, so he swam in the sea the way a crab scuttles on sand, and he made a little headway. Ada, meanwhile, was almost there. Mason found himself thinking about the great distance that lay between the dark green surface, chopped into patches of white by the wind, and the slithery, teeming ocean floor.

She was trying to support the dog's belly, it appeared, when Mason reached them. The whites of Murphy's eyes seemed enormous. As if to demonstrate his situation, his lips were drawn back so that the pink and black gums and yellow-white teeth were visible, the fangs clamped deep into the soft plastic of the buoy. Murphy twisted his head to release himself, but the teeth were firmly stuck.

"I've got you, little Murph," Ada said, breathing harshly. "I've got his tail and his gut, a little bit," she told Mason. "Can you—"

He tried to say, "Piece of cake." It came out as a wet warble. He did what he considered the treading of water, really a flailing kick—the bottom seemed *so* far below—that shook his torso and head. He didn't try to speak again. He worked his fingers into Murphy's mouth and made the noises, though not the shaped words themselves, of Here we go, boy. Here we go, boy. Here we go. His own head slid beneath the surface several times, but he worked at the teeth and then had them unfastened. He surfaced just as Murphy, in the jaws of panic, clamped his own jaws down again, this time on Mason's left hand. Mason howled shrilly and Murphy, with Mason's fingers in his mouth, turned with great interest toward the noise. Using his right hand, he persuaded the muzzle open and removed his fingers. Ada pushed Murphy off toward shore, and the dog swam eagerly. Mason tried to shift from his flailing into his crooked sidestroke, but he was down to the single hand that would cup against water and he merely rolled a little before his head went under.

He felt her hand in his hair, tugging, and then he was on his back. He tried to protest, but water poured into his mouth, and he could only gurgle. Her hand cupped his chin, pulling back, so that now the ocean stayed out of his mouth and he could breathe whenever he wished. What gifts to give a man, he thought: the fruits of her watchfulness, as well as a choice of when to breathe. She towed him as if he were a blunt, unseaworthy barge and she a gallant tug. She swam what he knew was an actual and very effective sidestroke that resembled his sideways jerk only in the way you said its name.

Although he was kept the length of a bent arm away from her, he was intimately aware of her body. He heard her breath go out on the water. He felt the strength of her fingers as they held his throat and chin. Sometimes her legs, when they scissored, brushed his buttock or the small of his back. His arms trailed, and he sensed that if he moved them up a little he might touch her, and he wanted to, though he kept them at his sides. His eyes were closed. The day had begun that way, he remembered: him on his back with his eyes forced shut. She surged, then relaxed, surged and then relaxed, and he could feel her purpose, the power of her long muscles, and none of the sorrow that bowed her shoulders when she stood on the shore.

Something brushed his trailing forearm, and he squinted to his right to see one of the mussel buckets, right-side up and slowly spinning out toward open sea. He shut his eyes again and thought it possible that, half drowning, his mangled hand a pulse that beat in syncopation to the rhythm of the progress of her stroke, he might actually fall asleep in the waters of this cold Atlantic cove. But she halted them. He could feel her tread water with a different kind of strength from that of her sidestroke. Then she swam him a little farther, paused again, and then began to walk with him still floating on his back, towing him through the shallows. Murphy had made it back, and he lay on a tilted, vast, refrigerator-shaped stone, looking down toward them while he panted at a ferocious pace, his tongue exhaustedly stiffened and stuck straight out. It was time to stand up, Mason knew, and he reluctantly climbed to his feet by holding with his unbitten hand on to Ada, who stood above him with the ocean pouring between her thighs.

"You're all right," she said, "aren't you?" She'd begun to shake.

He let go of her hand and stood before her on his own. He trembled, partly because of the cold. "Thank you," he said.

"No, that was a great rescue," she said. "Thank you from Murphy and thank you from me."

"And you," he said, breathing as fast as if he had pulled someone large through the ocean against currents, gravity, dog bite, and fear. "You saved my *life*, Ada."

"But we won't have mussels for dinner tonight. And I'm sorry. It would have been fun to give you that." He watched her head droop a little as her shoulders bent toward the sea.

Murphy shifted his demented glare from one of them to the other as he panted from above. Mason wanted to examine his hand to see whether the dog had only torn his fingers apart or had also broken a few, but he held it at his side with what he hoped was nonchalance.

"Another night," he said, "please."

"All right," she said. "Yes. But we're freezing here."

"We are," he said. But he was thinking of the nighttime heat in which they gathered at Checkpoint Eight One, the smell of the driver rising through the chemical stink of the rubber and plastic of the burning truck. His legs and loins cooked in the cab while the upper segment lay before them. The driver's remaining eye was wide as if in speculation about these Americans who shuffled closer and closer to the torn torso and its wrecked head.

Ada bent forward, suddenly, and she gathered her hair in a fist, reaching for a barrette that had been torn away by the sea. She stayed bent over, then looked up to see him watch her hair whip backward as she straightened and said, "I'm going up, I'm building a fire in the fireplace, and I'm making tea to pour brandy in. We'll deal with your hand, which looks a little lousy, I'm afraid. And I'm smoking plenty of cigarettes."

She turned from Mason to get herself past pitted, bleached-out boards and hanks of snapped rope that lay among the stones she climbed toward the house. Murphy went slowly ahead of her. Holding his beating right hand in his left, and knowing that he risked a fall on the slippery, yellow-green rockweed and the slimy bottoms of tidal pools, Mason followed them up.